Rave reviews for J.A. JANCE,
New York Times and *USA Today* bestselling author

"Addictive. . . . Jance will charm you into reading
everything by her you can find."
—*The Statesman Journal*

LEFT FOR DEAD

"Loyal fans and newcomers alike will be glad to join
feisty Ali in her latest adventure."

—*Kirkus Reviews*

"What is it that separates a good writer from a great
writer, interesting books from excellent books? Jance
has found the secret. By creating and developing mem-
orable characters, using for a backdrop the environment that is familiar to her and letting her imagination
develop complex plots, she has won millions of fans
who can't wait to read her next book."

—*Bookreporter*

"Engaging."

—*Publishers Weekly*

"An excellent mystery. . . . Jance deftly paints each of
her characters in full detail without stopping the action for long descriptions. Her flowing writing style
makes the reading easy and fun; she pulls no
punches. . . . *Left for Dead* should be next on your
reading list!"

—*Blogcritics*

FATAL ERROR

"The plot never stalls."

—Publishers Weekly

"In her inimitable, take-no-prisoners style . . . Ali manages to disarm."

—Kirkus Reviews

"An entertaining mix of sleuthing and human relationships."

—Booklist

"Jance continues to delight with her detail-filled suspense stories that capture so much of life."

—Library Journal

"A captivating page-turner."

—Lincoln Journal-Star

TRIAL BY FIRE

"Fast pacing, surprising plot twists, and a strong, principled heroine make for a satisfying read."

—Booklist

"Fans will not be disappointed with this new novel. It's a page-turner."

—Green Valley News and Sun

"Jance proves once again that she has mastered the nigh-impossible task of writing consistently (and convincingly) in three quite different styles, one for each of her series—no easy feat!"

—BookPage

CRUEL INTENT

"Compelling . . . satisfying."

—*USA Today*

"A fast-paced read with as many twists and turns as a county fair roller coaster."

—*Seattle Post-Intelligencer*

"Jance has honed her talent for writing entertaining, accessible mysteries that readers can zip through."

—*Booklist*

"An enjoyable and easy read . . . perfect for a weekend in front of the fireplace."

—*Sacramento Book Review*

HAND OF EVIL

"Entertaining. . . . Jance fits together the many pieces of this literary jigsaw puzzle into a coherent and satisfying whole."

—*The Tennessean*

"Jance at her best, weaving a masterful story of suspense."

—*The Sierra Vista Herald*

"A suspenseful climax."

—*Daily Camera*

WEB OF EVIL

"Gripping. . . . Jance's skills will keep the reader riveted. . . . Ali couldn't be better company."

—*South Florida Sun-Sentinel*

"Jance keeps the entertainment value at a steady level."

—*The Augusta Chronicle*

J.A. JANCE

LEFT FOR DEAD

POCKET BOOKS

New York   London   Toronto   Sydney   New Delhi

Pocket Books
A Division of Simon & Schuster, Inc.
1230 Avenue of the Americas
New York, NY 10020

This book is a work of fiction. Names, characters, places, and incidents either are products of the author's imagination or are used fictitiously. Any resemblance to actual events or locales or persons, living or dead, is entirely coincidental.

First Pocket Books paperback edition January 2013

POCKET and colophon are registered trademarks of Simon & Schuster, Inc.

For information about special discounts for bulk purchases, please contact Simon & Schuster Special Sales at 1-866-506-1949 or business@simonandschuster.com.

The Simon & Schuster Speakers Bureau can bring authors to your live event. For more information or to book an event, contact the Simon & Schuster Speakers Bureau at 1-866-248-3049 or visit our website at www.simonspeakers.com.

Manufactured in the United States of America

10 9 8 7 6 5 4 3 2 1

ISBN: 978-1-4516-2860-9
ISBN: 978-1-4516-2862-3 (ebook)

To the REAL Patty Patton

Prologue

Seventeen-year-old Breeze Domingo lay on a sagging leather couch in a filthy apartment that Thursday morning and tried to sleep, but sleep eluded her. She tossed and turned and spent the time wishing her life had been different. She wished she had listened to her mother and stepfather and stayed in school. She wished she had never set foot on Van Buren Street in downtown Phoenix and discovered how easy it was to make money if you didn't care what you had to do to get it. And she wished she had never hooked up with Chico Hernández.

Some of the other girls had warned her to stay away from him, but Chico was a smooth operator. When she first met him, she'd been new to the life, a fourteen-year-old runaway living on the streets. Chico was the one who had told her what she wanted to hear—that she was beautiful and that he would take care of her. That was the day a john had busted her in the jaw rather than fork over his money. Chico had taken her to urgent care and waited while she got stitched up. After that she owed him. After that she was his. She had ditched her given name of Rose in favor of becoming Breeze Domingo. Three years later, she still was.

In a way, Chico was like Breeze's stepfather: As long as she did as he said and didn't give him back-talk, they got along fine. For a while everything seemed A-OK with Chico, too. His girls stayed in three apartments in a not too run-down building near downtown Phoenix. All she had to do to earn her keep was put out on demand and turn over whatever money she earned to Chico. Breeze noticed that girls who tried to short him in the money department tended to disappear without a trace, so she made sure she paid him every last cent.

But then Chico got in some kind of money trouble. The girls who had lived in three separate apartments now found themselves crammed into one. Premium cable TV went away right after the two additional apartments. The food got worse. So did the clothing. That was bad for business, because if the girls didn't look the part, they didn't bring in the same kind of cash.

Having that single apartment made for difficult sleeping arrangements. Four of them shared the two queen-size beds in the bedroom with one sleeping solo on the sagging leather couch in the living room. That night Breeze's john had been old and drunk. He couldn't get it up. When he passed out, she had left him in his room at the Hyatt and caught a cab back to the apartment, where she had arrived early enough to lay claim to the couch.

The place was a disgusting mess, with dirty dishes piled in the sink; with fast-food containers and leftovers covering every surface, attracting swarms of cockroaches that scurried out of sight when the lights came on; with clothes strewn everywhere; with garbage and trash cans overflowing. At first, remembering her stepfather's amazingly clean house in Buckeye, Breeze had tried to clean up and make the others do their share, but she finally gave up. Chico didn't care. As long as the girls showed up for work clean, smelling good, and ready for action, he didn't give a rat's ass about the squalor they lived in.

Tonight, when sleep wouldn't come, Breeze thought about home, her real home, less than twenty miles but forever away.

It was hard to remember how life had been back then, when she was an innocent but rebellious girl named Rose Ventana. She had run away when her mother's new husband, Jimmy, had taken a look at her report card. Once he discovered she was flunking four subjects, he immediately canceled plans for her quinceañera celebration. First he returned the dress, a gorgeous thing and the only formal dress she had ever owned. Then, even though he'd already put down money for the caterer and the DJ, Jimmy canceled those, too, losing his deposits in the process. When Rose objected, Jimmy told her that the traditional party in honor of the fifteenth birthday was a privilege, not a right, and that she hadn't kept her part of the bargain.

It was true. Jimmy had warned her back in September when school started that if she wanted the party, she had to keep up her grades, help out with her younger sisters, and be home by curfew—ten o'clock on school nights; midnight on weekends. Rose's problem was she thought he was bluffing, the same way her mother, Connie, usually bluffed back when she was a single mother trying to raise three daughters on her own with the slim income she earned working part-time and irregular hours in a series of tattoo parlors.

Life with Connie alone had been one of not enough food and plenty of empty promises and equally empty threats. By the end of her long odd-hour workdays, Connie was too worn out by keeping food on the table and a roof over their heads to carry through on anything she said. The three girls had learned to function in a world where no one kept their word or did what they said they'd do.

Then James Fox, an electronics engineer who worked at the Palo Verde nuclear power plant, had shown up in their lives. He had come to the tattoo parlor, where Connie Ventana had inked a bright red fox on his arm. The next week he came back for another tattoo. Before Rose and her sisters knew what was happening, their mother had up and married the guy. Jimmy, as he told Connie's girls to call him, was someone who always did exactly what he said. He had promised them braces for their teeth, and he had delivered. He had moved them from the small Section 8 apartment that was all Connie could afford into his spacious air-conditioned home in Buckeye, where they had a heated pool to swim in and where Rose and her sisters each had a room.

In Jimmy's house, there was always plenty of food on the table. Rose and her sisters had new clothes to wear to school without having to shop at the Salvation Army thrift store. They no longer had to face the humiliation of eating "free" lunches at school, which every kid in the universe understands aren't really free at all. From that point of view, Rose's life had improved immeasurably when Foxy, as her mother liked to call him, became part of the family equation.

As far as Rose was concerned, however, all those improvements had come with a very steep price. Jimmy expected Connie's girls to mind; to be respectful; to listen to their mother; not to talk back; to do their homework; to do chores around the house. Three years later, a prostitute named Breeze Domingo could see that all Jimmy had done was try to impose some order on a chaotic family that had little to none before his arrival on the scene.

To the oldest child in the family, the sudden introduction of structure and discipline was something of a shock. Rose Ventana had been used to playing substitute parent to her younger sisters, and she resented the loss of authority a lot more than she appreciated the loss of responsibility.

Jimmy had told her he wanted to give her a chance to be a girl again, but she hadn't understood what he meant at the time, and she hadn't valued it, either. Now that she finally did realize what he had been trying to do, it was too late. She had been on the streets for too long even to think of going home. She had seen what happened to girls who tried to get out of the life. They usually didn't make it because their so-called families no longer wanted them.

A year earlier, while flipping through the channels on the second anniversary of the day she ran away, Breeze had been shocked to come across her parents being interviewed on a local television newscast. They both looked a lot older than she remembered. There were deep lines around her mother's eyes and dark shadows under them that Breeze had never seen before. All through the news segment, Jimmy had stood next to Connie, looking sad and patting his wife's shoulder encouragingly while she spoke into the microphones and cameras, asking anyone with knowledge of her daughter's whereabouts to please come forward.

Nobody did, because no one in Breeze's present life knew or even guessed who she once was. Rose Ventana had been replaced. Even before she changed her name, Rose had changed her looks. One of the first things she did when she landed on Van Buren Street was to dye her hair. With her naturally tanned skin, she made a convincing and striking blonde. She was also young and on her own in a very rough part of town. That made her a target, and Chico Hernández was the guy who had come to her rescue.

As part of Chico's stable, Rose was rechristened with the name Breeze. Chico liked his girls to have unusual and often weather-related names: Breeze, Stormy, Dawn, Rain, Sunny. Weird names aside, working for Chico wasn't such a bad thing. His girls were regarded as call girls rather than whores, and he forked over the money needed for them to dress the part. He had a particular clientele made up of guys who liked their partners to be girls, the younger the better, and Chico had people who usually handled the "bookings."

Rose had always been self-conscious about being underendowed in the boob department, but in her new line of work, being small was an advantage. It made it easy for Chico to pass her off as several years younger than she was, and Breeze had the added advantage of being pretty. The braces her stepfather paid for served her in good stead. In a business where lots of the competition came with meth mouth, Breeze's mouthful of straight white teeth offered yet another mark in her favor.

Breeze had been a part of Chico's team for three years, but tonight she found herself wishing she were back in Buckeye in a clean room with clean sheets and with nothing to do the next morning except get up and go to school.

At last she managed to fall asleep. All her roommates were home and sleeping when Breeze's cell phone rang at nine A.M.

"Okay," Chico said. "I've got you a date in Fountain Hills. Meet me down in the lobby at ten. And don't tell the other girls where you're going."

An hour later, with her roommates still sawing logs, it was easy for Breeze to do as she was told. She hurried downstairs without saying a word to anyone and found Chico waiting out front in his aging Lincoln Town Car. He gave her an appraising look as she climbed into the front seat.

"I told you Fountain Hills," he said. "Couldn't you do any better than jeans and a T-shirt?"

"Sorry," she said. "I didn't have time to do laundry."

"All right," he said. "We'll do some shopping on the way."

To her amazement, he took her to Biltmore Fashion Park, where a quick dash through Macy's netted her some very high heels, a slinky little black dress, and some silky black underwear, all of which he had her wear out of the store. Breeze was happy to have the new clothing, but she was also a little puzzled. If Chico was having financial difficulties, why would he spend that kind of money on her?

Once they left Macy's, it seemed to Breeze as though they drove forever. She never had any idea that Phoenix was that big. Chico was surprisingly quiet the whole way. Nervous, too. Breeze wanted to ask him what was going on and who the client was, but if life on the street had taught her any lessons at all, the most basic was not to ask questions, especially not when you didn't want to hear the answers.

At last they turned off a winding strip of pavement onto a smaller but still curvy street. Eventually, Chico stopped the Lincoln in front of an ornate iron gate, complete with a manned guard shack. At the end of a long uphill drive sat an imposing house.

"Get out here," Chico directed.

Breeze looked down at her five-inch heels. "In these?" she asked.

"Don't worry. Someone will run you up the hill in a golf cart."

"How do I get back?"

"Don't worry," he said. "Someone will come get you."

The other girls, the ones who had warned Breeze about Chico in the first place, had also warned her: Don't get stranded somewhere you can't get home from on your own steam.

Breeze glanced back the way they had come and realized she had no idea how to get back to the apartment in downtown Phoenix. "But—" she began.

"I said get out," Chico urged. "Do what they tell you. Understand?"

Breeze got out of the car, and Chico's Lincoln drove away. It was windy and surprisingly cold to be standing outside in a skimpy, sleeveless dress and a pair of sling-back pumps. She wished she had asked Chico to buy her a sweater, too. The guard opened the gate wide enough for her to slip inside the compound. As Chico drove away, the guard spoke into some kind of walkie-talkie. Minutes later, a golf cart came down the hill to get her. The ride in the open cart that brought Breeze up to the house left her shivering.

The cart stopped under a covered portico. Breeze stepped out of the cart and waited while the driver—a man wearing a uniform very much like that of the guard at the gatehouse—hurried up onto the porch, opened one of a matching pair of doors, and escorted her into a marble-floored entryway that was, she realized later, a beautiful entry into hell itself.

At the door the driver handed her off to a uniformed maid who led her into an ornate room that looked more like a museum or a hotel lobby than part of a house. There were huge paintings on the walls and groupings of furniture. At the far end of the room was a woodburning fireplace, alive with a roaring fire. A man stood as if posing for a photo shoot in front of the mantel. Holding a champagne flute in one hand, he watched as the maid led Breeze into the room.

"Ah, yes," he said. "The guest of honor has arrived. Let me take a look at you."

Breeze wasn't stupid. She knew why she was there, and it wasn't as anybody's guest of honor. The man carefully set his drink down on a table in front of the fireplace and then moved toward her. Breeze had become fairly adept at estimating johns' ages. This one was at least sixty and very ugly. The bulbous red nose spoke of too much booze, the leathery lizardlike skin of too much sun, and the narrow eyes of too much meanness.

He stopped directly in front of her and stared her up and down. "Not bad," he said at last. "Better-looking than I expected."

Breeze was accustomed to this kind of frank appraisal. Even so, the way his eyes trailed over her body made her nervous.

"I'm forgetting my manners," he said, giving her a leer. "Can I offer you some champagne?"

That was one of Chico's rules: DO NOT DRINK WITH THE JOHNS! Not even champagne, even though a sip of champagne sounded very good right about then.

"No, thank you," Breeze said.

"Lunch, then?"

"That would be nice," she said.

He turned to the maid, who had retreated to the doorway, where she stood, awaiting further instructions. "You can bring lunch upstairs to the library," he said.

Breeze had never been in a house with an actual library. Why someone would eat food in a library, she didn't understand. Libraries were for books. Dining rooms were for eating.

"This way," he said, reaching out and putting a proprietary arm around Breeze's waist. "I wouldn't want you to trip and fall on one of those amazing heels."

With his arm still around her waist, he led her up a long curving staircase. There were thick rugs on the floors. There was more colorful artwork on the walls of the long upstairs hallway. The room he led her into was indeed a library. Three walls were covered, floor to ceiling, in shelves loaded with leatherbound books. One wall was floor-to-ceiling windows that looked out over the entire Valley of the Sun. Breeze stood there staring while yet another uniformed maid rolled a linen-covered serving cart into the room.

There was a small table in the middle of the room. With deft movements, the maid covered it in a snowy white cloth and then set it for two, laying out as sumptuous an array of food as Breeze Domingo had ever seen.

"Since you won't have any champagne," her host said, "would you care for some iced tea?"

"Yes, thank you."

"Sugar?"

"Please."

She took the icy glass gratefully and swilled down the tea. That was the last thing she remembered for a very long time.

1

10:00 A.M., Friday, April 9
Sedona, Arizona

In the late morning, on a cold but bright Friday in early April, Ali Reynolds sat outside on her patio in Sedona, Arizona, ninety miles north of Phoenix. An outdoor heater hissed nearby, keeping the chill at bay. Around her, Sedona's iconic red cliffs glowed in the distance, but on this particular morning, Ali was immune to the view. Instead, she tried desperately to focus on the table in front of her, spread with a dozen paper-filled folders. Ali had been scrutinizing each of the files one at a time for the past hour and was more than ready for a break. She just couldn't concentrate.

How had she, intrepid reporter turned L.A. anchorwoman, then murder suspect, widow, and police academy graduate, wound up administering a private charitable fund as her primary duty in life? Surely she was too young to be put out to pasture.

"I'm going in to check on Sister Anselm's cassoulet," Leland Brooks said, stopping in front of the table on his way past. "While I'm there, would you care for some coffee?"

Leland was Ali's majordomo, her butler, her right hand, and her elderly but spry man Friday. Since Ali's return to Sedona, Sister Anselm, a Sister of Providence who lived in nearby Jerome, had become one of Ali's dearest friends. In the process Sister Anselm and Leland Brooks had become friends as well.

Sister Anselm served on the board of an organization that helped people dealing with substance abuse issues in several northern Arizona counties. On the second Saturday of each month, after a regularly scheduled board meeting in Flagstaff, she would often stop off in Sedona to enjoy one of Leland's signature meals. Cassoulet, a savory stew that the good sister had loved during her childhood in France, was one of her personal favorites. Even though it took Leland the better part of two days to make the stuff, he was always eager to serve it to such an appreciative guest. Sister Anselm had told him that eating it "transported" her back home.

All morning long, enticing aromas had leaked out of the kitchen and blown across the patio, setting Ali's mouth watering.

Looking up, she smiled. "The cassoulet smells delicious, even out here," she told him. "And coffee would be great."

Leland Brooks and Ali's newly remodeled house on Sedona's Manzanita Hills Road had come into her life as a package deal. Leland, a displaced Brit and a Korean War veteran, had managed the place for decades for its former owner, Arabella Ashcroft, and for Arabella's mother, Anne Marie Ashcroft, before that. When Ali purchased the property with the intention of restoring it, she had kept Leland on, supposedly for the duration of the restoration process.

The remodeling project was long since over. The house, a gem of midcentury-modern architecture, had been returned to its original glory but updated to twenty-first-century building codes and fully stocked with modern-day appliances and computer-driven convenience. In the meantime, what Ali and Leland had both envisioned as a temporary employment situation had become more or less permanent.

During the Ashcroft years, Leland had occupied the servants' quarters just off the kitchen. Now he lived in his own place, a fifth-wheel trailer parked on the far side of the garage, while Ali had the remodeled house to herself. Leland did the cooking and oversaw the cleaning. He had finally admitted that, at his stage of life, he could perhaps use a little help with the more rigorous chores. Nonetheless, he demanded perfection of all visiting crews of cleaners, window washers, and yard people, and having them available had allowed him to dive headfirst into a long-postponed project of creating a lush English garden in Ali's front yard.

When Ali had mentioned Leland's proposal to her parents, Bob and Edie Larson, her father immediately voiced his adamant disapproval. As far as he was concerned, putting a garden like that in the high desert of Arizona would be a colossal waste of time, effort, money, and water, but Ali was determined, and so was Leland; Ali because she'd always dreamed of having her very own "Enchanted Garden," and Leland because he'd promised the house's original owner that he'd complete her beloved project. During the "Arabella years," when Anne Marie's daughter had inherited the house and the butler, plans for the garden had been scrapped due to Arabella's lack of interest. Now, with Ali in charge, Leland was determined to bring Anne Marie's ambitious vision to fruition.

As far as gardening was concerned, Ali was well aware of her own personal limitations, one of which was having a perpetually black thumb. She had killed more indoor ficus plants than she cared to count. Initially, she'd been wary of such an undertaking, but it soon became clear that Leland was prepared to take the entire project in hand.

Leland had looked after Anne Marie's troubled daughter for years after Anne Marie's death, though his primary loyalty had always been to the family matriarch. When Leland first showed Ali the original garden plans, hand-sketched by Anne Marie on what was now wrinkled, yellowed sketch-pad paper, Ali knew what they needed to do.

She agreed to the project but on the condition that Leland's role would be strictly supervisory. That was why, for the better part of the past week, a crew of strapping young men had been busily digging trenches and turning the soil, first to install the irrigation system and then to prepare the garden plot for planting. After that would come the pouring of the foundation for the garden's centerpiece, a statue of a bighorn sheep created by Ali's son, Christopher. Only when the statue was in place would it be time to plant the colorful array of growing things that Ali and Leland had selected while trudging through what had seemed like miles of aisles at Gardeners World in Phoenix.

Once Leland disappeared into the house, Ali turned her attention back to the folders on the table in front of her. The materials included both printed and hand-written (often barely decipherable) letters of recommendation from various teachers, employers, and friends stating why one particular girl or another should be the recipient of this year's Amelia Dougherty Askins Scholarship.

Almost thirty years earlier, when Ali had received her own invitation from Anne Marie Ashcroft to come to tea at this very house, she'd had no idea that the scholarship program even existed, much less that she was a candidate. She had been quietly nominated by her high school English teacher, and receiving that unexpected scholarship had enabled Ali to attend college when she couldn't have done so otherwise. Now, through a twist of fate, she was in charge of doling out those same scholarships to a new generation of deserving girls, and although it was a job she loved, it was hardly enough to keep her busy full-time.

That morning Ali had started with a field of twelve semifinalists. She stacked ten of the folders on one side of the table and put those of the two finalists on the other.

Rubbing her eyes and stretching her shoulders, Ali looked off across a valley punctuated with Sedona's striking red-rock cliffs as Leland emerged from the house carrying a tray laden with coffee and a plate of freshly baked shortbread cookies.

"How's the selection process coming along?" he asked, unloading the tray and depressing the plunger in the French press. Leland came from a class-conscious English background. It had taken more than a little persuading on Ali's part to convince him to join her for an occasional cup of morning coffee. Leland was of the opinion that "familiarity" constituted a serious breach of employee/employer etiquette, but as Ali had pointed out, he wasn't in Kansas anymore, and he wasn't in Kensington Gardens, either.

Ali pushed the two finalists' folders over toward the spot where Leland had deposited his cup and saucer.

"I've narrowed it down to these two," Ali said. "Olivia McFarland and Autumn Rusk."

Leland nodded. "Excellent choices," he said. "They would have been mine, too."

During the previous months, as the nominations arrived, Ali had deputized Leland to be her "feet on the ground" and to discreetly gather "intel" on the nominees. Leland had been an unobtrusive presence in Verde Valley communities for many years, and his sleuthing had unearthed quite a few things about the various girls' backgrounds and family situations that were absent from the official school records.

For instance, Olivia's 3.5 GPA at Mingus Mountain High School was solid enough, but it might have been much higher if Olivia hadn't been charged with caring for her three younger siblings—two brothers and a baby sister—while their widowed mother worked two jobs to keep a roof over their heads and food on the table.

Ali also couldn't help but wonder what would happen to the younger children if Olivia were given a scholarship that took her away from home. Would receiving the award, a positive for Olivia, turn into a negative in the lives of her younger siblings? For that matter, would she even accept it?

Autumn Rusk also came from a single-parent home. In the economic downturn, her once prosperous family life had disappeared right along with her father's job. After the job was gone, the house went next, and after the house, the marriage. Autumn and her mother had moved from their upscale home in Sedona to a modest rental in Cornville, where Autumn's mother had resumed her long-abandoned career as a hairdresser.

The chaos in their lives had impacted Autumn's schoolwork, especially during her junior year, when she moved from Sedona High to Mingus. As a senior, she was back hitting the books and making headway in raising her GPA to its former level, but it was a tough road.

Three years before, faced with two equally deserving girls, Ali had opted to choose them both. Those two girls, Marissa Dvorak and Haley Marsh, were now juniors, attending the University of Arizona in Tucson and doing well academically and personally. In Ali's wallet, right along with photos of her own twin grandkids, she carried a school picture of Haley's bright-eyed son, Liam, grinning a five-year-old grin that was already minus one front tooth.

Giving someone an Askins scholarship meant a multiyear commitment from the endowment. The economic downturn that had cost Anthony Rusk his job had adversely affected the scholarship fund as well. And though it had received two recent generous donations that made up some of the investment shortfall, Ali wasn't sure she could justify giving two scholarships this year.

Leland poured the coffee and took a seat. "I don't envy your having to make the decision," he said, as though reading her mind. "But if you're thinking of awarding two scholarships, perhaps it's time to consider doing some kind of fund-raising effort."

"Long-term, you're probably right," Ali agreed, "but for right now I need to settle this so the girls and their families can make plans of their own."

When coffee was over, Ali returned to the file folders. By lunchtime she had made up her mind. She would invite both girls to the traditional tea but would meet with them separately. The scholarship for Autumn, who was interested in nursing, would be to any four-year institution of higher learning within the state of Arizona, renewable annually provided she maintained an acceptable GPA.

Olivia's, on the other hand, would pay in-state tuition, books, and some living expenses for her to attend Yavapai College in Sedona and in Prescott. It would also include a small stipend for child care for her siblings during study or school hours. Upon graduation, assuming she had maintained a suitable GPA, her scholarship could be extended for two more years if she transferred to a BA program at a school inside Arizona. That meant that Olivia's family would benefit from having her at home with them during those first two years of college, but she'd also be getting a start on her education.

Having made her decision, Ali set about writing the

required notes with a happy heart. She was confident that those seemingly trivial invitations to tea would change the course of at least two young lives, just as Anne Marie Ashcroft's much earlier invitation had transformed the future for Alison Larson Reynolds.

As she sat there on her sunlit patio, Ali took pleasure in a life that seemed placid and orderly, and she relished every moment of it.

2

3:00 P.M., Friday, April 9
Fountain Hills, Arizona

Breeze Domingo awakened alone in a windowless room where the walls and ceiling looked as though they had been covered with egg cartons. The black dress was gone. So were the silky black underwear and the high heels. She was naked and cold and lying on a hard metal table with thick leather bands restraining her arms and legs.

Fighting her way through the fog, she tried to remember where she was or what had happened. She remembered Chico dropping her off at the gate and riding up the hill in the golf cart. She remembered walking into the book-lined room where the ugly old man had been waiting for her. And then she seemed to remember being given something to drink. After that the world became fuzzy. She recalled the sensation of being thrown over someone's shoulder and carried, fireman-style, down a seemingly endless staircase, but that was all. She had no idea how much time had passed or even if she was still in the house in Fountain Hills. Where was Chico? He had said he would come back for her, but he hadn't. Why not? And what was going to happen to her? The possible answers to that question filled her with dread. Whatever it was, she knew, it wouldn't be good.

An invisible door—also covered with what looked like egg cartons—opened, and the ugly man walked into the room. He was wearing a bathrobe. He looked at her and smiled. "It's about time you woke up," he said. "Nap's over. The two of us will have some fun."

"Where's Chico?" she asked.

"Don't hold your breath waiting for him to come back," the man said. "I guess he didn't tell you. Chico owed me money. Quite a bit of money, and I agreed to take it out in trade. I tore up his IOU, and now you belong to me."

He paused long enough to light a cigarette and then stood over her, studying her naked body. "That's quite a tattoo you have there. Very pretty."

That was the one part of her fifteenth-birthday present that Jimmy Fox hadn't been able to cancel, because he hadn't known about it. Some girls begged to have their ears pierced. Rose Ventana had begged her mother for a tattoo from the time she understood what Connie did for a living. Her mother had always told her that, if she still wanted one, she could have one for her fifteenth birthday. That promise had been made long before Jimmy Fox appeared on the scene, and both Rose and her mother understood how much he would disapprove.

One day while Jimmy was at work, her mother picked Rose up early from school and took her downtown to the tattoo parlor to do the job. The pattern Rose chose was one to match her name, a bright red rose that was tucked out of sight on the inside of her right breast. Connie had positioned it in such a way that it wouldn't show, even under the low-cut neckline of Rose's formal—the one she had never worn; the one Jimmy had returned.

The rose was the only thing Breeze Domingo still had from her childhood; it was her only abiding gift from her mother. But she didn't tell the man with the cigarette any of that. She didn't want to give him that kind of power over her. Instead, she said nothing.

He shook his head sadly. "Chico told me that you were a good girl, that you would do what you're told. When I talk to you or ask a question, it's not good manners if you don't respond. Understand?"

With that, after taking one last drag on the cigarette, he deftly pressed the burning stub into the middle of the rose tattoo. Breeze howled in agony at the searing pain, and her anguish made the man smile.

"See there?" he said. "That's more like it."

Breeze Domingo was accustomed to giving men what they wanted, and what this monster wanted was to see her suffer, to hear her scream. For a time he would carry on a seemingly reasonable conversation, asking her inane questions: Where had she gone to school? What was her favorite subject? What was her favorite food? There was no way to tell in advance if he would find her answers satisfactory, but whenever he didn't, he burned her again, relishing her futile attempts to writhe out of reach. When he tired of the burning game, he pulled out a knife and played a bloody game of tic-tac-toe on the flat planes of her belly. Only then did he peel off the robe.

Breeze was relieved. After all, sex was what she had expected. He was an old man. How bad could it be? It turned out to be very bad indeed. Frustrated that he couldn't deliver with his own aged equipment, he railed at her for being an emasculating bitch. Then he pulled a billy club out of the pocket of his robe and came after her with it.

That was about the time when she passed out. He slapped her awake and kept the game going for what seemed like hours, pausing now and then for another cigarette and to lift a bottle to his lips and sip on something that smelled like straight tequila. Finally, with a satisfied sigh, he picked up the robe and put it on. Pulling out a phone, he snapped it open and dialed.

"Okay," he said when someone finally answered. "I'm done. Get rid of her."

That was the last she remembered until she awakened again much later. She had no idea how much time had passed. It could have been hours or days. She was bound and gagged, wrapped in what felt like a rolled rug, and lying in the dark on the floor of a moving vehicle that seemed like a panel truck, hurtling forward toward some unknown destination. When the truck went around a curve or a corner, Breeze rolled helplessly one way or the other, unable to stop until she slammed into the wall.

Her whole body hurt from the burns and the cuts. The inside of her body felt bruised and battered, and she needed to pee. She held back as long as she could. When at last she let go, urine ran down the back of her leg and across some of the cuts or burns, she couldn't tell which. All she knew was that it stung like hell.

She lay there, crying quietly. If the van had stopped, she might have tried banging against the side of the van with her legs, but the rug made that impossible, and they didn't stop, anyway.

For a time it seemed clear that they were on a freeway. She could hear the sounds of other traffic and the grumbling roar of traveling semis. Then they turned off onto a much quieter road—a slower road with a lot less traffic, though it was still paved. Much later, they pulled onto what felt like a rutted dirt track. As they bounced across the hard washboard surface, the van filled up with a cloud of dust. Breeze needed to cough and sneeze. All she could do was choke. Finally, the van stopped. The back door opened. The man who was standing there was the same one who had driven her up the hill in the golf cart.

"Okay," he said. "Come to Daddy. Humberto Laos may be the big boss, but he doesn't get to have all the fun."

3

5:00 P.M., Friday, April 9
Three Points, Arizona

Officer Alonzo Gutierrez slapped his Border Patrol SUV into park and then stepped outside to survey the nearby portion of mesquite-dotted desert landscape through a pair of high-powered binoculars as the sun drifted down behind the rockbound Baboquivari Peak in the Coyote Mountains to the west.

It was close to the end of Al's shift, and he was hoping to come up empty. So far his patrol of the sector from Sasabe north to Three Points hadn't yielded any illegals. If he picked up someone now, he'd be stuck doing paperwork on his own time because, according to his supervisor, overtime was currently off the table no matter what.

Al had grown up in Washington State, the son of migrant workers who had managed to put down roots in Wenatchee. The youngest as well as the tallest of three brothers, he had won a basketball scholarship to WSU. He was the first member of his family to graduate from college, and he should have been living the American dream with a good job and thinking about starting a family of his own. Except things hadn't worked out quite the way he had expected or wanted.

For one thing, his mother hadn't lived long enough to see her son graduate in his cap and gown. Once he was out of school with a business degree, the jobs he had hoped for hadn't materialized. He knew that in the current job market, his less than stellar GPA had hurt him. Jobs for new graduates were scarce to begin with, and even when he managed to get an interview, he never got a callback.

He could have worked with his dad in the orchards and maybe found an office job with one of the growers. After all, that was how he had put himself through school—earning money by working in the fields and orchards during the summer months. Stoop work hadn't been too good for his forebears, but since he had the benefit of an education, he wanted something more than that. And he sure as hell didn't want to hang around Wenatchee now that his father had hooked up with a new wife, Ramona.

As far as the old man was concerned, Al could have stayed at home indefinitely while he continued his job search. Except Ramona wasn't having any of that. The witch had made things so miserable at home that Al had taken the first job that presented itself—an offer to go to work for Border Patrol. When he signed up, he had ditched the name Alonzo in favor of plain Al. And when they had shipped him off to the Arizona desert, he hadn't minded a bit. The farther away from home the job was, the better he liked it. Or so he had thought.

But Al had come to realize that he hated the Arizona desert, and he hated the job. He missed his home state—the rolling hills and fertile farmland of eastern Washington and the snowcapped peaks and towering evergreens of western Washington.

As for the job? Some of the guys were okay, but others weren't. Some of them were beyond gung-ho. Al was there because it was a job and the only job he could get. The fact that he spoke Spanish, thanks to his mother, had worked in his favor. But along with the job came some very real danger, because there were some genuine bad guys out in the desert.

First and foremost were the drug smugglers, of course, who were often armed to the teeth. They tended to shoot first and ask questions later. Next came the people smugglers—the coyotes. They were generally well armed, too, as they transported vans full of illegals from Mexico and other South American countries across the border and into Arizona's interior. Their customers included the traditional illegals—the ones in search of jobs—but they also brought along the occasional would-be jihadists. More than once, Al had encountered troops of otherwise hardworking illegals who had been strong-armed into carrying drugs. The cartels gave them a simple choice: Turn into a mule and carry our drugs north or be dead, take your pick.

On a daily basis, though, Al's work brought him into contact with people who reminded him of his own family—people who crossed the border in search of the American dream, of making a better life for themselves and for their families. And every time he picked up people like that—people whose major crime was wanting to better themselves—he couldn't help but feel guilty, because his family had come north for the same reason. As he rounded up dispirited border crossers and loaded them into buses to ship back home, Al felt guilty because, but for the grace of God, that could have been him. Or his brothers.

Their grandfather had come to the States as part of the old *bracero* program. He had married a U.S. citizen and had become a naturalized citizen himself. Had it not been for Al's father's mother, Al himself wouldn't be here, riding around in a Border Patrol vehicle and doing this job. As conflicted as he somehow felt about all this, he continued to remind himself on a daily basis that it was his job—something he was sworn to do, like it or not.

Al had parked his vehicle on a dirt track on King's Anvil Ranch. Now he walked away from the SUV to the arroyo just out of sight from where he had parked. He knew that illegals often trudged north in dry creek beds, keeping to the sandy washes in hopes of staying out of sight and avoiding apprehension. That was where Al was when he heard the sound of an engine turning over. The engine was followed by a moan of pain that made the hair on the back of Al's neck stand on end. Drawing his weapon and crouching behind a clump of mesquite, he eased his way over to the edge of the wash. In the sand ten feet away, he saw what appeared to be the naked body of a woman lying faceup in the stream bed.

He stood there for a moment, trying to make sense of what he was seeing. The sand surrounding the victim was smooth and undisturbed, as though she had been rolled down the bank and left there.

In his months on the job, Al had seen his share of beating victims, but what he saw here went far beyond a mere beating. The woman's body was bloodied, cut, and bruised. Someone had carved tic-tac-toe games into her skin. Her body was dotted with scabs that he was sure were cigarette burns. But the worst of her injuries looked as though they had been inflicted by someone wearing steel-toed boots while they kicked the hell out of her.

The fact that she was bleeding told Al that she was still alive and her attackers hadn't been gone long. He suspected they had heard his approaching vehicle, and that was what had sent them packing.

Al was torn. It was possible that he could give chase and catch whoever had done this, but he knew that if he left the woman alone for very long, she might well die. That was when she moaned again. The agonizing sound galvanized him to action. He vaulted down the edge of the bank, dropping down beside her. She must have heard him land. Her eyes blinked open.

"Water," she whispered. "Water, please."

Not *agua*, he noticed. Not *por favor.* "Water, please," in English.

"Hold on," he said. "I'll be right back." He raced back to his vehicle, radioing for help as he went. He had no idea who her assailants were, which direction they were going, or what kind of vehicle they were driving, but he did the best he could.

"How bad is she hurt?" the dispatch operator wanted to know.

Al thought about the catalog of bloody bruises, cuts, and burns. "Looks to me like someone tortured her first," he said. "Then they threw her down in the sand and kicked hell out of her."

"Survivable?" the dispatcher asked.

"I don't know," he said. "She's hurt real bad."

"Ambulance or helicopter?" the operator asked. "Your call."

As a taxpayer, Al knew that each and every airlift of an undocumented—and, as a consequence, uninsured—alien was coming out of the pockets of legal Arizona residents at a rate of fifty thousand dollars a pop. Still, he didn't think the woman would live long enough for a regular ambulance to arrive, to say nothing of driving her the fifty or more miles to the nearest trauma center.

"Needs to be an airlift," Al answered.

"Airlift it is," Dispatch said. "I'll give you a call when I know their ETA."

"You've got my coordinates?" he asked.

"Yes, sir. Your vehicle's GPS position is right here on my computer."

Al wondered how things had worked back in the days before all the vehicles came equipped with GPS technology. Back then cops out in the boonies were probably a whole lot harder to find.

He collected a bottle of water and a lightweight blanket from the trunk of his vehicle, then made his way back down to the woman. Her eyes were closed again. Out of nowhere, a swarm of flies had appeared. She gave no indication that she even noticed them buzzing around her and made no effort to drive them away. He did.

"I brought you some water," he said, kneeling beside her. He knew it was dangerous to move a victim, but he did so anyway, lifting her as gently as he could into a semi-sitting position so he could give her some water. Her eyes flickered open briefly, and she moaned again. He held the open bottle up to her parched lips and tried to dribble some water into her mouth. He was afraid she might choke on it, but she managed to swallow a small sip. He offered her more, but she closed her eyes. Since the woman—a girl, really—had apparently passed out, he didn't dare give her more for fear of drowning her.

"They're sending a helicopter to take you to the hospital," he explained, covering her naked body with the blanket, more for modesty's sake than for warmth. She was already far too warm. "They'll be here soon," he added. "Hang on."

Most of the illegals he had met spoke some English, but only with prodding. This one had spoken English even under terrible physical stress. Her blond hair and olive skin constituted a mixed message. She might be Hispanic, but he wasn't sure she was an illegal. If not, who was she, and what was she doing here?

Al sat there cradling the injured woman and keeping the flies away until the helicopter showed up half an hour later. While they waited, he noticed the tape residue on her arms, legs, and mouth—evidence that she had been restrained by her captors either during the attack or before. As the air ambulance attendants moved her onto a gurney, Al noticed the tiny rose tattoo discreetly inked into the side of her right breast with what appeared to be a cigarette burn marring the center of the flower.

Not a prison tat, Ali realized. And not a DIY home-grown ink job, either. Al couldn't ever remember seeing a female illegal sporting a professional tattoo.

Relieved that she was still among the living, Al left her in the care of the air ambulance attendants and went looking for the crime scene. He found it on the other side of the wash, just opposite the spot where he had found her.

On the far bank, the rocky red dirt had been disturbed. From the way the grass was bent, it looked like something—a blanket, maybe, with something heavy in it—had been dropped on the ground. Unfortunately, there were no legible tire or footprints to be found. Broken stalks of dried grass and mesquite branches showed where people on foot had tramped through the desert. Here and there around the place where the blanket must have been, Al found what looked like blood spattered on the ground, as though much of the beating had been administered right there.

He was photographing the scene when his immediate supervisor, Sergeant Dobbs, showed up.

"What have you got?" Kevin Dobbs asked.

"Looks like the worst of the assault happened here," Al answered. "The victim is being airlifted to the trauma center at Physicians Medical in Tucson. If she doesn't make it, this will turn into a homicide. Do you want me to notify Pima County?"

"Naw," Dobbs said, shaking his head. "Don't bother. If you do that, you'll be stuck with a world of paperwork, and so will I. You found her and got her transported. She's an illegal. That makes her somebody else's problem."

Al knew that Sergeant Dobbs wasn't a fan of extra paperwork, either. "What if she isn't?" Al asked.

"Isn't what?"

"Isn't an illegal."

"You found her out here in the desert all by herself, in an area that is known to be full of illegal immigrants, right?"

Al nodded. "Right."

"Did she look like an illegal to you?" Dobbs asked.

"Yes, but—" Al began.

"But nothing," Dobbs interrupted. "If it looks like a duck and walks like a duck and quacks like a duck, then it is a duck. End of story. Go write up your report and hand it over. I'll take it from here, and I want you signed out at the time your shift is over. Got it?"

"Got it," Al answered.

But once he got back to his vehicle, he made a note of the location showing in his GPS. He thought it was likely that Dobbs would simply deep-six any investigation, but if Al needed to get back here with a local homicide detective and without the vehicle he had driven that day, he wanted to know exactly where he was going.

4

5:00 P.M., Friday, April 9
Sedona, Arizona

Late in the afternoon Ali's peaceful reverie was broken by the welcome arrival of twin tornadoes in the form of her two-year-old grandkids. Squealing with delight, Colleen and Colin raced onto the patio just ahead of their father, Chris.

"Mom, can you watch these two dust devils while I check on the footing forms for the cement pour?" Chris, who left nothing to chance and was determined that the sculpture would be spot-on perfect, had arrived carrying a diaper bag laden with kid stuff as well as a giant tape measure.

Seeing both things together made Ali smile. "Sure," she said, "they're safe with me."

When the twins were born, Chris had put both his teaching and his artwork on hold in favor of being a stay-at-home dad, while Athena, their mother, continued to teach and coach at Sedona High. Chris had done an excellent job of caring for the little ones, but as they grew older, Ali had seen evidence of his feeling frustrated and stuck, something she saw as the male equivalent of postpartum depression. Her decision to commission Chris to create the garden's centerpiece had helped snap him out of it. As the job progressed, the old Chris reemerged—energetic, humorous, and full of enthusiasm. And two more people who had seen the work in progress in his basement studio had commissioned him to do pieces for them.

As Ali watched the twins explore the patio—clambering off and on the furniture; chasing after fallen wisteria blossoms; examining an ungainly praying mantis; and asking nonstop questions—she smiled to think what her sophisticated friends from her newscasting days or from the police academy shooting range would think if they could see her now.

She had never been one of those women who spent years longing to be a grandparent, so the joy she took in getting to know Colin and Coleen was entirely unexpected. During the first few months, she had helped out a lot while Chris was trying to get his head around caring for not one but two newborns. With Chris's artwork bringing in extra cash, he and Athena had been able to hire someone to come in and help out as a part-time nanny. Not wanting to be regarded as an interfering mother-in-law, Ali had used the arrival of the nanny as an opportunity to step back. She found herself in the position of seeing the twins less and enjoying them more.

She loved watching their similarities as well as their differences. Did Colleen take after her mother? In some ways, yes. She was fiercely independent, but she also mimicked her father's more artistic side. She loved cooking "pretend" meals and, even more, "helping" a doting and exceedingly patient Leland with real cooking chores at Ali's house.

Colin, on the other hand, was introspective, almost dreamy. Needless to say, he was the quieter of the two. Yes, he played with blocks and could be persuaded to do "art," as in finger painting, but what he really liked was being cuddled and read to. He also loved animals to distraction.

"Where's Sammy?" Colin wanted to know when it got chilly enough to go inside, where they settled into the playroom off the kitchen.

Sammy was Ali's one-eyed, one-eared adopted tabby. She'd come into Ali's life years earlier, arriving as a particularly ugly sixteen-pound foster-care case. The fact that Ali had never had cats and hadn't cared for them all that much was irrelevant. She'd rescued the overweight aging cat as a favor to a dead friend, but over time, Sam had become her cat.

As Sammy had aged, she'd developed mobility issues. Ali and Leland had placed pet stairs here and there, which allowed Sam to reach her favorite spots—on the pillows of Ali's tall bed or on top of the warm clothes dryer. Two years ago, a sudden loss of weight had necessitated a regimen of daily insulin shots. A month ago, Ali had awakened to find Sam seemingly asleep in her usual spot on the bed, only she hadn't been sleeping. All that remained of Sam were the ashes in a polished elm wood box on the fireplace mantel in Ali's bedroom.

"I'm sorry," Ali reminded Colin. "Remember? Sammy's not here anymore."

"Where is she?"

"In heaven."

"Where's that?"

"Far away."

"But why isn't she here?"

"She's dead."

"What's dead?"

Ali had no compunction about tossing Chris under the bus. "Ask your father," she said.

Moments later, as if by magic, Chris returned to collect his offspring and helped oversee the process of putting away toys. After the exchange of sloppy toddler goodbye kisses, Ali went to her room to change out of her tracksuit.

Earlier in the day, B. Simpson had called. "I hope we still have a date tonight for dinner at my place."

"Of course we do. I was just going to change from my sweats into something more appropriate."

"Don't dress up," B. said. "The menu is pizza."

"What a surprise," Ali said. As a dedicated noncook, B. was big on eating out and taking out.

Ali and B. had both grown up in Sedona but fifteen years apart, far too long for them to have known each other. Given the name Bartholomew Quentin Simpson at birth, B. had shortened his name to a single letter in junior high as the result of too much teasing from classmates about the "other" Bart Simpson.

Like Ali, B. had left Sedona in hopes of making his mark on the world, and he had, earning a fortune designing computer games. In the aftermath of a failed marriage, B., again like Ali, had returned to Sedona to get his bearings. For months after coming back home, he had been a daily visitor at Bob and Edie Larson's Sugarloaf Café.

When Bob Larson had learned that his regular customer was in the process of starting a computer security company called High Noon Enterprises, he suggested that Ali look into using their services. At the time Bob made the introduction, he'd had no idea that he was acting as a matchmaker-in-chief.

Ali and B. had now been a couple for several years. During that time, B.'s business, although locally based, had developed into an internationally recognized computer security company with more than a few government contracts. Operating out of a former warehouse in nearby Cottonwood, High Noon employed almost fifty people, an economic boom in an area where many businesses, especially those involving tourism, had taken a big hit.

High Noon still did some private security work, though the company had morphed into one that specialized in providing anti-hacker services to both businesses and government agencies. Believing in fighting fire with fire, B. had attracted a cadre of talented young hackers who were willing to ply their high-tech trade in relatively rural Yavapai County, with its spectacular scenery and laid-back lifestyle. And the understated appearance of the corporate offices belied the multimillion-dollar contracts that routinely found their way into High Noon's in-box.

B. would have happily married Ali, anytime, anywhere, but she wasn't ready for that kind of commitment. She had yet to recover from the emotional damage left behind by the multiple betrayals of her previous husband, Paul Grayson, a serial philanderer who had cheated on her five ways to Sunday. In addition to Ali's trust issues, there was also the fifteen-year age difference between her and B. The idea of being labeled a cradle-robbing cougar was more than Ali could handle, although the label was out there anyway, wedding or no.

For now having pizza together was fine. Having fun together was fine. As for getting married? Not so much.

5

8:00 P.M., Friday, April 9
Nogales, Arizona

Deputy Jose Reyes squirmed in the driver's seat of his idling Santa Cruz County Sheriff's Department Tahoe, trying to find a comfortable position. He had the heat turned down, but with his uniform and Kevlar vest on, it was way too warm in the front seat of his patrol unit.

It was an unusually quiet night. He turned the thermostat down one more notch, leaned back on the headrest, and closed his eyes. It was hours before his shift was due to end, and Jose was more than a little bored.

He would have preferred to be on the prowl for some of the real bad guys in Santa Cruz County, the drug and people smugglers who had turned Nogales—both Nogales, Arizona, and Nogales, Sonora, in Mexico—into booming homicide centers. Instead, he was following orders from headquarters and hanging out on the far side of the Kino Ridge Country Club, waiting to see if he could pick off a likely-looking DUI suspect who would help him meet his moving-violation quota for the week.

Not that Jose had a quota, at least not officially. Unofficially? That was another story, and the retirees who frequented the relatively lowbrow Kino Ridge were more likely than the more upper-crust folks at Amado or Rio Rico to shut up and pay their fines than they were to hire criminal defense attorneys. Every deputy in the department had been told—off the record, of course—that when fines got paid without involving costly court cases, it helped keep the fiscal wheels turning in the Santa Cruz county government.

In southern Arizona, where border security was a top priority, it was also an incredibly divisive issue. People lined up on either side of the illegal-immigrant divide. Some wanted a completely airtight border, while others wanted to open the floodgates. Jose's boss, Sheriff Manuel Renteria, had staked his claim on the tiny sliver of middle ground between the two opposing factions.

As a relatively new officer on the force, Jose chafed under Renteria's "majoring in the minors" approach. He had campaigned for office as a law-and-order man, with a small L and a small O. It seemed to Jose that Renteria was far more concerned with keeping the state roads free of speeders and drunk drivers than he was with stopping the drug or people smugglers. The sheriff wasn't as interested in making a big name for himself as he was in maintaining the status quo by doing the little jobs of law enforcement rather than the big ones. Renteria had let it be known that problems related to the somewhat diminished flood of illegal immigrants and drug cartel smugglers flowing across the border and making their way up and down I-19 were Homeland

Security's problem, not the Santa Cruz County Sheriff's Department's.

Jose wasn't wild about his agency's low-key serve-and-protect focus, but he went along with the program, quietly and without a whole lot of enthusiasm. Nearly three years out of the academy, he had plenty of people counting on him, including a wife and two preschool-aged stepdaughters as well as a boy due to be born within the next few weeks. That meant Jose was grateful to have a job. Lots of the people he knew from the academy weren't that lucky. They had either been laid off or had never found jobs to begin with.

So Jose kept his mouth shut and his nose clean and did his job. This night it meant sitting there, waiting and resting. Once he picked up a speeder or a drunk driver, he'd be home free. Unless there was some kind of emergency call, hours of paperwork would help fill the time until the end of his shift, when he could go home.

Home. Jose was inordinately proud that, a year earlier, he and Teresa had been able to buy a three-bedroom double-wide mobile home on a one-acre plot just outside Patagonia. Jose considered Nogales a less than perfect place to raise kids; he had always dreamed of raising them in a country setting. When they found the place in Patagonia, Teresa hadn't been wild about the location, because it was closer than she liked to her former in-laws, but the price had been more than right—something they could afford on one income without Teresa having to go back to work.

It turned out that Teresa's concerns about her ex-in-laws had been totally unfounded. She hadn't heard word one from Olga and Oscar Sanchez. From what Jose knew about Teresa's vocal ex-mother-in-law, that was just as well. Jose was prepared to let that sleeping dog lie indefinitely.

Buying a house was a big deal for Jose. Both his grandfather Raúl and, later, his father, Carmine, had worked in Arizona's copper mines. Jose remembered growing up in low-cost company housing in San Manuel. At first Carmine had worked underground. Later on he had labored in the smelter in temperatures so sweltering that, on a few occasions, his hard hat had melted.

Both Carmine Reyes and his father before him had been "dusted," the copper miner's term for the lung diseases that plague miners the world over. Both Jose's father and paternal grandfather, neither of whom ever smoked, had succumbed to emphysema in their forties. Ill and dying, Carmine had returned to Santa Cruz County. On his deathbed, he had grasped his teenage son's wrist and begged him to find something to do besides kill himself working in a mine, and to live someplace where he wasn't stuck in company housing.

For a while after high school, Jose had walked on the wild side without ever getting into any serious trouble. He'd reached his mid-twenties before he got serious about his life and enrolled in Santa Cruz Community College to study criminal justice. He had just received his two-year degree when he met Teresa Sanchez. Recently widowed and pregnant with her second child, Teresa came with a ready-made family that included a toddler named Lucia. A beautiful child, Lucy had wormed her way into Jose's heart right along with her mother. When an opening turned up at the Sheriff's Department, Jose had jumped in with both feet. After being hired, he had spent the next month and a half attending police academy training in the Phoenix area.

He and Teresa had married shortly after Jose graduated from the academy and a month before her second child, Carinda, was born. As far as Carinda was concerned, Jose was her father, the only one she had ever known. Since Jose was the one who had driven mother and daughter to and from the hospital, he regarded Carinda as his own. Given the unfortunate circumstances surrounding Danny Sanchez's life and death, Jose was thankful neither Lucy nor Carinda had any real memory of their biological father.

Now. Almost two years later, Teresa was expecting again. This would be her third child and Jose's first. They knew the baby would be a boy, and they had decided to name him Carmine, in honor of his grandfather. Jose was looking forward to having a boy in the family, another male presence in a house that he teasingly told Teresa was overpopulated by females.

Jose hadn't been physically big in high school, but he'd been quick and smart. Years of weightlifting had given him strength that belied his size so that, as a senior, he was named outstanding quarterback on that year's all-state football team.

Since Teresa was tiny—just over five feet—Jose expected their son would be on the small side. Even so, Jose hoped he could raise the boy with the sense that you didn't have to be a big bruiser in order to make your mark in the world. He wanted to instill in this child the same things he had learned from his father and grandfather—that you worked hard, raised your family, kept your promises, and met your obligations. Jose wanted his son to be proud of him the way Jose had been proud of his father and the way Carmine had been proud of his father before him. That was the family legacy he hoped to pass along to his baby boy.

While Jose had been sitting there, several vehicles had come and gone. Two of them had edged up a couple of miles an hour over the posted thirty-five mile-an-hour limit, but that wasn't enough of a margin to get excited about, nothing that made them worth pulling over.

Then another pair of headlights swung into view, coming down the road behind him rather than from the golf course entrance. Jose already had his radar gun in hand, but even before it registered fifty-three he knew he had a live one. By the time the car, an older Buick, surged past him, he was turning on his lights and slamming the Tahoe into gear.

As the car sped past, Jose had the odd impression that he had seen it several times over the course of the evening, although there had been nothing about it then that had aroused his suspicion. He caught a fleeting glimpse of the driver, whose head was covered with a scarf and whose face was half covered by a gigantic pair of post-cataract-surgery, glare-stopping sunglasses.

"It's nighttime, lady," Jose told himself as he swung the Tahoe onto the narrow pavement. "Time to ditch the shades."

Already in pursuit, he tried radioing in his position, but the dispatcher was busy with some other problem. Since this was a routine traffic stop of a solitary speeder, Jose didn't worry about the communications situation all that much, though it did annoy him that the driver didn't pull over immediately. In fact, she didn't seem to notice he was there, even when he came right up on her back bumper with his lights flashing overhead.

What's wrong with her? he wondered. *Is she half blind or half deaf?*

When Jose let out another squawk from the siren, the Buick swerved in a slight jiggle that showed the driver was aware of his presence. Although the Buick slowed down, it didn't stop. Instead, the signals came on, and the Buick turned right onto a small unpaved side road where, after a quarter mile or so, it came to a stop in a cloud of dust.

It was only then, as Jose was opening his car door, that Dispatch got back to him. He spat out his location, said he was making a routine traffic stop, and left his vehicle. He approached the Buick as he'd been taught, walking up to the driver's side, hand on his holstered weapon, calling out instructions.

"Hands where I can see them," he ordered through the open window. Except by the time Jose actually saw the driver's hands, one of them was holding a drawn weapon—a handgun.

Jose closed his fingers around the grip of his own firearm, but before it cleared his holster, a point-blank gunshot caught him full in the gut inches below his vest and sent him sprawling backward onto the soft shoulder, where he tumbled head over heels down a steep brush-covered hillside. At the bottom, his body crashed into a man-size boulder before coming to rest facedown in the rocky dirt.

For a moment or two he lost consciousness.

When his brain came back online, Jose was dimly aware of noises coming from far above him. Warning signals beeped in the night, indicating that car doors had been opened while keys were in the ignition. Doors thumped open and closed while noisy footsteps scurried between at least two vehicles. Those noises were soon followed by the sound of something being smashed, something metal or maybe glass being beaten to pieces.

What the hell is she doing? he wondered. *Wrecking my car?*

He tried to sort out whether she was alone or if someone else had driven up to help her. Or maybe an accomplice of some kind had been hiding in the backseat. If there was someone with her, neither of them spoke, but Jose didn't need to hear any words to understand the gravity of his situation. It was no accident that the woman had pulled off on the deserted road. He'd been deliberately lured into a trap. But why? Were they after his patrol car or something in it? Did someone want him dead?

Far above, a car door slammed shut. The night went totally quiet as the insistent beeping of the ignition alarm was silenced. Footsteps rustled through dried weeds and grass on the shoulder above him, then the blinding light from a flashlight cut through the night. Jose knew that whoever was up there was looking down at him, getting ready to finish the job.

Injured and helpless, Jose could do nothing except lie there waiting for the kill shot he knew was coming. It was only in that final extremity that Jose Reyes remembered Miss Swift, the drama teacher in his senior year at Nogales High School. She had been new to town, a first-year teacher who was also surprisingly good-looking. Jose, along with half the guys in his senior class, had a crush on her.

Wanting to make a good impression on the townsfolk, Miss Swift had decided to bring some culture to town by staging a production of *Hamlet*. Jose had been chosen to play the part of the doomed Ophelia's brother, Laertes. At the very end of the drama, after a fierce sword fight between Laertes and Hamlet, the stage was littered with the supposedly dead bodies of several characters, including Queen Gertrude, the king of Denmark, Hamlet, and Laertes.

During rehearsals, Miss Swift had gotten down on the floor with the actors and coached them on how to slow their breathing and maintain the pose in which they had fallen. All those years later, lying at the foot of the steep bank, that was what Jose did. He stifled the urge to groan in agony. He forced his breathing to slow. He lay still. This time it wasn't make-believe. This time Jose's very life depended on it.

Above, the rustling footsteps came as far as the edge of the ravine and then stopped. The beam from the flashlight circled around and around until it landed on him, catching him and pinning him in an eerie orange glow. When the beam stopped moving, time stopped, too. Jose had no idea how long the killer stood there, peering down into the darkness with the flashlight raking back and forth across his fallen body.

"All right, then," a raspy voice said aloud. "That's that."

Jose couldn't tell if the speaker was talking to herself or someone else. If so, they seemed satisfied by what they saw. The flashlight clicked off. Darkness returned. Another car door slammed. An engine turned over. Headlights came on. Jose waited until the sounds of the retreating vehicle—a single one, it seemed—faded into the night. Only when the insect-humming silence of the desert night reasserted itself did Jose allow himself to take a full breath. And only then, with one danger gone, did he realize the full gravity of his situation.

Jose understood that his life's blood was gradually seeping into the thirsty sandy bottom of the wash that had cushioned his fall. Even if people came searching for him, they weren't likely to spot him lying here in the dark. Jose could tell that with fear-fueled adrenaline no longer pumping into his system, he was in danger of drifting into shock. He fought it, tried to focus. Far away in the distance, he could hear the busy chatter of the police band radio coming from his own vehicle.

The overworked dispatcher must have realized that Jose's radio had gone silent, but how long would it take for her to understand that the situation was serious enough to send people looking for him? And would they arrive in time?

Jose tried to move his right hand, hoping to find his weapon, but that small gesture was accompanied by an astonishing stab of pain. His right arm was broken at the wrist; useless. With agonizing slowness, Jose reached his left hand across his bloody belly. How could there be so much blood but not much pain? Nothing like the pain in his arm.

It occurred to him dimly that not feeling any pain might not be a good thing, but he pushed that thought aside. Jose managed to extract his personal cell phone from his pants pocket. He punched the green button twice, trying to call Teresa. She usually turned the phone to vibrate or silent once the girls went to sleep, so he didn't expect to reach her directly. All he wanted was the chance to say goodbye and to tell her one last time that he loved her. Gritting his teeth, he held the phone to his ear. Nothing. When he checked the readout on the glowing screen, he saw there was no signal.

Groaning in despair, he let the phone fall away. The last thing Jose Reyes thought as he lost consciousness was the final line of the Lord's Prayer: "Thy will be done, on earth as it is in heaven."

6

8:00 P.M., Friday, April 9
Sedona, Arizona

It was dark and cold when Ali pulled into B.'s driveway. As she walked up to ring the bell, the large, rustic front doors looked curiously forbidding. The first time Ali entered the house, it had been little more than a well-carpeted computer lab, with tables and wiring everywhere and banks of computers lining every wall. Soon after, the computers had been banished to the company HQ.

Once the electronics were gone, B. had hired one of Sedona's premier interior designers to transform the place. In the living room, angular side tables and sleek black leather van der Rohe sofas and chairs slung on chrome tubing set a masculine tone. What might have been a cold space was warmed by a two-sided gas fireplace and lots of Navajo rugs, in colorful contrast to the high-gloss birch flooring. Bright red acrylic cubes alternated with leather ones that functioned both as drink tables and, if needed, additional seating.

The stark lines of the furniture were further softened by subdued lighting that, when dimmed, glowed like candlelight. At night, a few brightly colored cushions and several blown-glass pieces provided a cozy and colorful shimmer to the room. During the day, the panoramic two-story windows came alive with unimpeded views of Sedona's red cliffs.

Ali liked the house, which she thought could be featured as a photo shoot for *Architectural Digest*. Although his house and hers were both aesthetically pleasing, hers was long on chintz and natural-grained wood. Based on furnishing style preferences alone, cohabitation in the near future looked unlikely, and maintaining their separate homes seemed like a good idea.

After greeting Ali with a breezy kiss, B. led her into his kitchen, where a red-and-white-checked tablecloth covered his round glass table, lending warmth to what was essentially an oversize stainless-steel catering kitchen. The table was set for two, complete with proper Bordeaux wineglasses. Ali handed over her bottle of wine—a 2004 Amarone bottled by Guiseppe Campagnola from grapes grown in the Caterina Zardini vineyards.

B. examined the bottle and laughed. "This should certainly do justice to Pago's pizza."

While he opened and poured the wine, Ali loaded plates with slices of pizza and mounds of Caesar salad.

"What did you do today?" B. asked.

"Sorted through the nominees for the scholarship," she answered. "Once again I ended up with two winners."

"Why doesn't that surprise me?" B. said with a grin. "What are their names?"

"Autumn and Olivia," Ali answered.

He raised his glass in a toast. "So here's to Autumn and Olivia, your two new Askins scholars."

"Thanks," Ali said, touching her glass to his. "Let's hope they do well. And what about you? When do you have to leave?"

He glanced at his watch. "I fly to D.C. tomorrow at four. I'm the Sunday-morning breakfast speaker at an international congress of security geeks. After the conference, I have meetings scheduled for most of the rest of the week. Should be back late Friday. If your dance card's not too full, maybe we can spend the weekend together."

Ali knew better than to ask for more detail. Most of what B. did these days was classified. Though he had a grueling travel schedule and work consumed most of his waking hours, he also clearly enjoyed what he did. He certainly didn't do it for the money.

Truth was, Ali envied his passion for his work. She remembered having that fire in her belly before it got extinguished, or rather, diminished, by a series of betrayals, both professional and personal. She knew now that she felt best when she was helping people.

"My week looks a lot less complicated than yours," she said. "With any luck, by the time you get back, the weather will have broken and we'll be ready to plant the garden."

"Speaking of that," B. said, "I hope you're not over-working poor Leland."

"Of course not," Ali said. "He's limited to supervisory work only."

"Good. How old is he, anyway?" B. asked. "Since he served in Korea, must be getting up there. Isn't it about time for you to let him retire?"

"When I mention that to him, he says he retires every night," Ali replied. "Besides, Leland and I have an understanding: He can work for me as long as he wants to."

"I see," B. said, helping himself to another slice of pizza. "Kind of like our understanding—that I'm welcome to hang around as long as I want to?"

Ali realized the conversation had gone from light-hearted to serious in the blink of an eye. "You're too young to have grandkids," she pointed out, "and I'm too old to have kids."

"I never said I wanted to have kids," B. replied evenly. "As far as I can see, skipping kids and going straight to grandkids seems pretty efficient."

"You might change your mind."

"I might," he conceded, "but I doubt it. I work too much to have kids. In the meantime, you and I apparently have an understanding. I can live with that."

Dropping the subject, he poured them more wine. When it was gone, they loaded the dishwasher and cleaned up the kitchen. Then they made their way upstairs to the combination study/bed/media room that B. referred to as his man-cave.

The furniture may not have been to Ali's liking, but what went on in the bed was more than fine with her. Under the soft duvet, their differences in style and age were beside the point.

Yes, in that massive four-poster bed, Ali Reynolds and B. Simpson were most definitely on the same page.

7

12:30 A.M., Saturday, April 10
Patagonia, Arizona

At a bit past midnight, summoned from a restless sleep, Teresa Reyes heard the doorbell and staggered out of bed with the sense of dread that all cops' wives live with day in and day out. She knew that whoever was out there ringing the bell in the middle of the night was bringing bad news. She flung on her robe and raced to the front door in hopes of keeping the noisy bell from ringing again and waking the girls.

When she turned on the porch light and opened the door, there stood Sheriff Renteria, his face distraught, shaking his head. Seeing him, she immediately assumed the worst—Jose was dead. She grabbed the door frame and used it to hold herself upright.

"I'm sorry to have to tell you this," the sheriff said, mumbling the words as he fought for control. "There's been an unfortunate incident."

"Oh, no," Teresa groaned. She stumbled backward into the room, reeling under the weight of the terrible news. She might have fallen all the way to the floor if Renteria hadn't reached out and steadied her.

"Please," she begged. "Don't tell me Jose is dead. He can't be."

"Shhh," Renteria said, pulling her to him. "He's not dead, but he's been shot and wounded. It's serious, Teresa. I won't lie to you and say he's going to be fine, because the EMTs told me it's bad. He's being transported to the trauma center at Physicians Medical Center in Tucson."

When those last few hopeful words penetrated Teresa Reyes's consciousness, she fought her way out of the numbing fog of despair and clung to them with grim desperation. "You mean he's really not dead?" she asked.

"He's still alive," Renteria allowed. "At least he was when they airlifted him out."

Teresa knew that airlifting was expensive, that it was used in only the most desperate cases, but the welcome news filled her heart with a thin thread of hope. "Why not University Medical Center?" she asked. UMC was the premier trauma center in Tucson.

"The EMTs told me that for this kind of injury, Physicians is the best bet," the sheriff said. Then he pointed toward a patrol car easing its way down the driveway toward the mobile home.

"Do you know Deputy Carson?" Renteria asked. "Jimmy."

Teresa nodded. "I've seen him around town, but I don't really know him."

"I asked him to come stay with you until you can get things organized. Then he'll drive you to the hospital. Under the circumstances, I don't want you driving yourself."

"You're right," Teresa agreed. "And thank you."

Once the sheriff left her alone, Teresa stood in the entryway, frozen into a block of indecision. What should she do? Wake the girls? Bring them along to the hospital? Or should she leave them here, sound asleep, while she alone dealt with the crisis? She considered calling her mother, but Maria Delgado lived in Nogales. After her recent cataract surgery, she was no longer comfortable driving anywhere other than her immediate neighborhood, and she didn't venture out at night at all. In addition to vision problems, Maria Delgado was frail. Not only did she have a debilitating heart condition, she also suffered from osteoporosis. Yes, she loved the girls dearly and could look after Lucy and Carinda as long as they were sound asleep, but she didn't have the upper-body strength to wrestle Carinda in and out of her crib, and she didn't have the energy to chase after the two lively preschoolers once they were awake.

There was only one option. In preparation for having the baby, Teresa had already packed a bag to take to the hospital. She grabbed a diaper bag and stuffed it with enough items to get Lucy and Carinda through the morning. Motioning Deputy Carson into the house, she handed him the bags and asked him to get Carinda's car seat and Lucy's booster out of the back of her minivan and put them in the back of his patrol car. With any luck, the girls would never remember that they'd been hauled out of their beds in the middle of the night. While Carson loaded the car, Teresa lugged the two sleeping girls out to the waiting vehicle and buckled them in. The deputy had started the engine. His car was warm. The girls stirred a little and were quiet.

The gate at the end of the driveway was closed. Jimmy started to get out to open it. "I will," Teresa said. She held it open while Jimmy drove through. Had Teresa looked to the right just then, she might have seen a car parked at the far end of the cul-de-sac with its lights doused and its engine running. Teresa's mind was elsewhere, however. Hurriedly, she closed the gate, fastened it, and climbed back into the patrol car. Then she sat quietly while Carson maneuvered the winding road that led back to the highway.

"What happened?" she asked when they turned onto the blacktop, where the deputy switched on his emergency lights and hit the gas.

"Didn't Sheriff Renteria tell you?"

"Some," she said. "But I was so upset, I wasn't really listening."

"Jose was out on patrol by himself," Carson said. "Down by the Kino Ridge golf course. He called Dispatch, saying he was doing a routine traffic stop. After that, his radio went silent. Dispatch sent someone looking for him at his last reported location. They found him shot and bleeding at the bottom of a ravine."

"Do they have any idea who did it?" Teresa asked.

Carson shrugged. "We sent out a Blue Alert, but we have no leads. It's early, though."

Blue Alerts were for injured cops what Amber Alerts were for kids. They went out to other police jurisdictions when an officer had been assaulted and the perpetrator was at large.

"What about his dashboard camera?"

"Smashed and then taken. Along with the rest of the system," Carson said.

"So there's no film of what happened?"

"The memory stick was in the camera, and that's gone," Carson said.

"What about Jose?"

"The EMTs transported him by ambulance back to the parking lot at Kino Ridge. There, an air ambulance picked him up and took him to Tucson."

Teresa spent the rest of the drive to the hospital in prayerful silence. Three years earlier she had made an eerily similar trip. That one had taken her from the rented home she had shared with her first husband, Danny, on Tucson's far west side to the trauma unit at UMC. That night a uniformed cop from the Tucson PD had knocked on her door to tell her that Danny Sanchez had been shot in a drive-by in South Tucson.

On the way to the hospital that time, she remembered what her mother had tried to tell her about Danny when she first started dating him: that he was bad news. Even though Danny came from a decent family—his father, Oscar, raised quarter horses in the San Rafael Valley—the boy was trouble.

The problem, of course, was that bad boys were always more exciting and interesting than the good ones. In the beginning Teresa had found it easy to ignore all of her mother's warnings. Besides, she wasn't worried. Danny promised her that once they had kids, he'd settle down, quit hanging around with his bad-boy buddies, and stop using drugs.

When Lucy was born, Teresa had fully expected

those promises would be kept, but they weren't—none of them. She soon found herself hassling Danny about everything: quitting drugs, ditching his friends, and getting a real job. The more she nagged, the worse things got. When they ran behind on the bills or needed money for groceries, Danny's mother—far more than his father—was there with a checkbook, ready and willing to bail out her mama's-boy only son.

Teresa hadn't wanted to be bailed out. What she'd wanted was for Danny to grow up. She wanted the two of them to have a real life together, functioning as a real family, without always having to be beholden to his parents, especially to Olga. Teresa had already figured out that Olga's purse strings were iron-clad apron strings.

By the time Lucy turned two, Teresa was pregnant again, and she and Danny were fighting more and more. Finally, she gave him an ultimatum. Either he grow up and get a job, or she was taking Lucy and leaving. She had been screaming at him when he stormed out of the house and drove away.

It was later that night when the cop knocked on her door. Still in a rage, Danny had gone to some of his favorite South Tucson hangouts, where he and his friends had done some serious drinking. Just before closing time, there was an altercation that went from inside a bar to outside. Out in the parking lot, one of the guys from the fight got in his car and drove away. A few minutes later, he came back, driving past where Danny and his friends were gathered. The driver's window rolled down. Danny was shot at point-blank range without the vehicle ever coming to a stop.

At the time, the car Danny was driving was registered in his mother's name. The address on his license was Olga Sanchez's Tucson address. For that reason, Danny's parents were the first to be notified of the shooting. They had been at the hospital for some time before Olga thought to send someone to let Teresa know what had happened. The cop who had rung her doorbell that night had been kind enough to take Teresa and Lucy to the hospital.

The next three days had been a nightmare. Danny's grim-faced doctors had made it clear from the beginning that it was unlikely their critically injured patient would survive. Even if he did, the kind of catastrophic brain damage he had suffered would probably leave him permanently paralyzed. While Danny's father had stayed in the background, Olga had been front and center, weeping hysterically and railing at her daughter-in-law. If only Teresa had been a better wife to Danny, maybe he wouldn't have been out partying in the middle of the night. As far as Olga was concerned, what had happened had everything to do with Teresa's behavior and nothing at all to do with her son's bad choices.

Teresa already had a toddler to care for and was expecting a second baby. The prospect of caring for a helpless and possibly bedridden husband was more than she could take. She was actually relieved when, three nights after he was shot, the lines on Danny's monitor went flat, announcing to the world that he was gone. Yes, she grieved for him, but more for what she had hoped to have with him rather than what she'd had.

Because Danny had no job, there was no group insurance. In fact, there was no insurance of any kind. Danny's parents had paid the medical bills, which Teresa suspected were astronomical. They also paid for the funeral at the old Catholic church on South Sixth and Twenty-second, only a few blocks from where Danny had been gunned down. At the hospital, Oscar had told Teresa that she and the girls were welcome to come live on the ranch with them. It was a generous offer, and it meant that Teresa's girls would have wanted for nothing. Teresa had been considering it right up until the scene at the funeral when Olga lit into Teresa again, proclaiming in public that Danny's death was all her fault.

For Teresa, that was the final straw. A few weeks later, when the rent came due and she had no money, Teresa didn't even consider accepting Olga and Oscar's help. Instead of taking the easy way out, Teresa had rented a U-Haul truck. With the help of Uncle Tomás, her mother's younger brother, and a couple of cousins, she had moved out of the house and back into her widowed mother's tiny place in Nogales. Her uncle had helped her get a job as a receptionist for one of the trucking companies headquartered in Nogales. That was where she was working when Jose came back into her life through a friend of his who was a driver for the same company.

Teresa and Jose had known each other slightly in high school, but he had been one of those boring good guys who, at the time, hadn't gotten a second glance. Jose had known Danny, too. They had played football together, but they hadn't been pals.

Teresa had been pregnant with Carinda when she started dating Jose shortly after Jose had been hired by the sheriff's department. They had married days after his graduation from the academy.

The last time Olga communicated with Teresa was the day of Danny's funeral, but just because she wasn't talking to Teresa didn't keep her from talking about her. Word of the rumors made their way back to Teresa. Olga told anyone who would listen that she was sure Teresa and Jose had been an item long before Danny's death. It hurt Teresa to think that the girls' grandmother had shut them out of her life—that in order to punish Teresa for something she hadn't done, Olga had resolutely turned her back on Lucy and Carinda. That was too bad for Olga, and too bad for the girls, but for Teresa, given the choice between having a relationship with her toxic former mother-in-law and having Jose Reyes as her husband, it was no contest.

Now Teresa's life was about to undergo another sea change. What if Jose died? Then she'd be on her own again, this time with three kids to support instead of two. She had become involved with Jose because he was Danny's exact opposite. Jose was a good guy. She had known instinctively that he would be a good provider. Yes, she had worried about him being a police officer. She read about police officers dying on the job all the time, but she had also read about officers who retired after thirty-plus years on the job without ever firing a round in the line of duty. When Jose put on his uniform and went to work, she simply closed her mind to the possibility that he might die.

With Jose lying unconscious in the ICU, Teresa forced herself to face facts. If he died, there would probably be some insurance benefits. Jose had put Teresa on the county paperwork as his beneficiary even before they tied the knot. Even so, raising kids was expensive. Teresa knew that she'd probably end up losing the house in Patagonia. It had been Jose's dream house but not hers, and Teresa alone wouldn't be able to cover the expenses. She'd have to go back to Nogales to live with her mother again; she'd have to see if she could get her old job back.

"Here we are," Deputy Carson said.

For the last twenty miles of the trip, Teresa had been so lost in thought that she hadn't said a word. They had driven all the way across the city without her noticing. They arrived at the hospital at almost three in the morning. Deputy Carson stayed in the car with the two sleeping kids while Teresa walked into the main entrance to get directions.

With Deputy Carson's help, Teresa eventually managed to get the two girls and all their stuff hauled to the waiting room outside the OR. Three hours later, with the girls waking up and asking nonstop questions, a surgeon emerged from the operating room. "Mrs. Reyes?" he asked, holding out his hand.

Teresa had tried to prepare herself for the bad news. Nodding, she stood up, holding Carinda on her hip while Lucy, suddenly shy, ducked out of sight behind her.

"Yes," Teresa said, taking the proffered hand.

"I'm Dr. William Lazlo, your husband's surgeon. The good news is that he's survived the surgery. He's being transferred to a recovery room. It's a miracle that he didn't bleed to death before he got here. The EMTs did a great job of stabilizing him. We've done what we could to repair the damage, but we had to resection his bowel. For right now he'll have a stoma—you know what that is?"

Teresa swallowed. "You mean like a bag?"

The doctor nodded. "Yes, a bag. There was also some damage to his lower back. Apparently, two of the vertebrae were damaged by the fall. We've managed to stabilize them, too, and we've lowered his body temperature in an effort to prevent swelling in his spinal cord. In other words, we're doing everything we can, but worst-case scenario, you need to be prepared for the idea that your husband may have long-term issues with both the intestinal damage as well as with his back."

"You mean he might be paralyzed?"

"Possibly."

Teresa absorbed that dire news in stricken silence.

"Can we see Daddy?" Lucy asked.

The doctor shook his head. "I'm afraid not, young lady," he said. "Your father's too sick to see anyone right now except maybe your mother."

Teresa managed to commandeer an abandoned wheelchair to transfer the kids and all their stuff from the OR waiting room to the recovery room waiting room. An hour after that, when Jose was moved from recovery to the ICU, she repeated the process. Once in the new waiting room, she came face-to-face with the ICU rules—no children under sixteen were allowed inside the unit. When Danny had been in the ICU, his parents had been there, too. They had looked after Lucy when Teresa went into Danny's room. Now, alone with two girls and a husband in the ICU, Teresa Reyes needed help.

Up to that point, she had resisted calling her ailing mother, but now she did so. While she waited for Maria Delgado to sort out transportation from Nogales to Tucson, Teresa settled back in one chair with her feet and swollen ankles propped on another. Her cell phone rang as she started to doze off. She expected the call to be from her mother. It wasn't.

"It's Donnatelle, from Yuma. I just heard what happened," Donnatelle Craig said. "How bad is it, and what can I do to help?"

Donnatelle and Jose had been classmates at the police academy. When Jose and Teresa got married, Jose had invited several of his fellow recruits to the wedding. Much to their mutual surprise, Teresa had hit it off with Donnatelle Craig, a black woman who was both a single mother and a deputy for the Yuma County Sheriff's Department. The two women had stayed in touch ever since, sharing the occasional e-mail.

Teresa had been holding herself together for hours, and Donnatelle's long-distance sympathy sapped her hard-won composure.

"It's real bad," Teresa said, her voice breaking. "Jose's in the ICU. He may not make it."

"Where are you? Which hospital?"

"Physicians Medical in Tucson."

"Who's there with you?"

"Nobody. My mother's on her way. Right now it's just the girls and me."

"You're there by yourselves?" Donnatelle demanded in disbelief. "You mean there's no one there from Jose's department?"

"Not so far. One of the deputies gave us a ride here. After he dropped us off, he had to leave again. I'm sure someone will show up eventually."

"Do they have any idea who did it?" Donnatelle asked.

"From what Sheriff Renteria told me, Jose was shot in the course of a routine traffic stop."

"Routine my ass," Donnatelle muttered. "And somebody from his department should be there with you."

That was what Teresa thought as well, but she didn't say so.

"Let me make some phone calls," Donnatelle said. "I'll get back to you."

Teresa closed her phone. Her mother was coming. Donnatelle would do what she could to help. What Teresa needed was a few moments of peace and quiet and maybe even a minute or two of sleep, but just then a firefight broke out between the two girls over who got which of the few toys Teresa had brought along. In the process of breaking up the fight, Teresa discovered that Carinda's diaper needed to be changed. By the time she did that, Lucy was announcing she was hungry.

No, for Teresa Reyes, there was no time to sleep.

8

2:00 A.M., Saturday, April 10
Vail, Arizona

Alonzo Gutierrez was up early even though he had barely slept. All night long, whenever he drifted off, he'd been plagued with a recurring nightmare about being burned with cigarettes. He knew where that came from. After starting coffee, he went outside to collect his newspaper.

Yes, Al was twenty-five years old. Yes, he had grown up in a world where microwave ovens were everywhere. He didn't remember a time when computers hadn't been readily available. Even though he was a full-fledged member of the digital generation and reasonably computer-savvy, he still liked reading newspapers; liked the feel of newsprint in his hands. Delivering newspapers back home in Wenatchee was the first job he'd ever had.

He and three other young Border Patrol officers shared a four-bedroom house in Vail, outside Tucson. The house had been built before the real estate crash. When it didn't sell, the developer had turned it and many of the other unsold houses in the neighborhood into rentals. It was a cost-effective place to live for four guys who weren't making tons of money.

Al was the one who paid for the newspaper subscription. He also endured plenty of teasing from his roomies about reading a "dead-tree" paper, although he noticed that once he finished with it, the sports pages, at least, got plenty of use from guys who never helped pay for them.

That morning Al scanned the news pages of the *Arizona Daily Sun,* checking for any mention of the Three Points assault and wondering if the woman was alive. The paper had a reporter named Michelle Skidmore who specialized in immigration issues and wrote an ongoing column called "Crossings" that often dealt with crimes against illegal immigrants. That day's column concerned vandals who routinely destroyed the watering stations that volunteers set up and supplied with potable water to keep migrating illegals from dying of dehydration.

The assault wasn't mentioned there or anywhere else in the paper, either; that and the fact that there was no mention of it on the morning news while he was eating breakfast made Al wonder if Dobbs had buried the report. If so, it wouldn't be the first time.

The whole idea disgusted him, but Al wasn't about to run up the flag to the media or to anybody else. The brass had made it clear that contact with the media was forbidden for guys like him. The officers who had made the mistake of complaining to reporters about being told to let up on taking illegals into custody had been put on unpaid leave, and spending time on unpaid leave was something Al Gutierrez couldn't afford.

As for calling in an anonymous tip? He had a feeling those were a lot less anonymous than advertised. Cell phone calls could be traced. E-mails could be traced. And if he tried going over Sergeant Dobbs's head, there would be hell to pay.

For right now, there was nothing for Al to do but put on his uniform and go do his shift.

Whatever had happened to that poor girl south of Three Points was someone else's problem, not his. And with any kind of luck, over time, maybe Al's resulting nightmares would go away.

9

7:00 A.M., Saturday, April 10
Sedona, Arizona

Awakening the next morning, Ali heard the steady thrum of B.'s treadmill and the muffled sound of a television news broadcast from the exercise room down the hall. Slipping into a tracksuit she kept at his place for just these occasions, Ali made her way to his tiny but well-equipped gym. When she showed up, B. moved from the treadmill to the free weights. Ali was about to step onto the treadmill in his place when her phone rang. A glance at the caller ID didn't help. The number was unfamiliar.

"Hello, Ali?"

"Yes."

"It's Donnatelle—Donnatelle Craig—from the academy."

"Yes, Donnatelle. How are you?" Ali's caller had enough confidence in her voice to make her unrecognizable. The realization made Ali smile. Clearly, this new Donnatelle was a far cry from the hesitant young woman Ali remembered from her time at the academy in Peoria.

Two and a half years earlier, Donnatelle had been in despair about her prospects and in danger of washing out of training. Ali had reached out a hand to help Donnatelle along, encouraging her with her firearms handling and target range shooting. In the end, Donnatelle successfully completed the course and graduated along with the rest of her class. The last Ali heard from her, Donnatelle was serving as a sworn deputy with the Yuma County Sheriff's Department.

"I hope I'm not calling too early."

"Not around here you aren't," Ali said. "I'm up and at 'em. How've you been?"

"I'm fine," Donnatelle said. "But I'm calling with some bad news. Have you heard about Jose? I just got a Blue Alert about it."

"You mean Jose Reyes from our class?" Ali asked.

"Yes," Donnatelle said. "He's been working for the Santa Cruz Sheriff's Department. He was shot last night."

Jose Reyes had been another academy classmate. Initially, he and Ali had butted heads, but by the time their training was over, they had not only buried the hatchet, they had acquired a genuine respect and fondness for each other. Jose had helped Ali care for a troubled friend named Brenda Riley when she had shown up in Peoria, drunk and begging for help. After that, Ali had returned the favor by helping Jose and Donnatelle master some of the academic aspects of their training.

It struck Ali as ironic that without her tutoring, neither Jose nor Donnatelle might have graduated from the academy. Almost three years later, they were both working in law enforcement, while Ali wasn't. What was that old saying? Something about those who can, do, while those who can't, teach.

"What happened?" Ali asked.

"He was on patrol a few miles outside Nogales. He was making a supposedly routine stop when he was shot at close range. When they found him, he was transported to a trauma unit. The last I heard, he was alive, but that's about all. It's bad."

"Will he make it?" Ali asked.

"I just talked to his wife, Teresa. The jury's still out," Donnatelle answered grimly. "He was airlifted to Physicians Medical Center in Tucson, where he's undergone surgery. According to Teresa, the hospital lists his condition as guarded."

"Doesn't sound good," Ali agreed.

"It gets worse. Teresa is eight and a half months pregnant. She's stuck at the hospital with her two preschoolers from a previous marriage."

Clearly, Donnatelle had stayed in closer contact with Jose and his family than Ali had. She had heard that he was married, but the last bit—about three kids being involved in this looming tragedy—hit Ali hard.

She understood more than most exactly how tough it was to raise even one baby without a father. She'd had to do that herself when Dean, her first husband, had lost his battle with glioblastoma weeks before Christopher was born. If Jose Reyes died as a result of his wounds, he would leave behind a widow with three orphaned children.

"Do you have any contact information for them?" Ali asked.

"Sure do," Donnatelle said. "Like I said, Jose's wife's name is Teresa—with a T-E rather than a T-H. About a year ago they bought a place in Patagonia."

Donnatelle reeled off both a post office box as well as phone numbers and an e-mail address. Ali jotted down the information.

"I'm just now going off shift," Donnatelle went on. "Tomorrow is my day off. It sounds like Teresa is completely overwhelmed and could use some help. My mom's coming over to look after my kids. As soon as she gets here, I'm on my way to Tucson."

"I can't come down today," Ali said. "I've got company coming for dinner. But I could show up tomorrow and stay for a day or so. You'll keep me posted?"

"Sure will," Donnatelle said.

"And speaking of your kids," Ali said, "how are they?"

"Fine," Donnatelle answered. "All three of them made the honor roll."

"Good for them," Ali said. "And good for you!"

That was the main reason Donnatelle had been determined to make it through the academy. She had wanted to set a good example for her kids, and she was obviously doing so.

They hung up after that. Ali stood with her cell phone in hand and her dialing finger poised to dial Teresa Reyes's cell phone number. Ultimately, she didn't call. For one thing, Teresa Reyes didn't know Ali from Adam, and in the midst of this crisis, she didn't need to be juggling phone calls from people she didn't know. Helping out in person would be different. Even now, years after her first husband's death, Ali could remember the people, some of them distant acquaintances or friends of friends, who had simply shown up unannounced at the hospital or at the apartment to help Ali with her dying husband and later with her newborn son.

Ali knew right then that she'd be on her way to Tucson first thing on Sunday morning. Maybe she didn't owe it to the Reyes family, but she did to the people who had helped her when she needed it. They had paid it forward, and now she would pay them back.

"What's up?" B. asked. He was still hard at work on the elliptical machine.

"Jose Reyes, one of the guys from the academy, got shot Saturday night."

"That deputy down in Santa Cruz County?"

Ali nodded.

"It was on the news a little while ago," B. said. "I thought the name sounded familiar, but I didn't make the connection. Wasn't he the one who blacked your eye just before that Labor Day weekend?"

"That's the one," Ali answered with a smile. "He's also the one who helped me out when Brenda Riley was in such bad shape. Donnatelle Craig, one of our classmates, heard about it on a Blue Alert and called from Yuma to let me know."

"Is he going to be all right?"

"Can't tell," Ali answered. "He's been airlifted to Tucson for surgery. According to Donnatelle, he and his wife are expecting a baby in a matter of weeks, and there are two older kids as well."

"Tough," B. said.

Nodding her agreement, Ali stepped onto the tread-mill and punched in her settings. "Sister Anselm is coming for dinner tonight, and Leland has been cooking up a storm. Tomorrow I'll drive down to Tucson and see what I can do to help. Being in a hospital waiting room with an injured husband and little kids is no picnic."

"Speaking of Brenda Riley," B. said after a pause, "what do you hear from her these days? Is she still sober?"

Brenda Riley and Ali Reynolds had been contemporaries working for sister television stations back in the days when Ali was a television newscaster in L.A. They had been forced off-screen about the same time, due to having reached the female equivalent of a pull-by date. Since that was about the same time Ali's second marriage blew up, she had come home to Sedona to get her life back in order and recover. Brenda had done the opposite. She had gone on a bender that lasted for a couple of years and nearly killed her.

While Brenda was in the process of sobering up, she'd had the misfortune of falling under the spell of a cyberstalker. When the situation had gone from bad to worse, Ali, with the help of a Grass Valley homicide detective named Gilbert Morris, had managed to pull Brenda's fat out of the fire.

Much to Ali's surprise, in the ensuing months, Detective Morris and Brenda had morphed into a romantic item, complete with a beachside wedding Ali had attended solo because B. was off on some business trip or other. After the ceremony, Gil and Brenda had laughingly told Ali that theirs was a match made in hell rather than heaven.

"Yes, she's still sober," Ali said. "She wrote a book that's due out soon. You do remember that her mother died, don't you?"

"Not really," B. admitted.

"Brenda's share of the estate evidently came to quite a chunk of change. Last month Gil was able to pull the pin on his job with the Grass Valley PD."

"He's a little young to be retired, isn't he?" B. asked.

"He's only retired from law enforcement," Ali answered. "He and Brenda are in the process of buying an operating B-and-B in Ashland, Oregon. Ashland isn't all that far from Redding, where Gil's kids live with his ex-wife."

"Sounds like a lot of work," B. said.

"Having an ex-wife?"

"No, running a B-and-B. It's a job description that automatically requires the owner to be civil to a bunch of yahoo customers first thing in the morning," B. said. "Before you even have your first cup of coffee. Spare me."

"Because you're a grump in the morning?" Ali asked.

"Pretty much," B. agreed.

When their joint workout was over, Ali and B. paused in the kitchen long enough to share a cup of coffee and two pieces of leftover pizza. Coffee beans kept in the freezer were the only fresh food that could survive B.'s long absences without going bad. Ali was grateful for the pizza. After spending the night living in sin at her place or B.'s, she was capable of showing up at the Sugarloaf and brazening it out with her parents, but she didn't like doing it.

"I'm going to miss you," Ali said.

"No, you won't," B. replied. "You'll be too busy planting that garden of yours to even notice I'm gone."

"You're wrong," Ali told him. "I'll notice."

Sometime later, knowing that B. needed time to get gathered up and packed, Ali kissed him goodbye and headed home, where she found she had the place to herself. Leland was out doing some last-minute shopping for dinner, while the house was filled with the tangy aromas of the duck-breast and sausage-laced cassoulet they would share that evening with Sister Anselm.

Stopping off long enough to pour herself a cup of coffee, she went into the library, where there was a distinct chill in the air. A storm had blown in overnight, driving away yesterday's bright blue sky. Outside her window, a few flurries of snowflakes drifted from an overcast sky.

"So much for spring," Ali muttered, lighting the gas log in the fireplace.

At her desk, Ali set her cup down in the empty space next to her computer and found herself missing her kitty.

For years, that spot on her desk had been one of Samantha's favorite perches. Trying not to miss Sam too much, Ali booted up her computer and began looking for articles about a recent officer-involved shooting near Nogales. She was busy reading through a collection of online news articles when her new-e-mail notice dinged. Checking the list, she found a message from Sister Anselm.

Sorry. Just had a call out. On my way to Tucson. Please give Mr. Brooks my regrets. So sorry to miss his cassoulet.

An energetic seventy-something, Sister Anselm split her time between serving as a resident psychologist at St. Bernadette's, a facility for troubled nuns in Jerome, and acting as a special emissary for the head of the Phoenix diocese, Bishop Francis Gillespie. A "call out" meant that she had been summoned to serve as the patient advocate for some unfortunate who had landed in a hospital somewhere in Arizona without anyone to act as an intermediary between the injured patient and the medical community.

The vast majority of Sister Anselm's patients were UDAs who came to grief while making the dangerous trek north and hoping to cross the border undetected somewhere in the wilds of the Arizona desert. Some of her patients came with injuries suffered in fierce car chases that routinely scattered dead and dying illegals along isolated stretches of Arizona roadways. Some of them, attempting to cross the border on foot, were abandoned by coyotes without sufficient food or water to survive in the unrelenting desert. Sometimes Sister Anselm's patients were found close to death from dehydration or starvation or sunstroke. Others were clearly the victims of vicious acts of violence perpetrated either by their supposed guides or by their fellow illegals.

The most seriously injured ended up in hospitals with no idea of what had happened to them or how they had come to be there. Isolated and alone, they found themselves being treated by doctors they couldn't understand. Usually they had no one to help them navigate the unknown health procedures that might or might not save their lives. In those situations, Sister Anselm often turned out to be their only ally. She knew what it was like to be lost and alone in a foreign land because it had happened to her.

Sister Anselm had been born as Judith Becker into a German-American family from Milwaukee, Wisconsin, prior to the beginning of World War II. When war broke out, her father, Hans, a recent immigrant, was arrested on suspicion of being a German spy and sent to a war relocation center in Texas, where he developed TB. His wife, Sophia, a natural-born citizen, renounced her U.S. citizenship and went to Texas to care for him, taking her two young daughters with her.

The father, Hans, died on board a Swedish ocean liner during an abortive prisoner-of-war exchange, leaving his widow and daughters to soldier on as displaced persons in war-torn Europe. By then Sophia had also developed TB. When she, too, died, her orphaned daughters were taken in and cared for by the sisters in a small convent in France. The older of the two girls had rebelled against her religious caretakers and come to a bad end on the streets of Paris by the time she was seventeen. The younger girl, Judith, had grown up to become a nun herself—Sister Anselm.

Blessed with a natural facility for foreign tongues, she was fluent in several languages and conversant in several more. Sister Anselm's personal history of utter abandonment while she was a child had left her with an affinity for people in similar circumstances. It was her skill as a translator that had brought Sister Anselm and her story to the attention of a young American priest named Father Gillespie at Vatican II in Rome. Years later, when Father Gillespie was appointed bishop of the Phoenix Diocese, he had sought out Sister Anselm and brought her back to the land of her birth where he put her to work interceding on behalf of people who otherwise would have no voice.

That was how Sister Anselm and Ali had first met— at the bedside of a critically burned woman who was terribly injured in a fire set by an ecoterrorist. Before it was over, the two women found themselves facing down a crazed killer in a desert shoot-out. With a relationship forged under a hail of bullets, it was hardly surprising that the two women had been fast friends ever since, but they both knew that when Sister Anselm was on call, she was on call.

Ali went straight to the kitchen to let Leland know their expected dinner guest would be a no-show. She knew he would be saddened that his cassoulet, two days in the making, would be wasted on just Ali and Leland. For her part, Ali was already regretting that she and Sister Anselm would miss the long philosophical conversation that often preceded and accompanied their shared meals. For Ali, those discussions were as much food for the soul as Leland's well-cooked dishes were food for the body.

In the kitchen, the yeasty aroma of baking bread had been added to the mix. When Ali gave Leland the bad news, he was clearly disappointed.

"How about if I invite my parents and Chris's family to come over?" Ali suggested. "Chris would probably jump at the chance to dodge making dinner."

Leland brightened at the prospect of having company. "If the little ones are coming," he said, "I should probably whip up a batch of mac and cheese. No doubt the cassoulet will be far too rich for them."

In situations like this, Ali usually checked with her daughter-in-law before checking with her son. She didn't want to be held responsible for bullying Athena into a social engagement she didn't really want. It turned out, however, that Athena was absolutely ecstatic at the idea of eating Leland Brooks's food, regardless of what it was. With Chris and Athena's invitation settled, Ali moved on to her parents, catching up with her mother at the Sugarloaf during a small lull in the weekend lunch crowd.

"It would have to be early," Edie Larson cautioned.

Unseen on her end of the phone, Ali rolled her eyes. It wasn't exactly news that Edie Larson went to bed with the chickens so she could be up at O-dark-thirty, in time to do the day's worth of baking at the Sugarloaf.

"It will be early," Ali promised. "Athena says her softball game should be over right around five. She'll come here straight from school. That means we should be able to sit down to dinner by five-thirty at the latest."

"You're sure Mr. Brooks doesn't mind cooking for all of us?" Edie asked.

"I'm sure," Ali said.

"Do you want us to bring something?"

"Just yourselves," Ali told her, "and your appetites." She went into the kitchen to give Leland a revised guest list. "Everybody's coming, twins and all."

"I think I'll do a flan for dessert, then," he said. "Colleen especially likes that."

His statement confirmed something Ali already suspected—that Colleen Reynolds had Leland Brooks wrapped around her pudgy little finger.

"Do you need any help?" she asked.

"Not at all," Leland said, but he gave her a disparaging look that, roughly translated, meant "Are you kidding?"

"All right, then," Ali said. "I'll leave you to it."

Taking another cup of coffee, Ali returned and found a few more late-breaking articles about the Reyes shooting, but they told her less than she had already learned from Donnatelle. Ali didn't know the exact distance between Yuma and Tucson, but it was bound to include several hours' worth of driving time. In the meantime, Ali used the address information from Donnatelle to send Teresa Reyes an e-mail:

Dear Teresa,
    My name is Alison Reynolds. Jose and I were in the police training academy together. Donnatelle Craig, another academy classmate, called today to tell me about what happened to Jose. I'm so sorry to hear the news. Please know that you and your family are in my thoughts and prayers. I know what it's like to

be stuck in a hospital setting with little kids.
Unless I hear from you otherwise, I'll show up
there tomorrow and see if there's anything I
can do to help.

Sincerely,
Ali Reynolds

Considering the catastrophe that had befallen the Reyes family, writing a note and offering to come help seemed like a puny gesture, but it was better than doing nothing.

10

It was early afternoon when a weary Sheriff Manuel Renteria pulled into the attached garage at his house on the outskirts of Tubac. He parked his dusty patrol car next to his refurbished candy-apple-red Dodge Charger and then sat there for a few minutes, gauging how tired he was. Halfway through his third four-year term of office, this had been his worst day ever on the job.

"I'm too damned old for this crap," he muttered to himself as he made his way into his too-quiet house.

The stucco tract home in Tubac was covered with trellises of bright pink bougainvillea that climbed the outside walls. Once, the house and the yard had been a lively place with kids coming and going at all hours and a dog or two racing to the gate or the door to greet him.

Back then, when he came home from work, the house was always filled with the smells of cooking, because that was the way Midge was. She loved to cook, and she always had something simmering on top of the stove or baking in the oven. Now there was no one here but him, and the only cooking that went on was in the microwave as he heated up an occasional Hungry-Man frozen dinner.

The kids were grown and gone, Midge had been dead for five years, and two months earlier he'd had to put down his aging German shepherd, Charger, named after the car, of course.

Manuel would never be able to admit it to his kids, but right now he missed Charger more than he missed Midge. He guessed that over time he had gotten used to her being gone. The loss of the dog was still too new. Up until a few weeks ago, he'd still been able to help Charger into the Dodge to take long Sunday drives. Charger loved riding shotgun, with his nose stuck out the window and mariachi music pounding through the muscle car's killer sound system.

Inside the house, Renteria hung his Stetson on the hat hook next to the back door. Stripping off his belt and his holstered 9mm Glock 17, he hung them there, too. Midge would have disapproved of his leaving his weapon in the kitchen, but she was gone now.

Grabbing a soda from the fridge, he stumbled into the living room. Yes, Midge was gone, but her influence lingered. He made sure he put the soda can on a coaster on the side table before dropping heavily into his recliner. The boots came off next. He wiggled his toes and massaged the aching balls of his feet. He'd spent almost eight solid hours tramping around the crime scene. In the old days, that wouldn't have bothered him. These days? Well, that was another story.

Dispatch had awakened him out of a sound sleep when they called to notify him of the Reyes shooting.

He remembered staring blearily at the clock face with 2:37 A.M. glowing in red letters as he picked up the phone. He had known before he ever said hello that it was going to be bad.

He was dressed and out of the house two minutes later. With siren blaring and lights flashing, he had raced to the scene, beating the air ambulance en route from Tucson by a good ten minutes. The local EMTs were there, doing what they could to stabilize their patient. Sheriff Renteria was the one who suggested they use the golf course parking lot as rendezvous point for the helicopter. He stood to one side, watching helplessly, as they loaded Jose's gurney into the chopper.

As the helicopter became airborne, Sheriff Renteria headed for Patagonia to tell Teresa what had happened. He had been a cop for a long time. He had done plenty of next-of-kin notifications in his time. Usually, the people involved were strangers. This was personal.

He had known the Reyes family forever. He and Carmine, Jose's father, had attended the same high school and played football and basketball together. He was shocked when Carmine died, and had seen his grieving son spend his late teens and early twenties skating on the edges of serious trouble.

As a member of the sheriff's department, Manuel Renteria had done what he could to help Jose along. Finally, things started to click. Jose had signed up at the local community college and started taking classes. It was pretty clear that Jose's interest in studying criminal justice was a direct result of the interest Manuel had shown in him over the years. In the end, however, what had made all the difference for Jose was Teresa.

The sheriff had been delighted when he heard that Jose had started courting Teresa Sanchez. Manuel had known her family, too—Midge had been good friends with Teresa's mother, Maria. Teresa was a struggling single mother, a pregnant widow with a toddler, when Jose appeared on the scene. The truth was, Jose's involvement with Teresa Sanchez was the main reason Sheriff Renteria had offered to hire Jose.

When Jose and Teresa married, the sheriff was invited to attend. He had been honored by the invitation, but Midge's death was still too raw and new for him to go to a church and hear anyone else repeat those fateful words "in sickness and in health." On the day of the wedding, he made sure something came up at the last minute that made it impossible for him to attend.

All this time, Sheriff Renteria had thought Jose was walking the straight and narrow. Now he didn't know what to think.

Yes, Sheriff Renteria had spent eight hours at the crime scene, but it wasn't his crime scene. Officer-related shootings had to be investigated by an outside agency. Renteria had spent all that time standing on the sidelines while investigators from the Arizona Department of Public Safety, led by Lieutenant Duane Lattimore, combed through every inch of the crime scene.

Lattimore and Renteria may have worked for different agencies, but they did so in the same general geographical area. Each was a known quantity to the other, and there was a good deal of mutual respect— too much for either of them to play games. Another DPS investigator might have sent Sheriff Renteria packing, but Lattimore didn't. As long as Renteria merely observed and kept his mouth shut, Lattimore let him stay. Unfortunately for Sheriff Renteria, they'd found far more than he had expected.

Jose's last radio transmission to Dispatch had said he was making a routine traffic stop, but it turned out there was nothing routine about it. Information about the stop should have been available on the dashboard camera in Jose's patrol car, but the camera had been smashed off its sticky pad mounting. Even the pieces were nowhere to be found.

What they had found, unfortunately, were two three-kilo bundles of grass as well as white powder that field-tested out as cocaine. It had all been stashed in the trunk of Jose's patrol car. In addition, there were several hundred-dollars in loose hundred-dollar bills inside the trunk and blowing around the crime scene.

It was possible that the drugs and the money were part of something Jose was investigating, but there had been no mention of any such investigation in Jose's paperwork or in his interactions with Dispatch. Lieutenant Lattimore and the other DPS investigators didn't say anything about all that to Sheriff Renteria. They didn't have to. Everybody understood what they were likely seeing—a drug deal gone bad.

As far as weapons were concerned, they found next to nothing. Jose's service weapon was located at the scene, near where he'd been found. Apparently, it had been drawn but not fired. The CSI team found a few shell casings that they'd send in to NIBIN—the National Integrated Ballistics Information Network. But there were so many weapons coming and going across the border these days, the idea that they'd come up with some kind of a match on the casings that would lead to first a weapon and then an actual owner was a long shot.

What wasn't a long shot, and what Sheriff Renteria had to face, was the likelihood that Jose was dirty. The evidence found in and around Jose's car was compelling, although until today, Sheriff Renteria wouldn't have entertained that as a possibility. He would have sworn on a stack of Bibles that Jose Reyes was true blue, but the evidence said otherwise.

Until that Saturday morning, Sheriff Renteria had been gearing up to run for a fourth and final term as sheriff, but that was now unlikely. If one of his cops was dirty, there was a chance that others were as well. His whole department could come crashing down.

If I'm no better judge of people than that, Sheriff Renteria told himself, *then maybe it's time for me to hang up the badge.*

He finished his soda and then sat dozing in the chair for the better part of two hours. At last he forced himself awake. He stripped off his bedraggled uniform and stepped into the shower. Half an hour later, shaved and wearing a freshly laundered uniform, he strapped his Glock on his hip and stuck his Stetson back on his head.

Earlier, he'd hated having to drive to Patagonia to give Teresa Reyes the terrible news that her husband was critically injured. This was even worse. Now he had to drive to Tucson and tell her that her hospitalized husband was most likely also a crook. Maybe she'd be as blindsided by the news as he had been. Then again, maybe not.

What if Teresa had suspected something and said nothing, or worse, what if she knew all about it? What if they were both crooks? Could a husband hide that kind of activity from his wife? Renteria knew he wouldn't have been able to get away with that kind of stuff with Midge, never in a million years.

Shaking his head, Sheriff Renteria turned the key in the ignition, and the powerful police pursuit engine roared to life. He had already decided he would go to Tucson and tell her. He'd use everything he had learned while working as a deputy for sixteen years and as sheriff for ten to read Teresa's reactions to what he had to say.

With any luck, she'd turn out to be completely in the dark. That's what he hoped, anyway. And if she wasn't? Then three little kids, one of them not yet born, were in for a very rough ride.

11

12:00 P.M., Saturday, April 10
Flagstaff, Arizona

When the first few bars of the "Hallelujah" chorus rang out from Sister Anselm's iPhone, no one in the board of directors meeting raised an eyebrow. Over the years her fellow board members had learned that the ring tone meant a call from Bishop Francis Gillespie at the archdiocese in Phoenix. It also meant that Sister Anselm would be hightailing it out of the meeting to go wherever she was needed. Her role as patient advocate trumped everything else.

"How's the weather up there?" Bishop Gillespie asked when Sister Anselm stepped outside the boardroom to answer.

"It's snowing here more than it was when I drove up from Jerome this morning," she said, "but it's not that bad. Why?"

"Because my office has just been notified that a UDA was transported to the ICU at Physicians Medical in Tucson yesterday evening. She's in bad shape, and there's no one with her. How soon would you be able to go?"

In the old days, it might have taken time to arrange for transportation, but that was before Sister Anselm was able to drive herself. Although past retirement age, with encouragement and lessons from her friend Ali Reynolds, and with permission from Bishop Gillespie, Sister Anselm had gotten a driver's license for the first time. After years of being driven to and fro, she now tooled around the state in her own all-wheel-drive red-and-white four-door Mini Cooper. Donated to the diocese by a generous parishioner, her Mini Countryman sported a whimsical bumper sticker that said, ACTUAL SIZE.

Sister Anselm glanced at her watch. Wherever she went, there was always a fully packed suitcase tucked into the Mini's "boot" for just this kind of contingency, so there would be no need for her to go home before leaving for Tucson. The trip would take the better part of four and a half hours, depending on traffic and road conditions.

"If I leave right now, I could probably be at PMC by five."

"Do you have chains?" Bishop Gillespie asked.

"And all-wheel drive," Sister Anselm answered. "And I know how to use both." She and Bishop Gillespie had become good friends, but she tended to get her back up when he fussed about her too much.

"All right, then," Bishop Gillespie said. "Travel safely. I took the liberty of calling All Saints to let them know to expect you."

The hospital now known as Physicians Medical Center had started out in the early twentieth century as a TB sanitarium under the auspices of the Sisters of

Providence. For almost a hundred years, the nuns of All Saints Convent had been in charge. In recent years, the facility had been purchased by a group of physicians and transformed into a full-scale hospital.

Although PMC was no longer an officially designated Catholic hospital, many of the All Saints nuns, most of them trained nurses, continued to work there. And when Sister Anselm's work took her to hospitals in and around Tucson, she preferred the structure and discipline of staying with her fellow nuns to staying at a hotel.

But having the bishop call to let them know she was coming counted as more unwarranted fussing. "I'll call there again myself," Sister Anselm said. "That way, if they've changed the gate or door codes, I won't need to awaken someone if I arrive after lights out."

Once off the phone with Bishop Gillespie, Sister Anselm sent an e-mail to Ali, offering her regrets about missing dinner. Her next call was to the convent in Jerome to let them know that she wouldn't be coming home until further notice. The call after that was to Sister Genevieve, the current reverend mother at All Saints. The call went straight through to the mother superior's cell phone.

"Good to hear from you," Sister Genevieve said. "Bishop Gillespie said you might be coming."

"Am I cleared for a late-night check-in if needed?" Sister Anselm asked.

Sister Genevieve's answering laugh was hearty and welcoming. "Absolutely," she said. "Your favorite guest room is ready and waiting."

"If you want to give me the entry codes, I can let myself in. That way no one will have to wait up for me."

"We haven't changed the entry codes," Sister Genevieve said. "But don't worry about showing up late. You know me, I'm a night owl. I hardly ever go to sleep before midnight. Whenever you get here, I'll most likely be on hand, ready and waiting to greet you and activate the gate."

"All right, then," Sister Anselm said. "I'm on my way."

Having anticipated cassoulet for dinner, Sister Anselm had skipped lunch in Flagstaff. By the time she hit Cordes Junction, she was out of the worst of the weather, but she and her "ride" were running on empty. Eating a fast-food burger was a very poor substitute for one of Leland Brooks's outstanding dinners, but fuel was fuel.

While in line at McDonald's, she reached into the pocket of her jacket to locate her change purse, encountering the recently acquired Taser C2 that she kept there. She suspected that the other customers in the restaurant would have been surprised to know that the nice older lady, the one wearing gold-framed glasses and a conservative pin-striped pantsuit, was not only a nun but also armed and dangerous.

When she'd had a driver to get from place to place, Sister Anselm had gone on her rounds armed with nothing but her rosary beads and prayers. Things had changed. For one thing, several years earlier she had been kidnapped from a hospital setting in Phoenix. After that unsettling event, Ali had talked with her about making sure she could defend herself. She had resisted strongly.

St. Bernadette's Convent in Jerome was a home for troubled nuns. Sister Anselm had spent the last three months dealing with an elderly nun—older than Sister Anselm anyway—who was recovering from hip replacement surgery as well as suffering from post-traumatic stress disorder. Sister Louise had been walking home from a pharmacy to her convent in Dallas when she was attacked by a carload of young thugs. They had thrown her to the ground and wrenched her purse and shopping bag out of her hands. No doubt hoping to find money and/or powerful painkillers, the thieves had gotten away with a little over six dollars in change, Sister Louise's three-month prescription for Boniva, and a box of Depends. Passersby had found her a few minutes later and summoned an ambulance. She had been taken to Parkland Memorial Hospital, where an orthopedic surgeon successfully replaced her damaged hip. What the Parkland physicians had not been able to fix was her sense of well-being.

That was Sister Anselm's job, and she had been working on it. But dealing with Sister Louise's troubles had brought home to Sister Anselm—more so than even her own kidnapping—that there were evil people in the world who were more than happy to target someone they thought to be helpless.

So now, when Sister Anselm drove from one end of the state to another, going about her business normally, there was one major difference. She had a weapon discreetly stowed in the pocket of her blazer. Her nonlethal protection was a gift from Ali, who'd warned that it should be carried on one's person and not in a handbag. In Sister Louise's mugging case, her purse had been taken out of play almost immediately.

Just because Sister Anselm was out in the world doing God's work, there was no reason to be a victim, not if she could help it. If anyone tried to take her out, they'd be in for a big surprise.

12:00 P.M., Saturday, April 10
Patagonia, Arizona

That Saturday morning, it took Phil Tewksbury longer than usual to run his mail delivery route. Everyone he met along the way wanted to talk about the Santa Cruz deputy who had been shot while on duty the night before. Phil knew the guy's name, Jose Reyes, and where he lived, because he was on Phil's delivery route, but that was all he knew. Details about the shooting itself were pretty scarce, although when they were available, Phil figured that the Patagonia post office would be information central.

Once his mail truck was back in its spot inside the fenced lot behind the post office, Phil hurried home and settled in to spend the rest of the weekend painting the weathered outside trim on his house and garage.

Considering the problems inside the house, including several thorny issues he was not yet ready to tackle, the paint and the new double-paned windows were like putting lipstick on a pig, but for the first time in years, he was working on the house with a sense of purpose rather than a sense of despair. To his amazement, he found himself whistling while he worked. That hadn't happened in a very long time.

Not that anything had happened. It hadn't. Not yet. But there was the possibility that something would happen. He had a hope that something might happen, and that made all the difference.

Finished with the trim on the dining room window, he moved on to the ones in the living room. That was when the whistling stopped. For years, the broken seal in the old windows had left a film of fog between the living room and the outside world. Through the blur, no one could see in or out. Now it was all there and clearly visible—Christine, or at least the shabby wreckage of Christine, and the dilapidated fifteen-year-old Christmas tree with its burden of dusty ornaments and strings of mostly nonworking lights.

He had told Christine years ago that once the last of the lights burned out, the tree was gone. No matter what she said, he was taking it down then. Recently, he had come to suspect that she must have a secret stash of lights hidden somewhere and was using the spares to replace one or two dead bulbs at a time. It reminded him of that lady in one of the old Greek legends he had read back in high school. Her husband had gone away on a trip and was supposedly lost at sea. Someone wanted to marry her, and she said yes, but she told her would-be suitor that she had to finish weaving a rug first. So every day she wove like crazy, and every night, when no one was looking, she tore up that day's work.

If that was what was happening, Christine was a lot

cagier about it than Phil had given her credit for being. On the other hand, maybe some of those old lights, made back in the day when Christmas lights came from the U.S. instead of China, were just that much better than the ones you could buy today. Better or worse, depending on your point of view.

Christine sat there now, in her chair next to the tree, watching him, but not with any kind of curiosity or connection or interest. He might have been a living color image performing on a television screen; not that she watched TV, either. She mostly stared at the tree, day after day, year after year.

Phil stopped painting and studied her. Trying to remember the old Christine, which wasn't anything like the old Christine who had been on television a year or two ago. His wife's hair had been reddish brown back then. She had worn it short and curly. He hadn't realized until much later that the curl came from the beauty shop and probably most of the color, too. Now it hung past her waist in long gray strands that were lank and greasy.

That was something Phil knew he'd have to deal with tonight—bath night. Once a week, on Saturdays, they waged the bath night war, and it was hell. Once a week, whether Christine wanted to or not, he insisted that she get up out of her chair and strip off that week's shapeless muumuu and grubby undergarments. After what was often a physical struggle, he'd maneuver her into the shower and turn on the water. He remembered seeing clips on *America's Funniest Home Videos* when people tried to bathe their cats. It usually ended badly, with the cats yowling and scratching, and this was the same thing.

Eventually, he would wear her down. She'd give up. She'd go ahead and soap her body and shampoo her hair, but it never happened without a fight. It made him glad that his grandfather had built his little house in the middle of five acres. Otherwise the neighbors, hearing the racket they made each week, might have assumed he was trying to kill her.

Which he wasn't. All on his own, Phil was doing what he could to care for Christine, or at least what was left of Christine, and doing it to the very best of his ability. He owed it to her. Because what had happened to her was his fault—all his fault.

Things were so different now, it was hard to remember how happy they'd been once. He and Christine had moved back home to Patagonia after Phil finished putting in his twenty years in the military. They had moved into the house his grandfather had built and which Phil had inherited when his grandmother died. He'd gotten the job working in the post office, and life was good.

By then it had seemed clear that he and Christine weren't going to have any kids, ever. They'd tried. It hadn't worked. End of story. At least that's what they thought. But then, much to their astonishment and right after Christine turned forty, she also turned up pregnant.

Christine was ecstatic when Cassidy was born. So was Phil. Life was wonderful for a time, right up to Christmas Eve fifteen years ago, the night everything changed. Phil and Cassidy had been on their way home from a last-minute Christmas-shopping trip to Tucson. Between Patagonia and Sonoita, a drunk driver came across the double line into their lane. Somehow Phil managed to avoid being hit, but he lost control of the car. It rolled. Cassidy died.

The original accident wasn't Phil's fault, but Cassidy's death was. Her mother always made sure Cass was properly belted in. Insisted on it. That day when they started home, Cassidy, who was seven, said she was tired. She wanted to lie down in the backseat to sleep, and Phil let her. When the car rolled, Cassidy was ejected, and the car landed on top of her. She died instantly. Sometimes Phil wished he had died then, too.

When he gave Christine the news, she didn't say a word. She didn't have to. Instead, she leveled an accusatory look that shriveled his heart. He had known right then that she would never forgive him, and she had not.

Cassidy's funeral was two days after Christmas. When they came home from the funeral, the decorated Christmas tree and all the wrapped presents were there in the living room, taunting them and showing them how much they had lost. Phil's first instinct had been to take it down and get rid of it, but Christine had stopped him. She told him that if he touched even so much as one decoration on the tree, she'd kill him, and he had believed her. The tree stayed up. Later, when they were still speaking occasionally, he'd managed to extract the agreement that the tree would stay up until the last light burned out. Fifteen years later, it was still there, and a few of the bedraggled lights continued to burn.

But that Christmas and Cassidy's death had been the

beginning of Christine's long retreat into herself. She stopped going out. For anything. She wouldn't go to the grocery store or to the gas station or to the doctor or dentist. Friends tried stopping by to see her or calling on the phone. She wouldn't open the door. She wouldn't answer the phone. She stayed in the house day after day, year after year. If it hadn't been for Phil's job delivering mail, he suspected he would have gone nuts, too.

Phil and Christine lived in the same house, but they slept in different bedrooms and existed on different timetables. When Phil left for work, Christine was usually asleep. Sometimes she prowled the house late at night, when he heard her pacing back and forth in her room. During the day, as far as he could tell, she spent most of her time sitting in the living room, watching the tree. He didn't know what she thought about all that time. She didn't seem to watch TV, had zero interest in current events. As far as he knew, she didn't read books.

With the house quiet and, except for the tree, mostly dark, he worried early on that someone might mistakenly think the house was empty and break in with her sitting right there in her chair. When he mentioned his concern to Christine, she gave him one of her scathing looks. Then she stood up, walked over to the Christmas tree, and picked up one of Cassidy's wrapped presents.

"I'll use this," she said, tearing the wrapping paper off the softball bat, a present Cassidy had never opened.

For months after that, Christine sat with the bat either in her lap or next to her chair. One day, though, for reasons Christine never explained, she stuck the bat in the trash. Rather than ask her about it, Phil rescued the bat, took it out to the garage, and left it there. By then he was at the point of wishing someone would break into the house. Maybe whoever it was would fix Phil's life for him. Give him back his freedom. After all, hadn't he earned it?

That, of course, was a pipe dream. Obviously, since he had brought this tragedy down on them both, Phil had no choice but to stand by his wife. He was resigned to that. He would take care of her until the day she died or until he did, but that was what made this new bit of brilliance in his life so miraculous. And who could blame him? After years of living with Christine's stony silence, no one would have thought twice about him having an outside interest—a side dish, as it were—a discreet side dish.

On the one hand, it was amazing after all this time to have someone who was actually interested in him, someone who laughed at his lame jokes and seemed to enjoy his company for those few minutes a day when it was possible for them to be together—on the side of the road, parked next to a bank of mailboxes, with cars going past, but together. She was often waiting for him when he stopped to deliver the mail. Sometimes she brought him treats—a plate of freshly baked cookies; a cup of coffee; a ham sandwich. No matter what she brought him, Phil was always pleasantly surprised and grateful. Their brief conversations were carried on in a kind of verbal shorthand that can happen only through shared experience, and they were a balm to Phil Tewksbury's wounded soul.

That was the most amazing part of all. In Ollie, Phil had found a soul mate, someone who understood exactly what he was going through. He didn't have to explain to her that he could never leave Christine to fend for herself, because she was dealing with the same situation. Not entirely the same, but close enough.

Having a husband wandering off into the world of early-onset Alzheimer's was slightly different from Christine's self-imposed and willful silence, but in other respects, Ollie's situation was very similar to Phil's—the isolation, the hopelessness, and the loneliness of being married to someone who was no longer there. Like Phil, Ollie wouldn't leave her husband, but she refused to betray him. In thought, maybe, but not in deed. What Phil and Ollie had together was a friendship—a circumspect friendship, one without phoning or texting, which would have felt more like cheating. They exchanged little notes from time to time, and Phil saved them all, reading them over and over sometimes in the privacy of his truck.

Rereading them gave Phil comfort. He could see that their connection had grown out of shared experience and came with the promise that someday, far in the future, when they were both free, there might be so much more.

That week in particular, Phil was grateful for the bit of misfortune that had left Ollie's little four-by-four with a flat tire. He had noticed it while they were chatting and had changed it for her. The culprit had been a stray roofing nail that had wormed its way through the balding tread of her tires. But the nail, the resulting flat, and the process of changing the tire had been a blessing in disguise because it had given the two of them twenty minutes or so of uninterrupted and utterly blameless conversation. No one was going to gossip about Phil being an everyday hero and changing some poor stranded lady's flat tire.

Finished with the trim on the living room window, Phil moved on to the kitchen window. With Christine's grim visage no longer staring accusingly at him through the clean glass, his spirits improved. His whistle returned.

Yes, for the first time in years, Phil Tewksbury felt that life was good. He'd finish painting the trim on the house today. Tomorrow he'd do the same to the garage. After that, he had plans to tackle the kitchen and the bathroom. Only after everything else was done would he bring up the Christmas tree. Now that people could see in as much as they could see out, it was probably time to bring up that troublesome issue and do something about it.

It was time.

13

12:00 P.M., Saturday, April 10
Sedona, Arizona

With more spare time on her hands than she'd ever had, Ali Reynolds had been making a conscious effort to read some of the classics she had previously only sampled or skimmed. After sending the note to Teresa Reyes, Ali tried turning her attention to her current read, *Don Quixote*, but the words on the page failed to move her. Too much real life had intruded on the author's fictional adventures.

The brightest spot in Ali's quiet afternoon was a phone call from B. just before he boarded his plane in Phoenix, heading for D.C. As she ended that call, her phone rang again. This time she recognized Donnatelle's number.

"I wanted you to know that I made it. I'm here at the hospital," Donnatelle said.

"How are things?"

"Not so good. Jose is still in the ICU. Teresa can go in to see him once an hour for five minutes at a time, but the girls can't. I brought them down to the cafeteria with me to give her a break, and to give the girls a break, too. They're lost. Lucy keeps asking why her daddy is so sick and why can't she go see him."

"Sounds like it's a good thing you're there."

"I'm the only one who is," Donnatelle said. "Teresa's mother was here for a while before I got here, but she's not at all well, and she's afraid to drive. A neighbor drove her here. Someone else is taking her back home to Nogales. What I want to know is where are the people from Jose's department? Why aren't they here?"

"They're not?" Ali asked.

"Not so far. Zip. Nada."

In her early news-broadcasting days, long before Ali climbed into a spot at a news anchor desk, she had reported on plenty of officer-involved shootings. She didn't remember a single one where members of the officer's department hadn't shown up at the hospital en masse to offer help and support. Why should Jose Reyes's shooting be any different?

"That's odd," Ali said.

"It's worse than odd," Donnatelle replied. "If Teresa didn't need me here looking after Lucy and Carinda, I'd drive straight down to Nogales and give the sheriff a piece of my mind."

Ali once again noted that Donnatelle had come a long way, baby. "I couldn't agree with you more," she said. "How's Teresa holding up?"

"She's been at the hospital since early this morning, and she doesn't have her car," Donnatelle said. "I offered to drive her home so she could take a shower, change clothes, and maybe a nap for a while, but she's not leaving."

"How about the kids?" Ali asked.

"They're kids," Donnatelle said, and the truth was, those words said it all. Kids and hospital waiting rooms didn't mix.

"How long are you going to stay?" Ali asked.

"Until tomorrow morning. After that I'll have to head back, because my mother has to work tomorrow evening."

"I'm planning on coming down tomorrow morning," Ali said. "I may not get there before you have to leave, but I'll be there shortly."

"Good," Donnatelle breathed. "That's a relief."

Ali was ending the call when the doorbell rang. Moments later, Leland came into the library announcing the arrival of Edie Larson.

"My mother without my dad?" Ali asked in surprise, but Edie Larson, who'd followed Leland into the room, protested.

"Your father and I aren't exactly joined at the hip, you know," she said. "I wanted to talk to you in private before everyone else gets here."

That sounded ominous. Sitting down to a family dinner with Ali's kids and her parents wasn't exactly public, but the anxious look on Edie's face sent a shiver of worry down Ali's spine. Whatever her mother needed to discuss had to be serious. Ali's first thought was that there was some looming health issue. After all, in terms of age, her parents were getting up there.

As usual, Leland picked up on the disquiet in the room. "Would you like me to bring some tea?" he asked.

"Please," Ali said gratefully.

Her mother sank into one of the easy chairs positioned in front of the fireplace. Unasked, Ali pushed an ottoman into place in front of Edie. The long hours Edie spent on her feet every day meant that she spent a lot of time each evening with her feet up.

"What is it, Mom?" Ali asked, trying to keep concern out of her voice. "Is something wrong?"

"Not wrong, really," Edie said. "Your father didn't want us to say anything until it's a completely done deal, but I don't think it's fair to keep something like this from the rest of the family. The kids are coming to dinner tonight, too, aren't they?"

Ali nodded. "Yes, they are."

"Good," Edie said, "so when your father spills the beans about all this, I expect you to act surprised. You can do that, can't you?"

It was sounding more and more serious by the moment.

"Of course," Ali said, "but what exactly are we talking about, Mom? What's going on?"

"We're selling the restaurant," Edie announced. "We're due to sign the paperwork first thing Monday morning. The new owners take over May first."

Ali's jaw dropped. Of all the news she might have expected, the sale of the Sugarloaf wasn't it. Her parents had entertained offers to buy the diner in the past, but for one reason or another, those sales had always fallen through, often because the prospective purchasers had wanted to come in and change everything. Those other times, Ali had always known about the possible sales well in advance. This time neither of her

parents had mentioned that a sale was not only pend-
ing, it was soon to be a fait accompli. Besides, the sale
of almost anything in the current economy was nothing
short of amazing.

"Really?" Ali asked a little lamely.

"Really," Edie replied.

Leland arrived with a tray laden with a teapot, cups
and saucers, sugar and cream. He placed the tray on
the table, then poured and served the tea before leaving them alone again.

There were a dozen questions Ali wanted to ask at
once—all those who, what, where, and when questions she had learned from studying journalism—but
she stifled the urge and contented herself with taking a
calming sip of tea.

Edie sighed. "For years your father harbored the
secret hope that one day Chris and Athena would
want to take over the business, but that's not going to
happen. Athena loves teaching, and now that Chris's
artwork is starting to take off, thanks to you, he's not
going to be interested, either. And when it comes to
running a restaurant, you're obviously not a likely
candidate."

Ali had in fact run the restaurant for a week a couple of years earlier so that her parents could take a
cruise, but it had taken a superhuman effort on her
part and help from Leland Brooks to make it work.
Besides, Edie's comment wasn't so much a snide remark about Ali's lack of cooking ability as it was an
honest assessment of her interests and aptitudes. Over
the years, Ali had spent enough hours working in the
Sugarloaf as hired help or observing from the sidelines

to have no desire to run the place. She knew how much work went on behind the scenes—the baking; the cleaning; the ordering; the organizing—all the scut work that no one noticed or appreciated unless it wasn't done.

"No," Ali agreed. "I'm definitely not. So who is it? Someone from here in town?"

"Their names are Derek and Elena Hoffman," Edie said. "Elena was raised in Scottsdale. Her family used to come up here during the summers, and it was always a big treat for them to come to the Sugarloaf for breakfast so Elena could have one of my sweet rolls. Her husband was raised back east somewhere. In Milwaukee, I believe.

"Derek is the chef in the family," Edie continued. "He and Elena met at culinary school, where they were taking classes. They both dreamed about being able to open their own restaurant. They came out to Arizona last February to visit Elena's grandparents. Derek has spent his whole life enduring those awful Midwest winters. He thought Scottsdale was splendid, but then Elena brought him to Sedona. He fell in love with Sedona, and he fell in love with my sweet rolls. They came back up last month and made us a generous offer."

"If they're just starting out, where's the money coming from?" Ali asked.

"Elena's grandfather is bankrolling them. He'll be a silent partner, but this way they can start in a restaurant that's already a going concern. For now they're not planning on changing anything. And they're cashing us out. The offers we had before always called for our carrying the note. You may not know this, but most new restaurants fail within the first year."

Ali did know that, and she couldn't help raising a few objections. "Just because this Derek guy is a chef doesn't mean he'll make a great short-order cook."

Edie smiled. "They're older than you think. Derek started slinging hash when he was with the marines in Desert Storm, so his initial cooking experience wasn't so different from that of your very capable Mr. Brooks."

Leland's humble culinary beginnings dated from the Korean War, where he'd been a cook in the British marines before immigrating to the U.S. Once here, he served as the man-of-all-work for, first, Anne Marie; and later, Isabella Ashcroft, turning himself into an excellent chef along the way. But knowing about Derek's military background went a long way toward explaining why Ali's father would be enthusiastic about having him take over the restaurant.

"Do they have kids?" Ali asked.

Edie nodded. "One—a daughter, Savannah. She's in kindergarten. That's always a problem when people move their kids over the summer. They end up not knowing anyone. Derek and Elena want Savannah to have the benefit of the last two months of kindergarten in her new school. That way she'll have a chance to meet some of her new classmates before summer starts. And I think it's wonderful that there'll be another little girl living in your old room."

"Wait," Ali said. "You mean they're buying the house, too?"

"They're buying the whole thing—lock, stock, and

barrel," Edie said. "The tax rolls consider the restaurant and house to be one property. To sell them separately, we'd have to subdivide, and chances are it wouldn't be allowed. The city of Sedona would be all over us."

It was bad enough to think of her parents selling the restaurant, but Ali bridled at the idea that they would no longer be living in the place she had considered home her whole life.

"But you'll have to move," Ali objected.

"Yes, we will," Edie said. "After so many years in one place, that won't be easy."

Clearly, the decisions had all been made, and since it seemed unlikely that anything Ali said would make a difference one way or the other, she didn't voice any more objections.

"That's great," she said, hoping she sounded sufficiently enthusiastic. "If anyone deserves to retire, it's you two."

"I told you we were selling the restaurant, but who said anything about retiring?" Edie asked. "Your father may have some harebrained idea about hopping in a motor home and taking off cross-country, but I don't have any intention of making like a turtle and hauling my house around on my back. Cooking meals in a camper doesn't sound like my idea of a good time, either. I want to go somewhere where someone cooks for me."

"Where are you going to live, then?" Ali asked.

"That's one of the little kinks we're having to work out. The new owners will take over the restaurant on May first, but we'll have until the end of June to move out of the house. We're thinking about moving either into a two-bedroom unit or a town house at that new retirement community, Sedona Hills Seniors. They should be ready for occupancy about the time we need to move. Their units come with a full-meal option."

Ali knew about Sedona Hills Seniors. Touted as "Luxurious Senior Living for Active Adults," it was being built along the highway just a few blocks west of the Sugarloaf.

"Are you sure you and Dad are ready for such a big change?" Ali asked.

Edie laughed. "More than ready, my dear. The dining room and clubhouse are lovely, and after a lifetime of cooking and serving meals, I'm ready to have someone else serve me for a change. Besides, they do all the upkeep, inside and out. What's not to like?"

"What about Dad?" Ali asked. "Where's he going to work on his Blazer?"

"Don't worry about that. Most of the units come with garages. As long as he has a place to keep his tools, we could go live in a tent for all he cares."

"Sounds like you've thought of everything."

Edie nodded. "Yes, I think we're both going to like living there. Best of all, Sedona Hills is inside the city limits."

"City limits?" Ali echoed. "What does being inside the city limits have to do with anything?"

Edie Larson beamed at her daughter. "I thought you'd never ask," she said. "I've decided to run for mayor. That guy they have now has never been in business a day in his life. He's been here what? Five years on the outside. I know everyone in town, and

I'm hoping you'll agree to be my campaign manager. I'm also hoping you'll help me break the news to your father."

"You mean you haven't told him?"

"Not yet," Edie said. "And chances are, he isn't going to like it."

14

6:00 P.M., Saturday, April 10
Tucson, Arizona

In the ICU waiting room, time passed with glacial slowness. Teresa's mother, Maria Delgado, showed up, dropped off by a neighbor who had driven her from Nogales to Tucson. In the early afternoon, Donnatelle Craig arrived as well, having driven over from Yuma.

Initially, the girls were shy around the tall black stranger, but gradually, Donnatelle won them over. The presence of the other two women in the waiting room made it possible for Teresa to spend five minutes each hour sitting at Jose's bedside.

Some time in the course of the afternoon, Teresa emerged from Jose's room and was astonished to find her former mother-in-law, Olga Sanchez, striding into the waiting room carrying two gigantic shopping bags with a pair of immense teddy bears sticking out of the top of one.

Teresa had assumed that Olga Sanchez was out of her life for good. And yet here she was, showing up at the hospital as though she had every right to be there, bringing along a treasure trove of goodies.

"What are you doing here?" Teresa asked.

Thin as a rail, Olga wore her lustrous black, streaked with white, hair pulled back into a complicated chignon. From the neck up, she resembled a prima ballerina, but neck down, she was cowgirl all the way, complete with skintight jeans, a western shirt, and glossy snakeskin boots. Her wide belt sported a massive silver and turquoise buckle worthy of a world cage-fighting champion.

"I just heard about Jose," Olga said. "I thought I'd come see if there was anything I could do to help, if that's all right. And I brought along a few things I thought the girls might like. It's high time I met little Carinda. She's my granddaughter, after all."

As far as Teresa was concerned, it wasn't all right, but for the moment, there wasn't much she could do about it. That was how Olga operated, all sweetness and light when she wanted something. She had done it with Danny, and she was doing it again with her granddaughters, but today Teresa was too tired to summon any outrage about it; too tired to tell the pushy woman to go to hell; too grateful to have someone else show up at the hospital, willing to help out.

"Thank you for coming," she said. "Bringing toys was a good idea. It's been a long day, and the girls are bored to tears."

Olga nodded in Maria Delgado's direction on the way past. Teresa noticed that her mother didn't respond. That was hardly surprising. Maria had never gotten over her outrage at the way Olga Sanchez had treated Teresa at Danny's funeral. Even if Teresa was willing to forgive and forget, her mother wasn't.

Donnatelle had the girls corralled in a corner of the room and was reading to them from the Dr. Seuss book Teresa had stuffed in her bag. They looked up warily as Teresa approached, bringing Olga and her shopping bags.

"This is your grandmother," Teresa said simply. "Your other grandmother."

"I'm your daddy's mommy," Olga said.

"But she's dead," Lucy said.

Jose's mother had died suddenly a year ago.

"I'm your real daddy's mommy," Olga said. "You can call me Grandma Olga. And look. I brought you some toys. Do you want to see them?"

Knowing she'd been outmaneuvered, Teresa paused long enough to introduce Olga to Donnatelle, then she walked away as the girls dove for the bags. With everything that was going on, Teresa understood that she had only so much strength. With that in mind, it was important to choose her battles. This was a fight for another day and another time, when she wasn't dog-tired and when she didn't have a possibly dying husband lying in a bed in the ICU. When she was stronger, she would sit down with her daughters and explain this mystery. Teresa had always intended to tell the girls about Danny and Oscar and Olga, but she had imagined that it would be at some time far in the future, when the girls were old enough to understand

"You shouldn't have let her get away with that," Maria whispered to her daughter when Teresa was back in earshot.

By then Olga had pulled a camera out of her purse and started taking pictures. Lucy loved posing for photos, and anything Lucy did, Carinda wanted to do, too. The girls mugged for the camera while Olga snapped away. What could it hurt if Danny's mother had photos of her granddaughters? Maybe it was time to get over some of those old hurts. Maybe it was time to move on.

"It's called turning the other cheek, Mother," Teresa said. "Right now, with everything else that's going on, I need all the help I can get."

"You'll be sorry," Maria predicted.

"Maybe," Teresa said. She leaned her head against the back of the chair and closed her eyes. "Right now I'm going to try to take a nap. Wake me in an hour."

15

6:00 P.M., Saturday, April 10
Tucson, Arizona

There had been a rollover semi accident on the bridge where I-10 crossed the Gila River. If Sister Anselm had been listening to the traffic advisories from her GPS, she might have known about the accident in time to choose another route and come down through Chandler or Apache Junction. But the constant chatter from the GPS lady's voice got in the way of Sister Anselm's thinking time. Since she knew the way to PMC with her eyes closed, she left the GPS off, and when she got caught up in the hour-long traffic delay, there was nothing to do but sit and wait.

When Sister Anselm finally arrived at the PMC campus on Tanque Verde, she parked her Mini in the far corner of the large lot. She was healthy enough to walk. It seemed important to leave the parking places closer to the main entrance for people who needed them.

People meeting Sister Anselm Becker for the first time would have thought they were encountering a retired businesswoman. In public she favored tailored pantsuits with no-frills blouses. In hospital settings she wore flowered scrubs that let her blend in with the other health care professionals. Her silver hair was cropped short. Her lined face was devoid of makeup. She walked with a slight limp from her hip replacement surgery years earlier. Her most striking feature, however, were her blue eyes. Beaming with cheerful intelligence, they offered a window on her soul through a pair of plain wire-framed glasses. Sister Anselm was a woman of faith, and that was where it shone through—in her eyes.

She had walked the halls of Physicians Medical many times. Once inside the lobby, she had no need to ask for directions. She made her way directly to the hospital administration office, where she signed in as a visiting service provider and was issued a temporary identification badge. From there she went to the ICU. Before looking in on Jane Doe, Sister Anselm tracked down the charge nurse at the nurses' station. Mona Lafferty was someone Sister Anselm had worked with on previous occasions.

"I wondered if you'd be able to come," Mona said.

"I got here as soon as I could," Sister Anselm answered. "How's she doing?"

"She's pretty heavily sedated but lucky to be alive."

"No ID?"

"None."

"Any distinguishing marks?"

"She's got a tattoo of a rose on her right breast," Mona said. "And what looks like cigarette burns and cuts all over her body."

Tattoos were common enough on male illegals. Less

so on the female of the species. As for the torture? That might have been used to extract information about friends and associates.

"Talking?"

Mona shook her head. "Not so far. Do you want to look at her chart?"

"Please. I'd like to take it to her room, if you don't mind."

Mona smiled. "Knock yourself out. Her room's the second one on the right."

With the chart in hand, Sister Anselm let herself into Jane Doe's room. She stood for several long moments, staring down at the injured and unconscious woman. Sister Anselm had encountered damage from beatings before, but in her experience, this was one of the most brutal. The real surprise was that the woman was still alive.

Her head had been shaved so the wounds on her scalp could be stitched together. Both arms and one leg were broken, but due to skin damage from the burns and cuts, the broken limbs were encased in splints rather than plaster casts. Her jaw was wired shut. What was visible of her face was a road map of stitched cuts and vivid bruises. It looked as though both her nose and one eye socket had been damaged and would require reconstructive surgery. Wherever bare skin was visible, so were the scabby tracks that burning cigarettes had left all over her body.

Settling into the room's single chair, Sister Anselm switched on a reading light and began to read. The list of injuries was appalling. At least four teeth had been knocked out of her mouth. So far Jane Doe had already undergone two separate surgeries to repair damage to her internal organs. The surgical intervention that had no doubt saved her life had also resulted in the removal of her uterus. The chart estimated the young woman's age to be late teens or early twenties. When Jane Doe awakened from what was at the moment a medically induced coma, she would discover that having children of her own was no longer an option.

But not having children might be the least of it. She had sustained several blows to the head. So far there was no sign of brain swelling, but with any kind of head injury, there was always a possibility that the patient would be left with impaired mental faculties, which could necessitate relearning things like reading and writing.

At the bottom of the chart was a notation that said that a rape kit had been taken. Sister Anselm didn't put a lot of stock in that. If the young woman had been attacked by fellow illegals, it was all too likely that the perpetrators who had raped, beaten, and tortured the girl and left her to die would never be identified, much less brought to justice.

As Sister Anselm went to return the chart to the nurses' station, she heard the sound of a raised female voice. "That's not true!" a woman declared heatedly. "My husband would never do such a thing!"

The speaker was a pregnant woman in her late twenties or early thirties. She was sitting a few seats away from the rest of her group of visitors, talking with an older man in a law enforcement uniform who was wearing a badge. His handgun was in its holster, and a white Stetson was in his hand, on his lap. A few yards away, a wide-eyed girl who looked to be five or so and another, younger one stood on either side of a seated black woman, whose arms encircled both of their waists. Their big eyes never left the pregnant woman, and they seemed disturbed.

"I'm so sorry about all this, Teresa," the man said in more hushed tones and looking around. "I'm sorry Jose is hurt, of course, but I wanted to let you know what's going on. What was found at the scene makes it look like drugs were involved. You need to be prepared for what's coming."

"This can't possibly be true," said the distraught woman, obviously trying but failing to speak quietly. "He must have stopped someone who was smuggling or transporting drugs. No matter what you say," she added vehemently, "my husband is not a drug dealer!" With that she burst into tears.

The black woman rose, ushered the girls over to a seated older woman, and came to put her hand on the pregnant woman's shoulder. She looked at the officer. "What exactly is it that's coming, Sheriff Renteria?" she asked.

The man turned to her. "And you are?" he asked.

"Deputy Donnatelle Craig," she answered. "With the Yuma Sheriff's Department. I'm a friend of the family."

"Since it's an officer-involved shooting—" he began.

"I understand all that," Donnatelle interrupted. "Just tell us who'll be investigating the shooting. DPS?"

"Yes. Lieutenant Duane Lattimore with the Department of Public Safety. I'm sure he'll be stopping by sometime soon—if not today, then tomorrow. I felt obligated to let Teresa know what's really going on." The sheriff reached into his shirt pocket and extracted a business card, which he handed to Donnatelle. "I'll be going, then," he said. "But here are my numbers in case Teresa needs to get in touch with me."

That's the problem with waiting rooms, Sister Anselm thought. *There's no such thing as privacy.*

But the drama wasn't over. As soon as the sheriff left the room, an older woman who was wearing jeans and cowboy boots approached the younger woman, who was in tears.

"I'm sorry, Teresa, but I couldn't help hearing what the sheriff was saying. Can this be true?"

The pregnant woman looked up, dazed. "Of course it isn't true! None of it!"

"Well," the other woman said in a huff, "I don't know Jose, but he's the stepfather of my flesh-and-blood grandchildren, and this is all very distressing."

"You ignore them for years and now act like they are yours?" Teresa asked, incredulous. "You have some nerve!"

"I stayed away out of grief for my son," the woman said. "I assumed you were a better mother to them than you were a wife to Danny, but now . . . well, I just don't know."

"Please, Mrs. Sanchez," Donnatelle said. She deftly stepped between the weeping younger woman and the irate older one. "You'd better go now. This isn't the time or the place."

"If what the sheriff said is true, you haven't seen

the last of me," Mrs. Sanchez continued, lowering her voice and almost hissing. "I won't have Danny's girls—my granddaughters—being raised in this kind of mess."

"Go!" Donnatelle ordered.

To Sister Anselm's relief, the older woman did as she was told. She stalked back over to the table where she had been entertaining the children and gathered up her belongings. Then she marched out of the waiting room. In the silence left behind, other than the muted beeps of lifesaving equipment, the only sound came from the brokenhearted sobs of the young woman. The two girls ran to her, one on either side.

"Don't cry, Mommy," the older girl said, hugging her thigh. "Please don't cry."

As quiet gradually returned to the waiting room, Sister Anselm retreated to Jane Doe's room. Once there, she used a wireless connection to access the hospital's monitoring equipment. An app on her iPhone allowed her to keep track of the patient's vitals as well as her periods of waking and sleeping even when Sister Anselm wasn't actually present. Then she settled into the chair next to the bed. For the next twenty-four hours or so, it was simply a matter of waiting and watching.

Sister Anselm was a great believer in 1 Thessalonians 5:17: *Pray without ceasing.* That was something else she kept on her iPhone—a prayer list app. Under Jane Doe's name, she added the names of the distraught little family out in the waiting room—Jose and Teresa as well as the angry woman who had just left,

Mrs. Sanchez. As an afterthought, she added Sheriff Renteria's name. He seemed to be hurting every bit as much as everyone else.

Just because Sister Anselm didn't happen to know any of those people personally didn't keep her from praying for them. That was part of her job, too.

16

10:00 P.M., Saturday, April 10
Sedona, Arizona

"You're not going to believe what's going on around here," Ali told B. later that night when he called to say good night. She went on to give him a shorthand version of what her parents had told her about selling the Sugarloaf.

"And that's not the half of it," she added. "My mother has no intention of retiring. Once they get moved, she's planning to run for mayor of Sedona. When she dropped the mayor bomb at the dinner table, I thought Dad was going to have a coronary on the spot."

To Ali's dismay, B. seemed to find the whole idea exceptionally funny. "That's what I like about your parents," he said. "They're always full of surprises. On the one hand, your mother figures she's old enough to live in a retirement community, but on the other, young enough to start a career in politics! Sounds like she wants to have it both ways."

"That's pretty much what my father said," Ali conceded. "And when she let on that she hoped I'd agree to be her campaign manager, he lit into me and accused me of keeping the whole mayor-run thing a secret from him."

"Had you been keeping it a secret?"

"Since I only found out about it this afternoon, I don't see how I can be considered guilty as charged."

"If your dad is as upset as you say he is, what are the chances he'll try to back out of signing the papers on Monday?"

"I suppose it could happen," Ali said, "but I doubt it."

"From my point of view, your mother could be a great mayor," B. added. "She's short on political theory and long on common sense. That might be an excellent combination for public office."

"Not according to my father," Ali said with a laugh.

"How are you with all this?" B. asked.

"I'm not sure. I should be happy that they have a chance to retire while they're young enough and healthy enough to do things they want to do . . ."

"I think I'm hearing an unstated 'but' in there," B. said.

"The Sugarloaf has always been part of our family," she said. "Even when I was living out of state and only home for the holidays, everything revolved around the restaurant."

"Change is tough," B. said. "Even change for the better."

"Thanks," she said. "I'll try to keep that in mind when I'm on my way to Tucson tomorrow."

"What for?"

"Donnatelle called tonight. Things have just gotten way worse for Jose and Teresa Reyes. Jose's boss, the Santa Cruz County sheriff, stopped by the hospital earlier to let Teresa, Jose's very pregnant wife, know that evidence found at the crime scene has put Jose under suspicion of drug trafficking. And Teresa's former mother-in-law evidently rode in on her broom this afternoon in time to hear all about the drug-dealing allegations. Now she's questioning if her granddaughters—her deceased son's children—are being raised in a 'suitable' environment. Donnatelle is concerned that she might be considering launching a custody fight."

"Alleging drug dealing is a long way from being convicted of same," B. observed.

"That's true," Ali agreed, "but with everything that's going on, I'm not sure Teresa can make that distinction. According to Donnatelle, the scene at the hospital was the straw that broke the camel's back. She's afraid Teresa might have a total breakdown, and she knows her pretty well. I'm going down first thing in the morning to see what, if anything, I can do to help."

"Like what?" B. prompted.

"Like be there," Ali said. "Sometimes that's the only thing you can do."

Lying awake after she got off the phone with B., Ali thought of something else she could do. While Teresa was dealing with the immediate health crisis, it probably hadn't occurred to her that Jose might need a good criminal defense attorney every bit as much as he needed quality medical care.

In the long run and as a police officer, Jose would probably qualify for help from the Arizona Police Officers' Legal Defense Fund, but that might take time and paperwork. But what about the short run? According to Donnatelle, the DPS investigator had not yet come by the hospital to interview either Jose or Teresa. Maybe that was something Ali could do—make sure that when it did happen, there would be someone on tap, looking out for their best interests.

17

8:00 A.M., Sunday, April 11
Tucson, Arizona

Sister Anselm hadn't meant to spend the whole night in the ICU, but she had. Much of that time had been in the waiting room rather than in Jane Doe's room itself.

When Sister Anselm first arrived at the hospital, her patient had been resting comfortably. Hours later, though, Jane Doe began to flail in her bed. Sister Anselm, noticing that her temperature had soared, ran to the nurses' station to summon help. Within minutes, the room was overflowing with doctors and nurses battling what Sister Anselm had suspected to be the onset of a serious infection that might well have led to sepsis without immediate corrective measures.

The fact that Sister Anselm had alerted hospital personnel right away probably made all the difference. Although there were screens and readouts at the nearby ICU nurses' station, the on-duty staff members were busy with other patients, and no one other than Sister Anselm had been watching the monitors.

While the staff was stabilizing Jane Doe, Sister Anselm had been banished to the waiting room, where three new sets of worried families came in, grabbing seats near their loved one's rooms or pacing and hovering nearby.

The young woman named Teresa, clearly tired beyond bearing, was numbly coming and going from her husband's room on an hourly basis, with her two little girls nowhere to be seen. No doubt someone—the black woman Sister Anselm had seen earlier, most likely—had collected the girls and taken them elsewhere. It probably had been done as a helpful gesture. In most instances, Sister Anselm would have agreed that hospital waiting rooms weren't suitable places for young children. When the two girls had been present, however, Teresa had made the effort to keep it together. With them absent, she seemed to be sinking into a state of exhausted despair.

"You look like you could use some water," Sister Anselm said, taking a seat next to Teresa and handing her a bottle she had liberated from her bag. "It's easy to get dehydrated in places like this."

Teresa looked at her questioningly, then opened the bottle and gulped down half the contents.

"Your husband?" Sister Anselm asked, nodding in the direction of Jose's room. She already knew the answer. She was simply making conversation.

"Yes," Teresa said. "His name's Jose. I'm Teresa. Are you a nurse?"

"No," Sister Anselm said. "My name is Sister Anselm. I'm not a nurse. I'm what's known as a patient advocate. The doctors and nurses are dealing with my patient's medical needs right now, which is why I'm out here. What happened to your husband?"

"He's a deputy sheriff," Teresa said. "He was shot last night." She paused and looked at her watch. "About twenty-four hours ago."

"I saw two little girls earlier. Your daughters?"

"My friend took them to a hotel. They were really tired of being here, and I don't blame them. I'm tired of it, too."

Sister Anselm pulled another chair within range and motioned for Teresa to put her feet up. Her ankles were swollen. So were her hands and fingers. At that stage of pregnancy, it could be a dangerous precursor to some serious medical issues.

"When's your baby due?"

Teresa looked down at her bulging belly. "About three weeks," she said. Her voice broke. "What if Jose dies? What if my baby never knows his father?"

"What does his doctor say?"

Teresa gave a halfhearted shrug. "That it's touch and go. Jose lost a lot of blood, and he was lucky to survive surgery. The doctor says that the next twenty-four hours are critical."

"So the doctors are looking after him," Sister Anselm said kindly. "Who's looking out for you?"

Teresa bit her lip and shook her head.

"Your baby's a boy?" Sister Anselm continued, ignoring the lack of response.

Teresa nodded. "We're going to name him Carmine," she whispered. "After his grandfather. After Jose's father. That's one of the reasons I married Jose. I thought he'd be a good father, like his father. And now . . ." She paused and shook her head. "The sheriff told me this afternoon that he may be involved with dealing drugs. I can't believe it. It doesn't seem like him, like the Jose I know, but . . . I don't know. I just can't believe any of this is happening."

Sister Anselm knew that was the real bottom line. The fact that Jose was injured was one thing. Learning about a possible betrayal made the situation that much worse.

"Let's take this one thing at a time," Sister Anselm suggested. "Your husband has been shot and may not make it. But what happens if you don't make it? What happens to Carmine then? Who takes care of your little girls?"

Teresa shook her head. Again she didn't answer, and she didn't have to.

"That's what I thought," Sister Anselm said. "Look. There's a sofa at the end of the room that nobody is using at the moment. I'm going to go ask the nurses for a pillow and a blanket. You lie down on that and rest for a while. I'll look in on your husband while you're sleeping. If his condition changes, I'll come get you immediately. All right?"

It seemed that was all Teresa needed—permission. She nodded and then plodded over to the couch in question. Within minutes of lying down, she was deeply asleep, despite the noise and activity around her. For the rest of the night, Sister Anselm moved from the waiting room to Jose's and then Jane Doe's making sure that all were sleeping soundly and that the monitors showed normal levels of respiration, heart rate, and blood pressure.

Earlier, when Sister Anselm read Jane Doe's chart, she had noted that the doctors estimated the patient was between seventeen and twenty years of age. Once the waiting room quieted enough to allow for concentration, Sister Anselm picked up her iPhone and scrolled directly to the website for the Center for Missing and Exploited Children.

Once at the website, Sister Anselm entered the words "rose tattoo" into the search engine. Within moments she had half a dozen hits. Several of them specified that the tattoo in question was on either a right leg or a left leg. One said it was on the right arm. Three of those had been found on the bodies of unidentified murdered young women whose information had been added to the listing by law enforcement agencies seeking both the girls' killers as well as their families.

At the very bottom of the list was the only one that mentioned a tattoo of a single rose on the inside of the right breast. That listing, for a girl named Rose Ventana from Buckeye, Arizona, was dated three years earlier, when the missing girl's age was noted as fourteen. The listing was accompanied by what appeared to be a school photo of a smilingly beautiful young woman, a photo that bore no resemblance to the shaved head and the shattered visage lying on a hard pillow in Physicians Medical's ICU.

Even so, Sister Anselm's heart quickened as she scanned through the information. From the girl's point of view, three years was a long time to be away from home. From a grieving parent's point of view, three years of waiting and hoping and dreading must have seemed like forever. Sister Anselm was convinced the distraught parents would welcome their long-lost daughter, damaged or not, with open arms, but she didn't pick up her phone to call them. Her first responsibility, as patient advocate, was to her patient.

Over the years Sister Anselm had learned that many of her patients had chosen to strike out on their own because of some conflict that existed in the family home. Until she was sure Jane Doe wanted to be returned to her family, Sister Anselm would keep the knowledge to herself.

She contented herself with doing a computerized search for articles dealing with the long-ago disappearance of Rose Ventana, who had left for school as usual one February morning and then simply vanished. Foul play was suspected, although no body was ever found.

Rose's mother, Connie Fox, a tattoo artist by trade, was the one who had created the tattoo, and she was the one who had mentioned it in the press. Articles included statements from James Fox, Rose's stepfather, who was briefly considered a person of interest in Rose's disappearance. He was quoted several times, as were Rose's two younger sisters. Subsequent articles done on the first, second, and third anniversaries of Rose's disappearance showed the mother and stepfather standing side by side. In all of the photos, the stepfather looked every bit as grief-stricken as the mother, but Sister Anselm wondered if that was true. In her work, she had seen much of the world's evil underbelly, and her knowledge was anything but theoretical. She knew the kinds of unsavory family situations that often drove children to run away.

Rose had been off on her own since she was fourteen. She might have been close to death from a beating and terribly dehydrated when she was brought to the hospital, but she certainly wasn't starving. In those intervening years, Rose had eaten well enough. So how had she managed to support herself and provide for food and shelter?

Sister Anselm knew that fourteen-year-olds weren't generally employable in the regular job market; prostitution remained the most likely occupation of choice for underage girls. She also understood that these days prostitution was seldom a solo endeavor. It was a world where freelancing was frowned upon by the guys running the show. If Rose Ventana had been absorbed into the shadowy world of prostitution, that was most likely the source of her attacker—a disgruntled john or an angry pimp. Sister Anselm worried that if the perpetrator learned his victim was still alive, he might well try again.

Yes, Sister Anselm was fairly certain she now knew the name of her Jane Doe patient. For the time being, she had no intention of mentioning that fact to anyone but the patient herself. Instead, when the charge nurse finally cleared her to return to Jane Doe's room, she settled into her chair, took her sleeping patient's hand, the one without the cast, and held it.

Earlier, thinking her patient was an illegal, Sister Anselm had spoken to her in both English and Spanish. She deemed that no longer necessary.

"My name is Sister Anselm," she said softly. "I'm here to help you."

18

7:00 A.M., Sunday, April 11
Patagonia, Arizona

Phil Tewksbury crawled out of his warm bed and started in on his Sunday chores. He went into the kitchen and turned on Mr. Coffee. Then he unloaded the dishwasher and got his weekly wash under way by loading that week's dirty uniforms into the aging Maytag. The uniform load went first. While the next load—bedding and towels—was washing, he'd get the uniforms ironed.

He checked the freezer. He had a selection of microwave dinners, enough to make it through the week. Next weekend he'd have to go shopping. Once he had made a real effort to cook decent meals. Now he barely bothered. Why should he? Microwave dinners worked fine for him. As for Christine? Oatmeal was what she wanted—that was all she wanted, three meals a day, 365 days a year.

Oatmeal with skim milk and brown sugar. Phil could hardly stand to look at the stuff anymore, but that was what she wanted and what she ate, so he cooked up a big batch every morning, dividing it into three separate containers—one for breakfast, when she bothered to get out of bed; one for lunch, which she ate usually while he was out delivering mail, and one for dinner. She often ate the third batch long after he had gone to bed. God forbid they should sit at the same table during dinner and actually talk.

When he was working, people knew him. Everybody nodded at the mailman. Little kids waved at the mailman, though they didn't know him particularly well because he avoided talking about himself and his difficult home situation as much as possible. Phil had broken his silence with Ollie because she was different and because she understood. As far as other people were concerned? The details of his life were nobody else's business. As far as Phil was concerned, explaining Cassidy's death to others and admitting what her loss had done to his marriage was far too painful.

A few months ago, with Ollie's encouragement, Phil had broached the subject with one other individual— his own physician. He had finally broken his self-imposed silence. Worried about the long-term effects of Christine's oatmeal-only diet on her overall health, Phil had mentioned the subject during his own annual physical.

Dr. Patterson was Phil's doctor rather than Christine's. Doc Manning, who had been her doctor once, had been dead for seven years. Since Christine refused to leave the house for any reason, finding a new doctor for her or even taking her to a dentist for a simple and much-needed cleaning or filling wasn't exactly an option.

Which was why Phil decided to ask his doctor for advice. "I was wondering if I could ask you some questions about my wife."

"Wife?" Patterson asked, looking dismayed. "All these years I thought you were a widower. I noticed you wore a wedding ring, but since you never mentioned having a wife, I assumed she was deceased."

"Not exactly," Phil said. "But she does have issues. For one thing, I'm worried about her diet. The only thing she eats is oatmeal."

"Oatmeal?" Dr. Patterson repeated. "As in oatmeal three meals a day? No protein? No vegetables?"

Phil shook his head. "Nothing but. Whenever I try giving her anything else, she tosses it in the garbage."

"How long has this been going on?"

"Years," Phil admitted. *Fifteen going on sixteen, like it says in the song*, Phil thought, but he didn't say it aloud.

"So tell me," Doc Patterson said. "What's the deal with the oatmeal?"

Phil took a deep breath before he answered. "It's what we used to eat for breakfast on Christmas morning, before Cassidy opened her stocking or her presents."

Dr. Patterson gave Phil a quizzical look. "Cassidy?" the doctor asked. "Who's Cassidy?"

Phil knew he was in for it now. That was the main reason he avoided talking about Christine—so he wouldn't have to go over the painful details of Cassidy's death, which had led, inevitably, to everything else. This time, though, more for Christine's sake than for his own, he told the whole story.

"So your wife blames you for your daughter's death?" Patterson asked when Phil finished.

Phil nodded. "Every day and in every way."

"And you've kept the same Christmas tree up and lit for fifteen years? Isn't it dirty?"

"She dusts it sometimes," Phil says. "When I'm out of the house or when she thinks I'm sleeping. She wipes off the ornaments and brushes off the cobwebs."

And replaces some of the bulbs, Phil thought.

That was the first time the bulb-replacement scenario had surfaced in his mind as a coherent thought, when he was talking to Dr. Patterson. He'd thought about it a lot since, but he hadn't said the words aloud—not to Doc Patterson and not to anyone else, either.

"Have you considered having a psych evaluation?" Patterson asked.

Phil grinned ruefully. "For her or for me?" he asked. "Because I'm probably as much of a nutcase as she is for putting up with it all this time. Seriously, the only way I could get her out of the house is by force, and I'm not going to do that. At first people told me she was grieving and that it would take time. Then they told me she was depressed. Now I think most people have forgotten about her. If they think about her at all, it's like, 'Oh, you know, the crazy lady who keeps her Christmas tree up all year long.'"

"Everyone has forgotten about her but you," Dr. Patterson said.

Phil nodded as tears stung his eyes. "It's my fault," he said. "That makes Christine my responsibility."

"So it's like that movie *Groundhog Day,*" Patterson

said thoughtfully. "Every morning she wakes up, eats her oatmeal, and thinks that your daughter is going to come out into the living room and open her presents. Are they still there, too?"

"All but one," Phil answered. "The rest of them are wrapped and unopened."

Patterson blew out a breath of air and considered for a moment before he spoke again. "It's a little difficult to diagnose a patient without ever seeing him or her. Would you say your wife is overweight?"

"No," Phil answered. "More like too skinny than too fat."

"Any mobility issues?"

"She can walk when she wants to. And I know she does when I'm not around. At night I hear her pacing in her room, but during the day she mostly just sits in the recliner in the living room and stares at the tree. I try to get her to shower once a week."

"She sounds depressed," Dr. Patterson said.

"I think so, too."

"Would she take medication if you offered it to her?"

Phil shook his head. "Probably not," he said. "I had some leftover antidepressants my old doctor had given me. I tried giving them to Christine. She accused me of trying to poison her."

"What about her teeth?"

"She's lost several so far. I begged her to go to the dentist. She says that since I'm the only one who sees her, what does it matter?"

"Presumably, your wife isn't in the best of health, but then neither are you," Patterson said. "Your blood pressure is off the charts. So is your cholesterol. If we don't get a handle on those, chances are she'll outlive you. Then what will happen to her?"

Patterson had posed that question aloud for the first time several weeks earlier, and Phil had been grappling with the issue ever since. They had no kids—no surviving kids—who could be called on to help out in the face of a long-term health crisis. As Christine had turned into more and more of a hermit, the people who were once their friends had slowly drifted away. So had their relations. For now this was Phil's fight and nobody else's.

That was what had prompted him to bite the bullet and replace the windows. It was why he was painting the exterior of the house and garage. His next plan was to redo the kitchen and replace the appliances. Next up after that would be the bathroom. And finally, the living room. If Christine was ever left alone with a caregiver, it would be in a house that was in the best shape Phil could manage.

Lost in thought, Phil absently stirred the pot of oatmeal. Once it was finished, he divided it into the three microwaveable plastic bowls and set them on the kitchen counter before putting the dirty saucepan in the dishwasher to run with yesterday's dishes. Then he moved the uniforms into the dryer and loaded the bedding into the Maytag. Glancing up at his grandmother's antique teapot-shaped clock, he saw that it was ten to seven—time for his one bit of daily self-indulgence.

Every morning before work and on weekends, too, Phil stopped by the San Rafael Café to have a leisurely breakfast and shoot the breeze. His breakfast choices at the café tended to include crisp bacon and over-easy eggs, something he had no intention of mentioning to Doc Patterson.

After breakfast, he'd come home, do the ironing, paint the garage trim, and do the rest of his chores, all the while hoping that Ollie would be waiting to see him when he delivered her mail on Monday afternoon.

19

11:00 A.M., Sunday, April 11
Marana, Arizona

On Sunday morning, heading down I-17, Ali used her Bluetooth to call Victor Angeleri, the criminal defense attorney who had been her go-to guy when she was accused of murdering her former husband and needed one. He had given her his home number back then, and she still had it. Fortunately, it was April and daylight saving time in most of the rest of the country. With Arizona and California in the same time zone at this time of year, she doubted she was in any danger of waking him up.

"Long time, no hear," Victor said cheerfully when Ali identified herself. "You're not offloading inconvenient husbands again, are you?"

"No," she said with a laugh. "And if you recall, I didn't do that the first time, either. Right now I'm calling for a friend of mine—a cop in southern Arizona who got shot the other night and is now under suspicion as a drug trafficker. He'll probably be able to get help from the local police officers' legal defense fund, but that will take time and paperwork. I'm looking for someone to step in sooner than that."

"I may have a contact or two in Tucson," Victor said. "Is Tucson close enough?"

"Tucson is exactly right."

"Can your friend pay the going rate?"

"Probably not. He's in the hospital with serious injuries and serious meds. Because it's an officer-involved shooting, it's being investigated by the Department of Public Safety. I'm worried that if the DPS investigator shows up for an initial interview while Jose is under the influence of medication—"

"That your friend may blow it."

"Exactly. I'm not offering to sign on for his whole defense, but I am willing to pay the freight for him to have representation during that initial interview process."

"It sounds like you're still busy spending your former husband's cash," Victor said with a laugh, "but let me see what I can do."

An hour later, as Ali approached Marana on Tucson's north side, her phone rang again. The number in the readout was unlisted.

"Ali Reynolds?"

"Yes."

"My name is Juanita Cisco. Victor Angeleri and I go way back. When he gives me a heads-up about something, I generally pay attention, which is why I'm calling. He told me that this concerns a friend of yours, a police officer who's in the hospital with gunshot wounds."

"That's right. Jose Reyes, a Santa Cruz County deputy, is the victim. Unfortunately, investigators now suspect that the shooting was the result of a drug deal gone bad."

"Jose is related to you how?"

"We're not related. We're friends."

"But you're the one who's hiring me, not him and not his wife. Why? What's your interest in all this?"

"As I said, we're friends. The shooting investigation is being handled by the Department of Public Safety. Eventually, Jose will probably have representation from the police officers' legal defense fund, but I want him to have someone on hand today if he ends up subjected to an initial interview when he's in the hospital and more or less out of it."

"I don't much like being called in as a pinch hitter," Juanita said, "but I suppose I could do it. You haven't asked me how much I charge, especially if I come in on a Sunday. My billing includes this phone call, by the way, and any necessary travel."

"Yes," Ali assured her. "Whatever it is, I'm good for it."

"All right. Which hospital?"

"Physicians."

"PMC isn't far from where I live, which is fine for today, but it's all the way across town from my office if the interview happens tomorrow or the next day. Are you at the hospital now?"

"Not yet. I'm on my way there."

"When did the shooting happen?"

"Sometime Friday night. Maybe Saturday morning."

"And the detective on the case made no effort to interview the victim or his family yesterday?"

"Not so far as I know."

"That could be bad. He's probably getting his ducks in a row before he comes calling. Do you have a name on the DPS investigator?"

"I believe Donnatelle told me that his name is Lattimore."

"I don't know him. Who's Donnatelle?"

"Another friend," Ali answered.

"Right. This Jose guy must be something, to have a wife and a whole raft of devoted female friends who are all ready to go to the mat for him," Juanita said. "Okay. Call if you need me. Here's the number. I should be home all afternoon, and I can be at the hospital in under ten minutes."

20

9:00 A.M., Sunday, April 11
Vail, Arizona

The fact that one of Al Gutierrez's regular days off was Sunday was a bone of contention with his roommates. He didn't venture out of his room until everyone else had either gone to bed or gone on duty. Someone had dragged the Sunday paper inside and rifled through it. The sports page had suffered a severe coffee spill. Fortunately, his roommates never bothered with the rest of the paper.

Once again, Al read through it carefully, looking for some reference to the assault incident. Despite his morning paper, he was far from a Luddite, so he logged on to the Internet. The whole time Al had been at work the day before, he had considered his options. Just because Dobbs was going to sit on this didn't mean that Al had to.

He put the words "rose tattoo" into the search engine. Google came up with over three million hits, many of them having to do with a rock-and-roll band named Rose Tattoo. Then he tried "missing women with rose tattoos." That gave him 305,000 hits. Disturbed and disheartened to think there could be that many missing women with rose tattoos on their bodies, he began scrolling through them. It was slow, painstaking work, and it took him the better part of the morning.

One of his searches led him to the website of *America's Most Wanted*. Al remembered when his mother used to watch that program, though he never had. Still, when he landed on their missing persons page, he tried "rose tattoo" again. This time it worked. Four hits. As soon as he hit the one at the bottom of the list and saw the name Rose Ventana and the words "Buckeye, Arizona," he believed he was getting somewhere.

He read everything he could about Rose Ventana— about her family's long search for their missing daughter and sister. He read the interviews they gave every year in February on the day Rose disappeared. Al wanted to pick up the phone and call them right then, but he didn't. He didn't want to give them the wonderful news that he might have found their missing daughter and that she might be alive only for them to discover that she wasn't.

Al's victim—Rose, he was sure—had been alive when the Air Evac helicopter lifted off to take her to Physicians Medical Center. Considering the extent of her injuries, he was convinced she was still there, if she hadn't died in the meantime.

That was when he hit on the idea of going to the hospital and taking some flowers to the injured woman. If the patient was dead, the hospital most likely wouldn't accept the flowers, would they? That was about the time he reconsidered the idea of making a phone call to Rose Ventana's family. With the help of a people-finding website, he was able to track down a Buckeye street address for Connie and James Fox.

Whenever there was a death, cops always made every effort to notify the next of kin in person. Was it out of respect for the dead, or was it to have someone there if emergency medical care were required? What about if the notification were about someone who wasn't dead? What if after being thought dead for years, that person suddenly turned up alive? Wouldn't that good news be just as mind-numbingly shocking to the grieving family members as bad news?

Al dressed in a U of A sweatshirt that he'd picked up during that year's March Madness celebration. He put on his Mariners baseball cap and pulled it down over his eyes. Looking at himself in the mirror, he had to laugh. He looked like any one of a number of would-be bank robbers. It wasn't much of a disguise, but he hoped it was good enough to keep Sergeant Dobbs off his back.

With that, Al headed for Costco. The one closest to the hospital was on Grant, near Wilmot. Wandering through the flower section, he saw the foil-wrapped Easter lilies and knew they were just right.

After all, Easter was about the resurrection. Wasn't this the same thing?

21

Teresa Reyes awakened when her daughters came racing through the waiting room, squealing, "Mommy. Mommy. Mommy."

"Look what Donnatelle got us," Lucy said gleefully. "A new dress. From Target."

It turned out to be two matching dresses, actually—one for Lucy and one for Carinda.

"Very pretty," Teresa said, peeling the girls off her and struggling to sit up. "Did you tell her thank you?"

Both girls nodded.

"Can we go show Daddy?" Lucy wanted to know.

"No," Teresa answered.

She looked at the clock on the wall and was astonished to see that she had slept for almost six hours. Just then Sister Anselm, the nun who might as well have been Teresa's guardian angel, emerged from one of the rooms on the other side of the unit.

"So you're awake," Sister Anselm said with a smile.

"You must have been exhausted, to be able to sleep that peacefully on a lumpy couch with people coming and going all around you."

"How's Jose?" Teresa asked. "I should probably go check on him."

"He's doing well," Sister Anselm said. "I checked on him about half an hour ago. Everything was fine. He's stable. No changes in his condition."

"When can we see Daddy" Lucy asked. "I want to see him. Now."

"Not until he moves out of this room and into another one," Teresa explained.

"Tell your mommy that we got some sticker books, too," Donnatelle said, taking charge of the girls once again. "Let's go play with those and give your mom a chance to wake up."

Teresa stripped off the blanket and sat up. Her shoes were on the floor, but when she tried to put them on, they felt like they were at least one size too small, maybe even two. "What about having some breakfast?" she asked the girls.

"We already ate," Lucy told her. "At the hotel."

"Thank you," Teresa said to Donnatelle. "For everything."

"No problem," Donnatelle said. "They were very good girls. We had breakfast first, and then we went to Target to look for dresses."

Looking from Sister Anselm to Donnatelle, Teresa couldn't help but be astonished by their kindness. Donnatelle had dropped everything and driven halfway across the state to help out. Sister Anselm had volunteered to look out for Jose so Teresa could grab a few hours of sleep. She would have to revise her thinking—two guardian angels, not just one.

With the girls happily occupied at a table in the corner of the room, Teresa limped into the restroom. Revived by sleep and refreshed by splashing cold water on her face and smoothing down her hair, she made her way into Jose's room. Sister Anselm was right. He was sleeping. She stood by his bed for some time. Was it possible that he had done what Sheriff Renteria had said? If so, Jose had succeeded in showing one face to her and his colleagues and another to the criminal world. Was it possible for the man she loved to be everything he had claimed to despise?

When Teresa was nervous or upset, she often twisted her wedding band, moving it around on her finger. This time, when she attempted to do that, the ring wouldn't budge. She looked at her hands. Her fingers looked swollen, but that was probably due to the way she had slept, lying flat on the couch with her hands beside her. She was sure that if she waited awhile, she'd be fine.

Leaving Jose's room, she realized she was hungry. She left the girls occupied with Donnatelle and made her way to the cafeteria. Her cell phone needed recharging, but there was enough power left in it to call her mother. Late in the evening, Teresa's uncle had driven Maria back home.

"If you need me to come back, I will," Maria said. "But I'm afraid I overdid it yesterday."

"That's fine," Teresa said. "You get some rest. I've made arrangements to keep Donnatelle's hotel room.

When it's time to go to bed, the girls and I will go there."

"But you don't have your car. Do you want me to ask Tomás to come get you?"

"Uncle Tomás has done plenty," Teresa said. "If we need to, we'll take a cab." Her phone beeped, letting her know the battery was low. "Sorry, Mom," she finished. "The phone is running out of juice."

Teresa arrived back at the ICU waiting room just as a new person—a tall woman with a blond ponytail—was added to the mix. Donnatelle left the girls with their sticker books and rushed across the room to greet the newcomer. When Sister Anselm emerged from her patient's room, she did a double take.

"Ali! For goodness' sake. What are you doing here?"

"I could ask you the same thing," the blond woman said with a laugh.

"I had a call out. I told you I had one, that I was going to Tucson. That usually means either this trauma unit or the one at University Medical Center. But why are you here?"

"She's a friend of Jose's," Donnatelle explained, answering for both of them. "I asked Ali to come help out because I have to leave for home shortly." She turned to Teresa. "I'm not sure you've met. This is Jose's friend Ali Reynolds, from Sedona."

Standing up to be introduced, Teresa was painfully aware of how short she was. Among those three towering women, she wished she were taller than her five foot nothing. She also wished she weren't so impossibly pregnant.

"I'm glad to meet you," she said.

"I'm guessing you didn't get my e-mail," Ali said.

"No."

"I told you I was coming. I'll be here to help out when Donnatelle has to go home."

Another helpful stranger, Teresa thought. She was grateful for the help but embarrassed that she needed it.

"You're from Sedona? I'm sorry you had to come all this way."

"It's not so far," Ali said. "And it was a beautiful drive, with all the wildflowers blooming. Besides, Jose really helped me out once. I'm here to return the favor. What needs doing?"

"Lucy and Carinda are working their way through their sticker books," Donnatelle said, nodding toward the girls, who were at the table with their heads tucked together in concentration. "When they run out of interest in that, they'll probably be ready for lunch. We had an early breakfast at the hotel. Come on. Let me introduce you to them, too."

Donnatelle and Ali walked away. As Sister Anselm returned to her patient, Teresa couldn't help wondering what kind of important person might be in the room across from Jose's. Whoever she was, she merited having Sister Anselm looking after her around the clock. Maybe it was a well-known politician or some kind of celebrity.

Teresa turned to go back to her temporary command center of waiting room chairs when her path was blocked by the sudden appearance of a large man who stopped directly in front of her. "Mrs. Reyes?" he asked.

In the generally hushed atmosphere of the waiting room, his voice was so loud that it startled her.

"Yes," she said. "Who are you?"

He was dressed in a sport jacket and a flashy tie. That meant he wasn't a doctor. In fact, she suspected the man was a cop even before he reached into a pocket and produced an ID wallet and badge.

As Teresa squinted to read the name on the badge, she realized that she had a splitting headache. Somehow she hadn't noticed that before. Now she did, discovering it at the same time as the letters on his ID wallet gradually sorted themselves into a name. Lattimore. The guy from the Department of Public Safety. This was the investigator Sheriff Renteria had told her about, the one who was investigating Jose's shooting.

"Yes," she said. "I'm Teresa Reyes."

"I'm Lieutenant Duane Lattimore with the Department of Public Safety. I'm charged with investigating your husband's shooting. I was hoping to talk to you about it."

When she looked up at the intimidating man looming above her, the room seemed to spin around him. For a moment she thought she might faint. She grabbed hold of the back of a chair to steady herself. Finally, she managed to focus.

"How's he doing, by the way?" Lattimore asked.

"Hanging in," Teresa said. "He's in the ICU and listed as stable at the moment, but the doctor says the next twenty-four hours are critical."

Tired of looking up at the man and worried that she was about to fall, Teresa staggered around behind him and managed to regain her chair. She felt surprisingly dizzy, almost as though she were drunk. Sitting down helped settle some of the vertigo.

"What do you need?" she asked. "How can I help?"

"You might start by giving me the names of some of your husband's associates," Lattimore said.

"Associates. You mean like the cops he works with?"

"Please, Mrs. Reyes," Lattimore said. "Let's not play games. We found evidence at the scene that indicates your husband is involved in a drug trafficking operation of some kind. We found even more evidence of that at your home earlier today."

"At my home," Teresa objected. "You went to my home?"

"We had a search warrant," Lattimore said. "A properly drawn search warrant. What we found in your husband's vehicle gave us probable cause to search his residence as well."

"My husband is the victim here," Teresa said, her voice rising in pitch. "He was shot. How dare you search our house?"

Pulling out a notebook, Lattimore made a show of opening it to the first blank page. Then he pulled a ballpoint pen out of his pocket. "Do you have any idea how long your husband has been involved in the drug trade?" he asked.

"Jose is not involved in the drug trade," Teresa declared forcefully. "He never has been involved in the drug trade. He's a police officer. He hates drugs. He hates people who sell drugs."

Lattimore gave no indication that he'd heard her objection. "When we searched your home, we found plenty of evidence that says otherwise. Now, if you'd be so kind as to give me the names of some of his business associates, perhaps we can move on to finding out who did this."

"You mean as in finding out who tried to kill him?" Teresa asked. "You're going to stand there and try to tell me that you even care about who shot him? This is about something else. This is all about proving to the world that Jose did something wrong. It's not about finding out who's responsible for putting him here."

Lattimore sat down beside her. "Now, now, Mrs. Reyes," he said soothingly. "There's no need to shout. Perhaps we should go somewhere less public so we can discuss this situation in private."

Teresa was abruptly aware that the entire waiting room had gone quiet as everyone there tuned in on this conversation. Some of her anger retreated, leaving her vulnerable and more than a little afraid. She hoped there was safety in numbers.

"We'll talk here," she said. "What do you want to know?"

As if responding to the uncertainty in their mother's voice, first Lucy and then Carinda abandoned the game they were playing with Donnatelle and came on the run. Once again, Lucy stationed herself protectively at her mother's side, while Carinda catapulted into her lap.

"These are your daughters?" Lattimore asked.

Teresa nodded.

"Cute kids," he said. He held out his pen, offering it to Carinda. She immediately reached out and grasped it with her short fingers. Before she could stick it in her mouth—ink end first—Teresa took it away

"She's two," Teresa said. "That's too young for pens."

When she handed the pen back to him, Lattimore immediately dropped it in his pocket and went searching for another one.

"Now back to business," he said. "Where were you on Saturday night?"

"You mean where was I when my husband was shot? Wait. Are you asking me if I'm the one who shot him?"

"Where were you?" Lattimore insisted.

"I was at home with my kids—these kids, Carinda and Lucy."

"Can they verify that for us?"

"Are you kidding?" she demanded. "Look at them. They're preschoolers. The younger one can barely talk. Neither of them can tell time. But I wouldn't go off and leave them alone, and if I were capable of doing what you suggested, I certainly wouldn't take the girls with me. What kind of a person do you think I am?"

"Perhaps someone called you at home that night," Lattimore suggested. "If you used your landline phone or your cell, we can use presence technology to verify exactly where you were at the time your husband was shot."

"I didn't talk to anyone on the phone. When the girls go to bed, I usually unplug the phone so it doesn't wake them."

"What about your cell phone?"

"Same thing. I turn it on silent or vibrate when they

go to bed, but nobody called me on Saturday night. I went to bed as soon as *America's Most Wanted* was over."

"You watch that?"

"Every week."

"Why?"

"Because we live in a place where we might see some of those people."

"I see," Lattimore said, sounding as though he didn't. "Back to the phone situation. In your husband's line of work, isn't turning off the phone when he's on duty a bit unusual? What if there was an emergency? What if his department needed to reach you?"

"There was an emergency," Teresa reminded him, feeling a flood of anger surge through her body. "Sheriff Renteria didn't call me on the telephone. He came to the house to let me know what had happened. In person."

Lattimore moved closer to her and lowered his voice. "Are you involved in the drug trade, Mrs. Reyes? Is it possible that both you and your husband are in this together?"

"That's the most ridiculous thing I've ever heard. I'm a mother with two kids. I'm expecting another one. Of course I'm not involved in the drug trade."

"Tell me about the money we found in your underwear drawer."

"What money?" she asked.

"Five thousand dollars in a plastic Ziploc container—all of it in hundred-dollar bills."

"I have no idea what you're talking about. There's no money in my underwear drawer."

"You're right about that," Lattimore said with a knowing chuckle. "Because it isn't there anymore. It's in an evidence bag and on its way to the crime lab."

"That's enough," a woman's voice said. "Leave her alone."

Teresa and Lattimore looked up in surprise as the blond woman Donnatelle had introduced as Ali Reynolds came striding across the room, cell phone on hand.

"And who might you be?" Lattimore asked. "The lady's attorney, possibly?"

"I'm a friend of the family. My name is Alison Reynolds. I'm not an attorney, but I have one on the phone right now." Ali handed her iPhone over to Teresa. "Her name is Juanita Cisco," Ali went on. "She's a criminal defense attorney here in town. I called her while you and this nice police officer were having your not so pleasant conversation, and she's been listening in on the speakerphone. You might ask if she's interested in representing you. If you can't afford her, I'm sure you can have an attorney appointed by the court, but given the circumstances, it seems to me that you need someone to represent you right now."

Teresa held the phone and looked at it warily, as though it might be an incendiary device set to explode. The same was true of Agent Lattimore's face. It, too, appeared close to exploding.

"I don't know who you think you are . . ." he began, shaking an outraged finger in Ali's direction. "You're interfering with an officer of the law."

That outburst was enough to move Teresa to action. She held the phone up to her ear, even though, with the thing set to speaker, holding it up to her ear wasn't necessary.

"Mrs. Reyes?" The voice over the phone bristled with urgency. "Did you hear what your friend said? My name is Juanita Cisco. I'm willing to serve as your attorney. All you have to do is say yes."

"Yes," Teresa whispered. "Yes, please."

"All right, then, hand the phone over to the officer."

Teresa did as she was told. She gave the phone to Lattimore. He took it reluctantly, scowling as he did so.

"Did you hear that?" Juanita asked. "Mrs. Reyes wants me to serve as her attorney in this matter."

"Yes," Lattimore muttered. "I heard."

"Would you like me to represent your husband as well, Mrs. Reyes?" Juanita asked, her voice booming through the cell phone speaker.

At first Teresa only nodded. Then, glancing at Ali's face, she realized her mistake. "Yes, please," Teresa said. "I want you to represent us both."

"And what's your name, Officer . . ."

"Lattimore," he replied. "Lieutenant Duane Lattimore. I'm an investigator with the Arizona Department of Public Safety. And there's no need to involve an attorney at this time. I'm merely asking Mrs. Reyes a few questions. After all, she's not a suspect."

"It sounded very much like you were treating her as a suspect, Mr. Lattimore," Juanita said. "So for right now, you're done. The conversation is over. Neither she nor her husband will be speaking to you again without my being present in the room. Understood?"

Lattimore knew he'd been outmaneuvered. "Understood," he said.

Without another word, he ended the call and thrust the phone back in Ali's direction. Turning, he strode out through the doors of the waiting room and disappeared down the hall.

To Teresa's surprise, the waiting room seemed to have filled with people without her noticing—nurses, orderlies, other visitors. They had all heard what was being said, and they understood instantly that this was a case where, against all odds, the little guy had beaten the big guy. Quietly, one person began to applaud. Soon other people joined in, and in a moment they were all clapping.

Teresa Reyes sat there, looking from one face to the other. Then her eyes rolled back in her head. Seconds later, as she slumped forward in her chair, the large purse that had been perched in her minimal lap fell to the floor, scattering possessions in every direction.

"I think she fainted." Teresa heard the words, but they seemed to be coming from very far away.

"Help me lower her to the floor," Sister Anselm said. "And somebody call a doctor."

That last remark was unnecessary, because the ICU charge nurse was already sounding the alarm.

12:00 P.M., Sunday, April 11
Tucson, Arizona

Ali watched as orderlies and nurses sprang into action. While one of them pushed an unoccupied bed out of one of the ICU rooms, a nurse slapped a blood pressure cuff on Teresa's arm and pumped it up. By the time the nurse finished taking the reading and listening to a stethoscope held to Teresa's chest, the expression on the woman's face was grave.

"We've got to get her to maternity," the nurse ordered. "Now!"

Several people stepped forward. Together they lifted Teresa from the floor and onto the makeshift gurney. As the gurney rolled toward the doorway, the two little girls tried to follow.

"Mommy, Mommy," Lucy wailed. "Where are you taking my mommy?"

Only Donnatelle's timely intervention kept the screaming children from following their mother down the hall. As they went through the door to the waiting room, the group almost flattened a uniformed hospital volunteer coming in the opposite direction, carrying a massive foil-covered, potted, and blooming Easter lily.

While Ali gathered the scattered contents from Teresa's bag, Donnatelle and Sister Anselm took charge of the children, trying to calm them. Pocketing Teresa's fallen cell phone, Ali handed the purse over to the charge nurse for safekeeping. Just then Ali's cell phone rang.

"Somebody hung up on me," Juanita Cisco complained when Ali answered.

"That would be Lieutenant Lattimore," Ali said.

"Maybe I should talk to my client again when we're not on a speakerphone."

"That's going to be tough," Ali said. "She fainted dead away. They put her on a bed and are rolling her to the maternity ward as we speak."

"She's pregnant?"

"Very."

"When do you think I'll be able to talk to her?"

"I have no idea. The nurses didn't say anything, but I have a feeling that whatever's going on is pretty serious. Do you think Lattimore meant what he said—that he suspects Teresa has some involvement in her husband's shooting?"

"The spouse or significant other is always suspect," Juanita replied. "You're the one who knows these people. What do you think?"

"I know Jose," Ali said. "I met Teresa for the first time this morning, but that's not the reading I'm getting."

"Lattimore was trying to scare her into talking to him. Which is why you were absolutely right to put me on the phone. So what about the husband?" Juanita asked. "When can I talk to him?"

"He's still in the ICU."

"Is he able to communicate?" Juanita asked. "If I talk to him, will he make sense?"

Ali glanced toward the charge nurse, who had taken the volunteer and her load of flowers in hand. "Those can't go in any of the ICU rooms, because they're supposed to be fragrance-free zones," the nurse was explaining to the woman, who was evidently new. "You can park them on one of the tables here in the waiting room. Then, when the patient is moved to a regular room, we send the flowers along. Who are they for?"

"The guy didn't give us a name. Just the woman who was found near Three Points on Friday."

The nurse gestured toward the room from which Sister Anselm had emerged much earlier. "Okay," she said. "I'll just write Jane Doe and tape it to the side, here. That way we'll know they're hers. I'm not sure how long she'll be in the ICU, but you can take charge of them, right, Sister Anselm?"

Bouncing the weeping Carinda on her hip, the nun nodded. "Will do," she said.

"Excuse me," Ali said, interrupting the flower discussion. "This is Mr. Reyes's attorney on the phone. She wants to know if she can come to the hospital to talk to him."

The nurse shook her head. "Not at this time," she said. "Family members only."

"You heard that?" Ali asked.

"Good," Juanita said. "If I can't talk to him, neither

can Lattimore. At this point, I'm working as your attorney as opposed to theirs. I'm assuming you want me on the job?"

"Yes," Ali said. "I want you on the job."

"Very well, then. At their earliest convenience, Ms. Reynolds, I'll need to have a signed document from all of you, saying that you, Ali, are paying for their legal services, but you might want to reconsider."

"Why?"

"Because you might be wasting your money. In order to have a search warrant in hand, Mr. Lattimore had to convince a judge that he had some reason to believe illegal activity had occurred. You may believe these people to be friends of yours, Ms. Reynolds, but I must warn you, search warrants aren't issued easily."

"I'm aware of that," Ali said.

"So let me ask you one more question," Juanita said. "Did you have an affair?"

"I beg your pardon?"

"You and Jose? I'm trying to figure out why you're riding to the rescue here—calling Victor; calling me. What business is this of yours?"

"Jose and I didn't have an affair," Ali declared. "He helped me once when I needed it, and I'm trying to help him in return. I'm also trying to help his family."

"No good deed . . ." Juanita said with a sigh. "Have it your way. Are you staying at the hospital?"

"For now I am. I don't know for how long."

"Okay. Keep me posted. Call me as soon as Mr. Reyes is moved out of the ICU and can have visitors. If that's what he wants, I'll come by at that point and sign him up. By all means, see to it that he talks to me before Lattimore gets in to see him. But be advised, if Lattimore decides that Teresa is really a legitimate suspect in the attempt on her husband's life, then all bets are off. If that happens, I'll have to represent one or the other of them. I won't be able to represent both."

"I understand," Ali said. "I'll call if anything changes."

By the time the call ended, the room was mercifully quiet. Donnatelle had collected the two girls and taken them to the cafeteria. Sister Anselm, in the meantime, was busy examining the flowers.

"That's odd," she said to Ali.

"What's odd?"

"I was looking for a card so I could let my patient know who sent them and who should receive a thank-you note. Usually, when people send flowers to hospital patients, they don't do so anonymously. They want to get credit where credit is due."

Ali pointed to the small orange tag on the side of the potted plant. "Those lilies came from Costco," she said. "That's a Costco product number."

"I wonder who delivered them," Sister Anselm mused, but Ali was far more concerned about Teresa than she was about the appearance of the flowers.

"What do you think happened?" Ali asked.

"To Teresa? If I were to hazard a guess, I'd say preeclampsia," Sister Anselm answered. "I advised her to talk to a nurse earlier this morning, when I noticed that her hands and ankles were swollen." She turned to the charge nurse. "Did she mention anything to you?"

"Not to me, and not to anyone else, as far as I know."

"Preeclampsia is serious?" Ali asked.

"It can be," Sister Anselm said. "It's potentially very serious for both the mother and for the baby."

Leaving the flowers where they were, Sister Anselm excused herself and returned to the room evidently occupied by her patient. In the meantime, Ali pulled Teresa's phone out of her pocket and scrolled through the list of recent calls. The most recent one was an outgoing call listed as MOM. Punching send, she waited until a woman answered.

"My name is Ali Reynolds," she said. "I'm calling from Physicians Medical Center. Are you Teresa Reyes's mother?"

"Oh, no," the other woman breathed. "Don't tell me. Is Jose gone?"

"You are Teresa's mother?"

"Yes. My name is Maria Delgado. I can't believe this. Please let me talk to my daughter."

"She's the one I'm calling about," Ali said. "Teresa can't come to the phone because she passed out here in the waiting room a few minutes ago. They've rushed her to maternity."

"But it's too early for the baby," Maria objected.

"I don't know any more about her condition than just that, and the staff here isn't going to tell me. I think you should come to the hospital right away."

"That'll take at least two hours. I can't drive that far. My brother will have to come from Tucson to get me, or maybe I can ask my neighbor again."

"Get here as soon as you can," Ali urged. "And you might want to come prepared to spend the night. I probably won't be given any more information about

Teresa's condition, but if I hear anything, I'll give you a call. Is this a landline or a cell phone?"

"Landline," Maria answered. "I don't have a cell phone."

"All right. I have Teresa's phone. You can call me on that if you need to reach me."

As Ali ended the call, the phone gave her a low-battery warning. Remembering that there had been a charger among the items from Teresa's purse, Ali went to the nurses' station to retrieve it. By the time the phone was charging, Sister Anselm came back into the waiting room. She looked unhappy.

"What's wrong?" Ali asked.

"The flowers," Sister Anselm said. "I don't like the idea that they were dropped off anonymously. I checked with the lady at the main reception desk. She said the same thing the volunteer said earlier, that the guy who dropped them off said they were for the lady who was found over by Three Points. I asked what he looked like. She said he was a young guy wearing jeans, a U of A sweatshirt, and a baseball cap."

"So?" Ali said, not following. "That sounds pretty ordinary."

"My patient was savagely beaten and left for dead," Sister Anselm said. "As far as I know, there have been no published news items about the attack, at least none that I've been able to find surfing the Net."

Ali still didn't get it.

"Most of my patients never receive flowers of any kind," Sister Anselm continued. "That's usually be-cause their friends and relations have no idea where they are, much less that they've been seriously injured.

Call me paranoid, but I'm worried that whoever sent these lilies has something in mind besides well wishes. So far the victim doesn't have a name. We know which patient she is, but no one else does. If there's someone out there who is interested in finishing the job, sending a distinctive flower arrangement or other gift is one way of locating her room inside the hospital." With that, Sister Anselm carried the plant away. Just as she left, Ali's phone rang.

"How's your day going?" B. asked.

"Way more eventful than I would have thought," Ali said. She spent several minutes bringing him up to date. She signed off when Donnatelle returned from the cafeteria with the girls.

"Have you heard anything?" Donnatelle asked.

"Nothing," Ali said. "Teresa's mother is on her way, but she won't be here for a while."

Donnatelle looked at her watch. "I'm going to have to leave soon."

"It's all right," Ali said. "I'll be able to look after the girls until Maria Delgado shows up. If she needs it, I'll help out after she gets here, too."

There was a fifteen-minute period of chaos while the girls adjusted to the idea of being abandoned by one relative stranger, Donnatelle, in favor of a different one, Ali. By the time Donnatelle took off, things were reasonably well in hand. In the past two years, Ali had spent enough time backstopping Chris with the twins that dealing with a two-year-old and a reasonably self-sufficient five-year-old seemed like a piece of cake.

Keeping an eye on her watch and wondering what

was going on in the maternity ward, Ali kept Lucy and Carinda corralled and occupied with the collection of toys, Crayolas, and coloring books that had accumulated in two days. After convincing Carinda that she really did need to take a nap, Ali read to Lucy until she, too, began to fade.

Both kids had nodded off when Sister Anselm returned to the waiting room with her forehead creased by an unaccustomed frown.

"What's wrong now?" Ali asked.

"I spent an hour working my way up the chain of command. When I connected with the hospital's head of security, I asked if I could review the security tapes. I told him all I wanted to do was to get a look at the guy who delivered the flowers. He said the only way to get access is to have a search warrant. That's not gonna happen. But if the guy walks into my patient's room this afternoon or tonight, I want to know who he is. And it seems to me the hospital would want to know who it is, too."

It wasn't such an outlandish idea. After all, Ali and Sister Anselm had some experience with people who came to hospitals hoping to finish off an inconvenient witness or two. The idea of the head of security insisting that Sister Anselm procure a search warrant in order to scan the security film was particularly irksome.

"If all you want to do is get a look at the tape," Ali said, "let me see what I can do."

"Thanks," Sister Anselm said. "Now I'd better go check on my patient."

Ali's relationship with B. Simpson had taught her that

people who know all about online security often come at it from a background of online insecurity. High Noon Enterprises was in the business of teaching companies and individuals how to safeguard their computer presence by knowing all there was to know about penetrating the very systems people counted on for protection.

Carinda had fallen asleep in Ali's lap. Ali shifted the child to another position, wrestled her cell phone out of her pocket, and speed-dialed High Noon.

It may have been Sunday afternoon, but Ali wasn't surprised when Stuart Ramey, B. Simpson's geeky second-in-command, answered the phone. As far as B. was concerned, Stuart was the perfect employee. When it came to computers, Stuart, like B., was a self-taught genius. He loved his work and had no outside interests. B. said he paid the guy a king's ransom, and he was worth every penny.

"Hey, Ali," Stuart said. "What's up?"

"We have a situation. My friend Sister Anselm has a patient here in Tucson at Physicians Medical Center. Somebody delivered some flowers to the patient, and we need to know who it was. I'm sure the guy's picture is on the hospital's security tape, but they won't let us look at it. I was hoping maybe you could—"

"You're asking if I could hack into their security system and lift the photo from their video feed?"

"Well, yes," Ali admitted. "That's pretty much it."

"And this is all because someone delivered flowers and didn't leave their name, address, and phone number?" Stuart asked dubiously. "It'll probably turn out to be some do-gooder who does this kind of thing all the time and wants to stay anonymous."

"Someone tried to murder this girl on Friday," Ali explained. "She should be dead right now. Sister Anselm is worried that the flower delivery guy may be working for the bad guys and is going to take another crack at her. I'm worried, too. If the flower guy turns back up, it would be a big help to know what he looks like. It's also possible that the flower delivery was a ruse attempting to nail down the girl's location inside the hospital for someone else. The third alternative is what you said—the guy is totally harmless—but do we want to take that risk?"

Stuart sighed. "All right. No doubt the hospital security system is password-protected, but breaking it will probably be a piece of cake. You want me to send the film directly to Sister Anselm's phone?"

"No," Ali said. "Send it to mine."

"Okay, so when did this questionable flower delivery happen?"

"Right around noon," Ali said. "The guy should be easy to spot. He was wearing jeans, a baseball cap, and a U of A sweatshirt. He was carrying a pot of Easter lilies with yellow foil wrapped around the pot."

"Okeydokie," Stuart said. "I'll get right on it. Anything else?"

On the drive down, Ali had been thinking about her parents and their plans to sell the Sugarloaf to a party or parties unknown. What if the purported buyers turned out to be some kind of flimflam outfit? Since one of High Noon's specialties was doing background checks, it didn't seem completely out of line to ask.

"Now that you mention it, there is one more thing," Ali said casually. "There are some people I'd like you to check out for me."

"No problem," Stuart said. "Who is it?"

Ali had to think a moment before she could dredge up the names. "Derek and Elena Hoffman," she said at last. "I'm not sure where they live."

"You mean the people from Milwaukee who are buying the Sugarloaf from your folks?" Stuart asked. "I already did a background check on them for your mother. Since she paid for the initial report, I should probably get permission from her before I copy you on it."

Chagrined, Ali felt herself blushing. She was surprised to think that it would even occur to her mother to have a background check done on the café's proposed purchasers, but these days there seemed to be any number of things about Edie Larson that set her daughter back on her heels.

"Never mind," Ali said quickly, trying to cover her embarrassment. "I didn't know she had already ordered one. I'll just get a copy from her."

23

2:00 P.M., Sunday, April 11
Tucson, Arizona

Breeze Domingo stirred in the bed. She had no idea where she was or how she had come to be there. She seemed to be in a hospital. It looked like a hospital, but the last thing she remembered was being in a house, a big house and . . . No, she didn't want to remember that or the man who was there, the one who had burned her and cut her. She could remember that, but she didn't want to. What she really wanted to know was where Chico was. Why didn't he come for her? Why had he abandoned her?

In the background, someone was talking—a woman. It was a voice rather than a presence. Breeze could hear the woman speaking, but she couldn't see her. She seemed to remember having heard the voice before, although she wasn't sure exactly when or why or who the woman was. *Is she someone I know?*

For a while—when was that?—the woman had spoken in both English and Spanish. That seemed weird. Why would she do that? Did she think Breeze didn't understand English? Now she had dropped the

Spanish and settled into English, telling a long complicated story.

At first Breeze thought the woman was speaking
about someone else. Finally, though, she realized she
was talking about Breeze—about what had happened
to her; about her being found in the desert; about her
being raped and beaten. She tried to stop listening. It
hurt too much to think about it. Now the woman was
talking about what had happened in the hospital.
There were surgeries and something to do with blood
poisoning and wiring her jaw shut. Breeze didn't care
about what the doctors had done or would do. It was
too complicated. Too much information. All she
wanted to do was go back to sleep.

But then the woman said something shocking—her
name! Her real name. Not Breeze Domingo but Rose
Ventana!

How did the unseen woman know that? How
could she possibly?

Now she was talking about Breeze's family, offering
to be in touch with them if that was what Rose
wanted, to have them come to the hospital to visit her.

Her family? Her family was so long ago that they
might well have lived in another universe. They
would be so disappointed in who she was now; in
what she had become; in how she had lived all this
time. She didn't want to see them. She was too
ashamed. She didn't want them to know anything at
all about her. No. No. No. Especially not her stepfather. Especially not him.

She tried to say the word aloud: NO! But nothing
came out of her mouth. So she shook her head instead.

"All right," the woman said comfortingly. "As you wish. I won't make any effort to contact them until and unless you say so."

Breeze wanted to say, *Thank you. And who are you?* And any number of other things. But that didn't work, either. With her jaw wired shut, it seemed impossible to speak. She felt the wetness of a single tear rolling down her cheek.

"Rest now," the woman murmured gently, wiping the tear away. "We've talked quite enough."

24

3:00 P.M., Sunday, April 11
Tucson, Arizona

Teresa's cell phone rang at ten past three. "Ms. Reynolds?" a male voice asked when Ali answered.

"Yes."

"I'm Tomás. Maria's brother. I drove down to pick her up. We're almost there. Have you heard anything?"

Ali was grateful that Teresa's uncle had a cell phone, even if Maria didn't. "No," she said. "I've heard nothing. I have a friend who might find out for us, but . . ."

"What about Jose? How's he doing?"

"He's stable, as far as I know."

"I don't have a handicapped sticker on my Taurus," Tomás said. "Maria has a tough time walking any distances at all. If I dropped her at the main entrance, do you think you could meet us and take her where she needs to go?"

The two girls had been growing steadily more restless and whiny. They were bored. They wanted their mother. They wanted their father. They had exhausted all interest in the collection of stuff Donnatelle and the other grandmother had brought in hopes of keeping them occupied. They wanted to go home.

"Sure," Ali said. "We'll meet you out front."

"Are we leaving?" Lucy wanted to know.

"We're going to go meet your grandmother," Ali told them. "Then we're going to go check on your mom."

A hospital wheelchair had been abandoned on the sidewalk outside the front door. Ali appropriated the chair and let both girls sit in it while they waited for Tomás to arrive in an older-model Taurus. When a frail, graying woman slowly stepped out of the passenger seat of the car, the girls went nuts. "Grandma, Grandma, Grandma," Lucy shouted.

Ali helped Maria into the wheelchair and deposited Carinda on her grandmother's lap, then they headed for the maternity unit with Lucy trailing behind.

Visitors back in the ICU waiting room had seemed trapped in the grip of grim despair. In the waiting room of the maternity wing, it was a different story. Here the very air seemed charged with light and an electric exuberance. Two men, each pacing nervously, were clearly expectant fathers who, for one reason or another, had chosen to await their baby's arrival outside the delivery room rather than in it. One family group included everyone from the grandparents on down to a toddler who would be the new baby's older sister.

Pausing by the nursery window, Ali spotted a bassinet with a hand-lettered card saying BABY REYES. Inside, a tiny, red-faced infant slept peacefully. Donnatelle had told Ali that Teresa had said the baby would be named Carmine. The "Baby Reyes" designation worried Ali and made her wonder if Teresa was okay.

While Maria Delgado tottered off to find a nurse, Ali held the two excited girls up to the nursery window one at a time so they could glimpse their baby brother. When Maria returned, Lucy raced up to her.

"Where's Mommy?" Lucy asked. "Can we go see her?"

Maria shook her head. "Not right now." To Ali she said, "There have been some complications. Preclamp something—"

"Preeclampsia," said Ali.

"Yes, that's it," Maria said. "They had to do an emergency C-section. She's in the recovery room."

"What's a C-section?" Lucy parroted.

"Don't worry," Maria told her granddaughter. "It's nothing."

Ali knew it wasn't nothing. It could, in fact, be very bad.

Weeks earlier, as part of her reading-the-classics project, Ali had read *A Tale of Two Cities* from cover to cover, metaphorically speaking, since she had read the book on her iPhone. It occurred to her that for Jose and Teresa Reyes, these were both the best and worst of times. Their son had arrived perfectly formed and in what looked like good health and with a bright future ahead of him. All that was cause for rejoicing. But for the boy's parents? Not only had Jose's body been compromised by injuries sustained in the shooting, but his career in law enforcement, as well as his very freedom, might be in jeopardy. As for Teresa? Ali wondered how would she manage to care for three young children by herself in the aftermath of her own major surgery.

It was clear that Teresa's mother was more than willing to help out, but Ali could see that Maria Delgado's physical condition severely limited what she could realistically do. Ali was willing to help out, too, but not indefinitely. She wanted to be back in Sedona soon so she could participate in the garden planting project. She for sure had to be home by the following Sunday. That was when the two new Askins scholarship winners were due to come to their individually scheduled sessions of tea.

That was when it hit her. Two of her previous Askins winners, the ones from three years ago, were here in Tucson going to school. Haley Marsh, who had finished high school as the single mother of a two-year-old, was a junior honors student in the University of Arizona's nursing program. A five-year-old of her own qualified her as experienced in looking after little kids. Maybe she'd be willing to pick up some pocket money by helping Teresa. Before Ali could call and ask, however, her phone sent an alert that she had received a text message.

Ali herded the girls and their grandmother into the maternity waiting room, then stepped back into the hallway to check her phone. By then there were several messages, all of them from Stuart Ramey, all of them featuring photographs of the man the hospital receptionist had described to Sister Anselm—red-and-blue sweatshirt, baseball cap, carrying the potted plant. Even in the tiny image on Ali's iPhone, the guy looked furtive, like he was deliberately concealing his face from the security cameras.

Ali was looking at the last photo when her phone rang with a voice call. This time Stuart was on the phone. "I think you and Sister Anselm could be on to something," he said. "Your guy looks suspicious as hell to me. He did a pretty good job of keeping his face from showing. He sure could be up to no good."

"The images you sent me are the best ones?"

"Yes."

Ali was discouraged. She had hoped that the photos would be a lot clearer. "Other than the clothing which could easily be changed, the photos don't give us much to go on."

"Don't be so sure," Stuart said. "I'm working another angle."

"What's that?"

"I probably shouldn't do it and for sure shouldn't talk about it on the phone," Stuart replied. "If it works, I'll let you know."

With that, he hung up. Ali went back to the waiting room. With Maria worried about Teresa, Ali decided to take the girls with her to Jose's waiting room. "I have an idea," she told them. "Why don't we go see if anybody has told your daddy about your brother?"

As the girls dashed ahead, Ali pulled out her phone. "Hey," she said when Haley Marsh answered. "How would you like to earn a few extra bucks doing some fill-in babysitting?" While Ali was talking to Haley, Lucy and Carinda disappeared into the ICU waiting room. They immediately bounded right back out.

"He's gone," Lucy wailed. "He's not there anymore. They took him away. Daddy's bed's gone, too."

Worried, Ali quickly ended the call. Fortunately, the charge nurse came hurrying out on the girls' heels.

"Don't worry," she said. "We moved your daddy to a different room, one where you can go see him. And I'm sure he'd like to see you, too. He was awake the last I saw, and he can talk, but he's still very sick. You have to promise to use hand sanitizer before you go into his room. Okay?"

"Okay," Lucy said. "Can Carrie come, too?"

"Both of you," the charge nurse said. "One other thing. You have to be very gentle around your daddy. You can't get on his bed, and he won't be able to hold you. He has a big owie on his tummy. Do you think you can remember all that?"

Lucy nodded. "Can we go right now? Should we bring a Band-Aid for his owie?"

The charge nurse shook her head. "I'm not sure a Band-Aid will do the trick."

Lucy was already on her way out the door, but Ali caught her and dragged her back. "Just a minute," Ali said. "I need to see Sister Anselm for a moment. You two wait right here."

Ali went as far as the doorway to Jane Doe's room and tapped on the frame. Both patient and attendant seemed to be sleeping. Sister Anselm came to attention and hurried over to the door. She might not have been as spry as usual, but considering she had just done an all-nighter, Ali was impressed.

"What's up?" Sister Anselm asked.

"Jose's been moved out of ICU. The girls and I are on our way to tell him that the baby is fine."

"How about Teresa?"

"In recovery," Ali said, "and the less said about that, the better. But here's something you should take a look at." She cued up Stuart's photos and passed her iPhone to Sister Anselm.

Sister Anselm studied the photos. "It looks like he's deliberately concealing his features."

"That's what I thought," Ali agreed.

"Can we go now?" Lucy insisted. "Please! And I need to go potty."

Taking the phone back and hoisting Carinda onto her hip, Ali set off toward reception. The hospital was laid out with wings spreading out from a central hub. After a stop at the first available restroom, they went to admitting, where they were given directions to Jose's new room.

Jose greeted them with a wan smile. "Hey," he croaked. "How are my girls?"

"Daddy, Daddy!" Lucy exclaimed. "We've got a brother. He's real little. And he's all red."

Jose looked to Ali for confirmation. "Isn't this too early?"

"Evidently not," Ali said. "We just came from the nursery. He's fine."

"And Teresa?"

"She's in recovery. She had to have a C-section."

"What's a C-section?" Lucy asked again. Ali hadn't answered the question the first time, and she didn't this time, either.

"Is she all right?" Jose asked.

"As far as we know," Ali said. "Your mother-in-law is with her. I've called a friend in Tucson to come help out with the girls." Whoever had transported Jose from the ICU had been kind enough to collect the stash of kids' stuff from the waiting room. Ali parked both girls in a chair, handed them a sticker book, and turned her attention to Jose.

"I can't believe it's Sunday," he said. "How can I have lost two whole days?"

"It's easy," Ali said.

"But what are you doing here?"

"I came to help when Donnatelle had to leave."

"Donnatelle? From the academy? From Yuma? She was here, too? Did I see her?"

"No. Teresa was the only visitor allowed in the ICU."

"How did Donnatelle find out about it?"

"A Blue Alert went out on Saturday morning. She came as soon as she got off her shift."

"It's like you all thought I was gonna die."

"You came very close," Ali said. "So who did this? Do you have any idea?"

He frowned. "It's fuzzy. I was at work. I was making a traffic stop, and then *bam*. The next thing I knew, someone—a woman, I think—shot me in the gut."

"Tummy," Lucy corrected from the chair. " 'Gut' isn't a nice word. Can we see your owie?"

"Did they catch her?" Jose asked.

Ali shook her head. "Do you know who it was?"

"Not a clue," Jose said. "That's all I remember: an older woman with cataract glasses. And a scarf, I think. Yes. She was definitely wearing a scarf."

Ali took out her phone and dialed Juanita Cisco's

number. "One of your clients is awake at the moment," Ali said when the attorney answered. "For someone who's been out of it for a day and a half, he's making pretty good sense. You'd better come talk to him before Lattimore gets a crack at him."

Jose was frowning when Ali got off the phone. "Who was that on the phone? And who is Lattimore?"

"Lattimore is the DPS agent investigating your shooting. The woman on the phone is Juanita Cisco, your attorney."

"Why would I need an attorney? I'm the one who got shot. The woman who shot me is the one who needs an attorney."

"That's what you'd think," Ali said. "Unfortunately, you'd be dead wrong."

25

3:00 P.M., Sunday, April 11
Tucson, Arizona

It took two and a half hours for Al Gutierrez to drive from Tucson to Buckeye and locate the address he had found online. The neighborhood was nicer than he had expected: fairly new houses, most of them with desert landscaping in the front and pools in the back.

Much to his frustration, when he arrived at the right house and rang the bell, no one was home. He went back to the car and waited there for a while. Eventually, he began losing heart. What if Rose Ventana's family had moved away for good? What if they were out of town on a trip of some kind? Finally, Al went knocking on doors and got lucky the first time out.

"Jim's at work," the woman next door told him helpfully. "He doesn't usually get home until almost dinnertime. On Sundays, Connie and the girls spend most of the day at church. I can take a message for them."

Al didn't want to leave a message. He had driven over a hundred miles, one way, to talk to Rose Ventana's family in person. That was the whole point.

"No, thanks," he said. "I'll go grab some food and come back later."

He went to a nearby Pollo Loco, where he stayed until a quarter past five. Al had gleaned a lot of information about the family from the articles. He wanted to be sure James Fox would be home when it came time to deliver the news. Al expected it would be easier to speak to the stepfather and harder to speak to the mother and sisters. It had been three years, but he was pretty sure they were still grieving.

When he drove up to the house the second time, a BMW sedan was parked in the driveway, and a man with a Michelob Ultra in hand sat on a lawn chair on a covered front patio. Al recognized the man from the photos. This was definitely the stepfather, although he had aged considerably since the first television interview three years earlier.

The whole time Al was driving, he had contemplated how he would approach the family. He wanted to be thorough, calm, and convincing. If it had been a matter of straight good news or bad news, he suspected it would have been simpler. He could tell them that he believed their daughter was alive. At least she had been alive the last time he saw her, and he hoped she still was, though there was always a chance that she would die before they could get there.

"Mr. Fox?" Al asked, holding out his hand. "My name is Alonzo Gutierrez."

James Fox ignored the hand and took a drink of his beer while studying Al's face with an unapologetic stare. "My next-door neighbor said somebody stopped by earlier looking for us. Was that you?"

Al nodded.

"She said you looked like a cop. Are you?"

"Not exactly. Border Patrol."

"Well, Mr. Border Patrol," James Fox said sarcastically, "what do you want?"

This wasn't starting off the way Al had anticipated. Fox seemed hostile and angry and not the least bit welcoming.

"It's about your daughter," Al said. "It's about Rose."

"Sure it is," Fox said. "First of all, Rose is my stepdaughter, not my daughter. Second of all, she's dead. She died three years ago. I suppose you're here claiming you found the body?"

"It's possible she isn't dead—" Al began.

Fox ignored the interruption. "In that three years, my family has been through enough hell to last a lifetime. We don't need any more worthless yahoos showing up trying to jack my wife around by lifting money out of her pocket. They always claim they know where Rose is and say they'll help us find her and all kinds of claptrap. Some of 'em are psychics; all of 'em are jerks; but they all have one thing in common: They claim they can tell Connie exactly what happened to her daughter, and all she has to do is cough up a thousand bucks. Or two. We're not playing that game anymore, and we're not going through this again. It hurts too much. Now get the hell out of here before my wife gets home."

"I'm not asking for money," Al countered. "I just wanted to let you know that I believe I know what happened to her—to your stepdaughter. Someone beat her up pretty badly on Friday and left her for dead. She was found near Three Points, which is west of Ryan Field. She's in the ICU in Physicians Medical Center. I believe she's alive, although I don't know that for sure."

Fox set his empty beer bottle down on a nearby table. Then he stood up and stepped closer to Al, invading his space. "And you know all this how?"

Al stood his ground. "Because I'm the one who found her," he said. "I was out on patrol and found her."

"If this is supposed to be some kind of official notification, why aren't you in uniform? Why didn't you show me your badge?"

"This isn't an official notification. As I said, I found an injured woman out in the desert—beaten, burned, cut. It looked like she had been through hell. Everyone thought she was an illegal immigrant, but she spoke English, not Spanish. I called for a chopper and had her airlifted into town."

"If this isn't an official notification, why are you here? What do you want?"

Al thought about that for a minute—about Kevin Dobbs and the apparently buried "official" report. "Because someone needed to do it," he answered. "And because no one else seemed to give a damn."

"Our Rose has been gone for three years. What makes you think this woman you found in the desert is her?"

"I saw the tattoo, Mr. Fox. A rose tattoo that's right here." He pointed to a spot on his chest. "This morning I sat down with my computer and started looking for missing persons with rose tattoos. That's how I found you. When I saw the picture of the tattoo on the Internet and the part about her being from Buckeye, Arizona, it hit me that the girl I found might be her."

The man's anger dissipated some. At least he was listening, and he no longer looked as though he were ready to punch Al's lights out. He seemed to want to believe what Al was telling him, but he wasn't quite there.

"And you came all this way to tell me?"

Al nodded.

"If you've seen the information on the various sites, did you look at the photos? Does the woman you found look like the girl in any of those photos?"

Al thought about the assault victim's bruised and battered face; her missing teeth; her misshapen features. "No," he said at last. "The way she looks right now, it would take dental records or fingerprints or DNA to tell for sure. She was messed up pretty bad. Whoever did it meant for her to be dead. She was supposed to be dead. If I hadn't come along when I did and chased them off, she probably would be dead."

"And she may still die?"

Al nodded.

"So you expect me to tell my wife that you may have found our long-lost daughter, but she may be dying. In fact, by the time you got here to the house, she might have already been dead. Is that right?"

"Yes."

"Okay," Fox said. "Maybe you're not like the other guys. Since you're not demanding money, maybe your heart's in the right place, but I'm not going to jump in the car and head for Tucson. Tomorrow I'll get in touch with the Buckeye Police Department and have someone look into this."

"Don't you want to tell your wife?" Al asked.

"No, I don't. Haven't you been listening? Every time somebody shows up saying they knew where Rose is, Connie gets her hopes up. And every time, when it turns out that they're lying or deluded or just plain wrong, it breaks her heart all over again. If and when the cops can verify this, I'll tell her. Not before. Even if the girl you're talking about is Rose, what would be the point of finding her and having her die anyway? Now get the hell out of here before my wife gets home. Please."

Clearly, the conversation was over. Al turned and started away.

"You got a business card on you?" Fox asked. "I'll pass your name along to the local guys."

The business cards in Al Gutierrez's wallet were all Border Patrol cards. At that point, however, it didn't seem to make much difference. Al took one of them out, walked back to Fox, and handed it over.

"Thanks," James Fox said, slipping it into his shirt pocket.

"You're welcome," Al told him.

As he drove away, Fox was standing in front of the house, watching him go. Al was surprised by the man's lack of urgency. If it had been his kid or his wife's kid, he was sure he would already have been in the car and on his way to Tucson.

The two-and-a-half-hour return trip seemed to take less time because Al now knew the way. He spent the whole trip beating himself up for being a fool and for not minding his own business. He had tried to do the right thing. It had blown up in his face. He had expected that Rose's parents would be thrilled to hear the news and they would come rushing to see their daughter. Instead, he had gotten the brush-off. The stepfather had said he'd contact the Buckeye Police Department. Somehow Al doubted it, but that wasn't his problem. If Rose Ventana's family didn't care whether she was alive or dead, why should he? What Al Gutierrez needed to do was go back to work on Tuesday and forget all about it.

But he couldn't. He had saved her life, and as he'd said, nobody else seemed to give a damn. Not her family. Not Kevin Dobbs. No one.

When Al reached the intersection of Grant and the freeway, he had a decision to make. Keep going east and go home, or turn off and go to the hospital. He turned off.

26

3:00 P.M., Sunday, April 11
Tubac, Arizona

It was while he was eating his lonely Sunday-night dinner when Manuel Renteria missed Midge the most—Midge and her tamales. Theirs had been a mixed marriage. They were still newlyweds when Manuel's mother had taken her Anglo daughter-in-law in hand and taught her how to make tortillas and tamales. When Midge was alive, that was what they usually had on Sunday nights—Midge's homemade tamales.

Now Sheriff Renteria pushed aside the leavings of his Hungry-Man microwave dinner and sat at his kitchen table, surveying a stack of documents he never should have had in his possession.

Santa Cruz County was too small and too poor to have a crime lab of its own. As a consequence, any forensic work the county needed done was sent to the state crime lab in Tucson on a contract basis. Sheriff Renteria had been in the law enforcement business in Santa Cruz County for a very long time. He knew most of the people who worked in the crime lab, not just the scientists in the labs but their bosses and their bosses' bosses. He also knew their wives and their kids—who played soccer; who was going to ASU; who had signed up for the marines.

In other words, Sheriff Renteria was connected. And when he called in his markers, the people at the crime lab delivered. In this instance, he had run up the flag on the Reyes shooting, even though it was not his case to investigate. Duane Lattimore's evidence was not Manuel Renteria's evidence, but he had it anyway.

Naturally, the reports from the crime lab went first to the DPS investigator, but after that and on an "unofficial basis," most of that same information turned up on Manuel Renteria's private fax machine at his home in Tubac. With any luck, Lattimore would never be the wiser.

Manuel Renteria knew, for instance, about the results from the search of Jose and Teresa Reyes's mobile home in Patagonia. Several plastic containers of grass, each in the neighborhood of three kilos and conveniently packaged for flat-rate USPS shipping, had been found on the floor at the back of the entryway closet. These were amounts that would automatically trigger charges that included the words "intent to distribute." The sheriff studied that notation for a long time, trying to come to terms with the very idea that either Jose Reyes or his wife, Teresa, could be involved in the drug trade.

Manuel had known both these people for years. He had seen the couple out in public with Teresa's two girls in tow on more than one occasion. They struck him as good parents—caring parents—and the idea that they would leave that much grass in a place that was so easily accessible to the girls didn't fit.

Then there was the money. According to the crime lab report, a stash of over five thousand dollars in hundred-dollar bills had been found in a plastic container in Teresa's underwear drawer. Only one set of fingerprints had been found on the outside of the container. Due to the location, it was safe to assume the prints would turn out to be Teresa's, although no copies of her prints were currently available. A notation from Lattimore indicated that her comparison prints were in process, but Sheriff Renteria wasn't sure what that meant.

The crime lab was proceeding with an examination of the cash, lifting fingerprints whenever and wherever possible. The bills from the dresser drawer, along with the ones that had been found lying loose at the crime scene after Jose's shooting, all had traces of cocaine and methamphetamines. As far as Sheriff Renteria was concerned, that didn't mean much. He suspected that most of the hundred-dollar bills currently in circulation in southern Arizona had been used in drug trafficking somewhere along the way and most likely held the same kinds of trace evidence.

The presence of flat-rate USPS shipping boxes in the search warrant inventory rang an unwelcome bell. He remembered seeing one of those on the ground near Jose Reyes's vehicle. Was that how crooks were transporting drugs these days? In a way that seemed smart—a lot like hiding something in plain sight—but if that were the case, how did they get the shipments past the various Border Patrol checkpoints where drug-sniffing dogs checked every vehicle?

Unidentified prints had been found on shipping

boxes but not on the packaged bags inside the shipping boxes. The prints had been run through the Automated Fingerprint Identification System, but so far there had been no hits. That was odd. If Deputy Reyes had handled the boxes, his prints would have been there, unless he had used latex gloves. Since he was a police officer, a record of his prints would be in the AFIS database.

So whose were the unidentified prints? Teresa's, maybe? If that turned out to be the case, three little kids were about to be left alone, not orphaned but worse. The very thought turned Sheriff Renteria's stomach. He went into the living room, retrieved a bottle of Jose Cuervo from the liquor cabinet, and poured himself a generous shot.

Back at the table, he looked through the blurry facsimile copies of the crime scene photos, trying to sort out how the shooting had occurred. There was a gravel road, a narrow single-lane track where it left the pavement, which widened into a turnaround at the spot where the shooting had taken place. Situated at the top of a small hill, it was unofficially dubbed Necker's Knob, because it was a known hangout for teenagers bent on drinking and/or screwing. After the shooting, the other vehicle had been able to drive away without leaving any identifiable tracks.

A battered lug wrench had been found on the front seat of Jose's patrol car. It was easy to assume that had been used to blast the dash-mounted camera off its perch. Pieces of the broken mounting system had been found at the scene, but none of the camera. The footage in the camera most likely would have allowed the identification of the vehicle and maybe even the shooter. But how many crooks bothered with that kind of detail? Scared of being caught in the act, they were usually far more preoccupied with getting the job done and then getting the hell out of Dodge.

There was a copy of search warrant requests that had been submitted on all of the Reyes family telephones, landline and cell phone alike. Phone records, both incoming and outgoing, made otherwise invisible connections obvious. The fact that Teresa's phone was included in the request suggested that Lattimore suspected her of involvement, at least in the drug movement system and maybe even in the attempted hit on her husband.

Initially, that had been Sheriff Renteria's inclination, too—to assume that both Jose and Teresa were involved in whatever was going on. The evidence found in the search of their home should have reinforced that idea. Instead, the sheriff found himself moving in the opposite direction. This was all too easy; too pat. If it was a setup, Teresa had been targeted right along with her husband.

So who was behind it and why? Who was easier to answer than why. The people who called the drug-dealing shots in and around Nogales were members of the feared Nogo Cartel, based in Nogales, Sonora.

For as long as he had been sheriff, Renteria had maintained a separate peace with the cartel, due in large measure to the fact that his cousin's son, Pasquale, a boy Manuel had once dandled on his knee, had risen to the top of the organization. Once Manuel was elected to the office of sheriff, he and Pasquale had hammered out a live-and-let-live agreement. The sheriff would keep his department's efforts focused on the needs of the people who had elected him while leaving the drug war to others—to the feds, the DEA, and the Border Patrol. In exchange, Pasquale had agreed not to target Santa Cruz County officers.

Sheriff Renteria wasn't someone who went looking for a fight, but if the fight came to him, he wouldn't shy away from it. If the Nogos turned out to be in any way involved in what was going on here, then all bets were off. Sheriff Renteria would do everything in his power to take them down, starting with Pasquale. Renteria would turn whatever he knew about his cousin and his cohorts over to Duane Lattimore.

Having made up his mind, Sheriff Renteria stacked his papers and locked them in his briefcase. Then, after pouring and downing one last shot of tequila, he went to the bedroom and fell into a dreamless sleep on what he still, after all this time, considered to be his side of the queen-size bed.

27

7:00 P.M., Sunday, April 11
Tucson, Arizona

Ali's decision to call Haley Marsh turned out to be nothing short of brilliant. Haley left her son, Liam, with her roommate long enough to come meet Lucy and Carinda and to take them in hand. Two long days in the hospital had taken their toll. The novelty had worn off. The girls were tired and cranky and wanted to be somewhere that wasn't a hospital waiting room or hallway. Within minutes of meeting Haley, Lucy and Carinda were more than ready to go play at what she assured them was a "real" house.

When it was time for them to leave, Jose was sleeping again. Ali was helping load the girls and their gear—clothing, toys, and car and booster seats—into Haley's minivan when she saw DPS Lieutenant Lattimore striding across the parking lot. Ali was on the phone to Juanita Cisco before he made it into the lobby.

Juanita had come by earlier and given Jose a retainer to sign, but she had told Ali she wanted to be physically present if Lattimore showed up for fear Jose might say more than was good for him. Ali hurried back inside and was waiting outside the door to Jose's room when the lieutenant came down the hall from reception.

"You again," he said when he saw Ali barring his way.

"Yes," she said. "Me again."

"I'm not sure what you're doing here or why you think it's okay to interfere with a police investigation," Lattimore said.

"Jose is a victim of a crime," Ali countered, stalling for time. "I think you've lost sight of that."

"I haven't lost sight of anything. When a crime victim is involved in illegal activities, it's usually a good place to start looking for the perpetrator. That's true even if the crime victim happens to be a police officer. I need to talk to Mr. Reyes and see if he can help me clear this case."

"He told me the shooter was a woman—a woman wearing a head scarf."

"So he's been talking to you, but he can't talk to me? And what did he mean by that—that she's a Muslim or something?"

"He said a scarf. Just a scarf. And sunglasses. Cataract-style sunglasses."

"I'd rather be hearing this from him than from you," Lattimore said.

Juanita Cisco arrived on the scene, wearing garden clogs and a loose-fitting smock. It was clear she'd come to the hospital straight from doing yard work. She was short and dumpy, with a set of jowls that made her face resemble that of a pit bull—an angry pit bull.

"I'm Mr. Reyes's attorney," she announced. "You won't be hearing anything at all from him unless I give you the go-ahead. Understood?"

Lattimore wasn't a happy camper, but he nodded. "All right," he said. "We'll do it your way."

Since no one told her otherwise, Ali followed the attorney and the detective into Jose's room. There were still machines and plenty of beeping monitors. Jose had been asleep when the girls left, but he was awake now.

"Jose, it's Juanita," the attorney said, reminding him in case the meds had interfered with his recall of her previous visit. "I told you about Mr. Lattimore earlier." She sat down in the only visitor's seat in the room, leaving Lattimore standing. "Mr. Lattimore is here to interview you about the shooting," she continued. "He's to confine his questions to that. If he strays into other areas, I'll direct you not to answer." She nodded in Lattimore's direction.

"So what can you tell me?" Lattimore asked Jose.

"It was a traffic stop. A woman."

"How old?"

"Older. Cataract glasses. And a head scarf—with flowers of some kind."

"What happened?"

"I turned on my lights, but she didn't pull over right away. Finally, she did, but instead of pulling over on the shoulder, she went up a side road. When she stopped, I got out and approached the vehicle. I told her to put her hands in the air, but by the time I saw her hands, she was already shooting."

"So you walked up to the car and she went kerblammo? No exchange of words?"

"Not that I remember."

"What kind of vehicle?"

"Older-model Buick sedan. A Regal maybe."

"This isn't someone you recognize or a vehicle you recognize?"

"No."

"You have no idea who she was?"

"No."

"Was the shooter alone in the vehicle?"

"I didn't see anyone else, but there might have been. I'm not sure. It was dark."

"Let's talk about the trunk of your vehicle. What was in it?"

"The usual stuff. Water, extra ammo, first aid kit, spare tire, a tool kit."

"Did you make any other stops of any kind that night?"

"I made a couple of traffic stops, but it was pretty quiet."

"Traffic stops only?"

"Yes."

"Nothing where you might have picked up some contraband?"

"No."

"So what would explain the presence of drugs in your vehicle?" Lattimore asked.

"What drugs? There weren't any drugs."

"Was it maybe evidence from another case, one you were working on and hadn't mentioned to anyone else? Maybe you hadn't quite gotten around to doing the paperwork on it."

"If you found drugs in the trunk of my car, someone else must have put them there," Jose said. "I didn't."

Juanita gave a warning shake of her head. It was meant for Lattimore and Jose. Both of them ignored it.

"Does any other officer drive that particular patrol car?"

"No. I'm the only one. I take it home at night."

"And where do you park it?"

"In my yard. In Patagonia. Outside Patagonia."

"Is the yard fenced and gated?" Lattimore asked.

"Both—a fence and a gate. I keep the vehicle locked at all times."

"So you're saying that it would be difficult for someone else to gain access to it when it's parked at your home?"

Jose nodded.

"I'm not liking the direction your questions are taking," Juanita said. "Let's go back to the shooting."

"Okay, let me understand you. You're saying that an unidentified woman lured you off the road, shot you, and then left money and drugs in the back of your car?"

Jose nodded again. "It would have to be. I didn't put them there."

"How many times have you pulled a crack pipe out of someone's purse or the central console on the car and had the person in custody try to tell you that the contraband wasn't theirs?"

"I'm telling you, if you found drugs in my vehicle, they're not mine. I don't use drugs. I don't deal drugs. That's one of the reasons I became a cop—to take drugs off the street."

"Tell me about your wife," Lattimore said.

"Teresa's great," Jose said. "She just had a baby today. Six pounds, three ounces."

"How long have you been married?"

"A little under two years."

"No marital discord?"

Juanita gave a warning headshake, which Jose once again ignored.

"With Teresa? Not just no, but hell no. She's the best thing that ever happened to me. Are you saying you think she had something to do with this?"

Jose had been answering the questions right along. For the first time, he seemed agitated. The beeping monitor sped up accordingly. Ali wondered if that was because Jose was offended by the direction of Lattimore's questions or because the questions were coming too close for comfort or because he was just getting tired?

"When it comes to suspects, the spouse is always on the short list."

"Not Teresa."

"She doesn't work?" Lattimore asked.

"Of course Teresa works," Jose told him. "We've got two little kids at home. Three as of today."

"But she doesn't work outside the home?"

"No."

"Have the two of you been experiencing any money problems?"

"No more than anyone else," Jose answered. "We have kids. We have a mortgage. It's not easy, but we're making ends meet. At least we were. Now I'm not sure."

"Would it surprise you to learn that Teresa had a substantial amount of money lying around the house?"

"Lying around the house? The only money we have lying around the house is in Lucy's piggy bank."

"This wasn't in a piggy bank. It was stowed in one of Teresa's dresser drawers."

"You had no business digging through my wife's dresser drawers."

"Mr. Lattimore evidently obtained a search warrant for your home, Mr. Reyes," Juanita interjected. "They executed it earlier this morning."

"I'm the victim here. Why are you treating me like I'm a crook?"

The beepers tuned up and began sounding more urgent as Jose's heart rate quickened and his breathing became labored. Before Juanita Cisco could put an end to the interview, an alert nurse appeared in the doorway.

"This visit is over," she announced. "Mr. Reyes needs to rest."

Lattimore left without another word. Ali followed Juanita Cisco into the waiting room where the attorney stopped and looked around. "Mr. Reyes is a wounded cop, so here's something I don't understand. Where are his fellow cops? Why aren't they here?"

"I have no idea," Ali answered.

"If he's a good cop, they should be all over the place. If he's a dirty cop, it stands to reason the other guys in his department would want to distance themselves. I wish I knew for sure. In the interview, Lattimore was making noises like he thinks Teresa might be involved in the shooting—as though she might be behind it. If this were my case long-term, I'd send an investigator down to Nogales to sort out some background information. It would be an added expense, but do you want me to look into hiring a PI to do just that?"

"Hiring a private investigator might be a good idea," Ali said. "Let me think about it. I'll let you know."

Juanita Cisco nodded and walked away, her rubber-soled clogs squishing on the white-tiled floor. Ali waited until the nurse was out of sight, then let herself back into Jose's room. He was awake and upset.

"If he thinks Teresa had something to do with shooting me, the man is nuts!" Jose declared. "And as for finding five thousand dollars in her dresser drawer? She's always stressing about not having enough money to buy groceries. Where would she get that kind of money?"

"They think she's dealing," Ali said. "They think you are, too."

"But I'm not," Jose insisted. "Neither is she."

"Then someone's trying to frame you. Who? Do you have any enemies?"

"Not that I know of."

"Are you having problems with someone at work?"

"No, not at all. Work is good."

"You were shot. Most of the time when cops are shot, fellow officers go to the mat for them. They come to the hospital. They offer support for the family. So tell me, why isn't that happening? Why aren't they here for you?"

"They haven't been?" Jose asked. He sounded surprised and hurt. Up to now he had been medicated enough that he hadn't noticed.

"Not as far as I know. Donnatelle Craig and I are the only cops or even semicops who have been here. I heard Sheriff Renteria dropped by for a while yesterday, but I have yet to see anyone else from the Santa Cruz Sheriff's Department."

Jose seemed genuinely puzzled. "That makes no sense. Why wouldn't they be here?"

"Good question. What can you tell me about your sheriff?

"Renteria's a good guy. We go way back. He knew my dad. His wife knew Teresa's mother."

"If he's such a good guy, maybe I'll go talk to him tomorrow," Ali said. "Since Lattimore, the cop who's supposed to be investigating your shooting, is apparently convinced you're a crook, I'm hoping Sheriff Renteria doesn't share that opinion."

Jose nodded vaguely. The nurse had administered some kind of medication, and it seemed to be working. He was starting to drift. "Did you see the baby?" he asked. "Did you see Carmine?"

When Ali had seen the baby in the nursery, he hadn't been given a name, at least not officially. "Yes," she said. "I've seen him. He's fine. So is Teresa."

"And the girls will be okay with your friend?"

"They needed a break from the hospital," Ali said. "And the hospital needed a break from them."

"Thank you," Jose murmured gratefully. "Thank you for everything."

He was asleep before Ali was out of the room. She

went straight to maternity. In the nursery, the name-plate on the Baby Reyes bassinet had been changed to Carmine Jose Reyes. Ali took that to mean that Teresa had recovered enough to verify the name. That was good. It was also good that the baby was asleep.

Visiting hours were officially over. There was no sign of Maria Delgado in the waiting room. Ali hoped her brother had taken her home or else to a hotel to spend the night. When Ali poked her head into Teresa's room, she was asleep, too. The entire Reyes family had been through enough in the past few days that they were all having an early night-night. Obviously, they needed it.

Ali was on her way back to the ICU to check on Sister Anselm when her phone rang. The readout showed Stuart Ramey's number at High Noon.

"I have some information on your mysterious flower guy," he said.

"You ID'd him?" Ali asked. "How?"

"We've done a lot of work for Homeland Security lately. I've got an in with some of their IT guys," Stuart said. "I asked one of my contacts to run the photos we had through their beta-release facial recognition software. Guess what? We got a hit."

"Really?" Ali said.

"Yup. His name's Alonzo Gutierrez. He's an agent with the Border Patrol. Works out of the Tucson sector. That's all I've got right now. I've got a call in asking for more info on the guy. As soon as I learn anything, I'll be in touch."

"Good," Ali said. "And thank you."

It was shocking to think that the person possibly

targeting Jane Doe was an actual Border Patrol agent, an active Border Patrol agent. It didn't matter why he was doing it; it mattered only that he was doing it. That was vital information that Sister Anselm needed to have in her possession. Now.

Ending the call, Ali took off for the ICU at a dead run.

28

8:00 P.M., Sunday, April 11
Tucson, Arizona

With the Reyes family no longer in attendance, Sister Anselm noticed that the ICU waiting room outside Jane Doe's door was relatively quiet. According to Mona, the charge nurse, Jose's condition had improved enough that he'd been moved into a regular room. Mona also said that Teresa and her new baby were doing fine.

That was a relief. Sister Anselm was weary and feeling the effects of her long vigil. Jane Doe's situation had worsened again during the afternoon. Sister Anselm had yet to go to All Saints. She was looking forward to it. She wanted to take a shower; to lie down; to sleep for a few hours. She knew that her phone would alert her if there was yet another crisis for her patient, someone the hospital officially listed as Jane Doe, although Sister Anselm knew otherwise.

During the afternoon, Sister Anselm had gone down to the administration offices and printed out copies of the photos Ali had forwarded to her. They were easier to see in a larger format, even if the features themselves were a little blurry. That was the real reason Sister Anselm was sticking around the ICU. She was worried that Rose Ventana's assailant would return to try to do her harm. If that happened, Sister Anselm would most likely be Rose's only line of defense.

While the machines murmured in the background, Sister Anselm slipped into a doze only to be startled awake by someone knocking on the door frame. The nun's eyes popped open in time to see a man's face appear in the doorway.

"Excuse me," he said. "I'm looking for the woman who was found out by Three Points on Friday. Are you a nurse?"

There he was, the very man Sister Anselm had been worrying about all afternoon. He was dressed as he'd been in the earlier security photos—jeans and a red-and-blue U of A sweatshirt. He was carrying the Mariners baseball cap instead of wearing it.

At first Sister Anselm thought she was asleep and this was a bad dream. But no, she wasn't. He was right there in the waiting room, outside Jane Doe's door.

Sister Anselm hustled to her feet and planted herself defensively between the doorway and her sleeping patient. Slipping her hand into her pocket, she searched for her Taser. As her fingers closed around the weapon, she pushed back the sliding cover, exposing the trigger button. That way, when she brought it out of her pocket, the Taser would already be activated; the red laser sighting light would be glowing.

"This is an ICU," she said firmly. "Are you a relative? If not, you'll need to leave immediately. Only authorized relatives are allowed to visit patients in this unit."

"Mr. Gutierrez?"

Sister Anselm heard what sounded like Ali's voice speaking urgently from the waiting room but outside the nun's line of vision. The man spun around to face the person who had spoken to him. As soon as he did so, Sister Anselm extracted her Taser and stepped toward the door, closing the distance between them. When she stopped moving forward, she was less than three feet from the intruder. At that distance, even a bad shot would hit the target.

He took several steps backward and moved away from the door. He glanced warily first to the left, then back at Sister Anselm, and finally down toward his chest, where two bright red laser dots had appeared.

"What the hell?" he demanded. "You've both got Tasers? Are you women nuts?"

While he continued to back away from them, Sister Anselm moved farther into the waiting room, pulling the door to Jane Doe's room shut behind her.

"What are you doing here, Mr. Gutierrez?" Ali demanded. She was out of breath and gasping between words. "What do you want?"

Sister Anselm had no idea how Ali knew the man's name, but clearly, she did. At least he acted as though she did.

"I'm trying to find out if she's alive," Gutierrez answered. "That's all I want to know—if she's alive or not."

The man didn't appear to be armed, and he didn't seem violent. Sister Anselm slid the lid back over the Taser's trigger, dousing the red targeting light, but she didn't return the weapon to her pocket. "Why do you need to know that?" she asked.

Gutierrez shook his head. "Never mind," he said. "This was a bad idea."

"You don't mean her any harm?"

"Are you kidding? You're both crazy. I'll just go."

"No, wait," Sister Anselm said. "You brought flowers to the hospital earlier today. Why did you do that?"

"Because before I went to talk to her parents, I wanted to know for sure that Rose Ventana was alive. I'm the guy who found her."

There was a moment of stark silence.

"You know my patient's real name?" Sister Anselm said incredulously. "You know my patient's parents?"

"Not both of them. I only spoke to her stepfather."

Ali's laser dot switched off as well.

"You spoke to James Fox?" Sister Anselm asked. "In Buckeye?"

Gutierrez nodded. "Yes."

"How did you know it was her?"

"I didn't, not for sure," Gutierrez admitted. "But I remembered seeing the rose tattoo when I found her out in the desert on Friday. Everybody thought she was an illegal. I tried to tell them that I didn't agree, because she spoke English not Spanish, but no one paid any attention."

"You reported that?" Sister Anselm asked.

"Yes, but it didn't do any good, so I did some looking on my own. Then this morning I ran across a website dealing with missing persons. That's where I found out about Rose Ventana, who went missing in Buckeye, Arizona, three years ago. I couldn't tell from the photos if she was the one, but it seemed like a good fit. So I drove up to Phoenix to give her parents what I thought was good news. Instead, Mr. Fox sent me packing. He claims he'll talk to the Buckeye Police Department, but until he has some kind of official verification from them, he won't even tell her mother. I was on my way back from Buckeye, and I decided to come by the hospital. I wanted to make sure she wasn't already dead."

"She's not dead," Sister Anselm said. "She's getting better." Those two sentences constituted a serious breach of patient confidentiality, but at this point, she was prepared to give Mr. Gutierrez a break. She held out her hand. "I'm Sister Anselm," she said. "This is my friend Ali Reynolds. And you are?"

"Al," he said. "Al Gutierrez. I'm with the Border Patrol. I found her on Friday and had her airlifted to the hospital here."

"Glad to meet you, Mr. Gutierrez. I've been assigned to serve as Jane Doe's patient advocate," Sister Anselm explained. "I've done my own research on the topic, and I happen to agree with you. The woman in that room most likely is Rose Ventana, but at this juncture, I must ask you to make no further effort to contact her or her family."

"Why not? If she's getting better, if she's not going to die, why not tell them?"

"Because earlier this afternoon, when I asked her if she wanted me to be in touch with her family, she answered with an emphatic no."

"She spoke to you?"

"Not in so many words. With her jaw wired shut, all she could do was shake her head, but that's enough of an answer for me. As her patient advocate, I'm honor-bound to abide by her wishes. Like you, I tracked down the family's current address in Buckeye. Unlike you, I've made no effort to contact them, and I won't until I have her full permission to do so. I'm asking you to do the same. To let it go."

Al had stumbled backward into the waiting room far enough to collide with a chair and collapse into it.

"But why wouldn't she want to see them?" Al Gutierrez demanded. "Her parents, I mean. And whether she's dead or alive, why wouldn't they rush right down here to see her? If she were my kid, I'd want to know the minute somebody found her."

"Not all families are alike," Sister Anselm said. "And until she tells me otherwise, I want to abide by her wishes. Are you with me on that, Mr. Gutierrez?"

"I suppose so," he agreed reluctantly. "But you and your friend here drew Tasers on me. You both drew Tasers. All I did was knock on her door, and you were ready to take me down."

"I've been sitting here guarding her with my life," Sister Anselm said. "Someone tried to murder her the other day. I was afraid that you were one of her assailants and that you had come back to finish the job."

"I never meant her any harm," Al objected. "In fact, it's just the opposite."

"I understand that now," Sister Anselm said. Al Gutierrez seemed very young to her right then. Reaching out, she patted his knee. "And I'm sure Ms. Doe—we need to continue referring to her that way—will be better served if we all work together rather than at cross purposes."

Al looked at her questioningly. "You really are a nun?" he asked.

Sister Anselm nodded. "I really am."

"What about her?" He nodded in Ali's direction. "Is she a nun, too?"

"No," Sister Anselm replied. "She was with the Yavapai Sheriff's Department for a while. Now she's a reserve officer."

Al looked from one woman to the other. "Well," he said, "if you ask me, Rose is very lucky to have the two of you in her corner."

"She's lucky to have you in her corner, too," Sister Anselm told him. "Even if it didn't work out the way you expected, you weren't wrong to try contacting her family."

He nodded and stood up. "Okay," he said. "I guess I'd better be going."

As the young man left the waiting room, Ali glanced at her watch. "It's been a long day. I'd better go, too. I need to find a place to sleep."

"How about a convent?" Sister Anselm suggested.

"A convent?" Ali asked. "I can't quite see myself staying in a convent."

"You'd be surprised," Sister Anselm said. "All Saints is right up the road. That's where I'm supposed to be staying, I just haven't made it that far. But Sister

Genevieve, the reverend mother there, is an old pal of mine. Since you're here on an errand of mercy, I'm sure she'd be glad to take you in for a night or two."

"Isn't that a little presumptuous?" Ali asked. "After all, I'm not even Catholic."

"No, you're not, but the fact that you're one of my friends makes up for a lot. Let me give her a call."

29

6:00 A.M., Monday, April 12
Patagonia, Arizona

Phil Tewksbury didn't exactly leap out of bed at six o'clock on Monday morning. The weekend of unaccustomed painting meant he had exercised muscles that were now mad at him. His aching right shoulder had kept him awake off and on overnight, and he felt stiff all over. Still, there was a smile on his face as he pulled on his clothes, brushed his teeth, and took some extra effort with his comb-over. Monday was the one day in the week when Ollie usually showed up, often bringing along something for a picnic. After being home with Christine all weekend long, Phil was ready.

Christine was in her bedroom, probably asleep, as he headed for the kitchen, but Phil did notice that at least one and maybe two of the remaining lights on the tree had burned out overnight. He made a mental note of their location in case the bulbs got replaced behind his back.

Now you really are being paranoid, he told himself.

He was in the kitchen by six-fifteen, making coffee and doing his usual oatmeal ritual—making the hot cereal, dividing it into separate bowls, and leaving them on the counter for Christine to find later. He had the timing down to a science. At six-thirty exactly, he picked up his wallet and keys, left the house, and headed for the garage and his aging F-150 pickup truck. That gave him an hour to have a leisurely breakfast with the guys at the café and be at the post office at seven-thirty to do the final sort of his mail. That was when Patty Patton, Patagonia's postmistress, would give him the Priority and Express Mail packages.

After all, despite rain, snow, sleet, hail, or even living in hell on earth, the mail must go through.

Phil stopped at the garage door and shoved the key into the lock, thinking as he did so how, back when his grandparents were alive, the garage door was never locked. A week or so ago, when he had misplaced his key ring, it had been a pain. Fortunately, he'd had a spare.

That was then, he told himself. *This is now.*

Phil pushed the door open. As he stepped into the garage, he was astonished to find himself tripping over something he couldn't see. Pitching forward, he fell headlong onto the concrete floor, landing hard on his elbow and whacking his shoulder on the pickup's passenger-side front fender as he fell. His thermos bounced once and rolled out of reach under the truck while his house key ring skittered away from him, coming to rest a good five feet away.

He lay there for a moment, trying to assess the damage. *What the hell just happened to me?* he wondered. *Did I break anything?*

Phil was on his hands and knees, attempting to scramble to his feet, when something slammed into the back of his head. The shattering blow sent him sprawling once again. It also knocked him senseless. He felt the first blow, but that was it. He was unaware of a dropcloth—his own much used dropcloth, it turned out—being tossed across him to keep bits and pieces of flesh from flying up onto his assailant. When the furious barrage of blows ended, he lay there, dead or unconscious, while his unseen and totally silent attacker walked away.

Unheard by Phil, the garage door opened and closed behind him. Soon the soft whine of a battery-powered screwdriver cut through the early-morning quiet as the screws that had held an invisible length of fishing filament in place a foot off the ground were removed and the holes left behind were plugged with tiny dots of white toothpaste.

There was no way to tell if Phil Tewksbury, buried under the dropcloth, was dead or alive when the door closed the second time, but that didn't really matter. One way or the other, it was over for him. From that moment on, whatever happened to Christine Tewksbury was someone else's problem.

30

6:00 A.M., Monday, April 12
Tucson, Arizona

Ali's cell phone awakened her in a simple but unfamiliar room. She had slept on a narrow cot that would have to be stretched several inches in every direction to duplicate a modern twin-size bed. The iron-barred headboard hadn't been constructed with reading in bed in mind. At last she located the buzzing phone on a rough-hewn bedside table.

"Good morning," B. said. "Sorry to wake you. On my way into a meeting in five minutes. Where are you?"

"A convent," Ali said. "All Saints Convent outside Tucson."

"A convent? How did you end up there?"

"I was going to go find a hotel, but Sister Anselm is in Tucson. She suggested I come here."

"What's Sister Anselm doing in Tucson?"

"Long story," Ali said. "Longer than I can explain in five minutes. The reverend mother at All Saints, Sister Genevieve, is a friend of Sister Anselm's, and she was kind enough to take me in. It's a bit Spartan, a dormitory room with a bed and a bathroom down the hall, but once I got here, Sister Genevieve made me hot tea and helped me raid the fridge."

"I didn't know convents had refrigerators to raid."

Somewhere on the grounds, something that sounded like a church bell tolled six chimes. From somewhere else came the scents of cooking—frying eggs, baking coffee cake, and brewing coffee. Doors opened and closed up and down the hallway, and quiet footsteps whispered past Ali's closed door.

"That was the call to prayer," she told B. "Since I'm not a Catholic, Sister Genevieve gave me a pass on prayers, but she said if I wanted breakfast, I'd better be in the refectory at six-thirty."

"So it's a good thing I rousted you out of bed."

"Yes," Ali agreed. "It's a good thing."

"How's your friend doing?"

"That's another long story. Jose's condition has been upgraded, and he's out of the ICU. His wife had her baby—an emergency C-section. And their two girls are currently staying with Haley Marsh."

"One of the Askins girls?'

"That's right. I needed someone to take care of two ankle biters, and Haley was a likely prospect. She doesn't have classes during the day today, so she's looking after them until this evening."

"So it's all good?"

"Not all. Jose and Teresa are being investigated for possible drug dealing by the cop who's supposed to be investigating Jose's shooting."

"And who's the flower guy?" B. asked. "Stuart told

me something about helping you track down a delivery guy."

"Turns out he's Border Patrol."

"How's he connected to Jose Reyes?"

"He's not," Ali said. "He's connected to Sister Anselm's patient, Jane Doe. You're going to have to call me when we have more time. This is way too complicated."

"All right. Here's my hat; what's my hurry?" B. said. "But I do need to go. And so do you, if you're going to make it to breakfast."

"Have a good meeting," Ali said. She was on her way to the bathroom with her phone in hand when it rang again. "I'm sorry I threw you under the bus at dinner the other night," Edie Larson said. "Since I didn't hear from you yesterday, I'm guessing you're still mad at me. But we'll be signing the paperwork later this morning."

"I'm not mad," Ali said. "I'm in Tucson, and I've been really busy. But if anyone needs to apologize, it's me. I acted like a spoiled brat. There's no one more deserving of retirement than you and Dad. I was way out of line not to be more enthusiastic that you've found some qualified buyers. I guess I was surprised more than anything, but since I don't ask you about every decision I make—including my trip to Tucson—the reverse should be true. So I'm sorry."

"Not telling people in advance was selfish on our part," Edie said. "And I had no business embroiling you in that mayoral discussion before I spoke to your father about it. Besides, if I'm expecting to have a future in politics, I need to put on my big-girl panties and fight my own battles."

Ali laughed at that. "Dad was probably caught as flat-footed on that as I was on your selling the Sugarloaf. You can't blame him. It's a lot of change to take on all at once."

"Your father has plenty of outside interests," Edie said. "He'll probably spend more time with that damnable Blazer of his than he will with me. And when he doesn't have to go to the restaurant every day, I'm sure he'll spend a lot more time on his homeless outreach."

Ali suspected that was true. For as long as she could remember, Bob Larson had spent every spare hour away from the business providing all kinds of essentials—from food to used furniture to firewood—for the homeless and working poor in the area.

"Once the Sugarloaf is gone, I'll be the one with no outside interests," Edie Larson continued. "I'm not about to take up golf or bowling at my age, but I don't want to sit around reading trashy novels and eating bonbons, either. I'll go completely stir-crazy. It's like that friend of yours Sister Anselm. She does twice as much as people half her age. It's what keeps her going. Running for office here in town is something I can do to make a difference."

"I'll do whatever I can to help," Ali told her. "Including serving as your campaign manager."

"Really?" Edie asked.

"Really. We'll have our first strategy meeting as soon as I get back from Tucson."

"Good," Edie said. "That'll give your father a little longer to get used to the idea."

Me, too, Ali thought.

"So what are you doing down there anyway?" Edie asked.

"Helping a friend," Ali said. She would have said more, but Edie cut her off. "Oops," she said. "Customers. Gotta go." And hung up.

When Ali had packed to come to Tucson, she'd expected to stay at a hotel where the bathroom would be included inside the room. At All Saints, there were two bathrooms, one at either end of a long hallway. Sister Genevieve had loaned her a bathrobe for that reason. Showered and dressed, Ali showed up at the refectory breakfast and found herself in the presence of a dozen nuns in habits. Accustomed to Sister Anselm's mostly business casual attire, Ali was surprised by the traditional dress. She was also surprised by the congenial atmosphere, the easy laughter, and the good food.

Over tea and leftovers the night before, Sister Genevieve had recounted a little of All Saints' history. The main building—the one with the kitchen, refectory, chapel, and Sister Genevieve's quarters—had once been the ranch house for the old Coughnour Ranch, which stretched from the Tanque Verde River bottom to the foothills of the Catalinas on Tucson's far east side. The ranch had been established by a man named James Coughnour in the early part of the twentieth century. As the second son in a wealthy East Coast shipbuilding family, James had headed west with his newly inherited share of the family fortune as well as a pair of badly damaged lungs. He had bought up huge tracts of land along the Tanque Verde River and turned it into a thriving cattle ranch that had morphed into one of Arizona's primary meatpacking companies.

When James's only heir, his beloved daughter, Caroline, expressed an interest in becoming a nun, James had come up with a plan that allowed her to have her way without his necessarily losing her. He agreed to let her go and to use his considerable fortune to create a sanatarium for lung-damaged patients so long as she joined an order that would take charge of running the facility. Caroline had gone on to join the Sisters of Providence. What had once been the main ranch house was transformed into the All Saints Convent. Caroline, renamed Sister Antoinette, had lived there for the remainder of her life.

Eventually the sanatarium was purchased by a group of physicians and turned into Physicians Medical Center, a hospital where most of the sisters of All Saints worked as nurses. Sister Anselm had first ventured into the community in her role as a counselor to troubled nuns when Sister Genevieve's predecessor as reverend mother slipped into age-related dementia. Ever since, All Saints had served as Sister Anselm's Tucson home away from home.

Breakfast was delicious, with slabs of warm homemade coffee cake and mounds of freshly scrambled eggs. Coffee was hot and plentiful, as was grapefruit juice from fruit that had been picked that morning from trees growing on the grounds. Sitting there with the congenial group of breakfasting nuns, Ali felt totally at home, benefiting from the fact that any friend of Sister Anselm's was a friend of theirs.

The meal was winding down when Sister Anselm

put in an appearance. She looked more tired than Ali had ever seen her. Sister Lucille, the cook, immediately bustled around, bringing her breakfast.

"We had another tough night," Sister Anselm said in answer to Ali's question. "But she's sleeping, so I'm going to grab some sleep, too. In an actual bed. They'll let me know if anything changes."

"No word from her family?" Ali knew that healing broken families was as much a part of Sister Anselm's mission as healing broken bodies.

The nun shook her head. "I was hoping we'd hear from them, but there's nothing so far, and that's probably just as well. She's too fragile to deal with the added stress. What about you? What's on your agenda?"

"I'm going to go check on all my charges—Haley and Lucy and Carinda. I'm hoping to locate some help for Teresa when she's released from the hospital and goes back home. And Juanita Cisco wants me to look into Jose's situation at the sheriff's department and find out why his fellow officers are treating him as a leper as opposed to a wounded hero."

Sister Anselm nodded. "I wondered about that, too."

31

8:00 A.M., Monday, April 12
Nogales, Arizona

Sheriff Renteria called into his office as he drove into town. "Going to get a haircut," he told his secretary. "I'll be in as soon as I can."

Sheriff Renteria didn't need a haircut so much as he needed information. In the old days, crooks and cops had found common ground in churches. They may have been good guys and bad guys, but they were Catholic good guys and bad guys, with priests functioning as the diplomats who moved back and forth between them.

That was no longer true. A lot of the younger people on both sides had moved away from the Church. Now the man who stood with a foot in both camps was Sheriff Renteria's cousin, his father's brother's son, the barber Ignacio.

When Sheriff Renteria arrived, the barbershop was empty. Ignacio was sitting in his barber chair, reading a newspaper. He smiled, picked up his cape, and shook it out. "Need a little trim?" he asked.

"A little."

Manuel didn't have much to trim these days. Ignacio fired up his clipper and went to work. As long as the clipper was running, neither man spoke.

"What do you hear from Pasquale?" Manuel asked once the shop went silent. They both knew what he meant—that they were talking about the shooting.

"He didn't do it," Ignacio answered at once. "The people he works for didn't do it, either. That was the agreement he made with you, that your guys wouldn't be targeted."

That was the informal peace treaty Sheriff Renteria had negotiated with Pasquale years ago, back when he was first elected. Some would have called it a deal with the devil. There had been nothing in writing. The sheriff had met with Pasquale in his father's barbershop. The two had spoken briefly, then they shook hands. That had been it. The drug business was like a many-headed hydra. An agreement with one division didn't necessarily cover another, but as far as the Nogales area was concerned, Pasquale had enough influence to make it work.

"Was Deputy Reyes dealing?" Manuel asked.

On the surface, it was a stupid question. Sheriff Renteria had seen the evidence himself—the plastic-wrapped packages in the trunk of Jose's patrol car; the hundred-dollar bills lying scattered on the ground like so many dead leaves.

"Pasquale says no," Ignacio said quietly. "At least not for the Nogos."

"What would happen if he was dealing for someone else?"

"That would mean he was poaching on Nogo territory," Ignacio said. "Pasquale wouldn't like it, and it would also take your deal off the table. What if somebody set him up to look like he was dealing?"

In the mirror, Manuel Renteria met and held his cousin's gaze. "Any idea who?"

Ignacio shook his head.

"We found drugs at the scene," Manuel said. "If they didn't come from Pasquale, where did they come from?"

"I'm sure Pasquale is asking the same question."

Ignacio brushed loose hair from the back of Renteria's neck, removed the cape, snapped it clean, and folded it up.

"Thanks," Sheriff Renteria said. "Tell Pasquale I said hello."

Standing up, he pulled out his wallet and pulled out five ten-dollar bills. One at a time, he counted them into Ignacio's outstretched hand—ten bucks for the haircut and forty bucks for the tip, in every sense of the word. As far as Sheriff Renteria was concerned, it was well worth it. Ignacio had hinted at a possibility the sheriff hadn't considered—that maybe Jose Reyes really had been set up.

He thought about it for a time, but not for long. As much as he wanted to believe it, he couldn't. There was too much compelling evidence that said otherwise.

32

9:00 A.M., Monday, April 12
Vail, Arizona

Al Gutierrez was returning from a morning run when his phone rang. "What the hell were you thinking?" Sergeant Kevin Dobbs demanded.

"Excuse me?"

"You had no business going off Lone Rangering it. Now I'm in deep caca with the higher-ups, and you're in deeper caca with me."

"What are you talking about?"

"I'm talking about the 'informal' visit you paid to Buckeye yesterday. You weren't in uniform. You weren't on duty. I just got off the phone with a homicide detective from Phoenix. She's all over my butt, asking all kinds of difficult questions. Before she called me, she tried calling Pima County to ask about the progress of the investigation on the assault near Three Points. When they didn't know what the hell she was talking about, guess what? She started nosing around with Border Patrol, and somebody pointed her in my direction. Thank you very much for that, by the way. Really appreciate it. I told her the paperwork on the assault must have gotten lost between here and Pima County. I expect you to back me up on that, by the way."

Al had found the injured girl on Friday afternoon. This was only Monday morning. "Paperwork gets lost all the time," he said. "What's the big deal? And why a homicide detective?"

"The big deal is that your 'assault victim' is evidently a missing person in two jurisdictions and a homicide suspect in another. It's like she's all over the place, and I'm the one left holding the bag. So while I'm straightening out the paperwork, you can expect a phone call from the homicide cop. I gave her your number. Her name's Rush—Detective Ariel Rush."

"What do you want me to tell her?"

"That we handed our report in on Friday and have no idea what happened to it afterward. That we're sending a duplicate over to Pima County. As for why you were following up on something when you were out of uniform and it wasn't your concern? Knock yourself out. Tell 'em whatever the hell you want, but if it comes back and bites me in the butt, you're looking at a minimum three-day suspension."

Call waiting buzzed, but Dobbs had already hung up before Al switched from one line to another.

"Al Gutierrez?" a woman asked.

"Yes," he said. "That's me."

"I'm Detective Rush," she said. "Detective Ariel Rush with Phoenix PD, Homicide."

"Sergeant Dobbs told me to expect a call from a homicide detective. What he didn't say is who died."

"I'm investigating the murder of a man who was

found dead from blunt-force trauma and dumped in North Phoenix sometime early Friday morning. He has since been identified as Enrique 'Chico' Hernández, who ran a high-end call girl operation in Phoenix. On Saturday, some young women—Mr. Hernández's employees—called to report that he and one of their roommates, a girl named Breeze Domingo—a young woman with a rose tattoo on her right breast—had gone missing sometime early Thursday morning. The reason the roommates came forward in the first place is that Chico's name was the one on the rental agreement for their apartment. He had fallen behind in the rent. Without him there, the other girls were worried about being tossed out on their butts with nowhere to go and no protection.

"It wasn't until Mr. Hernández's bloodstained vehicle was found abandoned in downtown Phoenix early yesterday afternoon that we were able to put the missing persons report together with the homicide. When we ran prints found in the vehicle through AFIS, we ended up getting a hit from another missing persons case, that of a fourteen-year-old girl named Rose Ventana who ran away from her home in Buckeye over three years ago. Since Rose was also reported to have a rose tattoo in a pretty distinctive location, I think it's safe to assume that Breeze Domingo and Rose Ventana are one and the same. Since her prints were found at the scene of a homicide, that suggests she's either a suspect or, at the very least, a person of interest."

"How did you make the connection to the Three Points case?" Al asked.

"Her father," Ariel said. "Initially, I called the house first thing this morning, thinking that if Breeze were in some kind of trouble, she might have turned to her family for help. The mother was completely in the dark. When I told her about finding the fingerprints, she was overjoyed, not because her daughter might be a person of interest in a homicide but because she was alive. That was the first hint she'd had in years that her daughter wasn't dead. About that time Rose's father came on the phone, and it turned out he already knew."

"Stepfather," Al corrected. "And yes, he knew because I told him yesterday."

"Right," Ariel agreed. "Stepfather. He was pissed. He thought you were the one who had called us into it. It wasn't easy to get the whole story from him, because by then his wife was in the background, screaming at him and telling him that if someone thought her daughter was alive, he had no right to keep the information to himself. At any rate, Mr. Fox gave me your name and phone number because you had given him your card. When I tried reaching you and you weren't in, they put me through to your supervisor."

"Sergeant Dobbs."

"Exactly," Detective Rush said. "Who wasn't at all overjoyed to hear from me. By now I expect James and Connie Fox are on their way to Tucson to try to see their daughter. Maybe not both of them, but for sure the mother. It turns out I'm headed for Tucson, too. From what I'm hearing, it seems likely that Breeze/Rose could be both a victim of a crime and a perpetrator. I'll need to talk to her to sort all that out.

I'd like to see you, too. I'd like to go out and take a look at the crime scene. Can you direct me to it?"

"Sure. No problem." Al said. "I'll be glad to take you there."

"Was any kind of crime scene investigation done at the time?"

Al thought about the possible implications of any answer he might give. None of them were good. "I took a few photos, but that's about it," he said finally.

Detective Rush laughed. "Let me guess," she said. "That would be because Sergeant Dobbs deliberately dropped the ball."

"I didn't say that," Al told her.

"No, you didn't," she agreed, "because you didn't have to. This isn't my first day, Agent Gutierrez. I can figure out one or two things on my own. I've spent the past twenty years dealing with people like Kevin Dobbs. Generally, I give them two simple choices: Get out of my way or get run over."

Detective Ariel Rush sounded like the polar opposite of Kevin Dobbs.

"I'm just passing Picacho Peak," she said. "That's the nearest landmark. Let's visit the crime scene first and then go to the hospital. I'll come by your place and pick you up."

Al gave her the address and directions and then added, "I should probably call Sister Anselm and let her know Rose's parents are on their way."

"Who's Sister Anselm?" Detective Rush asked.

"She's Rose's patient advocate."

"What does she do?"

"She's at the hospital in the ICU. As far as I can tell,

her job is to look out for Rose's interests, but in the hospital, she's listed as Jane Doe, not Rose Ventana."

"Got it," Detective Rush said. "See you in a few."

For a moment or two, after Detective Rush hung up, Al stood there, staring at his phone. Before he left the hospital, the previous night, Sister Anselm had given him her cell number. Should he call and warn her that Rose's parents were on the way? After finding the number, he punched send.

When the nun answered, she sounded groggy, as though he had awakened her from a sound sleep.

"Sorry to disturb you," he said. "But this is Al—Al Gutierrez. I just heard from a Phoenix homicide detective who figured out that Rose is still alive and called her parents. They're on their way to the hospital."

Sister Anselm switched to full alert. "Her parents are coming here? How soon should I expect them?"

"I don't know, because I don't know how long ago they left Buckeye," Al said. "Probably fairly soon. Within the next hour or so."

"Thank you so much for the warning, Mr. Gutierrez," Sister Anselm said. "I'll be sure to be there to run interference, should that prove necessary."

33

Patty Patton liked to say that she had worked for the post office in Patagonia since "Noah was a pup." In view of the fact that her career with the U.S. Postal Service had started on a part-time basis when she was in high school and her mother, Lorna DeHaven, was the postmistress, that wasn't far from wrong.

Patty had married her high school sweetheart, Roland Patton, two weeks after she graduated from Patagonia High. She and Roland, an "older man" of twenty, had planned on staying with her mother only long enough for them to get a place of their own. That plan had come to grief when, a month after the wedding, Roland had died in the crash of his crop-dusting aircraft.

Patty never remarried. She never left her mother's house, and she never left the post office, either.

From the beginning, Patty had worn her blond hair in a bob, held in place by liberal applications of Aqua Net. Almost forty years later, the bob had turned gray, but it was still held in place by the same armor-like hair spray. Although Patty kept thinking about retiring, so far, that was all she was willing to do—think about it. When it came to husbands, jobs, or hairstyles, Patty Patton wasn't interested in change for change's sake.

For years the Patagonia post office had been downsized to a two-person operation. Patty hoisted the flag up the flagpole each morning and took it down at night. She sorted the mail into the individual boxes and into the plastic cartons Phil Tewksbury loaded into his truck. Phil took care of the janitorial end of the operation and kept their one mail truck in good repair. He also delivered mail to customers in outlying areas who didn't have access to a post office box.

Over years of working together, the two of them had developed a fairly congenial relationship. They were both dependable and conscientious. They both came to work on time and went home on time. There were only two real bones of contention between them. One was Phil's long hair, which he insisted on wearing in a limp comb-over, and the other had to do with the NFL. Phil was an avid Broncos fan; she was dyed-in-the-wool Dallas Cowboys.

That morning the truck dropped off the mail bags at seven. By eight, Patty had it sorted and was ready to open the window. Most of the time, her customers were in a hurry and totally focused on the mail. They wanted to buy stamps or pick up their general delivery or mail their packages. That morning one customer after another wanted to linger and talk. It was as though, in her capacity as postmistress, Patty Patton was also the source of all local knowledge. Everyone wanted to know if Patty had heard about poor Jose Reyes getting shot over the weekend. Did she have any idea how he was doing? Did she know which hospital he was in? How was his pregnant wife coping? Was there anything anyone could do to help?

Patty was so caught up in her conversations at the window that at first she failed to notice that Phil Tewksbury hadn't arrived in his usually prompt fashion. At ten, she closed the window long enough for a restroom break. It was only then, when she went back to the loading area, that she was surprised to see his collection of mail-filled cartons stacked where she had left them.

Before opening the window again, she tried calling Phil's house. There was no answer. She knew that if Phil were at home and able to reach a phone, he would have called to let her know he wasn't coming in. As for Christine? Patty knew from things Phil had said that his wife had stopped answering their phone years ago.

Patty's first concern and first responsibility was getting the mail delivered. Her next phone call was to Jess Baxter, the guy who occasionally drove the route when Phil was out sick or on vacation. After making arrangements for Jess to pinch-hit the mail delivery and before she reopened the window, she called the café.

"Has Deputy Carson come in yet this morning?" Patty asked Sally Drummond, the owner of the San Rafael Café.

"Not so far," Sally answered. "He usually shows up around eleven. Is something wrong?"

Patty didn't want to push any panic buttons. That was one of the reasons she hadn't dialed 911. Patty was concerned, but she also knew that Phil was a very private man. Having a cop show up at his place with lights flashing and sirens blaring wouldn't be appreciated.

"No big deal," Patty said. "Just have him stop by when he finishes his lunch."

It was almost noon when Jimmy Carson presented himself at Patty's window. She remembered Deputy Carson from back when he was a little kid, missing his two front teeth. The first time he came to the window to buy stamps, he parked his two-wheeler, minus the training wheels, just outside the post office's front door. Once inside, he had to stand on his tiptoes to reach the window. Because of the missing teeth, the word "stamps" came out with a double lisp—"sthampths."

Today he was a hulking brute of a man in a starched, perfectly ironed uniform. His hairline was definitely receding. He wore a sheriff's department badge pinned to his barrel chest and a firearm on his hip. He still lived with his mother.

"Morning, Ms. Patton," he said. "Sally told me you wanted to see me?"

Patty smiled, noting the difference. Sally Drummond at the café was never referred to as Ms. Drummond. The postmistress was always referred to as Ms. Patton.

"Phil Tewksbury didn't come in today, and he never called, either. Would you mind running by his place, just to check on him?"

Deputy Carson glanced at his watch as if he might not have enough time to drive the several blocks between the post office and Phil's house. "Sure," he said. "I suppose I could manage that."

"You know about his wife, right?" Patty asked.

"You mean the Christmas Tree Lady?"

"Yes," Patty said. "That's the one. Be sure you talk to Phil himself. I doubt Christine will even come to the door."

34

10:30 A.M., Monday, April 12
Tucson, Arizona

When Ali arrived at the hospital that morning, she was relieved to learn that on the medical front, news for the Reyes family was much improved. For one thing, feeling was beginning to return to Jose's lower extremities. He could move his toes. According to his doctor, it was possible that lowering his body temperature to prevent permanent spinal cord damage may have worked. As for his damaged intestines? The fact that he had made it through another day with no additional signs of infection was considered remarkable. On the other hand, the stoma situation was dicey. There was no way to tell if it would be temporary or permanent.

Teresa's health situation was downright rosy, with doctors predicting that, barring further complications, she and the baby would be sent home the following day, "home" being the operant word. With Jose's condition improving, that was where Teresa wanted to be—at home, where she had a nursery set up for the baby and where she could provide a little bit of normalcy for her two daughters.

"Wouldn't you be better off staying at a hotel?" Ali asked.

Teresa shook her head. "Being in a hotel room with one child is bad enough. Being there with three kids, including a newborn? Not a a good idea, and not fair to the other guests."

"But driving back and forth to the hospital . . ."

Teresa was adamant. "As long as we have the minivan, we'll be fine."

"Where's the minivan?" Ali asked.

"In Patagonia, along with the infant seat. When Deputy Carson brought us to town, I had no idea how long we'd be here or that the baby would be so early."

Before Ali could sort out the logistics of getting the car, a nurse stuck her head in the room. "Your husband's awake now, if you and the baby want to go see him. I brought along a wheelchair in case you do."

A few minutes later, with Teresa and Carmine settled comfortably in the chair, Ali pushed them down one long tiled corridor and up another. She parked the chair next to Jose's bed and then retreated from the room, closing the door behind her to give them a few moments of privacy. She returned to the waiting room in time to see Maria Delgado sink wearily into a nearby chair. She had managed to make the trip from one wing to another under her own steam, but just barely. She was trembling with effort and out of breath.

"I don't know what we would have done if you and Donnatelle hadn't been here," Maria said gratefully when she was able to speak again. "There's no way I could keep up with the girls on my own. But what's going to happen when Teresa goes back home and Jose gets out of the hospital? How will she take care of him and the baby?"

Ali already knew those were questions with no easy answers.

A few minutes later, a raven-haired woman in tight jeans and worn cowboy boots strode purposefully down the hallway and stopped directly in front of Maria Delgado. "I came by to see if I could help out with the granddaughters," she announced. She paused and looked around. "Where are they?"

"They're not here at the moment," Maria said coldly. "Teresa had to have an emergency C-section yesterday. We asked a friend to look after them, just to have them out from under hand and foot."

"A friend?" Olga repeated. "Why didn't you call me? I told you yesterday that I'd be happy to help."

As far as Ali could tell, Olga's offer of help sounded more like a declaration of war. Donnatelle had told Ali about the previous day's firefight between Teresa and her former mother-in-law. This was evidently the beginning of round two, this time with Teresa's mother, who wasn't backing down, either. Ali stepped between the two belligerent women, hoping to defuse the situation.

"My name is Ali Reynolds," she said, offering her hand. "I'm a friend of Jose and Teresa's. And you are?"

"I'm Olga Sanchez. I'm Lucy and Carinda's grandmother. Their other grandmother," she added, glaring at Maria.

"The girls are fine where they are," Maria said carefully. "As I told you, they are being well looked after."

Maria might have been soft-spoken, but her understated antipathy wasn't lost on anyone, especially Olga Sanchez.

"I still don't understand why you didn't call me."

"The girls are actually with a friend of mine, a third-year nursing student at the U of A," Ali said. "She lives here in town, close by, and has a son about Lucy's age. They're better off there than here."

"They'd be even better off at my place," Olga said. "They'd be with a family member rather than a complete stranger."

"You're a stranger, too," Maria pointed out.

"Yes, and I'm sorry for that," Olga said. "I shouldn't have quarreled with Teresa at the funeral—I was grief-stricken. I'm sorry about what happened yesterday, too—that's why I'm here now, to apologize and to offer to do whatever I can to help."

"I doubt Teresa is interested—" Maria Delgado began.

The door to Jose's room opened. Teresa rolled herself and the baby through the doorway. "Interested in what?" she asked.

"Olga came by to apologize," Maria said, her voice dripping with sarcasm. "She says she wants to help."

Ali expected that Teresa would follow her mother's lead and come out swinging. She didn't.

"That's very kind of you, Olga," Teresa said. "I appreciate the offer, but I think we're all right for the time being. They won't be back until late this afternoon."

"All right," Olga said. "I'll be in and out of town all day today. If you decide you need any help . . ."

"I'll call," Teresa said. "I promise."

Olga looked as though she were going to say something else. Evidently, thinking better of it, she turned and walked away. Watching her go, Maria shook her head. "Are you kidding?" she demanded of her daughter. "The last time you saw her, she was raising all kinds of hell. Now you're going to let her off the hook with a half-baked apology? I wouldn't trust that woman any farther than I can throw her."

"It's all right, Mom," Teresa said. "Olga is the girls' grandmother, after all. With everything that's happened in the past few days, I don't want to fight anymore, not with her and not with anyone else. If she's willing to be civil, so am I, and if she wants to help, I'll let her."

Maria Delgado shook her head. "I don't see how you can be so forgiving," she said. "I know I wouldn't be. I would have told her to take her help and put it where the sun don't shine."

Teresa looked at her mother and grinned. "Oh yeah?" she asked. "Isn't that how you and Dad raised me to be—loving and forgiving?"

"You can take being forgiving too far," Maria said. "Especially where that woman is concerned."

"Don't worry about Olga Sanchez," Teresa said. "She's already lost her only son. If she wants to be a part of the girls' lives, what can it hurt?"

"What if she offers you money?" Maria asked. "If you accept it, before you know it, she'll be running the show the same way she did when you were married to Danny."

"But now I'm married to Jose," Teresa pointed out. "Big difference."

"I hope so," Maria Delgado said. "I certainly hope so."

"And not being at war with the girls' grandmother should be better for everyone," Teresa said, "especially for the girls."

Ali was impressed that Teresa had taken the high road and that she was willing to entertain the possibility of having a less fractious relationship with her former mother-in-law.

"We'd better get back to my room," Teresa added. "I can tell Carmine needs a new diaper."

It took two full trips with the wheelchair to get everyone back to the maternity wing, one for Teresa and the baby and another for Maria Delgado.

"We still haven't solved the problem with the car," Teresa pointed out.

"How about this for an idea," Ali said. "I was already planning to drive down to Nogales today to speak to Sheriff Renteria. I could go there by way of Patagonia. Do you have someone who could ride as far as Patagonia with me and then drive your car back?"

"My brother—Teresa's uncle Tomás—has been driving me back and forth," Maria suggested. "We could ask him. He might not mind."

Nodding, Teresa pulled out her cell phone. "I'll call him and see what he has to say."

35

Showered and dressed but still groggy from lack of sleep, Sister Anselm hurried out to her Mini and sped back to the hospital. She appreciated Al Gutierrez's early warning that Rose Ventana's family was headed to Tucson. Sister Anselm wasn't at all certain what she should do about it. After all, in their one-sided conversation, the girl had made it painfully clear that, for reasons unknown, she had no desire to be reunited with her family. Now, ready or not, that unwanted reunion was imminent.

Puzzling over Al Gutierrez's phone call, Sister Anselm remembered something else he had said—that he had been given the news about Rose's family by a homicide detective of some kind. What did that mean? Who was dead? Sister Anselm was tempted to call him back and ask, but she didn't. Instead, she rushed into the ICU and was grateful to see that the waiting room was relatively deserted.

The monitors indicated that Rose Ventana was sleeping peacefully. After the difficult night they'd had, Sister Anselm hated to awaken her, but she did.

"Rose," she said. "Rose. You need to wake up. I need to talk to you."

The girl's eyes blinked open briefly and then closed again.

"I understand that your parents are coming to see you. I'm not sure how they heard you were even alive, to say nothing of here, but they did. They're driving down from Phoenix. When they get here, do you want to see them?"

With her jaw wired shut, speaking was difficult. Rather than make the effort, Rose shook her head vigorously, even though it clearly pained her.

"I'm sure they love you," Sister Anselm said. "You've been gone for three years. They've probably missed you terribly. I'll abide by your wishes, of course. If you're adamant about not seeing them, I'll tell them that your condition precludes visitors. But you must understand. After all these years of believing the worst and thinking you were dead, they're probably overjoyed to find you're alive. Are you sure you don't want to see them?"

Rose shook her head again.

"Why?" Sister Anselm said. "Is it because of what you've done between then and now? Is it because you're ashamed?"

The question was followed by a long wait. Sister Anselm let it hang there in the room. Finally, Rose nodded—the tiniest of nods.

Sister Anselm took Rose's hand again, holding it carefully so as not to disturb the scabs that had started forming on the cuts and burn marks.

"It couldn't have been easy to make it on your

own once you left home. You were what, fourteen?"

Rose nodded.

"At that age, job opportunities are limited. I'm guessing you turned to prostitution. Is that how you survived?"

Another nod.

"There's a lot of that in the world," Sister Anselm said. "That's what happened to my sister after our parents died. It was after the end of World War Two. Rebecca and I were taken in by the nuns in a convent in France. Becka ran away and lived on the streets. She was only seventeen when she died, but do you know what would have happened if she had come home?"

A headshake—a small one.

"I would have forgiven her for leaving and welcomed her home. The nuns would have done the same thing. Your family will welcome you, too. They're going to be so thrilled just to see you alive that nothing else will matter. I'm hoping you'll give them a chance."

Rose Ventana shook her head. Her answer was still no.

"All right," Sister Anselm said. "You might change your mind. You go back to sleep now. When they get here, I'll come let you know."

Sister Anselm went out and closed the door behind her. She moved a chair next to the entrance so she was partially blocking the way into the room. Al Gutierrez's pot of Easter lilies, returned from its banishment to the reception desk, sat on a table beside her. Despite her assurances to Rose, Sister Anselm wasn't at all sure the family would welcome back their wayward daughter. The parable of the prodigal son was just that, and when the stray was welcomed home with joy and feasting, the son who hadn't run away wasn't exactly a happy camper. Even if it turned out that Rose's parents were thrilled to have their daughter back, there was no way to tell how their other daughters, Rose's two younger sisters, would react.

The other thing Sister Anselm worried about was the media. The family had made every effort to keep their daughter's disappearance in the public eye. What if they did the same thing with her return? Considering Rose's opinion about being reunited with her loved ones, having it happen in front of cameras would make a bad situation that much worse.

The entire Fox family—James and Connie and Rose's younger sisters—burst into the ICU waiting room half an hour later. Recognizing them from photos on the websites she had accessed and grateful that there was no accompanying media, the nun hurried to meet them. "I'm Sister Anselm, your daughter's patient advocate. You're Mr. and Mrs. Fox?"

"James and Connie," James Fox answered. "We were told our daughter was being treated here in the ICU, but they didn't have her name at the front desk."

"She's listed on our records as Jane Doe. When she was admitted, we had no way of knowing who she was," Sister Anselm told them. "But yes, at this point, I believe Jane Doe is your daughter." She turned to the younger girls. "And these are her sisters?" She asked the question, though she didn't really need to. The family resemblance between these girls and Rose's shattered visage was striking.

"Yes," Connie said. "Lily and Jasmine. But what can you tell us about Rose? Is she going to be all right? When can we see her?"

"Not right now," Sister Anselm explained, directing them into chairs. "Without her express permission, I can't provide any details about the extent of her injuries or her course of treatment, but you need to understand that she was seriously injured before she was brought here, and those injuries are likely to impact her health for some time. If you do see her, you need to prepare yourselves for the idea that she won't look like the person you remember."

"If we see her?" Connie asked. "What do you mean if? She's our daughter. She's here. We're here, and I don't care what she looks like. I just want to see her and to know that she's alive, that she's okay."

"Alive, yes," Sister Anselm replied. "Okay, no. The problem is, she doesn't want to see you."

"She doesn't want to see us?" Connie echoed. "I don't believe it. Why not? How can that be? We're her parents. We've been trying to find her for years."

"You're her mother," James Fox said. "She'll see you even if she won't see me."

Hearing the regret in his voice, Sister Anselm studied the man. She had heard the all too common horror stories in which running away was the only option for children stuck in abusive homes. More times than she could count, that abuse had been perpetrated by stepfathers. That wasn't the reading she was getting from this particular stepfather, however.

"You're saying you and she were at odds?" Sister Anselm suggested.

"I was a lifelong bachelor who had never been married when Connie and her girls came into my life," James Fox said. "Rose and Lily were already in their teens. I had never been a father, but I was an engineer. When I see something that's wrong, I want to fix it."

"What was wrong with Rose?" Sister Anselm asked.

"Nothing, really. Rose was smart. She had huge amounts of potential, but she couldn't see it; she seemed determined to squander it. I tried to push her too hard in one direction—toward doing better in school, getting her education. She wasn't interested. I thought all I was doing was trying to create a little order in their lives by giving them a better place to live, more opportunities. But I can see now that she must have thought I was bossing everybody around. I got smarter after she left. I've done a lot better with her sisters, don't you think?" he asked Connie.

Connie reached out, took his hand, and nodded. The younger girl, Jasmine, sidled up to him and gave him a hug.

"When that young man Al Gutierrez showed up at the house last night, he said he was with the Border Patrol, but he wasn't in uniform, and I thought he was trying to scam us," Fox continued. "That's happened before. I've seen Connie put through the wringer enough times by people claiming to know what happened to Rose when all they really wanted was Connie's money. When the detective from Phoenix called this morning, I figured out that Gutierrez must have been telling the truth—that Rose really was alive. And now that we know she may be involved in a homicide—" His voice broke. He stopped speaking abruptly.

"Did they say whose homicide?" Sister Anselm asked.

James Fox nodded. "The guy's name was Hernández—Chico Hernández. Rose evidently worked for him as a . . ." He paused, looked at Jasmine, and added, "A call girl. He was murdered late last week, and Rose's fingerprints were found in his vehicle. That's why Detective Rush called us this morning."

"Does that make any difference?" Sister Anselm asked. She didn't say "call girl" aloud, but that was what she meant.

"Damn right it makes a difference!" James Fox declared.

Sister Anselm's heart fell. *Rose is right,* she thought. *If they figure out she's been working as a prostitute, the family will disown her.*

"Haven't you been listening to a word I've said?" he demanded. "Rose is a person of interest in a homicide. I don't care if she wants to see us. That doesn't matter, but if she's mixed up in a murder, she probably needs our help. That's why we're here. Tell her that, please."

Which was not at all what Sister Anselm had expected. She stood up. "Wait here," she said. "Let me go talk to her. I'll see what I can do."

36

By the time Detective Ariel Rush showed up on Al Gutierrez's door-step in Vail, he had printed out the crime scene photos, the ones Dobbs had told him not to bother keeping. His printer wasn't the best, so neither was the resolution.

"I took these on Friday," he said, handing them over. "They're not very good."

"You'd be surprised," she said. "I'll go get my computer and copy what's on the memory stick so the lab can take a look at it."

By the time she returned with her laptop, he had taken the memory stick out of his camera.

"Anything else on here besides your crime scene photos?" she asked.

"My graduation picture," he said. "From the academy."

"We don't want anything to happen to that," Rush said with a smile. "Have you been on the job long?"

"Awhile," Al admitted. "I just don't take that many pictures."

In a way, Detective Rush reminded him of his old junior high principal from back in Wenatchee. Mrs. Baxter had looked scary but wasn't. Al suspected Detective Rush was pretty much the same.

"Ready to saddle up?" she asked, closing her computer and returning the memory stick.

"Yes, ma'am," he said. "Want me to bring my camera along?"

"Don't bother," she said. "I've got my own."

On the forty-five-minute drive from Vail to King's Anvil Ranch, south of Three Points, Al told Detective Rush everything he could remember about the incident on Friday afternoon and everything he had learned about the victim.

On Friday, he had carefully recorded the location of the crime scene from his GPS so he'd be able to find it again later. Now, as they headed toward the crime scene in Detective Rush's vehicle, that notation proved to be invaluable; without it, they would have been flying blind through the mesquite-dotted landscape. His note helped him make sense of the countless tracks that meandered here and there across the desert. Eventually, he spotted something familiar.

"Stop here," he ordered. "It's on the far side of that clump of mesquite."

Before they got out of the car, Detective Rush slipped off her black low-heeled pumps in favor of tennis shoes. Stepping from the vehicle, she brought along Al's crime scene photos as well as her own camera. Out on the desert floor, Al helped her down the bank and then led her to the spot where the roiled sand indicated a lot of activity. It was April. All weekend long the wind had blown in from the west, shifting sand into what might have been usable tracks. Comparing the photos to the landscape, Detective Rush combed the wash for twenty yards in either direction. Then she examined the part of the bank where Al suspected something had been rolled down the steep incline, taking photos of bits of broken grass, horse nettles, Tucson burr ragweed.

"Look here," she said, pointing toward a plant with a bit of fabric tangled in one of the spiky burrs. She held up both the burr and the thread before dropping them into an evidence bag.

"It's not from the victim's clothing," Al said. "She wasn't wearing any."

When it came time to exit the arroyo, Al climbed up the steep wash. Then he reached down and helped Detective Rush up and out.

"I thought this was where the attack took place, since this is where I found the blood spatters," he told her. "They were tiny, though, and it looks like they're pretty much gone."

He was right. Whatever spatters might have been there on Friday afternoon had been blown away over the weekend by a scouring windstorm.

"This seems like the back of beyond," Detective Rush said. "So why bring her here? If the incident began somewhere in the Phoenix area, they had to go to some trouble to get her this far."

"Because it *is* the back of beyond," Al said. "It was lucky for her that I turned up when I did. There are thousands of acres of empty desert out here. She might've lay dead in the wash for weeks or even months before someone found her. Illegals come through here all the time, and some of them die. As Sergeant Dobbs demonstrated, no one worries about it all that much. One dead illegal is pretty much like another. Whoever did this put her here because they thought nobody would pay attention. Turns out they were almost right."

"You never saw the vehicle?"

"No, I heard it start up. It sounded like a truck of some kind or maybe an SUV. I'm pretty sure they heard me coming and took off."

"On foot?"

"Yes. This track dead-ends at a barbed-wire fence about half a mile north of here. It's a private road, but it's better than the one we're on. Made for a faster getaway. I tried calling it in at the time, but if anyone saw the vehicle, it didn't seem worth stopping. Or else they missed it altogether. There's a security checkpoint just west of Three Points."

"There are cameras at those checkpoints?"

"Yes."

"I'll try to get a look at the films and see if I notice anything out of line. Maybe we can convince Sergeant Dobbs to help me out with that. What time was this again?"

"Late afternoon. The time should be in the report."

"If and when said report surfaces," Detective Rush said.

"I have it on good authority that it's been located and sent along to Pima County."

"I'm puzzled about those cigarette burns," she said thoughtfully.

Al had thought of little else. The deliberate burns on the victim's skin had haunted his nightmares for two nights. How could someone do that to another human being? "Burns and cuts both," he said. "What about them?"

"Fresh?"

"I'm no expert. Maybe a day old, but it could be more or less."

"You found her on Friday afternoon. If the burns were part of what could be called an 'enhanced interrogation,' what were her assailants looking for? Presumably, Chico, her pimp, was dead by then. So was this recreational torture only, or were they looking for specific information, something she knew and no one else did?"

Detective Rush pulled out her cell phone. She punched in a number and held it up to her ear. Al was surprised. There were plenty of places in this expanse of desert where cell phone communication was either spotty or nonexistent. Evidently, this wasn't one of them.

"I want you to check something for me," she said into her phone. "Go into the ViCAP database. I'm looking for unidentified female homicide victims with evidence of cigarette burns." She paused. "Let's say the last five years." Another pause. "No, anywhere in the country. Get back to me as soon as you can." Closing her phone, she looked back at Al. "You say this road dead-ends at a fence?"

Al nodded.

"Let's walk, then," she said. "You take one side; I'll take the other."

"What are we looking for?"

"Anything that doesn't belong."

Several yards short of the fence line but within view of the other road, Al came to a sudden stop. "When you say something that doesn't belong, would you mean like maybe a cigarette butt?"

Ariel hurried over to where he was standing. The filtered butt lay on the weedy shoulder of the track. "Looks relatively fresh," she told him. "Way to go. Good spotting. It's too far from the fence to have been tossed out by a passing vehicle, which means whoever dropped it was walking here."

Extracting an evidence bag from her jacket pocket, she collected the stub and examined it before slipping it into the bag and back into her pocket, along with the bagged cockle burr.

"Like I said, lots of illegals walk through here," Al cautioned.

"Yes," Detective Rush agreed. "I'm sure they do, but how many of them smoke filtered Camels?"

"They took off in a hell of a hurry when I showed up," Al said. "It doesn't seem likely they'd have taken time out for a smoke."

"Maybe not as they were leaving," Detective Rush said, "but what about on the way in?"

When Al and Detective Rush reached the fence, they found one additional bit of useful trace evidence. A tiny thread, similar to the one on the burr, dangled from one of the barbs on the wire.

"See there?" she said triumphantly. "They were in a hurry, and they got careless."

"Assuming they parked here," Al said, "how did

they transport her from here to the wash? Did she walk there under her own steam?"

Detective Rush looked at Al questioningly. "How big is she?"

"Hard to tell, but not very. Five-five or so. Maybe a hundred and twenty pounds."

"So most likely, one guy couldn't carry her that far by himself. It would take two, at least, to cover this much distance."

With Detective Rush in the lead, they started back the way they had come. When her phone rang, she stopped to answer and listened for a time.

"Okay," she said finally. "If you've got any connections across the line in Mexico, you might see if there are any similar cases down there. In the meantime, we've got another victim with similar injuries. Only so far, this one isn't dead."

"What?" Al asked when she closed her phone.

"So far we've found three similar cases. Unidentified victims. Cigarette burns. Found in areas frequented by illegals. One in New Mexico, one in southern California, and another one over by Yuma, here in Arizona."

"So it's a serial killer?"

"That's my first guess."

"What happens if the killer finds out Rose Ventana isn't dead?"

"Maybe we'd better go try to talk to her, and to that nun you told me about, and let her know that the patient might be in danger."

"I think she already figured that out," Al said. "Last night, when I showed up unannounced, she pulled a Taser on me."

Detective Rush stopped short. "Really? A Taser?"

Al nodded.

"My kind of nun," Detective Rush said with a laugh. "Definitely my kind of nun."

"Are we going to stop by Pima County and let them know that the delayed assault report may be connected to a series of homicides?"

Rush thought about that before she answered. "I think we'll just let it sog for a while. So far all Pima County has is an attempted homicide on their books. I have more than that in my jurisdiction because the victim, Mr. Hernández, is dead. The last thing I need is to be caught up in some kind of jurisdictional pissing match when I really want to clear my case. And I don't want anyone swooping in and screwing up my trace evidence. If Pima County comes online and starts working the case, we'll cross that bridge when we come to it."

"What do we do next?" Al asked.

"We're going to stop by your office and see about getting a look at those checkpoint videos."

"And meet Kevin Dobbs?" Al asked.

Detective Rush grinned at him. "Remember what I said about people like that?"

"You mean you go around them or over them?"

"With Sergeant Dobbs," she said, "I'm choosing the go-around option. Since you'll be working with him after I leave, that'll be a better choice than a direct confrontation."

Doesn't matter, Al thought. *No matter how you slice it, Kevin Dobbs is going to be pissed as hell!*

37

For Ali, pulling the pieces together for the drive to Patagonia was a lot like herding cats. When Teresa had said she'd call her uncle Tomás, it sounded easy, but it wasn't. Tomás Kentera was Maria Delgado's brother. Unlike her, he had a cell phone and no landline. Unfortunately, he had forgotten to recharge the battery. As a consequence, his cell phone wasn't working. Ali had to drive to his house on the far west side of town to find him and then convince him to ride along with her to retrieve Teresa's minivan.

They were on the freeway and headed for Patagonia when Ali's phone rang.

"We closed the restaurant right after breakfast and gave ourselves some extra time off," Edie Larson announced. "The agreement is signed, sealed, and delivered. The Sugarloaf is sold. Your father is over the moon, and so am I. Can you believe it?"

"I do believe it," Ali said. She couldn't remember her mother ever sounding so excited. "Congratulations."

"In the meantime," Edie continued, "we've got an appointment later this afternoon to take a look at the available units at Sedona Hills. Since we really will be moving in a matter of weeks, we need to get our ducks in a row about where we're going. One thing is for sure—we'll need to have a yard sale or two."

"What about the mayor thing?" Ali asked.

"Yes," Edie said, "the mayor thing is still on. Your father hasn't exactly come around, but I'm guessing he will eventually."

Ali thought so, too. "He usually does."

"Now, wait a minute," Edie objected. "When you say it that way, you make your father sound henpecked."

"What I'm really saying is that you deserve each other," Ali said. "You both have your moments."

"All right, then," Edie said, changing the subject. "How are things on your end? How is your friend doing?"

"Better," Ali said, looking at Teresa's uncle, sitting in stolid silence in her front seat. "Better but not completely out of the woods."

A few miles later, Ali's next call was from Leland Brooks. The cement pour had gone well. Neither of the Askins nominees had RSVPed, but it was early days, the two teas were almost a whole week away. As for the garden? The long-term weather report indicated that some of the hardier items could start being planted the following week.

"So things are moving forward?" Ali asked.

"Absolutely, madam," he said. "You didn't think I'd let you down, did you?"

"No," Ali said. "Actually, I didn't."

Feeling guilty about carrying on not one but several telephone conversations in her passenger's presence, Ali switched her phone off. By then they had turned off I-10 onto Highway 83. Ali was trying to figure out how to initiate a conversation with this relative stranger when Tomás Kentera did it for her.

"Why do you think Sheriff Renteria ordered his people to stay away from the hospital?" Tomás asked.

"He what?" Ali demanded.

"I know lots of people in Nogales, and that's what they're saying—that Sheriff Renteria ordered his people to stay away from the hospital and from Jose."

Ali was astonished. "That can't be."

"Have you seen any people from the sheriff's department at the hospital?"

"No, but—"

"Someone should ask the sheriff about this," Tomás said. "I would really like to know."

"Believe me," Ali said determinedly, "so would I."

Teresa and Jose's mobile home was located in a housing development that had mostly failed to develop. Ten acres had been divided into ten one-acre lots, seven of which remained empty. Two other mobile homes, one obviously a derelict, were situated on the property. The Reyes lot was the only one that was completely fenced.

It was just past noon when Ali stopped at the gate. Tomás got out to open it. The minivan sat in a free-standing carport at the back of the house. Teresa had told Ali that the car keys were in a drawer in the kitchen and that a spare house key could be found under an empty flowerpot sitting next to the front steps. The key wasn't there, but by the time Ali reached the front steps, she realized no key would be necessary, because the front door stood ajar.

Ali knew that Duane Lattimore had executed a search warrant on the house, but it seemed unlikely that he would have gone off leaving it unsecured. She suspected that an enterprising burglar might have decided to take advantage of the current uproar in Teresa and Jose's lives. If so, it was possible the intruder might be inside the home.

Holding up one hand and motioning for Uncle Tomás to stay where he was, Ali eased her way up the wooden steps. By the time she was ready to pull the door open the rest of the way, she had her Glock 17 out of its small-of-the-back holster.

Ali peered around the door frame and came to an abrupt stop. During the time she had worked with the Yavapai County Sheriff's Department, she had seen the messy aftermath of several executed search warrants. This wasn't anywhere close to messy. Everywhere Ali looked, she saw wanton destruction.

Living room and dining room furniture had been overturned and the upholstery shredded, spilling fill into snowdrift-like piles of cotton. Lamps had been flung to the floor and broken; a glass coffee table had been smashed into thousands of shards. In the kitchen, the fridge had been tipped over on its side, spilling contents into a sticky, broken-jarred mess on the floor. Drawers had been removed from the cupboards, dumped, and then stomped apart. Dishes and glassware had been pulled out of cupboards and smashed to pieces. Something that looked like super glue covered the glass stove top. What appeared to be a collection of cookbooks had been thrown to the floor, and something wet and sticky, like Karo syrup, had been poured over them, swelling the covers and sticking the pages together in a sodden mass.

Picking her way through the debris field as carefully as possible, Ali searched the remainder of the house, feeling more and more heartsick as she went. In the room Jose and Teresa had prepared for Carmine's nursery, Ali found the wreckage of a crib and mattress as well as a demolished changing table. Diapers, tiny clothing, and piles of receiving blankets had been thrown on the floor and then covered with a thick substance that appeared to be a mixture of the contents of two Costco-size containers, one of baby powder and one of lotion. The last bedroom—the one at the far end of the mobile, which evidently belonged to Lucy and Carinda—seemed to have been spared, making Ali wonder if the intruder had run out of time or energy or both.

On the opposite end of the house, in Teresa and Jose's master bedroom, the level of destruction once again escalated. Gaping holes had been slashed into the mattress and box spring. Clothing had been pulled from the closet, ripped apart, dumped on the floor, and soaked with bleach from an empty two-gallon jug that lay nearby. Bottles of still-tacky nail polish had been spilled onto the torn bedding, sparing none of it. Bottles of shampoo and conditioner and lotion had been poured into an oddly flowery-smelling soup in the bathtub. Chunks of jaggedly broken glass left in the bottom of that mixture presented a cutting hazard for anyone trying to clean up the mess.

After searching the house from end to end and finding no intruders, Ali returned to the living room, where she found Tomás Kentera standing dumbstruck, staring at the destruction.

"Who would do such a thing!" he exclaimed. "And why?"

Ali had no ready answer for that question. Shaking her head, she put away her Glock, pulled out her cell phone, turned it on, and dialed 911.

"Nine-one-one," the operator replied. "What are you reporting?"

"A burglary," Ali said. She read the address Teresa had given her to program into the GPS. "That's just north of Patagonia, between Patagonia and Sonoita."

"I'm aware of where it is," the operator said. "Is anyone injured?"

"No. Someone broke into the house while no one was home."

"And the intruder is no longer at that location, is that correct?"

"Yes," Ali said, "but—"

"That address is in the county, so responders would be coming from the Santa Cruz Sheriff's Department. However, many of their personnel are currently involved in a complex emergency situation. If there's no immediate threat to life or property at your location, I'll need to take a report. They'll send someone out as soon as a deputy becomes available. What is your name, please?"

Ali gave her name, but before she could say anything more, the operator interrupted.

"I'm sorry. I'm going to need to take another call. Someone will be there as soon as possible."

With a click, she was gone. When Ali turned to look at Tomás, he was bent over and reaching into a pile of what looked like the debris of a kitchen junk drawer. He pulled out a key fob, held it up, and waved it triumphantly in the air.

"Look what I found," he said. "The minivan keys. Why didn't they steal it?"

"That's what I'd like to know, too," Ali said.

She scrolled through the numbers on her phone and dialed the one listed as Juanita Cisco's office number. She was astonished when Juanita answered her own phone.

"What's up now?" the defense attorney asked. "Has Lattimore showed up at the hospital for a return engagement?"

"This is something else," Ali said. "I'm standing in the middle of Teresa and Jose's house in Patagonia. It's a wreck."

"Maybe Teresa's not a good housekeeper," Juanita suggested cheerfully. "After all, if someone came into my house unannounced, they'd say the same thing about me—that my house is a wreck. Give the poor woman a break. She's got an armload of little kids. What do you expect?"

"You don't understand," Ali said. "This isn't a housekeeping problem. This is a breaking-and-entering problem. Maybe not so much breaking. Teresa told me there was a spare key hidden outside. It wasn't there when I got here, but someone has torn the place apart."

"What about the search warrant?" Juanita asked. "Maybe Lattimore's DPS guys are responsible for what you're seeing. Do you want me to ask him?"

"You can if you want," Ali returned, "but I don't think we can lay this at Lieutenant Lattimore's door. He's a cop. He may be a jerk, but from what I could see, he pretty much goes by the book. This looks like a frenzy of absolute destruction with a whole lot of malice thrown in on the side. I'm talking about broken dishes, smashed furniture, sliced mattresses, dumped food. Someone went through this house in a deliberate fashion, systematically destroying everything they could lay hands on."

"Have you reported it?"

"I tried," Ali said. "It turns out the local sheriff's department is totally preoccupied with something else at the moment. Believe me, once I leave here, I'm going directly there and then to Sheriff Renteria himself."

"If Teresa is released from the hospital tomorrow, will she be able to go home?"

Ali looked around at the ugly mess. "No way. The place looks like what you'd expect in the aftermath of an F5 tornado. Everything is wrecked—food, clothing, furniture."

Juanita sighed. "All right," she said. "If you'll handle the police report, I'll be responsible for letting Teresa know what's happened. I'll try to find out who carries her homeowner's insurance and see if I can get them to call out an adjuster. I'll also let Teresa know that she'll probably need to make other arrangements for a place to stay once she leaves the hospital."

"Thank you," Ali said.

"All right," Juanita said. "Considering the circumstances, I guess this set of phone calls is off the clock. In the meantime, you need to get out of the house so you don't get accused of messing up the crime scene."

"Believe me," Ali told her, "there's no way I could make this crime scene any worse than it already is. And thanks."

"You're welcome," Juanita said. "Just remember, the next time you talk to Victor Angeleri, tell him he owes me."

Ali stowed her phone and turned to Tomás, who stood in the middle of the shattered room, seemingly unable to move.

"What are we supposed to do now?" he asked. "Should we start trying to clean things up?"

"We can't even begin that process until after the cops have been here to make an official report," Ali said. "A police report has to be in place for insurance coverage to come into play."

"So who did this? A bunch of juvenile delinquents?"

Ali thought of the nail polish spilled on the bed. Nail polish didn't pour in a hurry. She thought about Teresa's wrecked cookbooks, with the sodden pages permanently glued together.

"I doubt it," she said thoughtfully. "Whoever did this devoted a lot of time and energy to the effort. The nail polish on the bedding wasn't completely dry, so this didn't happen all that long ago, probably sometime this morning. Today's a school day. That makes kids' involvement unlikely."

"Illegals, then?" Tomás asked.

"Maybe," Ali said, "but the level of destruction suggests this is a lot more personal."

"What do we do, then?" Tomás asked. "Just walk away?"

"No," Ali said. "I have a better idea. I'm going to document as much as I can."

Disregarding Juanita's advice, she went back through the house room by room, using her iPhone to snap one photograph after another. There were places on the carpet, especially in the hallway near the wrecked nursery, where a trail of baby-powder shoe prints remained, the white print in stark relief against the gray carpet. Ali did her best to avoid marring the prints in any way. If they were evidence, she wanted them left intact.

She was almost done taking photographs when Tomás came to find her. "I'm heading back to town," he said, holding up the minivan keys. "I just got off the phone with Teresa. She knows what's going on, and she's terribly upset, but I told her that she and the kids and even Jose, if necessary, can stay with me until we can get this place cleaned up and livable again. It'll be crowded at my place, and I'll need to move furniture around, but it'll be better than having them try to come back here."

Ali and Tomás stepped outside. After he drove away, Ali examined her surroundings. The house was set back from the road with empty lots on either side. The nearest house was three lots away, and the road was far enough that it seemed doubtful anyone driving by would have noticed or paid attention to what cars were parked at which house.

On her way out of the development, Ali stopped and banged on the door of the two neighboring houses, hoping that someone would have noticed something out of the ordinary. At the first house, a dog barked, but no one came to the door. At the second one, Ali was greeted with total silence. No one was home, and from the general air of neglect, it looked as though no one had been in or out of the house in weeks. Most likely, the person who had broken into the Reyes's household had done so secure in the knowledge that there would be no witnesses.

After Ali left, it took her a little over half an hour to drive to Nogales, the Santa Cruz County seat, where she was hoping to make contact with Sheriff Renteria. He wasn't there, and the only information his secretary handed out was that the sheriff was "currently unavailable."

Rebuffed, Ali returned to her vehicle and her iPhone. Logging on to one of the local Tucson television channels, she found a breaking-news alert that the Santa Cruz County Sheriff's Department was currently investigating a reported homicide in Patagonia.

Ali didn't try to find out the exact location of the homicide before she headed back to Patagonia. She didn't need to.

She figured the town was small enough that she'd be able to find a homicide crime scene there on her own.

38

11:30 A.M., Monday, April 12
Patagonia, Arizona

Aside from the delivery guys, the Patagonia post office itself was a one-woman operation. Patty Patton might have made a pitch to the higher-ups, asking to have some part-time help to cover the windows during lunchtime and breaks, but she didn't want to rock the boat. There was a lot of talk these days about shutting down "underperforming" post offices, and she didn't want hers to be one of them.

As a consequence, between eleven and twelve each day, Patty closed the window and then sat at the sorting table to eat her peanut better and jelly sandwich and to down the remains of her thermos of coffee. Once upon a time, she had imagined her life would be different, that she and Roland would travel around the world and dine in all kinds of exotic places. She hadn't expected to live her whole life without venturing outside the confines of Patagonia. But those were the choices she'd made and the way she'd lived her life, and most of the time she had few regrets.

It was quiet in the back room. Over the bank of

mailboxes, she could hear people chatting and greeting each other. At some point, while she was eating dessert—a container of banana yogurt—she heard a siren or two. She wondered about them, but not that much. She was a lot more perturbed by the fact that Jimmy Carson hadn't bothered to come back by to let her know what was going on with Phil. That seemed odd—out of character. Jimmy was usually far more dependable than that; his mother, Eunice, had seen to that long ago.

At twelve sharp, Patty downed the last slurp of coffee and put away the remains of her lunch. She didn't want people from out front looking through the service window and thinking she used the sorting table as a cafeteria.

Patty was not a tall woman. In order to reach the window and conduct business, she had to spend most of the workday perched on a three-step stool hidden behind the counter. When Patty opened the window after lunch, Maxine Browning, Patagonia's ace gossip, was waiting outside the window, drumming her fingers on the counter and looking pointedly at her watch.

"It's not like you to be even a minute late," Maxine complained. "But I suppose with what's going on over at Phil's, we're lucky you're open at all. I'd like a sheet of those breast cancer stamps, please."

"What is going on over at Phil's?" Patty asked, trying not to sound too concerned or alarmed as she retrieved the page of stamps.

"Something bad, I guess," Maxine said. "There are cops all over the place. I wouldn't be surprised if that woman finally got around to putting a bullet in her head. Christine Tewksbury has been crazy as a loon for all these years. I'm surprised Phil didn't place her in some kind of home long ago. I probably would have. Having that ugly Christmas tree around year after year would have driven me batty."

Patty felt a clutch in her stomach. If it had been something wrong with Christine, Phil would have called. This had to be something else, maybe something far worse.

"And what about Deputy Reyes?" Maxine continued. "I'm hearing that the reason he got shot is that he was dealing drugs on the side. With his poor wife pregnant and everything. I swear, if the cops are crooked, who are you supposed to trust these days?"

At that point, the woman behind Maxine, Annie Davis—who was head volunteer in the all-volunteer town library—jumped into the conversation. "That's right," she said. "I heard they found drugs galore when they searched Jose Reyes's house. The sheriff's department isn't releasing squat about it—they're claiming that the Department of Public Safety has taken over the case, but all that's doing is giving Sheriff Renteria a chance to save face. If he's got a bunch of crooked drug-dealing cops working in his department, that man is history. There's no way in hell he'll be able to weather that kind of scandal and get reelected."

Patty knew Jose and Teresa Reyes because she knew most everyone in town, but she was far less concerned about them than she was about Phil and Christine Tewksbury.

"What can I do for you, Annie?" Patty asked, trying

to maintain her focus and move the process along. She needed to get the customers out of the way so she could think.

"My cousin in Fargo asked me to send her eight pints of my prickly pear jelly," Annie replied. "She wants to give a jar to each of the members of her bridge club. Flat rate is the way to go, right?"

"Medium or large?" Patty asked.

"I don't know," Annie said. "What do you think would hold eight pints of jelly?"

"Large, most likely," Patty said. "You'll want to put in plenty of packing. You don't want jars of sticky jelly knocking together and getting broken."

Patty had to scramble down off her stool to go over to her box bin. That morning, when she'd been helping Jess do the mail load-in before running Phil's route, Patty had discovered that Phil had squirreled away a dozen of the large flat-rate boxes in the back of his truck. No doubt someone on the route had asked for them, but since Patty's inventory of flat-rate boxes was getting dangerously low, she'd dragged the boxes back inside. If someone on the route needed them, they'd have to come to the post office and pick them up.

"Since this is where Phil works, it seems to me as though someone would have the simple courtesy to come tell you what's going on," Annie complained. "It's not fair to leave you in the dark like this."

That was Patty's opinion as well. Another twenty minutes crawled by. Patty collected box rent. She made arrangements for several return-receipt-requested items that were being sent to the IRS. She sold a roll of

Forever stamps. When the phone rang behind her, she leaped off the stool and raced to answer it. Eunice Carson, Deputy Carson's mother, was on the line.

"When I saw they had Jimmy outside Phil and Christine Tewksbury's house directing traffic, I couldn't stand it any longer," Eunice said breathlessly. "I had to go check. You're not going to believe it. He told me Phil is dead. When they dragged Christine out of the house, she was screaming like a banshee."

Patty was glad she wasn't standing on her stool when she heard the news. For a moment the room seemed to spin around her. "Phil is dead?" she repeated. "You mean like a heart attack or something? I know he went to see his doctor a few weeks ago, but according to him, it was just a routine physical. I didn't think there was anything seriously wrong with him."

"Definitely not a heart attack," Eunice said. "She evidently beat the crap out of him with a baseball bat."

"She who?" Patty asked.

"Christine," Eunice responded. "Who do you think? According to Jimmy, when he got there late this morning, she was sitting in a chair in the living room next to that godforsaken Christmas tree. The bloody bat was right there with her the whole time. She didn't even bother trying to hide it. I can hardly get my head around the idea that those kinds of things can happen right here in Patagonia."

"Hello," Shelley Witherspoon called to Patty from out front. "Is anybody there?"

"Thanks for the call," Patty said. She put down the phone and returned to the window.

As soon as Shelley saw Patty's ashen face, her jaw dropped. "Patty, you look terrible. Are you all right?"

"I'm not feeling well," Patty Patton said. "You'll have to forgive me. I'm afraid I won't be able to help you today."

For the first time in her entire career with the United States Postal Service, Patty Patton put the CLOSED sign in place and shut the window for the day shortly after noon. Taking her keys, purse, and lunch bag, she went out the back way and locked the door behind her. Jess hadn't returned from running the route, but he'd be able to leave the mail truck inside the building's lockable chain-link fence and drop the keys in through the mail slot.

One of the things Patty had always loved about her job was the commute—a two-block walk along the edge of a busy highway. Today it seemed to take forever, and once she got home, she didn't stay. Instead, she got in her aging Camaro, one her mother had bought new back in the seventies, and drove out to Phil's house.

There were half a dozen cop cars in evidence, including one she recognized as being Jimmy Carson's squad car. Traffic cones had been set up, creating a temporary DO NOT CROSS barrier that Patty made no effort to enter. She parked her car well away from the cones. Before exiting the car, she grabbed a pack of cigarettes and a lighter out of her glove box. Yes, Patty was a smoker, but she didn't want to be tempted into creating a smoking room outside the back door of her post office. So the cigarettes stayed in the car and the car stayed safely at home when she was working. This afternoon all bets were off.

Wearing an orange traffic jacket, Jimmy stood in the middle of the small side road that led to the Tewksburys' house, doing nothing while he waited to direct nonexistent traffic. "Hey, Ms. Patton," he said when he saw her. "Sorry."

What does that mean? Patty wondered. *Is he sorry to see me; sorry Phil's dead; sorry he didn't come back to give me the news?*

"Your mom called," Patty said.

Jimmy nodded. "I thought she would."

No doubt Jimmy had been instructed to keep his mouth shut, but Patty Patton had known him all his life, and she didn't hesitate to play that card. "Is it true Phil is dead?"

Jimmy nodded. "Yes, he is. The body's already on its way to the morgue."

"What's going on in there, then?" she asked, blowing smoke in the air and nodding in the direction of the house. Most of the activity seemed to center around the free-standing garage a short distance away from the Tewksburys' kitchen door.

"Crime scene investigation."

When Eunice had told Patty that Christine was responsible, Patty had assumed the deadly assault had played out inside the house. "You mean it happened inside the garage?" she asked.

Deputy Carson sighed before he answered. "I shouldn't be talking to you like this, Mrs. Patton, but yes, it happened inside the garage, and Christine has been taken into custody. When I came by this morning to check on Phil, the way you asked me, I rang the door and nobody answered. Since it was a welfare check, I let myself in, and there she was, sitting in the living room. I asked her if she knew where her husband was. There was a bat sitting on the floor next to her chair. She picked it up and told me to get out. So I did.

"But on the way out, I decided to check the garage. I looked in the window and saw the tarp there on the floor with a pair of feet sticking out from under it. The door was locked, so I broke it open to check on Phil. He was already dead as a doornail, with his head bashed in. I immediately called for backup. When we went back into the house, Christine was sitting there, still holding the bat. I guess I'm damned lucky that she didn't use it on me."

"I don't believe it," Patty declared.

"I'm sorry," Jimmy said. "Phil really is dead. He must have been dead for a couple of hours before I found him."

But Patty was looking at the distance between the back door to Phil's house and the stand-alone garage. "I mean I don't believe Christine did it," she said. "According to Phil, she hasn't set foot outside the house in years. He claimed she was agoraphobic—that the very idea of leaving the house caused panic attacks."

"I'd call it a rage attack, not a panic attack," Jimmy observed. "She went off again a little while later when Sheriff Renteria showed up with the chief detective. One of the crime scene guys told me that the bat has something on it that looks like bits of blood and hair. They'll have to examine it before they know for sure if what's there belongs to Phil. Christine must've been ashamed, because she even covered the poor guy with a dropcloth before she finished him off."

Patty was sure this was Jimmy's first homicide ever. He was visibly excited and talking way too much. She also doubted that anything she said to him would be given much credence. "I want to talk to whoever is in charge of the investigation," she said.

"That'll be Detective Zambrano," Jimmy agreed. "But you'll have to wait until he's done in there."

"All right," she said. "I'll wait."

Finished with one cigarette, Patty lit another, then retreated to the Camaro and leaned against the back of the trunk to wait. Minutes later, a blue SUV—a fancy one Patty didn't remember seeing before—pulled up to the barrier. When a tall blond woman got out and started toward the house, Jimmy rushed forward to head her off.

"Sorry," he said. "It's a crime scene. You can't go there."

"My name is Ali Reynolds. I'm looking for Sheriff Renteria. Someone has broken into the home of one of his deputies. I'm here to report it."

"He's busy."

"Then I'll wait."

"Okay," Jimmy said, motioning toward Patty. "You and everybody else."

39

Al Gutierrez didn't know when he'd ever had a better day off. At the Border Patrol headquarters in Tucson, he and Detective Rush bypassed Sergeant Dobbs's office and went directly upstairs. That was the location of the massive library where miles of temporary checkpoint security videos were transferred onto permanent DVDs and cataloged by date and location. Within twenty minutes, Al and Detective Rush were in a viewing room with one of the library techs, scanning through the videos recorded the previous Friday afternoon at the Three Points checkpoint.

One vehicle after another passed without eliciting any interest. Most of the drivers and passengers were clearly Tohono O'odham, going and coming from one of the villages on the reservation, or elderly RV-driving snowbirds heading north after wintering in Arizona. Some were clearly ranch vehicles, a few of them pulling livestock trailers with and without livestock.

"Wait," Ariel Rush said. "Go back. Let's take a closer look at that white van."

Al was pretty sure Detective Rush was quite capable of running the video monitor on her own, but Homeland Security rules meant that only a properly qualified technician was allowed to handle the DVDs and the controls.

"Can you freeze those frames and expand them?" she asked the tech once the white van reappeared on the screen. "If possible, I want to get a look at the driver and the passenger as well as the license plates. And what's the logo on the side?"

Because the resolution was high enough to capture license plate information, the images offered a good deal of other information. The faces of both the driver and passenger were clearly visible. They were ordinary-looking guys who were waved through, traveling westbound, without any question. The logo on the driver's door was easy to decipher: RUG RUNNERS OF SCOTTS-DALE.

A quick Google search on Ariel's laptop showed lots of sites about runner rugs for hallways and entryways but no firm of that name anywhere in the country. A quick check of the license plate revealed that it had been stolen from a Lincoln Town Car parked in a long-term lot at Sky Harbor Airport sometime during the preceding week.

On Friday afternoon the van with the switched-out plate had driven through the checkpoint westbound at 3:58 and returned eastbound at 5:02. On the second trip, the van was examined by a drug-sniffing dog before it was waved through.

"If you're driving westbound on Highway 86, how far could you go in half an hour?" Detective Rush asked.

Al shrugged. "Not far," he said. "You'd have to push it to get from there as far as Sells and back in that amount of time. There are a few ranch houses out that way in between, and some smaller Indian villages, but I can't think of many places where someone would be buying an upscale rug. Most of the people I've met on the reservation are more likely to do their shopping at Home Depot or Target or Wal-Mart than they are in some arty kind of shop in Scottsdale."

"That sounds like racial profiling to me," Ariel said.

"It's more like reality profiling," Al said. "Those people don't have buckets of cash hanging around."

They left the library with the requested images safely stored on Detective Rush's computer.

"Where to now?" Al asked.

"Physicians Medical Center," Rush said. "I want to see if we can keep Rose's family from going public. We've got a potential survivor of a serial killer. I want to keep Rose Ventana alive."

Once outside the building, Detective Rush was back on her phone. "Okay," she said to one of her cohorts in Phoenix, "I think I may have a line on the vehicle in the Chico Hernández homicide. We need to check security tapes of all businesses in the area where the body was found. We're looking for a white panel van. There's a Rug Runner logo on it—at least there was on Friday, but I'm thinking it may be one of those magnetic signs that can be changed out in a minute. So look for a white van with any kind of logo; or no logo, for that matter. The plates that were on it were stolen, so the license number isn't going to help us much, but I want you to put both the plate number and the sign information out on a BOLO. Right this minute those are the only tentative pieces we have on this puzzle, and we just might get lucky."

By the time she finished the call, they were back in Detective Rush's patrol car and headed for the hospital.

"Thanks," Al said.

"For what?"

"For treating me like I have a brain."

"You have a brain, all right," Detective Rush said. "And it's because of your taking the initiative that we have a chance of solving this case."

"Sergeant Dobbs isn't wild about any of his people taking the initiative."

"That's his problem," Detective Rush said. "One of his problems," she added. "And before we're finished, he may have several more."

"Sweet," Al Gutierrez said as he buckled his seat belt. "It doesn't get any better than that."

40

2:30 P.M., Monday, April 12
Patagonia, Arizona

Settling in to wait, Ali studied the silent woman who stood next to an old red Camaro. From the pile of cigarette butts at her feet, she had obviously been here for some time, watching the police activity.

"Friend of yours?" Ali asked, nodding toward the house across the street, where most of the activity seemed to center around a detached one-car garage.

"Yes," the woman said. "Name's Phil Tewksbury. He was a coworker. Hell of a nice guy."

"I'm sorry," Ali murmured.

"Me, too. And who are you?" the woman asked. "Don't think I've seen you around these parts before."

"My name is Ali Reynolds. I'm from Sedona. Jose Reyes is a friend of mine. I came down to help after I heard what happened to him. He's in Physicians Medical Center, and now so is his wife. She had her baby."

"I'm Patty Patton," the woman said. "I run the post office. So what'd Teresa have, a boy or a girl?"

"A boy. Carmine's a few weeks early, but he's fine, and so is his mother."

"How about Jose?"

"Better," Ali said. "At least he's out of the ICU. That's a big improvement."

"Tough for Teresa, though," Patty said. "New baby. Sick husband. I overheard you say something about a break-in. Not their house, I hope."

"It was their house. And it's not just a break-in. Someone went to a lot of trouble to mess up everything within reach."

"Jerks," Patty said. "When it's time to put together a cleanup crew, you let me know. I'll put up an announcement on the bulletin board at the post office."

Ali smiled inwardly to realize that she had stumbled into a place where the post office was still more important than Facebook.

A man in a law enforcement uniform emerged from the garage. As soon as he put a white Stetson on his head and headed for one of the parked cars, Ali figured he was most likely Sheriff Renteria. Leaving Patty Patton behind, Ali hurried to catch up with him. "Excuse me," she said. "Sheriff Renteria?"

He stopped, turned, and removed the hat. "Yes?" he said. "What can I do for you?"

"My name is Ali Reynolds," she said. "I'm a friend of Jose Reyes. Are you aware that someone broke into their house?"

"You'll have to forgive me," he said. "We've been a little busy around here today. I am aware of the break-in. Since there were no injuries, I determined that it wasn't urgent. I've only now been able to spare a deputy long enough to send one out there. He's probably there by now. "

"It is urgent," Ali objected. "What's going to happen to the family? Jose is seriously injured. Teresa just underwent a C-section. They'll be coming home with three kids, including a new baby, to a house that is virtually uninhabitable."

"Unfortunate, of course," Renteria said. "And I and my department will do everything in our power to find the people responsible and bring them to justice."

"Sure you will," Ali said. "And will the people doing the investigating be the same people you've forbidden to visit Jose's hospital room?"

Sheriff Renteria looked pained. "I'm not sure where you're getting your information, but you're right. I did issue an order telling my people, sworn officers and civilians both, to stay away from PMC. This is a part of the country where dealing with Mexican drug cartels is a way of life. I have a very small department. I warned my people to stay away because I didn't want to put them at risk. For people like that, groups of cops can be an inviting target. We're already struggling to fill shifts and answer calls when we're just one officer down. If we ended up losing a couple more, it would be devastating."

"But not supporting an injured officer—"

"I'm sorry you disagree with my take on the situation," Sheriff Renteria said, "but you're evidently not from around here. I doubt you understand."

"It looks to me like you've simply abandoned the Reyes family, especially since the man who is supposed to be investigating the shooting seems to be far more concerned with accusing Jose and his wife of engaging in unlawful behavior than he is with finding out who shot him."

"I know Lieutenant Lattimore," Sheriff Renteria said. "I'm sure he's conducting his investigation to the very best of his ability. It's not my investigation, and I'm not commenting on it one way or the other."

"What if Jose is being framed?" Ali asked.

"If you have reason to believe that's true, you should take your concerns to Detective Lattimore. Now, if you'll excuse me, I need to go."

The sheriff got in the car and drove away, leaving Ali to fume. Just then three people—all of them wearing uniforms—emerged from the garage. One carried a banker's box. The other two, wearing latex gloves, each carried two red, white, and blue flat-rate postal boxes.

At the sight of those, Patty Patton sprang to life. "Hey," she said, dropping her most recent cigarette butt and hurrying after them. "What are you doing with those flat-rate boxes? They belong at the post office."

The third man in line stopped. He turned back to Patty and held his burden in her direction. "I don't think so, Patty," he said. "Take a whiff."

She stepped forward, sniffed, and then made a face. "Yuck. What is that?"

"That would be marijuana," he said. "I don't think you want this stuff going through the U.S. mail."

Patty Patton looked stricken. "Are you kidding me? You found that in Phil's garage?"

Another man emerged from the garage. This one wore gray slacks and a navy blue sport jacket. Ali immediately pegged him as a detective. He stopped long enough to lock the door before slapping a string of police tape across the doorway.

"Get that stuff out of here, guys," he ordered over his shoulder to the deputies serving as evidence techs. "You're not supposed to discuss this with anyone—no one at all."

As the deputies scurried away to deposit their respective loads in the back of an unmarked patrol car, Patty turned her attention from the postal boxes to the newcomer. "What's going on, Detective Zambrano?" she demanded.

"I'm investigating a homicide," he replied. "As it happens, you're one of the people I'm going to need to interview. When's the last time you saw Phil?"

"Saturday," Patty said. "At work. But where did the marijuana come from? How did it get into a flat-rate box?"

"I'm sure Phil could have answered that question," Zambrano answered. "Unfortunately, he's dead. It's possible Christine could have told us, too. Unfortunately, she's a raving maniac, and she's not talking to anybody. She's a lot more into screaming than she is into talking. Bottom line, I'm assuming Phil's the one who put it there. You always think of drug dealers having exotic smuggling arrangements. I have to say, packing it up and sending it through the mail has a certain understated elegance."

"Phil Tewksbury was not a drug dealer," Patty Patton said.

"Look, Patty," Zambrano said with a sigh. "I'm sorry. I'm sure you thought you were close to the guy, but we don't always know nearly as much about other people as we think we do. If you were to ask me about Jose Reyes, the same thing happened to me with him. I would have sworn Jose wouldn't be caught dealing drugs. Turns out I was just as wrong about him as you are about Phil."

"But this makes no sense," Patty objected. "Besides, Phil knew the ropes. Border mail gets spot-checked by sniffer dogs right along with everything else. The boxes wouldn't have made it past the dogs."

Zambrano sighed again. "Look, Patty, we found the drugs right here in Phil's garage, packaged and ready to tape shut and ship. We've lifted prints off the boxes. I'm willing to bet you any amount of money that those prints will turn out to belong to Phil Tewksbury. Maybe his wife figured out what he was up to and de- cided to put a stop to it. Or else maybe after all those years of living as a recluse, she finally blew a gasket and beat the crap out of him."

"Christine did not do this," Patty declared. "No way. Couldn't be."

"If you'd been the one she came chasing after with a bloody baseball bat in her hand, you might be sing- ing another tune."

"Softball bat," Patty said.

Zambrano nodded. "Softball," he agreed.

Watching this exchange from the sidelines, Ali wondered how it was that Patty knew what kind of a bat it was.

"I don't care if she came after you with a broom- stick," Patty said. "Christine definitely didn't kill Phil, not if he died in the garage. Is that where it hap- pened?"

Zambrano nodded.

"Well, then," Patty said, "trust me. Christine hasn't

left the house for years, hasn't so much as stepped outside. It's what, forty feet from the back door of the house to the door to the garage? She wouldn't go that far on her own. Ever."

"Look," Zambrano said, "I've heard all about that—the whole deal with the dead daughter and the Christmas tree and not leaving the house. I'm not buying it."

"Where is she?" Patty asked.

"Christine? She refused to respond to police orders. When we tried to remove her from the residence, she became combative and had to be restrained. She's been transported to the hospital in Nogales. From there she'll most likely go to Catalina Vista in Tucson, where she'll undergo a psych evaluation."

"What's wrong with you people?" Patty demanded. "You're dealing with a woman who hasn't set foot outside the four walls of her house in at least the past ten years, that I know of, so you can be pretty sure she's troubled to begin with. Then you turn up—burst into her house—and tell her that her husband is dead. What would you do in that situation, Detective Zambrano? Maybe you'd go berserk, too, especially if someone was bodily carrying you out of your own house. I'm pretty sure I would."

"We felt she was a danger to herself and others," Zambrano countered. "We did what we had to do." His cell phone rang. "Right," he said after a pause. "I'll go get 'em. On my way." He turned back to Patty. "Sorry," he said. "I need to go. If it's okay, I'd like to stop by the post office in the morning to do an official interview."

"Knock yourself out," Patty muttered as he walked away. "I don't care what you say. Christine didn't do it." She turned to go to her car and ran directly into Ali. "Oh," she said. "I forgot you were here."

"I've been listening to every word," Ali said. "It sounds as though, despite the evidence, you don't believe your friend was dealing drugs."

"I don't," Patty said. "Absolutely not! Phil was a worker, not a dealer; a saver, not a spender. It nearly killed him a couple of months ago when he had to cough up money to replace the windows on his house. Drives an old Ford pickup. Drove," she corrected. "Doesn't anymore."

"So not a flamboyant lifestyle."

"Hardly. As for Detective Zambrano's idea that Phil was trying to ship drugs in flat-rate boxes? Ridiculous. They'd never pass muster at the Border Patrol checkpoints. Phil wouldn't be that stupid."

"What about his wife?" Ali asked. "Would she be involved in any of this—the drug dealing, any of it?"

Patty shook her head. "No."

"And what about her husband's death?"

"Christine may be a lot of things, but she's not a killer. I believe somebody did this and they're trying to make it look like she's responsible because they know she's incapable of defending herself."

"Why?" Ali asked. "What's the matter with her?"

"With Christine?"

For the next little while, Patty recounted what she knew about Phil and Christine's history together, about the death of their only child and the painful aftermath. Patty didn't count it as gossiping, exactly.

Other people might be busy pointing the finger at Christine, and the only way she could make that stop was to tell what she knew.

"And she never left the house after that?" Ali asked.

"Not as far as I know. Wouldn't set foot outside, including walking as far as the garage. That's how come I know for sure she didn't kill Phil." Patty ground out her last cigarette. "I'd better go," she said. "I need to track Jess down and let him know what's happened."

"Who's Jess?" Ali asked.

"My substitute driver," Patty said sadly. "My permanent substitute driver. And I'll be back at work in the morning so I can talk to that damned detective, if nothing else. If you want to get hold of me to help organize that cleanup, that's where I'll be—at the post office. If you need to call me, my number's in the book."

41

2:00 P.M., Monday, April 12
Fountain Hills, Arizona

Humberto Laos had become an old crook by being a smart crook. He paid his people good money, and he expected them to earn it. When Tony and Sal had come back from dumping the girl's body, he had taken them at their word and hadn't given the matter another thought. They'd told him she was dead; he believed the girl was dead. He had told them to dump her in the desert. With any kind of luck, it would be months before someone stumbled across her body.

Because Humberto had plenty of money, he had plenty of sources of information. There were people in various cop shops and media outlets who, for a hefty cash payment made by a discreet third party, would provide the inside scoop on things that interested him, in this case the murder investigation into the death of Chico Hernández. When Humberto heard from one of his informants that a person of interest in the case was a seventeen-year-old girl who had been missing for three years, that made sense. The girls Chico pimped hadn't fallen out of trees. They had to come from somewhere.

So far, that was all to the good. Humberto knew that the girl the cops were looking for—presumably, the one whose prints they had found in his vehicle—was lying dead in the desert somewhere. As long as they were looking for the dead girl, they weren't looking at Humberto.

But Humberto believed in being thorough. So he checked with two more sources, both of whom were inside Phoenix PD. There he learned that the person of interest, the missing girl, was named Rose Ventana. She had run away at age fourteen and was thought to have a rose tattoo on her right boob.

Humberto knew for a fact that the part about the rose tattoo was true. The girl Chico had called Breeze definitely did have a rose tattoo, one with a few recent additions to the original design. Again, he wasn't especially concerned, but then things started to go south. One of his media sources came up with a very disturbing piece of information—a rumor, a tweet from Rose Ventana's sister—that maybe Rose wasn't dead at all; that she had been found badly injured on Friday and was being treated at an as yet unnamed hospital somewhere in Tucson.

Humberto was appalled. He could afford a lot of things, but he couldn't afford to have Breeze Domingo or Rose Ventana or whoever she was alive and able to talk. That was unacceptable. It was time for serious damage control, and it had to happen right away.

Humberto didn't call Sal and Tony in and read them the riot act. Instead, he opened the safe in the wall behind his desk and took out seventy-five thousand in cash. Then he went online and found photos of some of the known players—especially the parents and the homicide cop—anything that would help identify the targets.

With photos and the money loaded into a briefcase, Humberto left his chauffeur and the Bentley behind and drove himself to Phoenix in his silver Carrera. He parked outside a building that contained a high-end detail shop. Tossing his keys to an attendant, he went inside to look for Angel Moreno. Angel's company, Starshine, specialized in auto detailing. Angel himself was into another kind of work altogether.

"I've got a job for you," Humberto said, setting the briefcase on Angel's Formica-topped desk. "Three of them, actually. The sooner the better."

42

2:30 P.M., Monday, April 12
Tucson, Arizona

In her years as a patient advocate, Sister Anselm had dealt with plenty of challenging family situations, and this one was no different. She let Rose know that her family was waiting outside, but that was all. Her patient's wishes were paramount. It wasn't her responsibility to convince Rose to change her mind. It was a matter of watching and waiting. That was something Sister Anselm knew how to do. She was surprised, however, that the Fox family as a group seemed prepared to do the same thing—wait indefinitely.

They settled into the ICU waiting room and did just that. By midafternoon Rose's condition had improved enough that there was a good possibility she'd be moved out of the ICU later in the day. That was another bit of good news Sister Anselm couldn't share with Rose's anxious family, not until it actually happened.

Then Rose surprised her. "Still here?" she asked. With her jaw wired shut, the words came out in a distorted whisper, almost baby talk, but she was making the effort to speak, and Sister Anselm got the message.

"You mean is your family still here?" Sister Anselm asked.

Rose nodded.

"Yes, they are," Sister Anselm told her, sensing that something had changed. "They're waiting right outside."

"Sisters, too?"

"Yes, I've met Lily and Jasmine. They're lovely. You can only have one visitor at a time. Which one would you like me to send in first?"

There was a pause before Rose whispered, ". . . father."

That was not the answer Sister Anselm had expected. "That's who you want to see—your stepfather? Mr. Fox?"

Rose nodded. "Please."

"Right now?"

Rose nodded again.

Sister Anselm went to the door. "Mr. Fox? You can come in now."

He looked stunned. "Who, m-me?" he stammered.

"Yes, you," Sister Anselm said.

"But what about her mother?" Fox asked, giving his wife a questioning look as he rose to his feet. "This must be a mistake. Are you sure?"

"I'm sure," Sister Anselm said. "You're the one she asked for."

Once inside the room, Sister Anselm was prepared to leave them alone. "Stay," Rose ordered.

James Fox moved toward the bed. When he saw Rose's shattered face, he couldn't conceal his shock and dismay. Or his tears.

"Look awful," Rose managed.

"Oh, no," he said. "You're beautiful."

She shook her head. "Sorry," she said. "For running away."

"My fault," he said. "All my fault. We just want you home, Rose. We want you to get better."

"Good father," she said.

The unexpected praise caught James Fox by surprise. He sank into the room's only chair, covered his face with his hands, and sobbed while Sister Anselm looked on in wonder. She knew she might have played some small part in making this miracle happen, but she wasn't sure how.

By the time James Fox's five minutes were up, he had managed to quit crying. "We'll be outside," he said. "I'll send your mother in next."

Rose nodded. "Not yet," she said. "Later."

"See there?" Sister Anselm said to Rose once Fox left. "I told you your family wants you home."

"Yes," Rose whispered. Then, exhausted by the conversation, she drifted off to sleep. For the first time, there was a slight smile in the curve of her swollen lips.

Leaving Rose to sleep, Sister Anselm stepped into the waiting room where the Fox family was huddled together. Just then Al Gutierrez arrived with a middle-aged woman in tow. As soon as Al saw James Fox, the younger man stopped short, as if unsure what to do—stay or turn around and go. Fox solved the dilemma for them both by rushing over to him, grasping one of Al's hands in his, and pumping it. "Thank you," he said. "We can't thank you enough for finding her and saving her. And I'm sorry about last night."

By the time Fox's effusive greeting ended, the woman stepped forward to introduce herself. "I'm Detective Ariel Rush," she said. "You're Rose's family?"

The two parents and the two sisters nodded in unison.

"And you must be the patient advocate, the one Al told me about."

"Yes. I'm Sister Anselm."

Detective Rush looked around the room. "Has there been any public announcement about this—about your finding her?"

"Not yet," Connie answered. "We wanted to check with Rose before we said anything."

"Excellent," Detective Rush said. "Now, is there a conference room of some kind where we can have a private conversation? There have been some serious new developments in the case."

"Like what?" Connie asked.

"Your daughter may not be the only victim here," Detective Rush said. "In fact, she may be one of several. So far as we know, she's the only one who's still alive. As long as her killer doesn't know that, we have a better chance of catching him, because if he doesn't feel threatened, he may not go to ground. On the other hand, if he discovers she's alive, that may put Ms. Ventana's personal safety at risk. The sooner we can get her out of the hospital and into a more secure environment, the better I'm going to like it. For the time being, we have to keep Rose's situation out of the public eye. No interviews. No announcements. Even without media attention, someone could use the air ambulance records to track her here to the hospital."

"You really think she's in danger?" Connie asked.

Detective Rush nodded emphatically. Sister Anselm noticed that the two girls exchanged wary glances at that point, but she was too focused on solving the problem of Rose's safety to give the gesture any more than passing notice.

"I might have an idea about that," she said. "It can't be done immediately, but when Rose is well enough to be dismissed from the hospital, I believe I know of a place where she could stay in relative safety."

"Here in town?" Detective Rush asked.

"In a convent just up the road," Sister Anselm replied. "All Saints. There would be a lot less public access than there is here."

"Would the people at the convent go along with the idea?" Detective Rush asked.

"The reverend mother there is a friend of mine," Sister Anselm said. "I'll speak to her about it, and I'll also mention it to Rose's physician."

"Is there a chance I could interview her today?" Detective Rush asked. "I need to know if there's anything she can tell us that will help identify her attackers."

"There's nothing I can do as long as she's in the ICU. Visitors there are family members only. But it might be a good idea to hang around a little while longer, in case she's moved to another unit."

As far as patient confidentiality was concerned,

Sister Anselm knew she was pushing the envelope, but still . . .

"Was she sexually assaulted?" Detective Rush asked, handing Sister Anselm a business card.

Sister Anselm thought for a moment before she answered. "If there's an official protocol for the handling of rape kits, you might want to look into that."

Detective Rush got the hint. "Thank you," she said. "I will."

43

3:30 p.m., Monday, April 12
Tucson, Arizona

With Patty gone, only the young deputy was left at the scene. Gawkers had come and gone from time to time, peering curiously out of windows and pointing in the direction of the Tewksburys' house, but the deputy had waved them all on. Now he stepped aside so Ali could drive past, giving a respectful salute as she did. She suspected that the gesture was intended more for her exotic vehicle, her Cayenne, than it was for her.

Between Sonoita and I-10 on Highway 83, Ali was stopped at a Border Patrol checkpoint. There were several other vehicles in line, including three eighteen-wheelers, all of which were thoroughly checked by a drug-sniffing dog. As the dog carefully worked his way around and under each of the vehicles, Ali realized Patty Patton had been right. There were checkpoints along every route leading north from Nogales. Regardless of who was involved in the drug dealing, there was no way those flat-rate boxes could have been shipped in a regular mail truck without being detected. If they weren't leaving Santa Cruz County on mail trucks, where were they going, and how were they getting there? And what was the point of those marijuana-filled flat-rate boxes they had seen being carted out of Phil Tewksbury's garage?

What about Christine? Would she really step outside her house for the first time in years for no other reason than to murder her husband in cold blood? The detective was evidently convinced she was responsible; Patty was not. Just as Lattimore was convinced Jose Reyes was guilty of drug dealing but his wife, Teresa, claimed to know him better than that.

Driving back to Tucson, Ali found herself comparing those two incidents side by side. Patagonia was a small town—a very small town—with two drug-related violent crimes in as many days. No one had come right out and said that the incidents might be related. No one had even mentioned it, but Ali wondered about that. Perhaps if she could get to the bottom of what had happened to Phil and Christine Tewksbury, she'd be able to learn something about what had happened to Jose and Teresa Reyes, too.

Despite the supposed evidence against him, Jose continued to maintain that he was innocent, that he had nothing to do with drug dealing. If he had died as a result of his injuries, the evidence found in his vehicle most likely would have been accepted at face value. No one would have been around to claim otherwise, and no one other than his immediate family would have cared. Crooked cop dies in drug deal. So what?

Ali's belief in Jose's innocence remained unshaken. It appeared, however, that someone had gone to a great deal of effort to frame him. And what if the

Tewksbury situation were more of the same? If Phil could be dismissed as a drug dealer—yet another dead drug dealer—who would remain in his corner? And if you were going to frame someone for murder, who would be a better target than Christine—a troubled woman, someone the whole town seemed to have dismissed as being a hopeless nutcase?

To answer that question, Ali decided to attempt going straight to the source—the nutcase herself. There was always a chance that Christine wouldn't be allowed visitors. She might be under sedation, or she might simply refuse to speak to a complete stranger. On the other hand, she might be happy to tell her side of the story to someone who wasn't a cop and was somewhat sympathetic. Before getting on I-10, Ali stopped the car long enough to find the address of Catalina Vista, a psychiatric hospital in Tucson, and program it into her GPS.

On the way there, Ali worked out what she hoped sounded like a reasonable cover story to help her gain access to the facility and to Christine. She wasn't surprised to find that the lobby of Catalina Vista looked more like an upscale residential hotel than a psych ward. A young woman who looked terminally bored sat behind a granite-topped reception counter, reading a paperback Joanna Brady novel.

"I'm here to meet with Christine Tewksbury to make preliminary arrangements for her husband's funeral," Ali announced brusquely, slipping one of her business cards across the desk.

Other than her name, address, and phone numbers, the only word on the card was "consultant." It didn't say what kind of consultant and gave no additional information, but that didn't seem to matter. It passed muster with the young woman, who barely looked up from her book as she shoved a clipboard in Ali's direction.

"Sign in here," she said. "I believe Mrs. Tewksbury is in the dayroom at the moment. That's at the end of the hall. Press the button next to the door. I'll buzz you in and out."

When Ali entered the dayroom, she found at least a dozen people gathered there, most of them clumped around a flat-screen television. The television viewers all seemed deeply engrossed in watching an episode of *Judge Judy*. Three people sat at a table playing dominoes. In the far corner of the room, a solitary woman in a hospital gown and robe paced anxiously back and forth in front of a floor-to-ceiling window.

She was thin to the point of being gaunt. Long, stringy gray hair hung past her narrow waist. Of all the people in the room, she looked like the one Ali wanted.

"Christine?" Ali asked uncertainly. "Christine Tewksbury?"

With her face distorted by what looked like fury, Christine spun around and strode toward Ali, forcing her to take a cautionary step backward.

"Who are you?" Christine demanded. "Are you a doctor? Are you a nurse? They're keeping me here against my will. I want to go home. I want to go back to Phil. I know he doesn't love me anymore, and I don't blame him for that, but he's a good man, really, and he takes very good care of me. Please. Make them let me go home."

Ali realized then that what had appeared to be anger was more likely despair. The desperation in Christine's voice was heartbreaking. She wanted to go home. She seemed to have no understanding about what had happened, why she was there, or even that her husband was dead. Or maybe Christine Tewksbury was an excellent actress who understood everything about her situation and was dealing with it in the best way possible.

"My name is Ali Reynolds," Ali explained. "Patty Patton is a friend of mine. She told me about what had happened to you. I thought I'd come by and see if there's anything you needed."

"Patty works with my husband," Christine said, nodding. "And I do need something. I need Phil. Where is he? Is he still at work? Tell Patty that as soon as he gets done with his route, he needs to come pick me up. I don't know why those men broke into my house like that. I tried to make them leave me alone—I was screaming at them—but they put handcuffs on me and brought me here. They tried to tell me that Phil is dead, but I don't believe it. It's not possible. He was fine yesterday. Why would he be dead today? Someone needs to let him know where I am so he can come get me."

Christine's state of denial was so complete that Ali decided the best approach was to go along with it and pretend that Phil was alive.

"I'm sure your husband loves you very much," she said.

"Yes, he does," Christine agreed. "Although I'm sure he loves Ollie, too."

"Ollie?" Ali asked, taking a seat in a nearby chair. "Who's Ollie?"

After a moment's hesitation, Christine stopped pacing and sat down beside Ali. "Ollie is Phil's girlfriend," she explained. "I don't mind that he has a girlfriend, you see, but I wish he wouldn't bring her to the house. That's not right. Not with me living there. It's disrespectful. I don't like it. Cassie won't like it, either."

Ali had picked up enough of Christine's life story to know that Cassie, Phil and Christine's daughter, had been dead for years. If Christine somehow thought her daughter was alive, how much of the rest of the story was true? At this point, did Christine Tewksbury have any idea what was real and what wasn't? For that matter, what was her grasp on the difference between right and wrong? But the idea of a girlfriend thrown into the mix put the whole situation in a different light. And since Christine was willing to answer questions right then, Ali went right on asking them.

"Phil has a girlfriend?"

"Oh, yes," Christine said, "for months now. It's supposed to be a big secret, and I haven't let on that I know, but I found a letter he wrote to her. He left it sitting on the counter. It was silly. 'Dear Olive Oyl,' he said. And in the middle of the note, he called her Ollie, and he signed it, 'Love, Popeye.' That was the only part of the letter that was silly. The rest of it was real. He was telling her all about me—about what's wrong with me. That wasn't right. What's wrong with me is nobody else's business, especially not hers."

Patty had said that Christine hadn't left the house in years. Had Phil Tewksbury been so thoughtless as to bring the other woman in his life into the house with Christine still there?

"You're saying Ollie's been to your house?" Ali asked.

"Oh, yes. She was there this morning," Christine said confidently.

"Did you see her?"

"No, but I smelled her perfume. At least I think it was her perfume. It wasn't mine. Who else's would it be?"

"Did you tell the officers who came to your house earlier that you suspected someone else had been there?"

"I didn't tell them anything. I wanted them out of my house. I wanted them to leave me alone, but they wouldn't."

"This is important, Christine," Ali said. "Do you have any proof that some other person was in your house today?"

"Only the bat," Christine said. "Cassie's new bat. It wasn't there in the living room last night when I went to bed. I thought Phil had gotten rid of it, but this morning it was there by my chair as if by magic, and just when I needed it, too, when all those people came charging through my house without my permission. You do believe me, don't you?"

In a way, Ali did believe her. Part of the story sounded like the fantastical ravings of a madwoman, but part of it sounded like undeniable truth. Ali knew that the Tewksburys' house had been searched earlier in the day. Chances were that if Phil had entertained a girlfriend there, they would have found some evidence of her visit. And if there had been correspondence between Phil and Ollie squirreled away, that would have been found, too. Under the circumstances, the fact that Phil had had a girlfriend would be another black mark for Christine. In a homicide investigation, it was often only a short step from insane to insanely jealous.

But what about the presence of another person in the house that day, as either a possible perpetrator or a possible witness? Had Christine tried to tell Deputy Carson or Sheriff Renteria about that earlier when they had accosted the poor woman in her home? The presence of another person might be vitally important, but with Christine screaming at them and brandishing a lethal weapon, Ali doubted the officers on the scene had paid close attention to what she said. After all, everyone in town seemed to be convinced that Christine Tewksbury was crazy, and listening to crazy people was . . . well . . . crazy.

"Do you happen to know someone named Jose Reyes?" Ali asked. "Is he a friend of your husband's?"

Christine shook her head. "I don't recognize the name. He might be one of the guys at the café. Phil goes there every morning for breakfast."

"What about drugs?" Ali asked.

"What about them?"

"Is there a chance Phil might be involved in the drug trade?"

"What kind of drugs?"

"Marijuana," Ali said.

"Phil?" Christine said with a harsh laugh. "Are you kidding? He doesn't even smoke cigarettes. What would he do with marijuana? Besides, he's too busy working. That's all he does, really—he works, and he looks after me."

Ali glanced at her watch. Haley had an evening class to go to, and it was close to time for her to drop off the girls. Ali wanted to be back at the hospital in case she was needed to help chase after Lucy and Carinda. She stood up. "I'm sorry, Mrs. Tewksbury," she said. "I need to go now."

"Can I go with you?" Christine asked. "Please? What if Phil doesn't come get me today? What if he doesn't know I'm here?"

In some part of Christine's tangled reality, she truly believed that her husband was alive and coming to get her. It wasn't Ali's responsibility to convince her otherwise.

"I'm sure he does," she said reassuringly. "And I'm sure he'll come for you as soon as he can."

"But what if he doesn't?" Christine asked. Distress took over. Her voice rose to a keening wail. "What if I have to stay here forever? Please take me with you. Please."

By then, alerted to the disturbance by Christine's raised voice, a pair of uniformed attendants rushed into the room. While they tried unsuccessfully to calm Christine, Ali hurried to the door and buzzed to be let out. All the way down the hall and out through the lobby, she could hear that terrible, despairing cry. She felt guilty. Ali's presence was what had caused Christine's outburst, but Christine was the one who would suffer the consequences.

Back in her vehicle, Ali had to call information to get Patty Patton's telephone numbers. She tried both the home number and the one listed for the post office. In each case, the phone rang and no one answered. Patty was a landline person, and she evidently wasn't home.

"Patty, it's Ali Reynolds," Ali said into what sounded like an old-fashioned desktop answering machine. "It's about Christine, and it's important. Give me a call when you get this."

44

5:30 P.M., Monday, April 12
Tucson, Arizona

In the course of the afternoon, Sister Anselm ushered family members into Rose Ventana's room in the ICU. She knew that the visits were wearing on Rose, not only emotionally but also physically. The difficulty of communicating through her wired-shut jaw made speaking exceptionally difficult. Between each visit, she needed time to rest and regroup.

Sister Anselm was also aware that Detective Rush had taken her words of advice to heart. She and Al Gutierrez had spent the afternoon sitting on the sidelines. Sometimes Al seemed to be fielding phone calls while Detective Rush worked on her computer. Sister Anselm knew they were hanging around in hopes of interviewing Rose Ventana.

That opportunity came at five-thirty in the afternoon, with Rose's long-awaited move from the ICU to a regular wing of the hospital. Since her new room was only a few doors away from Jose Reyes's new room, many of the people Sister Anselm met in the corridor and in the new waiting room were familiar faces.

Shortly after the move, when the Fox family left for dinner in the cafeteria, Sister Anselm turned to her charge. "There's someone else in the waiting room who would like to speak to you."

"Who?"

"Detective Ariel Rush, a homicide detective from Phoenix, and Al Gutierrez, the Border Patrol agent who found you."

"Do I have to talk to them?" Rose asked. Her mumbled words were understandable, but just barely.

"You don't have to," Sister Anselm said, "but they'd like you to. Detective Rush needs your help."

"Why? Who's dead?"

Sister Anselm had noticed that during their brief visits in the course of the day, Rose's parents and sisters had all managed to avoid any discussions of Rose's life as Breeze Domingo. They also hadn't mentioned anything about Chico Hernández's murder, leaving it up to Sister Anselm to break the bad news.

"A friend of yours," Sister Anselm said. "Chico Hernández."

"He's dead?"

"Detective Rush is investigating his murder. She seems to think his killer may also be responsible for what happened to you. So if you'll speak to her, you may be able to help."

Rose thought about that for a moment, then nodded. "All right."

Sister Anselm went out into the corridor, caught Detective Rush's eye. "You can come in now," she said. "Do you want me to leave?"

"Not necessary," Detective Rush said. "This is a

preliminary interview only. With Agent Gutierrez and me here, she'll probably be more comfortable with you here as well."

As they entered the room, Rose's eyes followed Al, who was carrying an oversize briefcase. "You found me?" she asked him.

It seemed to take him a moment to understand her. When he did, he nodded.

"Thank you," Rose said.

That sentence was entirely understandable. Al's face broke into a wide grin. "You're welcome," he said.

During this exchange, Detective Rush was busy placing her open computer on the movable table next to Rose's bed.

"Good afternoon, Ms. Ventana," she said. "Ariel Rush from the Homicide unit of Phoenix PD. I'd like to record this. There's a video device loaded into my computer. If you don't mind, we'll be using that to record this session."

Rose nodded. "It's okay," she said.

After listing the time, place, and people present, Ariel Rush launched off on her questions.

"With the help of Agent Gutierrez here, I'm currently investigating the homicide of one Chico Hernández. Since you and he were both reported missing by your roommates on Saturday, I assume you know him?"

Rose nodded.

"I also have a slide show that I've loaded onto my computer," Detective Rush continued. "I'd like you to take a look at the photos and let me know if any one of those individuals is someone you recognize."

The montage contained ten photographs in all. Watching from several feet away, Sister Anselm noticed that most of them were mug shots and some were simple head shots. Two of them had a grainy texture that looked as though it might have come from some kind of security video. As Detective Rush clicked through, Rose watched the photos; Sister Anselm followed them while also watching Rose. The young woman's eyes widened in shock at the third photo in the group, and again several shots later.

"So do you recognize anyone here?" Detective Rush asked.

The answer was obvious, and Rose didn't try to deny it. She nodded.

"I'm going to go back through the photos one at a time," Detective Rush said. "You'll notice each photo in the montage is numbered. If you recognize one of them, please tell me the appropriate number."

Rose stared at the computer screen while the photos reappeared. "Three," she mumbled a few seconds later. "And eight."

"You recognize two of them?"

Rose nodded again. Nodding was clearly easier for her than speaking.

"And can you tell me how you know these gentlemen?"

Rose's eyes sought out Sister Anselm, asking for guidance on whether she should answer the question. During Rose's time in the ICU, a remarkable bond of trust had grown between the patient advocate and her charge.

"You need to tell her," Sister Anselm said gently. "You need to tell Detective Rush all of it."

"Those men in the pictures. They took me to the desert," Rose said. "Left me."

"They're the ones who dumped you?"

"Yes."

"Did they do anything else?"

"Hit me; kicked me."

"Anything more?"

This time Rose said nothing.

"Tell me about Mr. Hernández," Detective Rush continued. "Was he your employer?"

Rose hesitated but finally nodded.

"Your pimp?"

Again there was no answer forthcoming.

"Ms. Ventana," Detective Rush said. "As you are no doubt aware, girls on the street often don't bother reporting rapes. They think they won't be taken seriously by the law enforcement community, but that's not true for me. Just because you may have worked as a prostitute in the past doesn't make you fair game. So tell me about the two men in these photos—number three and number eight. In addition to beating you and kicking you, did they do anything else? Did they sexually assault you, for example?"

There was another long pause before Rose's whispered answer. "Yes."

"Earlier today, Mr. Gutierrez, the Border Patrol agent who found you, and I visited the crime scene near Three Points. We came away with trace evidence that may include DNA from one of your assailants. Unless you want to, you can't be compelled to give me any information about your medical condition or the course of treatment, but it would be a huge favor to me and to my investigation if I were to know some of the details of your treatment. For example, at the time you were admitted to PMC, do you know if a rape kit was taken?"

Rose looked questioningly at Sister Anselm, who nodded.

"Yes," Rose said finally. "It was."

"And if we can identify your attacker, is it your intention to press charges?"

Again Rose looked to Sister Anselm for confirmation. Another nod.

"Yes," Rose said. "It is."

"I'll need your signature on an actual police report to make that official," Detective Rush said. She took possession of the briefcase, opened it, and dug out a piece of paper. For the next several minutes, she scribbled on it before handing it over to Rose. "I know signing with your hand in a splint is tough. If you can make an X at the bottom, we'll have Sister Anselm and Mr. Gutierrez sign as witnesses. That way, I can make sure the kit is sent along to the crime lab so they can start processing it."

When the paper was properly signed and witnessed, Detective Rush returned to the interview. "Now, please tell me about the last time you remember seeing Mr. Hernández."

"Thursday. Going to Fountain Hills."

"To Fountain Hills?" Detective Rush confirmed. "Why there?"

"Client," Rose replied.

"What client? Did you know his name?"

"No."

"Was the client in the photo montage?"

"No."

"So you went to a house in Fountain Hills to see a client. What happened there?"

"He burned me," Rose whispered. "Cut me. Raped me. He liked hurting me."

"Do you know his name? Do you remember an address or a street name?"

Rose thought for a long time before answering. "Big house," she said. "Last street. Backed up to the desert."

"More than one story?"

Rose closed her eyes as if trying to concentrate. "Two," she said, "and a basement."

"Anything else?"

"Big gate, guardhouse, steep hill."

"If I brought you photos of gates in Fountain Hills, would you be able to recognize the right one and choose it?"

"Maybe."

"I hope so," Detective Rush said. "We want to find the guys who dumped you, the ones in the photos, but I believe the guy in the house in Fountain Hills is a big-time bad guy. We know of at least three other possible victims, all of them dead but all showing injuries similar to yours—evidence of burning and of cutting."

"All dead?" Rose asked.

Detective Rush nodded. "Dead, but with no DNA."

"Condom," Rose muttered.

Detective Rush paused. "Wait. He used a condom when he assaulted you?"

Rose nodded.

"But the guys who dumped you did not?"

"No."

"That probably means one of two things," Detective Rush said. "It could be that the guy in Fountain Hills is worried about picking up a local garden-variety STD. It's also possible that he's worried about leaving DNA lying around because he knows it may already be listed in the DNA database."

Detective Rush seemed to be casting around for another set of questions, but Sister Anselm called a halt. "That's all Rose can do for right now. She needs to rest."

The detective closed her computer. "That's all right," she said. "She may have given me exactly what I need to know."

45

5:00 P.M., Monday, April 12
Patagonia, Arizona

Once in her Camaro, Patty Patton drove away from the Tewksbury crime scene with every intention of going straight home. But then she started thinking about those flat-rate boxes. At this point she was still prepared to shout Christine's innocence from the rooftops, but she was no longer so sure about Phil.

How dare he pull her post office—her blemish-free post office—into this kind of controversy? And if he had used the flat-rate boxes to move drugs around, had he carried them from one place to another in his mail truck, a vehicle that was assigned to her operation?

That ugly realization hit home, leaving Patty so upset that she could barely see to drive. When she came to the driveway of her house, she drove straight past it. Instead, she returned to the post office and pulled in back, next to the locked storage yard with the mail truck sitting inside, safe and secure under lock and key.

The truck looked harmless enough, sitting there all

by itself. There was nothing sinister about it, nothing to indicate it had participated in any kind of wrongdoing, but for Patty's own peace of mind, she needed to know. Was Phil Tewksbury true blue, or had he played her for a fool all these years?

Making up her mind, she put the Camaro back in gear, made a rooster-tail U-turn, and drove two blocks farther east to the parking lot of the San Rafael Café. It was getting on toward dinnertime, and there were several cars parked in the lot. Eventually, she found the one she was looking for: Border Patrol K-9 unit #347.

Several of the local Border Patrol agents, young bachelor types looking for lower rent, had taken rooms in various houses around town. Mark Embry, of unit #347, and his German shepherd, Max, were Patty's hands-down favorites.

Once a week Mark's mother sent her son a care package—homemade cookies and/or books—in a flat-rate box. The packages, shipped special delivery, came every Friday morning like clockwork, and Friday afternoon, once he was off shift, Mark would come by the post office to pick up his goodies. When he came in to pick up the mail, he always ignored the NO DOGS ALLOWED sign and brought Max inside. When Max was the dog in question, Patty ignored the sign, too.

As expected, the dog was waiting patiently in the backseat of Mark's vehicle. That meant Max's handler was in the restaurant chowing down on dinner. When Patty went inside, she found Mark seated at the counter. As Patty slipped onto the stool next to him, he looked up from his hamburger plate and smiled.

"Afternoon, Ms. Patton," he said. "How are things?"

Patty didn't know how much he knew or didn't know about the situation with Phil Tewksbury. She wanted to have Mark's help without having to reveal too many details.

"I hear that dog of yours is pretty smart," she ventured.

Mark nodded. "Max is the best," he agreed.

"He can tell if drugs are in a vehicle, right?" she said.

"Absolutely. As soon as he smells them, he alerts and lets me know."

"What about if drugs were there and aren't anymore?"

"Once we have the alert, it's my job to locate the merchandise. There are times we know that a certain vehicle has been used in the drug trade even though the drugs aren't actually present when we search it."

"So there's a residual scent."

"You and I probably wouldn't notice it, but Max does. Why? What's this all about?"

"Since you're not on duty, I'm wondering if you and Max could do me a favor. An unofficial favor."

"Sure thing," Mark said. "Whatever you need."

"I'd like you to bring Max and follow me around to the back of the post office."

Without further objection and leaving money on the counter to cover his tab, he followed her out of the restaurant. When they reached the back of the post office, she used her key to let Mark and his dog into the yard where the truck was parked. Issuing the command "find it," Mark let the dog go. Max trotted around the whole expanse of yard, and absolutely nothing happened—not one thing.

"Try leading him over to the truck," Patty suggested.

Mark obliged, but again, there was no reaction.

"I don't know what you're looking for," he said, "but I don't think it's here."

"Thanks, Mark," Patty told him. "I appreciate the help."

Patty's heart was lighter as she watched them leave. Whatever Phil had been doing, he hadn't been using the truck. That was a huge relief. After closing and re-securing the gate, she decided on a whim that she'd go back to the café and have some dinner.

46

6:30 P.M., Monday, April 12
Nogales, Arizona

Sheriff Renteria went back to his office, sat behind his desk, considered his options, and waited for a phone call.

He was faced with two entirely separate cases, only one of which was his to solve. He didn't have to call Duane Lattimore and ask to review the Reyes crime scene photos because he remembered what he had seen there all too well. The scattered money; the drugs; the bullet casings; and something that had seemed more puzzling than important at the time—an empty flat-rate box from the United States Postal Service. Now that he had been to the Phil Tewksbury homicide scene, and now that he had seen those other flat-rate boxes, all of them stuffed full with plastic-wrapped containers of marijuana, he knew that the cases were related. Knew as in knew in his gut. What he was waiting for now was the fingerprint evidence.

Flat-rate boxes with fingerprints had been found at both crime scenes and in the course of the search warrant execution at the Reyes residence. The same prints had been found on the lug wrench at the scene of the shooting. Because of his connections inside the crime lab, Sheriff Renteria already knew that none of those prints belonged to either Jose or Teresa Reyes, and when the prints had been run through the Automated Fingerprint Identification System, there hadn't been any hits.

Sheriff Renteria hoped that tonight all that would change. He had sent Detective Zambrano on a mission to the coroner's office to pick up a set of prints from Phil Tewksbury's body and take them to Tucson. He was hoping that the prints, along with the stack of other evidence found in Phil Tewksbury's truck—the head scarf, wig, and sunglasses—would seal the deal. As far as Renteria was concerned, the story seemed pretty straightforward. Phil shoots Jose Reyes; Christine bashes Phil's head in; Christine gets shipped off to the funny farm; end of story; two cases closed. What he needed was to find solid leads that would link the two men.

When his phone rang, Renteria grabbed it during the first ring.

"Okay," Zambrano said. "I've got Phil's prints from the coroner, and I'm on my way to the crime lab."

"Have you spoken to Lattimore about all this?"

"Yes. I figured we'd have to clue him on what we had on the Tewksbury case so we could get access to what he has on the Reyes shooting. But even though we may have identified Lattimore's shooter, he's not backing off his investigation."

"He's still going after Jose and Teresa for possible drug dealing?"

"Yup. He's got that bit in his teeth, and he's running with it. I suggested we get together at the department tomorrow morning around ten and figure out the next step. He's not going to like it, but from where I'm standing, we're all going to have to work together. Reyes and Tewksbury may be two separate cases on paper, but it's looking more and more to me like they're related."

"What's next on your agenda?" the sheriff asked.

"I had hoped to get Patty Patton's interview out of the way tonight," Zambrano said, "but by the time I get back from Tucson, it'll probably be too late. I'd rather interview Patty at home than at the post office. Once news gets out about what happened to Phil, that place is going to be like Grand Central Station. For right now I'm planning on interviewing her as soon as we get the Lattimore meeting out of the way."

"You can only do what you can do," Sheriff Renteria said. He didn't add the words "with the least amount of overtime possible," but he could have. "When you do get around to interviewing Patty, be gentle with her. She's taking Phil's death pretty hard."

"That's not surprising," Zambrano said. "They worked together for twenty years. That's longer than I've been married."

"What's the situation on obtaining those additional search warrants?"

"We're hoping to have the warrants for the phone and bank records by noon tomorrow. On the other hand, there's a chance they'll come through tonight. I've got a deputy out chasing a judge."

"Good.

Renteria wondered if a search of Phil Tewksbury's

phone records was where they'd find some meaningful connections between Phil and Jose Reyes. So far, the only thing they knew for sure was that Phil had delivered the mail to Jose and Teresa's home.

It pained Sheriff Renteria to think that both Phil and Jose, two supposedly fine, upstanding men, had somehow been enticed into the deadly easy-money world of illicit drugs. And that was only part of the sheriff's worry. That old saw about one bad apple kept running through his mind. He wondered how many other people, ones who were also considered pillars of their Santa Cruz County communities, would also be implicated before the two investigations came to an end.

For a time after Zambrano hung up, Renteria remained at his desk, staring at the photo of Midge that still sat on the credenza on the far side of his office. That picture was a particular favorite of his, taken during Midge's senior year in high school. He kept it there as a reminder not only of their own marriage but also as a reminder of what marriage was all about. That brought him right back to Phil and Christine Tewksbury.

Unfortunately, the sheriff knew a good deal about the tragedy that had wrecked Phil and Christine's lives. A deputy back then, Renteria had been one of the responding officers summoned by Phil's frantic 911 call the night of the accident. Phil had been charging through the underbrush along the shoulder of the road, desperately searching for some trace of his missing daughter, who, he claimed, had been asleep in the backseat. At first, when there was no sign at all of the girl, there had been some concern that maybe Phil was mistaken, that injuries from the accident had left him confused, making the distraught father think his daughter had been with him when she really wasn't.

Everyone but Phil himself had pretty well given up searching for Cassidy when the tow truck arrived on the scene. The driver had asked several of the people gathered there—deputies and onlookers—to line up on the passenger side of the vehicle and see if they could manhandle it back onto its wheels. Renteria had been one of the six or seven men who turned their shoulders to the task. When they succeeded on the third try, that was where they found the lifeless body, pinned flat beneath the wreckage.

The end of Cassidy Tewksbury's short life marked the beginning of her parents' never-ending tragedy. In the days between Christmas and New Year's, Deputy Renteria had been in and out of their house several times, filling out necessary paperwork and gathering information for his written reports. What still haunted him about those long-ago events were the contrasts he had seen everywhere he looked.

The house had been gaily decorated in anticipation of Christmas. A lovely artificial tree, surrounded by a stack of brightly wrapped gifts, stood in front of the living room window. A collection of handblown crystal angels stood atop the wooden mantel on the fireplace, and three hand-decorated but empty stockings hung there, waiting for Christmas morning.

Wild with grief, Christine's starkly pale, tearstained face had been completely at odds with the colorful holiday decor. Phil had answered the questions with terse replies that bristled with grim self-recrimination. At the time Manuel Renteria already knew that many marriages weren't strong enough to withstand the death of a child, and he had wondered if Phil and Christine's relationship would ever recover.

At first the only thing most people noticed was that Christine stopped coming out of the house. No one else seemed to be going inside it. Phil emerged. He went to work; he went to the store and did the shopping; but there was no sign of his wife. As time went on, people noticed the bedraggled Christmas tree and began speculating about how long it would be until it went away. All these years later, the forlorn tree stood there still, decorated but only partially lit.

Manuel Renteria realized that in all the intervening years, he had never laid eyes on Christine Tewksbury, not even once, not until today, when he and Deputy Carson and Detective Zambrano had knocked on Phil and Christine's door and let themselves into the house. It had been like stepping into a time capsule. Nothing in the room had changed—not the tree, not the presents, not the dusty crystal angels on the mantel, not the hanging Christmas stockings, and not the furniture, either. The room hadn't changed, but Christine had.

Back then Renteria remembered her as a well-built woman, a little old to have a daughter as young as Cassidy, but attractive and fit. There was nothing attractive or fit about the enraged woman they found lurking in the Tewksbury living room today. Christine was little more than a gaunt, snaggletoothed hag. A shapeless shift that appeared to be several sizes too big now swamped her sallow body. Long gray hair, lank and greasy, hung past her waist. She was missing several teeth. Sitting in a filthy recliner, she had a clear view of an old-fashioned television console, but the set wasn't turned on. Next to the recliner stood a grimy TV tray with what looked like the remains of a half-eaten dish of oatmeal.

That was something that took Sheriff Renteria's breath away. Christine Tewksbury had slaughtered her husband, then she had gone back inside and calmly eaten her breakfast. That was beyond cold-blooded.

The three men had entered the room in single file but without drawing their weapons.

"What are you doing here?" Christine demanded.

"We're here to talk to you about what happened to your husband," Renteria said.

"No," Christine insisted. "No one is supposed to come here when Phil isn't home. Come back when he's here."

"You know we can't do that," the sheriff said. "Phil is dead."

Christine's response to that was one of immediate rage. "No!" she shrieked, half rising out of her chair. "That's a lie! Phil's at work!"

On the way to the house, Renteria had anticipated finding Christine a wheelchair-bound invalid. Deputy Carson had warned them in advance about the bat, and it was a good thing. Reaching down to pick it up, Christine had exploded out of the recliner like a crazed jack-in-the box. While she screamed and brandished the weapon, it had taken all three officers and two shots from Detective Zambrano's Taser to subdue her enough to put her in cuffs.

Ultimately, they managed to wrestle her out of the house and into the back of a patrol car, where she continued to scream and pound her head against the window as she was driven away.

Once she was gone, Sheriff Renteria had spent hours at the house and in the garage, following his crime scene techs as they photographed the scene and searched for evidence. Renteria gave the guys full credit. They had found two tiny and almost invisible screw holes in the outside of the door frame on the garage door. The holes had been plugged with a dollop of toothpaste that was crusty on the outside and still semi-soft on the inside.

From the distinct straight lines visible on both of Phil Tewksbury's legs, they had deduced that Christine must have used something—most likely a string or a wire—to trip him. So far, they had found no evidence of string, wire, or wire screws in the house or in the trash. Tomorrow the sheriff planned to have his officers perform a grid search of the entire property to see if Christine had disposed of the evidence by tossing it into the yard.

In other words, what had happened was obvious, but as he stared at Midge's smiling face in the photo, what Manuel Renteria still wanted to know was why. After all those years of being cared for by her husband, why had Christine Tewksbury suddenly snapped? What was it that had driven her over the edge and into a murderous rage?

If, as Patty Patton claimed, Christine hadn't set foot outside the house in years, why had she done so now, not once but twice—once to lay the trap with the trip wire and once to do the actual killing? Why kill her husband in the garage when she could just as easily have attacked him in the house—when he was asleep in bed, for instance? If she'd been intent on murder, wouldn't it have been easier to do the deed inside the house? Why go to all that trouble of setting the trap outside? Was it to deflect suspicion?

More than that, why do it at all? And then, almost as though Midge had spoken aloud, Sheriff Renteria had his answer. He immediately picked up his phone and called Detective Zambrano again.

"Whenever you see Patty, ask her about Phil's private life."

"What do you mean his private life? Like an affair or something?"

"Exactly," Sheriff Renteria said. "If he was having an affair, that might supply a motive. What if Phil Tewksbury was fooling around with some other woman and Christine found out about it?"

"After what we saw today," Zambrano said, "you could hardly blame him."

"Maybe you couldn't blame him, but Christine sure as hell could," the sheriff said. "And if he did have an outside interest, Patty will know about it."

"What if the other woman turns out to be Patty Patton?"

That one set Sheriff Renteria back on his heels. He hadn't even thought about that.

"Crap," he said. "I don't know. I guess you'll need to ask her."

He hung up the phone and went back to staring at Midge's silent photo.

If Patty turns out to be Phil's girlfriend, Renteria told himself, *there goes another pillar of the community.*

47

6:30 P.M., Monday, April 12
Patagonia, Arizona

By the time Patty made it home from dinner, she was done. Eating at the café had been a tactical error, because she'd been forced to do far too much talking. Was it true Christine Tewksbury had murdered her husband? People had heard rumors that bundles of drugs had been found in Phil's garage. How was it possible that the nicest guy in town was actually a drug dealer? In other words, everyone wanted to know what Patty knew and how long she had known it.

When she came in the front door and saw the voice-mail light blinking on her phone, she was tempted to ignore it. After all, it was bound to be more bad news. But when she saw the number listed on the display and realized it was Ali Reynolds calling, she picked up the phone and dialed back.

"Sorry it took a while for me to get back to you," Patty said. "I stopped off and had some dinner on the way home."

"I'm doing the same thing on the way to the hospital," Ali said. "Some relative or other of Teresa's showed up this afternoon to help with the little ones, so I got a break. But I did stop by to see Christine."

"And?"

"She seems to think Phil had a girlfriend."

For a moment Patty said nothing. This was not news to her. She had suspected Phil had a girlfriend for a long time, and why shouldn't he? He was devoted to Christine, but Patty was of the opinion that, after years of being punished for his daughter's death, he deserved to have some kind of life and some kind of fun.

Months ago Patty had noticed Phil starting to take a little more pride in his appearance: He didn't wear the same uniform two days in a row; he took more trouble arranging his comb-over; sometimes he even whistled or hummed as he took the mail bins out to his truck.

Yes, Patty had noticed, and she hadn't said a single word about it to Phil or to anyone else, either, because it was no one else's business. That didn't mean she hadn't wondered, though. Who was it? Where had he met her? Phil wasn't the kind to hang out in bars. Maybe it was someone he had met at the café, but if that were the case, someone probably would have noticed and mentioned it. When she noticed he was often late coming back from his route, especially on Mondays, Patty concluded that it had to be someone on his route.

The idea that Phil would casually pull his mail truck off into someone's yard and park it while he indulged in a nooner was more than a bit disturbing, but obviously, he and his gal pal were incredibly discreet, because not a whisper of it ever came back to Patty. The previous week, when he had come back later than usual, claiming he'd had to help a stranded motorist change a tire, Patty had started to tease him about it, but then she had let it go. She had already decided that if Zambrano asked her about it in his interview, she would keep it under her hat. For one thing, it was nothing more than a rumor. Patty knew no details of any kind.

Besides, why bring something up like that at a time when all it would do was hurt Christine? Now, to her surprise, word about a possible girlfriend had come from Christine herself.

"Hello," Ali asked. "Are you still there?"

"I'm here," Patty said. "Just a little taken aback is all. What did she tell you?"

"That she found a letter he had written sometime back—a letter to someone named Ollie."

"That's an unusual name for a woman," Patty said. "It's not one I recognize."

"It was like a pen name or something," Ali said. "He signed his letters Popeye, and Ollie was evidently short for Olive Oyl."

Patty blinked in surprise. That was the tune she remembered hearing Phil whistle on occasion, the theme song to that old cartoon—"I'm Popeye the sailor man."

"What's really important," Ali continued, "is that Christine thinks Ollie, or whatever her name is, was at their house this morning."

"She saw her?"

"No. Christine claimed she smelled the girlfriend's

perfume, and she was offended that Phil would bring another woman into the house when she was right there."

"Offended enough to kill him?" Patty asked.

"According to her, more like hurt," Ali answered. "Besides, at this point, I don't think Christine understands that Phil is dead. She's sitting there fully expecting him to get off work, come pick her up, and take her home. But you're sure you have no idea who this Ollie person might be or where we could find her?"

"None at all," Patty answered. "But if Phil did have a gal pal, she'd have to live on or near his regular route."

"Could he have met her anywhere else?"

"Not that I can think of," Patty said.

"Whoever she is, we need to find her," Ali said. "Right now the cops have only one suspect in Phil's homicide, and that's Christine. If someone else was at the house, there's a possibility that the person may have either witnessed or been involved in what happened."

"I'll see what I can do," Patty said.

She put down the phone and stood staring at it, thinking about what Ali had told her. Christine had found a letter. That meant a letter on paper. Not an e-mail. Not a text. But a letter, and where there was one letter, there might be more.

Making up her mind, Patty picked up her purse and her car keys and left again. She drove straight back to the post office. What she and Phil had always referred to as the sorting table was really an antique partner desk that Patty's mother, Lorna, had bought from a used-furniture auction in Tucson thirty-some years ago. The desk had two knee wells and two sets of drawers, one set on either side. For years, one of those sets had been Patty's private domain. The other was Phil's.

Once inside the back room, Patty ignored another blinking message light and went straight to Phil's side of the desk. She found what she was looking for—a packet of envelopes fastened with a rubber band—squirreled away in the back of the bottom drawer. There were no stamps or postmarks. The letters hadn't been sent through the mail. Written in flowery, feminine script on the outside of each envelope was a single word: Popeye.

Patty Patton had spent her entire life believing that handling the mail was a sacred trust. She didn't pry, not even so much as to read the notes on picture postcards back when more than a handful of people sent them. Her whole being recoiled at the idea of reading a letter that was addressed to someone else, but with Phil Tewksbury dead and with Christine's life hanging in the balance, Patty didn't feel as though she had any choice. She picked up the top envelope and removed the single piece of paper.

Dear Popeye,
   Up all night with Oscar. He's still bad this morning. I can't leave him for more than a few minutes.
   Won't be able to see you today. Miss you.
                                                    Ollie

And that was it. As far as Patty knew, there was only one Oscar living in the area—Oscar Sanchez. Oscar's quarter horse ranch out in the San Rafael Valley had to be one of the last stops on Phil's mail route. And if Oscar Sanchez were the topic of the note, then the person writing it, Ollie, had to be Olga Sanchez. Patty stood staring at the paper, thinking about Olga Sanchez, about the way she wore her hair—pulled back and wound in a knot at the back of her neck, just the way Olive Oyl in the cartoons wore her hair. Olive Oyl and Popeye.

But maybe there was more to it. Wasn't Olga the former mother-in-law of Teresa Reyes, and a seriously estranged former mother-in-law at that? It seemed like an odd connection between Jose's shooting and Phil's murder, but surely it was more than a simple coincidence.

With the letter still in her hand, Patty picked up the telephone receiver. The last call had come from Ali Reynolds's number. She pressed redial.

"Christine is right," Patty said when Ali answered. "I found a packet of letters hidden in one of Phil's drawers here at the post office. Ollie is probably a woman named Olga Sanchez. She and her husband, Oscar, live on a ranch called the Lazy S that's on Phil's mail route, between here and Lochiel."

"Wait," Ali said. "Olga Sanchez? Teresa Reyes's former mother-in-law? I've actually met her. Thin. Black hair pulled back in a bun."

"Yes," Patty said. "Just like Olive Oyl, Popeye's girlfriend in those old cartoons. That's where the Ollie part comes from, but you've met Olga? How?"

"She came to the hospital where Jose is being treated, offering to help out by looking after Teresa's two older girls."

"Her granddaughters," Patty added.

"She even apologized to Teresa for some of her past behavior."

"I'm glad to hear that," Patty said. "It's about time. Life is too short to carry grudges around like that, and there's been bad blood between Teresa and Olga for a long time. Olga always blamed her daughter-in-law for her son's death."

"Was Teresa responsible in some way?"

"Not in any legal sense. The way I heard it, Teresa and Danny had a big fight, Danny went out drinking with his pals and ended up in another fight—this one in a bar—and died as a result of a drive-by shooting. It's a relief to know that they're finally getting over it," Patty added. "It'll be better for them and certainly better for the daughters."

"Who are being raised by Jose Reyes, her daughter-in-law's second husband," Ali said. "Was the bad blood between Olga and Teresa serious enough that Olga would target Jose?"

"I don't think so," Patty said. "I've known Olga all her life. Her father came from Mexico years ago and worked as Oscar's foreman. Olga grew up on the ranch and ended up marrying Oscar after his first wife died. She was twenty, and he was a lot older, but as far as I can tell, it's been a good marriage. Oscar has had some serious health issues in the last few years. Olga seems to have been his devoted caregiver."

"Like Phil with Christine," Ali said.

While they'd been talking, Patty had removed another letter from its envelope. As she unfolded the paper, she noticed that a faint hint of lingering perfume came off the page as she scanned through it.

"This letter is all about Oscar's medical problems and going to Tucson to see doctors. So that's something Phil and Olga shared, being caregivers. Based on my experience looking after my mother, I can tell you, it's a pretty thankless task."

Patty opened another envelope. This one was about the picnic lunch they'd had together. Olga had brought tuna sandwiches and some chocolate chip cookies; Phil had supplied the sodas. They'd eaten lunch on a blanket under a tree with his mail truck parked nearby.

"So far this all seems pretty innocent," Patty said. "More like pen-pal stuff than love letters. And nothing salacious. Nothing about meeting somewhere and making mad, passionate love. More like having someone to talk to who knows what you're up against."

And nothing about drug dealing, either, Patty thought. *Not a word about that.*

If Phil had been involved in drug dealing, his gal pal, Olga, was probably as much in the dark about it as Patty was. And Christine.

All afternoon, since the moment Eunice Carson had told her Phil was dead, Patty had been grieving for the man. Now, for the first time, she was pissed at him instead. All the time he had been pretending to be one thing, he had evidently been busy *being* something else.

"I think you need to go to Sheriff Renteria with this," Ali said.

"With the letters?"

"Yes, with the letters. The cops need to know that there's another woman in Phil's life, a woman who isn't Christine."

"But won't that make things worse for her?"

"I don't see how. Christine already knows Phil had at least one outside interest," Ali said. "Maybe there was another one we know nothing about. If nothing else, knowing about the letters between Olga and Phil will give the detectives someone to investigate who isn't Christine. In any event, you can't withhold this information. It's a homicide investigation. If you don't call Sheriff Renteria about it, I will."

"Why don't I go talk to Olga first? Shouldn't I give her some kind of advance warning?"

"Are you asking my opinion?" Ali asked.

"Well, yes," Patty said. "I suppose I am."

"Talk to Sheriff Renteria. Do not talk to Olga," Ali advised.

"All right," Patty agreed. "I will."

She ended the call and put down the phone. Then she sat there and read through all the letters. The last one in the stack, the most recent, was a simple thank-you card—to Phil for changing Olga's flat tire. As far as Patty could see, this was all harmless, innocent stuff. Olga Sanchez was a neighbor, a local, someone Patty Patton had known all her life. Ali Reynolds was an outsider; a stranger.

In the small-town world of Patagonia, that's what tipped the scales for Patty Patton that night—insider versus outsider; neighbor versus stranger. Olga was in; Ali was out. Patty knew she would call the sheriff eventually because she had said she would, but not until after she had given Olga Sanchez a heads-up. Patty knew how what appeared to be a perfectly platonic relationship between Olga and Phil would be viewed through the prism of Patagonia's small-town gossip, and it wasn't going to be pretty.

Patty stuffed the packet of letters into her purse. Picking up her keys and shutting off the light, she locked the door behind her and headed out. The Lazy S was only ten miles south of Patagonia on Harshaw Road, but it would take the better part of an hour to get there. It was full dark out. Much of the unpaved road was open range, where wandering cattle made nighttime driving treacherous.

It was fine for Patty to head out on what she regarded as an errand of mercy. It was not fine to wreck the Camaro in the process. She drove carefully and smoked one cigarette after another along the way.

When her tires lumbered across the cattle guard at the entrance to the Lazy S, Patty could see the house in the distance. With no lights glowing in any of the windows, she guessed no one was home. Still, having come that far, she decided not to leave without at least going to the door. A minivan was parked next to a gate that led into a small fenced yard, and she pulled up next to it. When the Camaro stopped, a small dog, barking frantically, came racing to the front gate. The dog, a Jack Russell terrier–like creature, sounded completely prepared to go into full-attack mode, and Patty was glad he was apparently locked inside the yard.

It wasn't until she looked away from the dog that she saw, caught in her still-glowing headlights, the figure of a man sitting in a chair near the front door of the covered front porch. Despite the fierce racket from the dog, he sat with his chin resting on his chest as though he were asleep.

Warily, still worried about the dog, Patty rolled down the window. "Hello," she called. "Are you all right?" The man didn't move or respond in any fashion.

Patty switched off the engine and her headlights. Left in darkness, she got out of the car, opened the trunk, and dug out the powerful trouble light she kept there. She wished she had the doggie bag of dinner leftovers she had taken home from the café, but those were already at home in her fridge. She would have to talk her way around the fierce little dog without the benefit of food.

She approached the gate. The dog had retreated to the porch but he immediately came charging back to the gate.

"Sit!" Patty ordered. She gave the command with feeling and was amazed when it worked. The dog sat.

"Stay!" she ordered as she eased open the gate. That command worked, too. Patty Patton wasn't a dog person. "Sit" and "stay" were the only commands she knew, but it turned out they were the only ones she needed.

Leaving the dog next to the gate, she walked up the gravel walkway. She was almost to the porch and shining the light on the man when she saw the blood pooling on the wooden-plank flooring under the chair. Oscar Sanchez wasn't asleep. He hadn't heard the barking dog because he was dead.

For the first time in her life, Patty Patton wished she had a cell phone. For a time she stood there, staring at him, while the flashlight trembled in her hand. Raising the light, she walked behind the man and saw the hole in the back of his head, a small hole that went into the base of his skull and angled down through his body. There was very little blood in the entry wound. The blood had to come from somewhere else—a place she couldn't see.

Patty stood transfixed, staring at the body. Should she go back to town and summon help, or should she try the front door?

Mindful that this would be a crime scene, she used the tail of her shirt to try turning the doorknob. It opened. As she let herself inside, she worried about finding another body in the room, but there wasn't one. She saw no sign of a struggle, and no phone, either. Nothing seemed to be out of order. Picking her way across the room, she stepped into the kitchen, and that's where she found an old-fashioned dial phone mounted on the wall next to the kitchen cabinets.

Her hand was shaking. It was all she could do to get her dialing finger into the proper holes.

"Nine-one-one. What are you reporting?"

"I'm at the Lazy S Ranch on Harshaw Road," she said, trying to keep the panic out of her voice. "Oscar Sanchez is dead. I think he's been shot."

48

6:00 P.M., Monday, April 12
Tucson, Arizona

Angel Moreno had spent a very busy but very profitable afternoon. When he told Sal and Tony that Humberto had a job for them, the two dopes came along as nice as you please. They were now disposed of, wrapped in a roll of orange shag carpeting and dropped off in the landfill north of Coolidge.

Long experience had taught Angel Moreno that orange shag was the best bet for that kind of job. Even when things started to leak, the colors more or less matched, and no one went near orange shag these days if they could help it. He had left the landfill with an empty panel truck and a feeling of accomplishment. Two down; one to go.

Another thing experience had taught Angel was that there was no disguise quite as effective as pretending to be a janitor with a mop. Or, in this case, a janitor with an immense floor polisher. He had brought one along in his van when he drove down from Phoenix, just in case. And he had been right. It turned out that the long hallways at Physicians

LEFT FOR DEAD | 357

Medical Center were uniformly in need of polishing.

The one thing he had expected to be a real challenge—laying hands on a hospital employee badge—had turned out to be no challenge at all. Halfway through his second pass in the parking lot, he found a Van Pool van complete with a conveniently unlocked door and a valid PMC employee badge lying right on the dashboard. Angel was able to filch it without setting off so much as a beeping auto alarm. That was the thing he really liked about auto alarms—if doors weren't properly locked, an alarm didn't make a sound.

Armed with the badge lanyard attached to the pocket of a pair of anonymous scrubs, he was ready. The polisher was mounted on the front of a wheeled cart that held a tall plastic container with a convincing collection of mops and brooms. The bottom of the container held a small canvas bag with one particular item that wasn't remotely related to janitorial supplies.

Pushing his way across the parking lot, he used the badge to enter a locked door at the rear of the building next to the Dumpsters. That was the most dangerous time, getting inside the building. Once he was in, however, he didn't rush. He checked the map in the lobby so he knew where to find the ICU, but he was in no hurry to get there. In fact, the later he arrived, the better. All he had to do in the meantime was polish floors like crazy. As long as he kept the ID tag so the name didn't show, and kept his face averted around security cameras, Angel was secure in the knowledge that no one would notice.

Except this time they did notice. Everywhere he

went at Physicians Medical, people smiled at him or greeted him, asking him things like "How's it going?" That was not a good situation for someone accustomed to being invisible while in plain sight.

It was unsettling, but not enough so for him to back off or give up. After all, Humberto had paid him in advance, and Angel had no intention of screwing this up. Angel Morales knew all too well what happened to people who promised something to Humberto Laos and then didn't deliver.

49

Ariel Rush closed her computer and hustled out of Rose Ventana's new room, leaving Al Gutierrez to trail along in her wake. By the time they were in the hospital corridor, Detective Rush already had her phone to her ear.

"Yes," she said into it. "I want the name of that friend of yours who left Phoenix PD to go to work in Fountain Hills. That's Tim Barrow, B-A-R-R-O-W. Don't worry about the phone number. I can get that." She ended the call and turned back to Al. "How does hospital cafeteria grub grab you?"

Now that the interview was over, Al had expected to be on his way back to Vail, sooner rather than later. He was grateful for the opportunity to hang around a little longer. "Better than starving."

They made their way to the cafeteria, where she gave him money and sent him off to fetch burgers from the fast-food line while she set up her computer once more. When he returned with the burgers, she was back on the phone.

"Okay, Captain Barrow," she was saying into the

phone. "No, I don't have an address, just a description. This is what we've got. A two-story-plus-basement house in Fountain Hills. It's supposed to be set on a large lot that backs up to the desert. There's a long steep driveway with wrought-iron gates at the bottom of the drive and a guard shack by the gate. Any of that sound familiar?"

Ariel Rush paused to listen and then laughed. "Somehow that doesn't surprise me, but put it out to your patrol division. I think it's possible that you've got a serial killer sitting right there in town, and he's finally made his first mistake—a homicide victim who didn't quite die. We need to get to this guy and take him down before he figures out we've got a witness."

She cradled the phone on her shoulder long enough to apply ketchup and mustard to her burger. "Okay," she said. "You've got my number? And if you find it, I need someone to send me a photo of the gate and the driveway."

Detective Rush put down her phone and took the first bite from her burger. Al's was already half gone.

"You really think he's just going to sit there and wait for us to come find him?"

"Actually, I think he will. From what Rose told us, he's got money. He likes to torture girls, but he likes his creature comforts. He's also arrogant as hell. He's got people on the payroll who do his dirty work for him. The two guys who dumped Rose Ventana without properly finishing the job won't be eager to let him know they screwed up."

"Which gives us time," Al said.

"Some time," Ariel Rush allowed. "Some but not a lot. While we wait for Fountain Hills to get back to us, let's collect that rape kit and deliver it, along with our Three Points cigarette butt, to the crime lab to check for DNA."

"Isn't that expensive?" Al asked. "Who's going to pay for the testing?"

Detective Rush looked at him and grinned. "If this case turns out to be as big as I think it is, we're going to have all sorts of people lining up to have the evidence processed, up to and including the FBI. But we're not bringing in anyone else until I'm damned good and ready. Got it?"

"Got it," Al agreed. "Let's do it."

Just then her phone chirped. "Text message," she said. She pressed a button, glanced at the screen, then passed the phone to Al. "I believe we have a bingo," she said. "Let's go show it to Rose."

Al studied the photo on the screen. It showed a pair of ornate gates in front of a driveway that led up a very steep hill with what appeared to be a guard shack off to the left. The caption beneath the photo said 15568 CENTIPEDE CIRCLE, FOUNTAIN HILLS, ARIZONA.

Al looked from the photo to Detective Rush. "It can't be this easy," he said.

"Sometimes it is," Detective Rush said. "First we'll show this to Rose Ventana, then we'll see."

When they got back to the hospital, Rose's mother and Sister Anselm were still in Rose's room. As soon as the young woman looked at the photo of the gate,

Ariel Rush knew they were on to something. "That's it?" she asked. "That's the place?"

Rose nodded.

"All right, then," Detective Rush said. "You get better while we go to work."

"How did they know which house it was?" Al asked.

"The guard shack," she said. "That's what gave it away."

She was back on the phone by the time they were halfway down the corridor. "Okay, Tim," she said. "That's the right house. Send me anything and everything you have on this guy." She listened for some time. When she ended the call, she turned to Al.

"Back to Vail for you," she said, "and then I'm headed back to Phoenix. Our suspected bad guy's name is Humberto Laos, and he's very busy. He runs several companies, including a janitorial supply house and an exterminating company, with any number of white panel trucks registered to the company. The feds think he's using those companies as fronts to do money laundering for the Mexican cartels, with a bit of loan sharking on the side. The panel trucks do dual duty. When he's not using them for business, I'll bet they help out with the other more sordid parts of his life. I'm pretty sure we'll discover that one of those vans was used in the hit on Chico, and either the same one or a different one was used to transport Rose."

"And now Rose, the one who got away, may be the one who will bring him down," Al said.

"Yes," Detective Rush said. "Thanks to you. But

the really good news is this: The feds have had his property under video surveillance for some time. Tim says there are vans coming and going all the time, with a clear shot of Chico's Lincoln dropping Rose off on Thursday. They gave her a ride up the hill in a golf cart. There's no film showing her coming back down."

"What are you going to do next?" Al asked.

"I'm going to get myself a warrant and see if we can find some of Rose's DNA in Laos's basement before he figures out a way to get it cleaned up."

"What am I going to do?" Al Gutierrez asked.

He already knew the answer. He would go back to work and take more of Sergeant Dobbs's crap.

"If you can, stay in touch with Sister Anselm," Detective Rush said. "The sooner we can get Rose out of that hospital and into the convent, the better. Since you almost got into her room the other night, someone else could, too."

"You think Laos is that dangerous?"

"I do."

"Okay," he said. "When I'm not working, I'll be there."

They drove the rest of the way to his place in Vail in silence. When he got out of the car, Al Gutierrez felt let down. Something special had happened to him that day. Now it was over.

"Thanks," he said, reaching out to shake her hand. "It's been a trip."

"It has been," she agreed. "For me, too. You're a smart guy, Al, and a cop at heart. If you ever get tired of chasing illegal immigrants through the mesquite and decide that the Border Patrol isn't for you, call me. I happen to have more than a little pull with the hiring guys at Phoenix PD. I'll see to it that they give you a chance."

"And I can tell Kevin Dobbs to go to hell?"

"Be my guest."

Detective Rush drove away and left him standing there alone but feeling altogether better.

50

7:00 P.M., Monday, April 12
Nogales, Arizona

Sheriff Renteria was dozing at his desk when the phone rang. "Okay," Detective Zambrano said. "The two cases are definitely a package deal. The prints on all postal boxes track back to Phil Tewksbury, and his prints match the ones on the lug wrench from the Reyes shooting scene."

"Have you talked to Lattimore about any of this?"

"Touched bases. He's planning on meeting with us at the department tomorrow morning at ten."

"What about the bundles of drugs?" Renteria asked.

"I went into the evidence room and took a look at them. They're all pretty similar in terms of size and shape. Unless dope smugglers are into some kind of uniform packaging, I'd say they're all from the same source."

"Any prints on those?"

"Not a single one."

"In other words, whoever was doing the packaging wore gloves," Renteria suggested.

"Seems likely," Zambrano agreed.

"What about the sunglasses we found in Phil's truck?"

"Wiped clean, although they may be able to obtain DNA evidence from the nose pads, hinges, and earpieces. I've also asked the crime lab to check both the wig and the head scarf for prints. Finding prints on fabric is more difficult than finding prints on hard surfaces, but it's also harder for crooks to wipe fabric clean, because you don't wipe prints you can't see."

It was just what Renteria had hoped. The fingerprint evidence was telling them what they had expected to find—that the two cases were connected, and Phil Tewksbury was most likely responsible for the Reyes shooting.

"What about prints on the bat?" the sheriff asked.

"Those definitely point to Christine. There were actually two sets of prints on the bat—a very old set that belongs to Phil Tewksbury and several brand-new prints that match Christine's."

"What about the rest of it?" Renteria asked.

"The crime lab guy said what he saw on the working end of the bat looks good for possible brain matter, but official verification will take time."

"How much time?"

"I got the feeling that it depends on who's asking," Zambrano said. "You might have better luck than I did. I just heard that the phone company warrants came back tonight, earlier than I expected. I plan to work on phone records first thing in the morning, before our meeting with Lattimore. If we can connect some communication dots between Reyes and Tewksbury, it'll make our lives a lot easier. I'll do the Patty Patton interview after we finish up with Lattimore."

"Where are you now?"

"Stopping off at the Triple T to grab some dinner. There's nothing like good old-fashioned deep-dish apple pie to take my mind off spatters of brain matter."

The second line on Sheriff Renteria's line lit up. "Okay," he said. "Let me take this other call." He clicked over. "Sheriff Renteria."

"We just had a nine-one-one call from Patty Patton," the watch commander said. "She's out at the Lazy S Ranch south of Patagonia. She says Oscar Sanchez has been shot. He's dead."

Renteria was already on his feet, reaching for his Stetson. "Okay," he said. "I'm on my way. Any idea where Mrs. Sanchez is?"

"None."

"What kind of car does she drive?"

"I'll find out and get back to you. According to Patty, there's a minivan parked in the front yard. No signs of struggle inside the house."

"Patty went inside the house?"

"She had to go inside to use the phone."

"All right," he said. "I'm on my way to my car. Call Zambrano on his cell and tell him he'll need to order that deep-dish pie to go. He needs to meet me at the Sanchez place ASAP. Can we get Patty Patton to call me back on my cell? I need to talk to her."

"I can't," the operator said. "She called on the Sanchez home phone, but I told her that since the house is now a crime scene, she should go outside and wait for us to get someone there."

Sheriff Renteria knew that was the right move, but he was beyond frustrated. "Why the hell doesn't the woman have a cell phone?" he demanded.

"I don't know," the operator said. "You'll need to ask her when you get there."

Forty minutes later, Renteria pulled into the front yard at the Lazy S and parked his patrol car next to Patty's Camaro. She was sitting inside the open passenger door, cuddling a shivering Jack Russell terrier.

"His name is Bert," she said without looking up. "It says so on the tag. I think he must have been Oscar's dog."

"Did you touch the body?"

"No, but I know he's dead."

Not content to take her word for it, Renteria went to see for himself. It was true. Oscar Sanchez was propped in a chair. The bullet had been shot into the back of his head at an angle and exited through the bottom of the chair. As far as Manuel Renteria was concerned, it gave a whole new meaning to the term "execution-style slaying." Patty had left the front door open, and the sheriff was able to peek into the living room without having to step inside. Patty was right—there was no sign of a struggle. Nothing seemed to be out of place.

Renteria went back to the Camaro. Since Patty was still in the passenger seat, he slid in behind the steering wheel. "What are you doing here?" he asked.

"I came to see Olga, but she's not here."

"Lucky for you," Renteria said. "But why did you come to see Olga?"

"About these," Patty said. She opened her purse, pulled out a packet of envelopes, and handed it to him. "I wanted to let her know about it before I turned these over to you."

Renteria searched around the visor until he found the switch for the reading light, then he had to pat around in his pockets to find his reading glasses. "Popeye," he said once he could see the top envelope. "Who the hell is Popeye?"

"That would be Phil Tewksbury," Patty said. "After Christine told Ali that Phil had a girlfriend—"

"Wait, wait, wait. Who's Ali?"

"Ali Reynolds. Jose's friend. You met her today when she came to report the vandalism at Jose's house. When she went back to Tucson, she stopped by Catalina Vista and talked to Christine—"

"Christine actually talked to someone?"

"Ali said Christine was waiting for Phil to come get her, that she didn't seem to understand he was dead. Christine also said something about being upset because Phil's girlfriend was at their house earlier this morning."

Sheriff Renteria stared at Patty. He had wondered about Phil's love life—if he had one—and whether Patty herself might have been the object of Phil's affection. That was evidently wrong, but how the hell had Ali whatever-her-name-was gotten Christine Tewksbury to stop screaming and start talking?

"Christine told her that Olga Sanchez was Phil's girlfriend?"

"No. She just said that he had a girlfriend, a woman named Ollie—that she had seen a letter Phil wrote to someone named Ollie. And Christine claimed that Ollie had been at the house this morning—at Phil's house—that she had smelled her perfume."

Renteria felt a clench in his gut. Somewhere in the midst of the pitched battle in Phil Tewksbury's living room, while they were grappling with Christine and trying to wrench the bat out of the madwoman's hands, he seemed to remember her screaming something incomprehensible about perfume, but she had been a raving maniac at the time. He hadn't really paid attention. He had been too busy trying to keep from having his own head bashed in. Even in the patrol car, Christine hadn't made any sense. She had kept right on screaming and pounding her head against the window.

"Since Christine said she had seen one letter," Patty was saying, "I wondered if there might be others. If so, obviously, Phil wouldn't have left them lying around the house, where Christine could find them. I went back to the post office and looked in his set of drawers in the sorting table. That's where I found them. They're from Olga, but she signs them Ollie, short for Olive Oyl. I guess it's like a joke or something, but because she mentioned Oscar, I knew who she was. Since Christine claimed Olga had been at her house, I knew I'd need to turn these over to you, and I wanted to let her know."

"That was probably a really stupid idea," Renteria said.

"Yes," Patty agreed. "I know that now."

While they waited for the overworked county coroner and the crime scene techs to show up at Santa Cruz County's second homicide scene of the day, Sheriff Renteria decided to read the notes. First he went to his patrol car and retrieved a pair of latex gloves from the trunk. Then he came back to the Camaro.

What he found in the envelopes were notes rather than letters—notes that made arrangements for future meetings. There were brief comments on things Ollie and Phil had done, where they had been, and how things were at home with Oscar's increasingly precarious health situation. It wasn't until Renteria got to the last one, the thank-you note, that it all came together for him. As soon as he saw the part about changing the tire, he knew what had happened.

Phil Tewksbury hadn't shot Jose Reyes. He'd been set up—framed by someone who made sure his prints were on the lug wrench left at the crime scene. Olga had tried to murder her former daughter-in-law's new husband, first by passing the blame on to Phil and then by blaming Phil's murder on Christine. Now, with Oscar Sanchez dead, Olga had no one else to blame.

The sheriff pulled out his cell phone and dialed the office. "Have you located all the Sanchez vehicles?"

"Yes. They own a 2008 Dodge Caravan, a 2006 Range Rover, and a 1998 Buick Regal."

"Okay," he said. "I want you to put out a statewide BOLO on the Range Rover and the Buick. Olga Sanchez is now a person of interest in three separate homicides. Tell people to be on their guard. She could be armed and dangerous."

"Three?" Patty Patton asked. "You mean you no longer think Christine murdered her husband?"

Sheriff Renteria sighed and shook his head. "No," he said. "I'm afraid when you're right, you're right."

51

7:00 P.M., Monday, April 12
Tucson, Arizona

Detective Rush had been gone only a few minutes when the first reporter showed up at PMC. Hearing raised voices in the hall outside Rose's room, Sister Anselm went out to find a reporter, backed up by a cameraman, attempting to interview Connie Fox.

"What's going on?" the nun demanded.

Connie nodded in the reporter's direction. "What should I do?"

The reporter stepped forward and held up her ID for Sister Anselm's perusal. "My name is Abby Summers," she said. "I'm with the FOX affiliate in Phoenix. Someone who knows I've been following Rose's story for years sent me a tweet about it—a tweet from someone named Jasmine—claiming that Rose had been found and was being treated here."

In her head, Sister Anselm replayed the telling glance that had passed between Jasmine and Lily Ventana when Detective Rush had been explaining the need not to go public with Rose's situation. It seemed clear that even then the cat was already out of the bag. Sister Anselm also knew that if one reporter was here, others were bound to follow. And no telling who else. So if the strategy of keeping quiet wasn't going to work, maybe it was time to do the opposite. She thought it might be time for a media circus of her own making.

"I think you should go ahead and tell Ms. Summers the whole story," Sister Anselm said decisively.

Connie Fox's eyes widened. "All of it?"

"All of it."

"Are you sure?"

"Yes, I'm sure," Sister Anselm said. To the reporter, she added, "I think doing the interview right here in the waiting room will be fine."

As the reporter and cameraman moved into position, Sister Anselm set out on a brisk walk through the hospital, looking for something that didn't fit. She found what she was looking for in the next wing over when she walked past a man pushing an enormous floor polisher.

She looked at the man, smiled, and nodded. When he ducked his head and looked away, she knew. This was the guy.

One of the terms of sale between the nuns of All Saints and the doctors who created PMC had been a written agreement that, wherever possible, the hospital would make use of workers from a nearby sheltered workshop that was also operated by All Saints. Developmentally disabled adults from there did much of the hospital's grunt work, from the laundry to routine janitorial functions. One glance was enough to tell Sister Anselm that the guy pushing the floor polisher wasn't developmentally disabled.

She stopped off in a restroom long enough to dial Bishop Gillespie's number. "I need some help," she said when he answered. "I want an anonymous but urgent tip to go out to every media outlet in both Tucson and Phoenix."

Bishop Gillespie had a reputation for being well connected inside the law enforcement community, but his media savvy was just as extensive. "About?" he asked.

"I need a flash mob of reporters here at PMC as soon as you can drum one up. Tell them that Rose Ventana, a teenager from Buckeye who went missing three years ago, has been found outside Tucson. She was the victim of a vicious assault and is currently receiving treatment at Physicians Medical Center."

"Are you sure?" Bishop Gillespie asked. "This doesn't sound like you."

"I'm sure," Sister Anselm said. "And I need those reporters here ASAP."

She made three more calls before she left the restroom. The first one was to Detective Rush. "Where are you?" the nun asked.

"I just dropped Al off in Vail and I'm on my way back to Phoenix. Why? What's up?"

"I think we have a problem. There's a guy here running a floor polisher in the wing next to Rose's. I think he's a ringer."

"What do you mean?"

"I mean he's someone who's pretending to be a PMC janitor who isn't a PMC janitor."

"Do you think he poses a danger to Rose?"

"I don't know for sure, but I think it's a very real possibility. Enough that I think we need her out of the hospital immediately."

"All right," Detective Rush said. "I'm on my way back to the hospital right now."

"No," Sister Anselm said. "I want you to go straight to the All Saints Convent. It's on San Pedro Road. The entrance is on the left, about a mile and a half beyond the hospital. Ask for Sister Genevieve. She'll know what to do."

"But—" Detective Rush began.

"Please," Sister Anselm urged. "Just go. I'm working on a plan to smuggle Rose out of the hospital, and I need to make two more calls."

The next call was to Sister Genevieve. The one after that was to Dr. Lazlo. When she left the restroom, the floor polisher was still working his way down the corridor. Once again, she smiled at him as she passed. Once again, he looked away. By the time she got back to the hospital's main lobby, the first Tucson-based camera crew was already arriving on the scene.

Thank you, Bishop Gillespie, she thought.

Outside Rose's door, Abby Summer was finishing her interview. As the second crew came down the hallway, Sister Anselm motioned for them to stop. "Mrs. Fox will be doing interviews one at a time on a first-come, first-served basis," she announced to the woman leading the charge.

"Not a press conference?" the reporter asked.

"No," Sister Anselm said. "Individual interviews only."

And the longer they take, the better.

Sister Anselm nodded encouragingly to Connie Fox on her way past. She hadn't told Rose's mother what she was planning, for fear she wouldn't be able to carry it off. Right now she was better off not knowing.

52

7:15 P.M., Monday, April 12
Tucson, Arizona

When Angel Moreno reached the next hallway, he was shocked by what he saw. Most of the hallways had been relatively deserted. This one was jammed, and not just with people. There were reporters and cameras—way too many cameras.

During his briefing, Humberto had given him a series of photos, and Angel immediately recognized one of the faces in the crowd. The woman being interviewed was Connie Fox, the target's mother. So this was the right hallway and the right waiting room. No doubt the door to the right of where the mother was sitting was the room where he needed to be.

Pushing his supply cart into the hallway, he parked it as close to the target room as he was able to, then took the polisher to the far end of the hallway and went to work. The people with cameras and microphones gestured that they wanted him to turn off his machine, but he ignored them.

At one point, an elderly nun pushing another nun in a wheelchair appeared at the lobby end of the corridor. She deftly threaded her way through the milling reporters and went into the target room. They went in and came out in under a minute, then went back to the lobby.

Angel was at the wrong end of the hallway. Turning off the polisher, he followed them, but it took time to fight his way through the crowd. He arrived at the front entrance in time to see a wheelchair-accessible van speeding away from the front door so fast that he didn't catch a glimpse of the license plate. He wasn't sure exactly what had happened, but he didn't think it was worth making a mad dash across the parking lot in hopes of giving chase.

Two nuns had gone into the room; two nuns had come out. The girl's mother was still there, calmly talking to reporters. On his way back down the crowded corridor, Angel paused by the open doorway to the target room long enough to see that the patient was evidently still in her bed. Relieved, he went back to the polishing. All he had to do now was wait for the damnable reporters to finish what they were doing and get the hell out.

53

7:30 P.M., Monday, April 12
Tucson, Arizona

After a solitary but relaxing dinner at McMahon's and a forty-five-minute decompressing phone call with B., Ali pulled into the Physicians Medical parking lot at seven-thirty and was surprised to see that the place was full of media vans. Her initial concern was that Jose's condition had taken a turn for the worse. So she was relieved when she entered the lobby and Lucy came running toward her to give her a quick hug.

"We're over there with our cousin," Lucy said, pointing toward a table in the corner of the room. "We're playing Chutes and Ladders. I'm winning."

"Great," Ali said. "I was never any good at Chutes and Ladders."

A dark-haired teenager, chatting on a cell phone, came after Lucy and caught her up while Carinda stayed at the table, hugging a teddy bear that was almost as big as she was.

"I'm Julie," the girl explained. She closed the phone and stuffed it into the pocket of her jeans. "Tomás is my grandfather. My mom and I came over from Silver City to help out."

"I'm Ali Reynolds from Sedona. I'm here to help, too."

As Julie led Lucy back toward the board game, Ali headed for Jose's room. Once she was in the corridor, she could see a crush of media people in the waiting room beyond Jose's room. They were interviewing a woman Ali didn't recognize. Relieved that the media attention was on someone else, she hurried into Jose's room. A tearful Teresa, with little Carmine in her arms, sat in the visitor's chair.

"She's upset about the mess at the house," Jose explained. "I told her it's one of those things. We'll just have to get through it. Juanita Cisco got on the phone to the insurance company. They'll have an adjuster out at the house first thing tomorrow morning."

"Good," Ali said. "And I talked to Patty Patton, the woman who runs the post office. She says she'll be happy to help organize cleanup crews when you get to that point."

Jose turned to his wife. "See there? We won't have to do it all ourselves. That's why we're living in a small town—neighbors helping neighbors."

"I took some photos at the house," Ali said tentatively. "I'm not sure if now is a good time to look at them."

"Please," Jose said. "We need to know how bad it is."

Ali opened the photo app and passed her phone to Jose. Grim-faced, he scrolled through them all, then passed the phone to Teresa.

"But all the things I picked out for Carmine . . ." Teresa began, bursting into tears once more. "Our good dishes, our bedding, our furniture. It's all gone."

"Those are things," Jose pointed out. "We're alive. That's what's important, right?"

Teresa took a deep breath, attempting to pull herself together, then nodded in agreement. "You're right," she said. "At least we're all alive." She handed the phone back to Ali. "Thank you for handling the police report."

"You're welcome," Ali said. "It took longer than it should have because of the other homicide in town."

"Another homicide?" Jose asked. "Where?"

"In Patagonia," Ali answered. "I thought you might have heard about it. Phil Tewksbury was murdered sometime this morning."

"Phil Tewksbury—the mailman?"

"Yes."

"Too bad," Jose said. "I've met Phil a couple of times. Hell of a nice guy. Do they have any suspects?"

"Christine, for one," Ali said.

"You mean the Christmas Tree Lady?" Teresa asked.

Ali nodded. "There might be one more suspect. Someone you know."

"Who's that?"

"Patty Patton found a packet of letters in one of Phil's drawers at the post office. It turns out Phil was evidently carrying on quite a correspondence with your former mother-in-law."

Teresa looked genuinely shocked. "With Olga? Are you kidding? What about Oscar? He's always been good as gold to her. How dare she carry on with someone behind his back? And after the things she said about Jose and me getting together after Danny was dead . . ."

Just then Julie poked her head in the room. She was carrying the board game box and the teddy bear. "Can I leave these here?" she asked.

"Where are the girls?" Teresa asked.

"They went to Baskin-Robbins," Julie said. "With their grandmother."

"Their grandmother? Olga?" Teresa demanded. "You let them go off somewhere with her without even asking me?"

Julie seemed taken aback. "She said it's just a few blocks from here. That they'll be right back."

"Did you give her the car seats?" Teresa asked. "They're in my room."

"She said that since they weren't going far, she didn't need car seats. I hope I didn't do anything wrong, but when she offered ice cream, both girls wanted to go. It didn't seem like that big a deal."

It might not have been a big deal to Julie, but it certainly was to Teresa. Ali was already on her feet. "Look," she said. "It's not a problem. I'll take the car seats and go find them. I'll bring the girls back here as soon as they finish their ice cream."

Julie followed her out of the room with her cell phone ringing again. Ali suspected that her interrupted conversations were part of the reason she was happy to hand off the girls and let them be someone else's problem for a few minutes.

"If you'll go get the car seats," Ali told her, "I'll go get my car."

While she waited for Julie to bring the seats, Ali

pulled up to the front door. A quick Internet search showed her that the nearest Baskin-Robbins was under two miles away, on Wrightstown Road.

"I hope they're not mad at me," Julie said as she stuffed the seats into Ali's Cayenne.

"No one's mad at you," Ali assured her. "We'll take care of it. What kind of car was she driving?"

"I don't know. A white one? And like with four doors or something."

"A sedan, then?"

"I guess."

Julie's vague description wasn't a big help, especially since, when Ali arrived at the Baskin-Robbins parking lot, there were no white sedans in attendance. A white Toyota Tundra pickup truck, yes, but no four-door sedans of any kind. There was no sign of Olga Sanchez and the girls, either.

They must have left the hospital several minutes before I did, Ali thought, *so they should have already been here.*

Ali got out and went inside. She waited impatiently while a family of four did multiple taste tests before making their final flavor choices. She asked the solo employee, "Did a lady with black hair and two little girls come in a while ago? The lady wears her hair pulled back. There are white streaks in her hair."

The clerk behind the counter shook her head. "Not that I remember."

The first inklings of real concern leaked into Ali's consciousness. She went back out to the car and watched up and down the street for several minutes. Maybe Olga had decided to stop off somewhere on the way to the ice cream shop. While Ali watched on-coming traffic, she called Teresa. "I'm at Baskin-Robbins," she said. "They're not here."

"Where else would she have taken them?" Teresa asked.

Ali heard the rising panic in Teresa's voice. She didn't want to cause the poor woman any additional worry, and so, although Ali herself was feeling genuine alarm, she tried to keep it from showing.

"Maybe she went to a different branch," Ali suggested. "Or maybe she decided to go somewhere else first. Is it possible she took them home? She offered to do that earlier, didn't she? Where is home?"

"That would be either the ranch, the Lazy S, south of Patagonia, or else to her house here in Tucson."

"Where's that?" Ali asked.

"On Longfellow Avenue," Teresa said. "Right around Hawthorne. I don't remember the exact number."

"The streets are named for writers?"

"Yes," Teresa said. "It's an area in the central district called Poet's Corner, mostly homes from the for-ties and fifties."

"How will I know which one is the right one?"

"It's a brick house that's been painted white," Te-resa said. "Blue trim. If you're driving southbound be-tween Speedway and Fifth, their house in on the right side of Longfellow."

"What kind of car does Olga drive?" Ali asked. She was programming Longfellow Avenue into her GPS as she spoke.

"She and Oscar may not still have the same car, but

they used to keep an older-model Buick at the house in Tucson to use when they were in town."

"What color?"

"White."

"Two-door or four-door?"

"Four." Teresa added, "They have a Range Rover that they mostly keep on the ranch and a minivan conversion that holds Oscar's wheelchair." There was a momentary silence on the phone before she asked, "Do you think I should call the police?"

"Not yet," Ali said. "Let me drive by the house on Longfellow. The GPS says it'll take me just under twenty minutes to get from here to there. If there's no sign of them at the house, or if Olga hasn't brought the girls back to the hospital by then, that'll be the time to bring the cops in."

And issue an Amber Alert, Ali thought.

It occurred to her that while she was checking on the house in Tucson, Patty might be able to find out if Olga had retreated to the ranch. As Ali made her way across Tucson, she tried redialing both of Patty Patton's landlines, but there was no answer at either one.

Remembering what had happened on Sunday, Ali dialed Stuart Ramey's number.

"Hey, Ali," he said. "What can I do for you today?"

"Can you get back into the Physicians Medical's CCTV system?" she asked.

"Another evil flower delivery guy?" he asked. "How did all that turn out, by the way?"

"The flower guy turned out to be a good guy," Ali said. "I should have let you know. But now we've got a grandmother who may have gone off the rails. She came to the hospital sometime within the last half hour, loaded two kids—two little girls—into a vehicle, and took off. We need to get the kids back."

"She took the kids without permission?"

"Yes."

"So this is urgent?"

"Very."

"Let me get back to you."

He hung up. No more than a minute elapsed before he called her back. "Okay," he said. "I've got it. Looks like a Buick Regal from the nineties. Here's the license."

"I'm driving," Ali said. "Can't write it down. Can you send it to me?"

"Will," Stuart said. "But there's something else you should know. Those kids, the older one in particular, didn't look very happy to be getting in that car."

By then Ali had turned off Alvernon onto Second Street. Longfellow was two blocks in. She spotted the Range Rover parked on the street as soon as she turned the corner onto Longfellow. Not only was the Range Rover parked out front, there was a white Buick parked under the carport at the end of the driveway. A quick comparison revealed that the license number matched the one Stuart Ramey had sent to her phone minutes before.

"Bingo," Ali told herself. "Got her."

The xeriscaped front yard wasn't fenced. A concrete walkway led through a collection of prickly pear, yucca, barrel cactus, and palo verde. Growing along both sides of the house was a foolproof burglar deterrent—a thicket of seven-foot-high cholla. Backlit by the setting sun, the five-inch-long needles resembled an evil halo. Blinds on all the street-facing windows had been pulled tightly shut. Had it not been for the car in the driveway, the house might have been deserted.

Ali pulled in behind the Buick, effectively blocking it. If Olga planned to leave in the Ranger Rover, there wasn't much Ali could do, but if she planned to drive the Buick out of there, she would have to go through Ali's Cayenne to do it.

Ali rang the bell. When nothing happened, she rang the bell again. Eventually, despite the fact that there was no sound from inside, the light in the peephole went out.

"What do you want?" a woman's voice asked.

"I'm Teresa and Jose's friend, Ali Reynolds. I've come to pick up the girls."

"Whatever would make you think they're with me?"

"Come on, Mrs. Sanchez," Ali said. "Julie, the girl who was looking after Lucy and Carinda, told us you had taken them for ice cream. We have the security tape that shows you leaving the hospital with the two girls in your car."

Olga Sanchez gave an audible sigh. "Oh well, then," she said. "I suppose you should come inside."

When the door opened, the first thing Ali saw was the weapon, a .38, aimed directly at her midsection. What she missed more than anything in that moment was her Kevlar vest. She had her Glock; her Taser was in her pocket. Olga would have no way of knowing Ali was armed, but at that point, carrying the weapons did Ali no good at all. She knew she'd be dead before she had a chance to use either one.

"Come in and shut the door," Olga ordered.

Ali did as she was told. She stepped into a room that looked as though it hadn't changed in decades. With the blinds closed, the only light in the room came from what were most likely genuine Tiffany lamps on the tables at either end of an immense old-fashioned leather couch. A blanket that Ali took to be an antique Navajo rug—reminding her of B.'s—was draped casually over the matching leather chair.

On the surface, the room seemed comfortable and comforting, completely at odds with the disturbed woman standing there holding a weapon. There was no sign of the girls anywhere—none.

After surveying the room, Ali turned back to Olga. That was when she noticed the collection of luggage sitting next to the door. There were three suitcases altogether, two large ones and a smaller roll-aboard, all of them on wheels. That could mean only one thing—Olga was definitely on her way out of town. But was she planning on leaving with the girls or without them?

At that point, Ali's police academy training kicked in. When faced with an armed assailant, try to initiate a conversation and defuse the situation.

"Please, Mrs. Sanchez," Ali said. "You don't want to do this. Right now we can still fix it. If it goes on longer, or if the police have to be involved, it will be a far more serious situation. You could be charged with custodial interference or even kidnapping. I'm sure you don't want that."

"You have no idea of what I want," Olga said. "And this is none of your business. You shouldn't have come."

"Where are the girls?"

"They're not here," Olga said. "By the time you find them, it'll be too late."

Ali's heart gave a lurch. "What do you mean too late?"

"I gave them a little something in their ice cream," Olga said. "They're sleeping."

Ali was aghast. "You poisoned them?" she demanded.

"Not poison. Just a little something to help them sleep. I didn't want to frighten them."

"You gave them a sedative?" Ali asked. "What if you gave them too much? What if they die?"

"Then Teresa and I would be even, wouldn't we?" Olga said. "I lost my child. It's only fair that Teresa should lose hers. If I could have taken her new baby, too, I would have."

Ali's heartbeat ramped up. If the girls had been given an overdose of some medication, they might already be dead. She had to do something, and she had to do it fast, but for right now she needed to stay calm and keep the conversation going.

"You hate Teresa that much?" Ali asked.

Olga shrugged. "Danny's dead. Jose is alive. What's fair about that?"

That was when it all shifted into focus. Wasn't that what Jose had told Ali when she asked him about the shooting—that the woman who had shot him had been driving a Buick? But she remembered clearly that he had said she wasn't anyone he recognized.

"Have you even met Jose Reyes?" Ali asked.

Olga smiled. "I don't have to meet the man to know

all about him or to hate his guts. He stepped into Danny's place and took over. He claimed to be everything Danny wasn't—a real goody-goody, but his squeaky-clean reputation should be crap about now. He may be alive, but I'll bet he won't be a cop much longer."

As far as Ali was concerned, those words explained everything, including the vandalism at Teresa and Jose's house, where the least amount of damage had been done to the room shared by Lucy and Carinda. Now the very lives of those two little girls hung by a thread, and Ali Reynolds was it. Everyone had been only too ready to assume that Christine Tewksbury was the crazy one, but standing in that dimly lit living room, Ali came face-to-face with the idea that Olga Sanchez was beyond deranged.

Ali's cell phone chirped in her pocket. Though she hoped the caller was Teresa, she made no attempt to answer. Teresa had known where she was going. Maybe, if there was no answer, she would figure out there was a problem and summon help.

"You're taking a trip?" Ali asked, changing the subject.

Olga nodded. "One of Danny's friends keep a plane at Ryan Field. I'm supposed to meet him there in a little over an hour. He's going to fly me over the border into Mexico. Maybe you'd like to give me a ride there."

"To the airport?"

Olga nodded again.

Ali feared that an hour would be too long. Would the girls survive if they didn't receive medical atten-

tion? Her cell phone buzzed, letting her know someone had left a message. Again she ignored it.

"You've been planning this for a long time, haven't
you?" Ali said.

Olga nodded again. "Yes. It's taken almost a year to
put it together, and the only thing that went wrong is
that Jose didn't die."

Ali had noticed the hint of perfume wafting out of
the house when Olga first opened the door. Another
set of dots clicked together. The perfume Christine
had mentioned in the Tewksbury house that morning.

"Jose didn't die, but Phil did," Ali said.

Olga's eyes glittered in the lamplight. "Phil who?"
she asked.

The eyes had given it away. "You know," Ali said.
"Your good pal Phil Tewksbury—aka Popeye—the
guy who had his head smashed in with a baseball bat
early this morning. Patty Patton found some of the letters you wrote to him. He had them stashed in his
desk at work."

"How did she find out about it? Did Oscar tell her?
Did Phil?"

"Christine Tewksbury is the one who told us about
you, Ollie," Ali said. "But if your husband knows, too,
it's pretty much all over for you, isn't it?"

This time Olga changed the subject abruptly. "We
need to go," she said. She stepped over to the window
and lifted the blind outside. "It's dark enough that the
neighbors won't notice. We'll take your car. You can
carry the luggage. We'll have to make two trips."

"Three, I think," Ali corrected. "I don't think I can
handle more than one of those at a time."

All through this conversation, Olga had kept the .38 trained on Ali. By now, Ali guessed, Olga's wrist and grip were probably tiring. Once they were in the Cayenne, Ali thought she might risk a slow-speed crash into a fire hydrant. The explosive deployment of the airbags would most likely be enough to knock the weapon out of Olga's hand. But would Ali be unaffected enough to take advantage of it? She had to be. Since Olga had just confessed to two murders, she wasn't going to let Ali walk away once they reached Ryan Field, wherever that was. No, Ali would have to do something about it before they reached what could otherwise be her final destination.

Ali's phone rang again. "I should answer that," she said.

"No," Olga said. "Leave it alone. Better yet, shut it off. I'm tired of the damned thing ringing every two minutes."

Ali reached into her pocket, pulled out her phone, and made a show of turning it off. When she returned the phone to her jacket pocket, she thumbed open the trigger guard on her Taser. Her best bet would be to take Olga down with that before they ever got in the car. To that end, she decided to feign complete compliance.

"Which bag goes first?" Ali asked.

"That one," Olga said, pointing to the larger one nearest the door. "Open the door and lead the way. If you try to pull anything, I promise I will shoot you."

Ali knew that wasn't an idle threat. The moment she opened the door, however, she heard the wail of approaching sirens. Olga heard them, too. There were several nearby major cross streets. It was possible the sirens were headed somewhere else. Ali hoped they weren't.

"Back inside," Olga barked. "Now. You sit on the couch."

Ali let go of the suitcase, walked over to the couch, and sat. Olga edged to the window again and peered out through the slats of the closed blind. Even with the blinds closed, Ali could see the pulsing blue flashes from at least one arriving patrol car.

"Crap," Olga said. "They're already here."

With Olga's attention focused on what was happening outside, Ali had managed to ease her Taser out of her pocket, but she left it lying in her lap, out of sight under her hand.

There was a sharp rap on the door. "Police," an officer said. "Open up."

"They've got you, Olga," Ali said. "Give it up. Just tell me where the girls are."

For an answer, Olga Sanchez dropped the slat of blind and turned back to Ali. In one fluid motion, she raised the gun to her own head and fired. As Olga tumbled to the floor, the front door burst open. Weapon drawn, a uniformed patrol officer bounded into the room. He stopped just inside the doorway and took in the whole scene. He looked first at the fallen woman and then at Ali. "Are you Ali Reynolds?" he asked.

She nodded.

"Are you all right?"

"Yes." Ali held up her Taser with two fingers. "I was going to Tase her, but I didn't have a chance. And

I've got a Glock 17 in a back holster. What about that?"

"I'll need to take those for the time being," the officer said. Once Ali complied, he walked over to Olga, reached down, and felt for a pulse. After a moment, he shook his head. "She's gone. What about the little girls? We were told there should be a pair of little girls here as well."

Ali stood up. "She wouldn't tell me where they are. She evidently gave them some kind of sedative before I got here."

"You haven't seen them?"

"Not so far."

"We'd better see if we can find them," the officer said.

Ali started toward the room that had to be the kitchen with the cop on her heels.

On the kitchen counter, Ali found an almost empty container of pralines-and-cream ice cream. In the sink, there were two dessert dishes and two teaspoons, as well as an ice cream dipper.

"Don't touch anything," the cop cautioned.

"I'm not," Ali said. "But if Olga brought the girls here for their ice cream, they must be here somewhere. They didn't have that much of a head start on me."

Room by room, Ali and the uniformed officer went through the entire house—kitchen, bedrooms, bathrooms, closets, and utility room—without finding any sign of the girls. None. Ali had let herself out through the back door and was wondering where else to look when she saw the Buick that Olga had been prepared to leave parked in the driveway while she flew off to Mexico.

By then the cop had gone back inside to deal with the arrival of a slew of other officers. Ali tried the driver's door. It was locked. She could have gone inside and searched for the key, but she didn't. Instead, she ventured far enough into the xeriscaped yard to pick up a fist-size hunk of river rock, which she flung through the driver's-side window.

A young uniformed cop who had been left out on the street to keep an eye on the scene came racing up to her. "Hey, lady," he demanded. "What do you think you're doing?"

Ali had already unlocked the door, pulled it open, and hit the trunk release. By the time the officer reached her, Ali was at the back of the vehicle, staring into the trunk. Both girls were there—unconscious and scarily still, but both of them were breathing.

"I need an ambulance!" Ali yelled. "Two of them. Now!"

The young cop skidded to a stop next to her, looked down into the trunk, and reached for his radio.

54

8:00 P.M., Monday, April 12
Tucson, Arizona

Eventually, the crowd cleared out. It was a good thing, too. Angel had been manhandling the polisher for hours, and his shoulders were killing him. As the last of the news crews began gathering up equipment, Angel did the same. He unplugged the polisher and rolled up the cord. Then he went outside and moved his van to an empty spot in the front row of the parking lot. Next he rolled his cart and polisher outside and loaded them into the van. When it was time to leave, he would need to leave in a hurry.

He returned to the corridor as the news crew was leaving and as the mother, finished with her interview ordeal, disappeared into her daughter's room. She came out a minute or so later and headed for the lobby.

Angel was relieved to see her go. That meant there was only the girl and the elderly nurse left. He took a seat in the waiting room, sat down, and waited, all the while wondering how long it would take. Under five minutes later, the nurse emerged. She paused in the doorway, looked around, and then headed for the nurses' station.

Angel knew he had moments to make this work. As soon as her back was turned, he darted into the room, easing the loaded syringe out of his pocket as he went. He was all the way inside the darkened room and reaching for the form on the bed when the charge from a Taser knocked him senseless.

Someone might have told him to drop it, but Angel couldn't be sure. When he came back around, the Taser dart was stuck to his chest and his arms were secured by a pair of handcuffs.

"I don't know who you are," a woman's voice said, "but you're under arrest. What's in the syringe?"

"What syringe?" Angel said. "I don't have any syringe."

The nurse came back then, too. She was smiling and talking on a telephone. "It worked like a charm, Bishop Gillespie. We got him!"

The nurse seemed to think this was funny. Angel Moreno did not, because he knew he was a dead man. If the cops didn't kill him, Humberto Laos sure as hell would.

55

9:00 P.M., Monday, April 12
Tucson, Arizona

When the ambulance got to Olga's house on Longfellow, it practically took an act of Congress to get the EMTs to agree to take Lucy and Carinda to Physicians Medical instead of Diamond Children's Hospital. The point was, with the rest of the family at PMC, it made no sense to send the girls anywhere else.

Crime scene investigators had found an empty prescription bottle for Ambien in the trash in Olga's kitchen, so the medical personnel had a fairly good idea what the girls had been given. When the ambulances pulled out, Carinda's was in the lead. Ali had picked up enough information from the EMTs to understand that for some reason, the younger child was considered to be in more critical condition.

Ali managed to hold it together until both ambulances pulled away. Then she dropped into the passenger seat of the Cayenne, covered her face with her hands, and wept. That was where she was when the Tucson PD Homicide detective Adrian Howard came looking for her. They were partway through the interview when Ali's phone rang.

Both calls that had come in during the confrontation with Olga had been from Teresa. Ali answered this one fearing that one or the other of the girls hadn't made it, but when she checked caller ID, it wasn't Teresa's number.

"Ms. Reynolds?" a male voice asked. "This is Sheriff Renteria calling. I came back to Patty Patton's home in Patagonia. She gave me your number and asked me to let you know that we've had a disturbing evening out here. Oscar Sanchez has been murdered, and we have a BOLO out on his wife. Patty wanted me to call and warn you in case Olga turns up there."

"Thanks for the warning, but it's a little late," Ali told him. "And you can rescind that BOLO. Olga Sanchez committed suicide at her home in Tucson about an hour ago. She kidnapped her own granddaughters and was holding me at gunpoint. When the cops showed up outside, she put a bullet through her head. I'm in the process of giving a statement. Before she died, she took responsibility for shooting Jose Reyes and for murdering Phil Tewksbury."

"She confessed to shooting Jose?" Renteria asked.

"Yes. I have no idea why she murdered Phil Tewksbury," Ali said.

"I think I do," Renteria said. "She was setting him up to take the blame for the Reyes shooting."

"According to her," Ali continued, "the only thing that went wrong with the execution of her plan was that Jose didn't die, but that wasn't quite true. Somehow or other, Oscar must have found out about Olga's relationship with Phil Tewksbury. She thought Oscar was the one who told us about the relationship when it was really Christine."

"So Oscar either found out or figured it out on his own," Renteria said.

"I don't know which," Ali said. "I don't think Olga knew, either."

"Whichever it was, it sent her completely around the bend," Renteria said.

"There's something else," Ali added. "She didn't come right out and say as much, but I'm pretty sure she's responsible for the vandalism at Jose and Teresa's house. I wouldn't be surprised if the crime lab doesn't find trace evidence from that on the soles of her shoes. Boots, rather. She was wearing cowboy boots, not shoes."

The sheriff sighed. "I can see now why Oscar is dead. He was a good man and a proud one. He wouldn't have taken that kind of thing lying down. Having a wife messing around behind his back? He would have had to do something. If I'd been him, I would have filed for divorce. I'm assuming Olga had no intention of sticking around to face the music."

"That's right. She had a pilot all lined up to fly her out of town tonight," Ali said. "She had three packed suitcases. Two of them were filled with clothing. The third one was filled with cash, so she was going somewhere—Mexico is what she told me—and she wasn't coming back. Two detectives from Tucson PD are out at Ryan Field right now, looking for the pilot. He's supposedly one of Olga's son's pals."

"Figures," Renteria said. "Danny didn't run in the best circles. But did I understand you to say that

Olga kidnapped Teresa's daughters, her own grand-daughters?"

"And gave them an overdose of Ambien with their ice cream. They're both in the hospital. I haven't heard anything new on their condition. And the homicide detective is still waiting to finish the interview. I'd better get back to him."

"If you don't mind," Renteria said, "you might want to put him on the line. Sounds like we'll need to get together with him and Lieutenant Lattimore first thing tomorrow morning and see if we can pull all these pieces together."

Detective Howard was on the phone with Renteria for several long minutes. When he relinquished it, he said to Ali, "I think you had a couple of calls that came in while I was using your phone."

When the interview ended and Ali was leaving to go back to the hospital, she was finally able to check her phone. The actual number of missed calls turned out to be two—one from Sister Anselm and one from Stuart Ramey. She called Sister Anselm first.

"I thought you'd want to know that Lucy and Carinda are both in the ICU," Sister Anselm said. "Teresa told me that they're both still in critical condition. If you hadn't found them when you did, it's likely neither one of them would have made it."

"Thank God," Ali said.

"Yes." Sister Anselm chuckled. "With a capital G. But how are you?"

"A little shaky," Ali admitted. "Watching someone blow her brains out right in front of you comes as a bit of a shock to the system. If I had used the Taser, I might have saved her life."

"Some people don't want their lives saved," Sister Anselm observed. "Some people don't deserve it, either."

"How are things with your patient?"

"She's out of the hospital."

"She's well enough to leave?" Ali asked.

"She wasn't well enough, but we moved her all the same. She'll still be under her doctor's care and under mine as well, but rather than being in PMC, she'll be staying at All Saints. We figured out tonight that someone had come to the hospital hunting her, hoping to keep her from testifying against her attackers. Moving her to the convent was the closest thing we had to putting her into protective custody, and it took a whole lot less paperwork."

"Doesn't Sister Genevieve have something to say about that?" Ali asked.

"Actually, I believe she thinks it's a bit of a lark to have the nuns from All Saints venture into the witness protection business."

"Speaking of All Saints," Ali said, "I'll stop off at the hospital for a few minutes after I leave here, but I'm looking forward to getting back to my room at the convent. It's been a tough day all around."

Her next call was to Stuart Ramey. "You saved the day," she said. "Again. Thank you."

"And the two girls are all right?"

"Let's hope so," Ali told him. "Originally, Olga denied having the girls with her, but you'd already told me about the video, so I knew better. As soon as I saw the Buick in the carport, I knew I had her. This isn't going to get you in trouble with B., is it?"

"Let's just say it would be better if none of this shows up in any court action."

"It won't," Ali assured him. "I'm not saying a word about it. For one thing, with Olga dead, there probably won't be any court proceedings. And if there are, I'll tell the truth and nothing but the truth, but maybe not the whole truth."

Stuart laughed at that.

On her way back to the hospital, Ali called B. and caught him up on everything that had happened between the last call and this one.

"You're okay, though?" he asked.

"Yes," Ali said. "Okay but very tired. Drained."

"Could you please consider finding something else to do that doesn't put you in the line of fire with people like this?"

"Believe me," she said, "I didn't do it on purpose."

By the time the call with B. ended, Ali had pulled into the parking lot at PMC. She could have saved herself the trouble. Teresa and Carmine were asleep in the maternity wing. Jose was asleep in his room, and the girls were sleeping in the ICU. Even Sister Anselm had decamped for the night, so Ali left, too. When she pulled up to the gate at All Saints and rang the bell, Sister Genevieve's cheerful voice greeted her and buzzed her in.

"Come on up to the main building," Sister Genevieve said. "Sister Anselm and I are sharing a cup of tea—decaf chamomile, of course. I hope you'll join us."

Ali did so. Tea at All Saints, served in mugs, was accompanied by some delicately flavored lemon bars that Leland Brooks would have been proud to claim as his own. Somehow Sister Anselm managed to steer the accompanying conversation away from a rehashing of the day's events and into a spirited discussion of the days and times of Don Quixote. The book had always been a particular favorite of both nuns, who had read it in Spanish rather than English.

Instead of drifting off to sleep with visions of Olga Sanchez's lifeless body tumbling to the floor, Ali thought instead of Don Quixote and the loyalty and friendship of his somewhat reluctant squire, Sancho Panza. Which brought her around to thinking about her somewhat unorthodox friendship with Sister Anselm.

If one was going to go around tilting at windmills, real or imaginary, it was always a good idea to have a friend there to back you up. Sister Anselm Becker was exactly that kind of friend.

She had told Ali on more than one occasion that life had a way of showing you what you were meant to do. That was what had happened today. By the simple act of offering to take the car seats to the girls, Ali had ended up saving their lives.

With that one final thought in mind, Ali Reynolds drifted off into a deep and restful slumber.

56

10:00 P.M., Monday, April 12
Patagonia, Arizona

By the time Sheriff Renteria got off the phone with Detective How-ard and Lieutenant Lattimore, Patty Patton had made a pot of coffee and was frying up a pan of scrambled eggs. It had been a long time since the sheriff had sat at a kitchen table while someone else took charge of the cooking.

All he had to do was hold the traumatized dog, who, hours after the event, continued to shake. To-gether Sheriff Renteria and Patty had agreed that there was no way either one could walk away and leave Bert, the devastated little Jack Russell, alone at the crime scene. Sheriff Renteria had gone into the house in search of dog gear. In the kitchen he had located a pair of dishes—a water dish and a food dish—as well as a bag of dog food. In a corner of the master bed-room, he found a small dog bed and a few well-chewed toys. All of that had been brought back to Patty's house in Patagonia.

"I suppose I should turn him over to the pound," Renteria said.

"Try it," Patty said. "You'll take that poor little animal to the pound over my dead body. If someone from the family comes forward to claim him, fine. Otherwise, Bert is mine!"

"Yes, ma'am," Sheriff Renteria said. They both laughed. It was the laughter that night when there should have been no laughter that took them both completely by surprise.

They ate scrambled eggs, put the dog on a bed in the corner of the room, and then talked for hours. It wasn't an interview. Patty Patton needed to talk to someone about losing her good friend and coworker, Phil Tewksbury, and about the horror of discovering Oscar Sanchez's lifeless body. That night Manuel Renteria wasn't a sheriff so much as he was what Patty needed—a good listener.

"What's going to happen to Christine?" Patty asked when she started to run down.

"I don't know. We'll see what the psych evaluation says. After that, we'll do what we can to get her the help she needs."

"Thank you," Patty said. "I was hoping that's what you'd say."

When Sheriff Renteria left Patty's house to drive home to Tubac, it was almost four in the morning. But he wasn't tired. He felt better than he had in years. Something had changed for him.

He was relieved to know he hadn't misread Jose Reyes all that time. He was confident that when ballistics finished with Olga Sanchez's .38, they'd be able to link her weapon to the Reyes crime scene as well as to Oscar's murder. Renteria was also convinced that once they were able to track the drugs from Jose's vehicle and Phil's garage back to their original source, they would be found to have come from one of Danny Sanchez's old cronies.

The pilot who had been scheduled to fly Olga Sanchez out of the country had been surprised when cops had shown up instead of his client. He was reportedly spilling his guts, and that was a very good thing. It seemed that raising horses was no longer nearly as lucrative as it had once been. Once Danny was gone, Olga had taken over his contacts and had been operating her own boutique drug-running business ever since. She had been willing to sacrifice a big chunk of product and profit in order to bring down Jose Reyes.

As Sheriff Renteria pulled into his own garage, he looked at his shiny red Dodge Charger and thought about Patty Patton's shiny red Camaro, both of them almost the same color and both of them of similar vintage. A love of old red cars, scrambled eggs, good coffee, and dogs was a lot for two people to have in common from the get-go.

Yes, maybe he'd need to consider going on a diet and getting back into shape. And if he and Patty ended up getting together? Manuel Renteria was pretty sure Midge would approve.

57

10:00 A.M., Tuesday, April 13
Tucson, Arizona

On Tuesday morning, Al Gutierrez walked into the office for the morning briefing, expecting all hell to break loose. He had spent the whole night worrying about it and wondering what stunts Sergeant Dobbs would pull to make Al's life as miserable as possible.

To his surprise, the watch commander stood up and read a fax from the Phoenix Police Department citing that one of the Tucson sector's agents, namely Al Gutierrez, had provided major assistance to Phoenix PD in breaking one of their recent homicide cases. The note ended by saying that kind of cross-jurisdictional help was all too rare most of the time and, as a consequence, was greatly appreciated.

Al managed to sneak a glance at Sergeant Dobbs's stony face while the letter was being read. He didn't look happy.

Al, on the other hand, was happy. Lighter than air. Thanks to Detective Rush, he had public acknowledgment that he had helped with something important, and he wasn't done helping, either. He planned to contact Detective Rush to let her know that he'd be happy to go straight back to PMC to continue looking after Rose Ventana the moment his shift was over. And if Dobbs gave him any grief about it? Tough.

Al Gutierrez had been looking for a job when he found this one. And if push came to shove, he could always go apply at Phoenix PD.

58

10:00 A.M., Tuesday, April 13
Tucson, Arizona

During the two-and-a-half-hour drive from Tucson back to Phoenix, Detective Ariel Rush managed to scare the hell out of Angel Moreno. With a prosecutor backing her up and the possibility of a plea deal on the table, Moreno was ready to talk. And talk he did.

By nine o'clock the next morning, the detective had enough probable cause to get a search warrant for Humberto Laos's Fountain Hills mansion. She was determined to move forward in a hurry. Detective Rush knew that once Laos realized Angel Moreno was in custody, the big guy would pull a disappearing act. He had the means to flee, and she was convinced he would do so. She was also concerned about gaining access to that basement room while there was a chance of retrieving damning DNA evidence.

She knew she had the goods on the guy, but it was rewarding to be in the room and watch as the luminol spray on Laos's basement floor lit up like a Christmas tree.

Detective Rush had left two cops in charge of Laos

while she went down to the basement with the crime scene techs. She came bounding back up the stairs with a smile on her face.

"Mr. Laos," she said, turning him around and slipping on a pair of cuffs, "I'm placing you under arrest for the murder of Chico Hernández, Sal Lombardi, and Tony Verdugo. You're also being charged with the attempted murder of Rose Ventana."

"Who?" Laos asked, trying to look genuinely puzzled. "I never heard of anyone named Rose Ventana."

"Right," Detective Rush said, securing the cuffs. "And your friend Angel Moreno didn't have a syringe filled with enough ketamine to kill a horse, either."

She saw the surprise register on his face when she mentioned Angel's name. That was when she pulled out the card and began reading. "You have the right to remain silent . . ."

59

10:00 A.M., Tuesday, April 13
Tucson, Arizona

As soon as Ali got to the hospital the next morning, she could see there had been a sea change. Not one but three Santa Cruz County sheriff's vehicles were parked in the parking lot. Since Jose Reyes was no longer officially off-limits, there were three uniformed deputies in his room, chatting and laughing.

Ali found Teresa and Carmine in the ICU waiting room. Maria Delgado was there, along with her brother and a much chastened Julie.

"I don't know how to thank you," Teresa said to Ali. "If it hadn't been for you, my girls would be gone."

"How are they?"

"The doctor says Lucy should come out of the ICU later this morning. Carinda may take a little longer."

"Good."

Teresa was quiet for a moment. "I can't believe that Olga hated me enough to do all this."

"I believe it's a safe bet that Olga Sanchez had a couple of screws loose," Ali said. "It's probably terrible of me to say so, but I think she did the world a favor by ending it the way she did. At least it's over. Nobody has to go to court. Nobody has to testify. Items found in her trunk—the remains of Jose's dashboard camera and the fishing filament used to trip Phil Tewksbury—link her to both crimes, and they are currently considered closed."

Teresa nodded. "Juanita Cisco called me a little while ago. She said Lieutenant Lattimore called and told her we're no longer under investigation. That's thanks to you, too."

"No," Ali said. "I think it has a lot more to do with Patty Patton, the lady who runs the post office in Patagonia, and with Sheriff Renteria. They're the ones who got Lattimore to back off."

"And then there's the will," Teresa said.

"What will?" Ali asked.

"Oscar's will. The ranch, the house in Tucson, all of it goes to the girls—to Lucy and Carinda. They're Oscar and Olga's only grandchildren and their only heirs. I'm sure it's going to be complicated, but . . ."

"Yes, depending on how the will is written, there will be probate issues, and the properties will need to be sold or held in trust for your girls. There may even be other relatives who come crawling out of the woodwork, hoping to grab some share of the pie. Your lives will be different and probably far more complicated than you ever would have thought possible. And far more interesting. After what you and

Jose have been through this week, I think you're up to the task."

Late that afternoon, Ali headed home to Sedona. She wanted to see her bighorn sheep. She wanted to see the plants going into her garden. She wanted to sleep in her own bed. She wanted to tuck in to some of Leland Brooks's cooking. When he heard she was coming home, he promised to have some roast beef hash ready to cook the moment she walked in the door.

When Ali knew Donnatelle would be off shift, she called to give her the lowdown.

"I knew Olga was trouble the moment I met her," Donnatelle declared, "but I had no idea she was as bad as all that. Now, though, thanks to her, Lucy and Carinda get everything?"

"That's how it looks," Ali said. "The ranch and the house in Tucson."

"Sweet," Donnatelle said. "So some things do turn out right in the end."

A full moon was rising as Ali pulled into the driveway at Manzanita Hills Road. She left the car inside the garage and walked around the outside of the house. Her bighorn sheep was just visible at the far end of the front yard. He looked for the world as though he might come to life and scramble up and over the man-made cliff that was his home. In that moment, Ali Reynolds couldn't have been more proud of her son, Christopher. He was indeed a talented young man.

The porch light snapped on, and Leland Brooks

came out through the front door. "What do you think?" he asked.

"It's beautiful," she said. "Breathtaking."

"Yes, it is that. Come on in this way," he added. "I'll go fetch your bags from the garage."

Ali stepped onto the porch and inhaled the delicate scent of wisteria. The gnarled old tree was heavy with blooms, just as it had been years earlier when Ali had stepped onto the porch the first time, coming to hear the surprising news about being the recipient of an Askins scholarship.

Inside the door on the entryway table, she saw the mail, neatly stacked. She thumbed through it and opened the two small envelopes that contained the RSVPs for Sunday's tea. Not surprisingly, both Olivia McFarland and Autumn Rusk would be coming to tea on Sunday, Olivia at two o'clock and Autumn at four.

"They're both coming?" Leland asked as he returned from the bedroom, having dropped off Ali's luggage.

"Yes, they are."

"I supposed I'd best start planning the menu," he said.

"I saw Haley and Marissa while I was down in Tucson," Ali said. "They're both doing very well. So is Liam."

"Not surprising," Leland said. "Not surprising at all. And what about Sister Anselm? Will we be seeing her anytime soon?"

"She's fully occupied at the moment," Ali said. "But she'll turn up eventually."

"The hash should be ready in about ten minutes or so. Will you be eating it in the dining room?"

"No," Ali said. "The kitchen, please. And break out a bottle of wine. I'd like to share it with you while you tell me all about the garden."

"Very good, madame," Leland Brooks said. "Whatever you wish."

Turn the page
for a sneak peek
at the next Ali Reynolds novel

DEADLY STAKES

by *New York Times* bestselling author

J.A. Jance

Coming soon from Touchstone

Even for June it was ungodly hot as Gemma Ralston pulled her Mercedes SLK into an almost deserted parking lot and stopped outside the brick-and-mortar offices of Video-Glam. Despite the name, Video-Glam appeared to be anything but glamorous. The office was located in a mostly dead and partially repurposed strip mall at Indian School Road and 43rd Avenue. Video-Glam occupied a single storefront at one end of the complex. At the other end, two units had been combined into one to serve as a Spanish-language Baptist church. In between were three empty units, their boarded-up windows a colorful catalog of three-foot-high graffiti.

For a moment, Gemma sat in the Mercedes with the engine running, wondering if she wanted to bother going inside. From out front it didn't look the least bit promising, even though the membership consultant at Hearts Afire, a dating site for "mature singles," had suggested that Video-Glam was the only place in Phoenix that they recommended as a source for uploadable videos.

"It's like Glamour Shots," the young woman had told her, "only with, like you know, videos instead of just pictures."

That comment had told Gemma a lot about the age and general qualifications of her membership consultant without engendering a whole lot of confidence in the process itself.

She was considering putting the SLK in reverse and backing out of the lot when a car pulled in beside hers. It was a dusty-green Subaru months beyond needing a complete detailing. A collection of doggy noseprints on the inside of the backseat window obscured the interior of the car but let the world know that a large family dog of some kind was often a passenger.

The woman who hopped out of the driver's seat, a bedraggled thirtysomething, matched the car in every way. She looked harried and overworked and, from the way she hotfooted it inside, she was most likely also late for her appointment. She was dressed in faded black sweats topped by someone's well-worn Glendale High School football jersey. The whole woebegone outfit was underscored by a pair of blue rubber flip-flops. Stringy, dishwater-blond hair was pulled back into a scrunchy-style ponytail. In other words, as far as Gemma was concerned, the woman looked like crap.

Gemma's first thought was, *Here's someone desperately in need of a little glamour*. Her second thought was along the lines of, *If that's the competition, I'm home free*.

Gemma couldn't help being a little curious if anyone at Video-Glam would be able to wave a magic wand at the poor unfortunate creature who stood before the reception desk just inside the front door. Without really thinking about it, Gemma switched off the ignition and grabbed a small suitcase with her changes of wardrobe off the floor on the passenger side and her out-of-season mink off the seat beside her.

Once inside, the woman ahead of her at the reception counter was in a full-scale case of hysterics. "I know I have to move on," she sobbed, dabbing at her tears. "But I just don't know how to do it. I've been out of the dating scene for so long that the whole idea scares me to death."

"You'll be fine," the much-pierced young woman behind the counter reassured her, passing along a box of tissues. This was evidently a situation she had dealt with on more than one occasion. As the weeping woman grabbed one of the offered tissues, Gemma noticed the pale spot on the skin of the woman's ring finger from which, most likely, a wedding band had recently been removed.

Gemma felt a tiny stirring of irritation. It made no sense that she'd be in even remotely the same boat as this unfortunate creature. If Charles had simply manned up and done what she had expected him to do—which was live up to his potential—things would never have come to this pass. He had told her initially that he planned on becoming a surgeon, and that's what she had expected. Had he done so, Gemma would have gotten a reasonable return on her investment, and she wouldn't have had to dump him. Instead, after one stupid mistake—and one lost patient who probably wouldn't have survived anyway—he had backed away from surgery and become a do-gooder. The money he made looking after Alzheimer's patients was fair, but not what she had hoped for. And they were all going to die, too, so what was the point.

Gemma had decided to cut her losses and look for greener pastures while she still could. Fortunately, she was starting over with a lot more going for her than Ms. Flipflops, who was still standing as if frozen in front of the receptionist, who slid a credit card and a receipt across the counter. Still weeping, the woman signed it and stuffed her copy into her purse. At that moment, a young woman dressed entirely in black stepped through an interior door into the reception area.

"Oh, hi, Noelle," the receptionist said. "Here's your stylist, Rachel. She's the one who'll be helping you today. Just go with her and don't worry about a thing."

Looking more than a little lost, Rachel allowed herself to be led away while Gemma stepped up to the receptionist and tossed her fur onto the counter.

"Is she here for Hearts Afire?" Gemma asked, nodding toward the door through which Rachel and her stylist had disappeared.

"Oh, no." The receptionist's smile was one step short of a purr. "We do videos for several different sites, but if you're here for Hearts Afire, you must be Gemma."

Gemma had to beat back her first inclination, which was to say, "Ms. Ralston to you." Instead she nodded. "I'm here for my ten o'clock," she said, pulling out her Amex card.

"You're aware of our charges?" the receptionist asked. "You're paying for the shoot as well as your initial upload. We keep the videos on file and you're charged a nominal fee each additional time you ask to have them uploaded to another site."

"Yes, yes," Gemma replied impatiently. "That's fine."

Now that she was here, what she wanted more than anything was to get the process over and done with—sort of like going to the dentist for a root canal. She already knew it was going to be bad. The only question remaining was how long would it take.

The receptionist ran her card and then passed both the card and receipt to Gemma as the interior door opened again and yet another black-clad young woman appeared.

"This is Roxanne," the receptionist announced to Gemma. "She'll be your stylist today."

Roxanne was young—probably no more than twenty-five—but as Gemma examined her hair and makeup, she could find nothing to complain about. Naturally good-looking to begin with, Roxanne's carefully applied makeup and precision cut bob added to her appeal. So maybe, Gemma thought hopefully, with any kind of luck and having someone like that do the styling, it wouldn't be all that bad.

Gemma picked up her coat and suitcase and then allowed herself to be led into the next section of the building, which turned out to be a tiny but exceedingly well-equipped beauty shop. There were four stations in all, two for hair and two for makeup. Off to the side was a walled-off section with a door marked WARDROBE.

"Most people stop here first and choose their outfits. That way we can be sure we have the right makeup," Roxanne explained. "After you've chosen what you'll wear, we'll also select which of our backdrops you'll want once we get to the studio."

"I don't need any of this stuff," Gemma told her stylist. "I brought my own."

As they walked by the wardrobe door, Gemma noticed that Rachel, the dishwater blonde, was still inside, trying on a Harley-Davidson jacket. A discarded stack of obviously fake furs lay on the floor beside her.

At a table outside the wardrobe room, Gemma set down the valise and laid out the three different outfits she had brought along. Eventually they settled on her favorite, a chartreuse silk sheath and a pair of high-heeled strappy sandals.

Roxanne nodded approvingly and then brought up a series of photos on a laptop. One showed a summery garden through the railing of what was evidently a front porch. "We have a porch swing that we use with this one," she said. "That will be perfect with the dress."

"What should we use for the mink?" Gemma asked, wanting to be certain Roxanne understood her coat was the real thing, not some rip-off.

Roxanne clicked through a series of photos. "What about this one?" she said, pausing at what looked like a snow-covered Swiss chalet. "I think this one will do it justice," she said. "Believe it or not, back in the studio we have some perfectly wonderful faux snow that looks just like the real thing."

By the time they finished background shopping, Rachel had emerged from Wardrobe, and the change was nothing short of miraculous. Noelle had evidently persuaded her charge to skip the Harley-Davidson jacket in favor of a sapphire blue wraparound dress with a plunging neckline and simple, flowing lines, which could evidently be adjusted to fit almost any figure. The flip-flops had disappeared, replaced by a pair of classy pumps that had been dyed to match the dress. The wardrobe department at Video-Glam evidently had a large selection of all kinds of shoes in multiple sizes to go with the very adjustable dress.

Roxanne went to work shampooing Gemma's hair. When she was finished, Gemma noticed that Rachel's formerly drab locks had been lightened by some kind of rinse and were being swiftly but deftly trimmed. The revised hairdo was followed by the meticulous application of makeup that took a full ten years off Rachel's face. Watching from the sidelines while her own hair was being shampooed and styled, Gemma couldn't help but be impressed. The new, sophisticated look made Rachel a different person, smiling and laughing and maybe enjoying herself for the first time in a long time. But the change in appearance didn't change the fact that Rachel had arrived for her shoot in a filthy Subaru with dog snot all over the inside windows.

"Noelle's really great," Roxanne commented. "She's especially good with the broken birds. She makes them look good, but she also makes them *feel* good."

"What about me?" Gemma asked.

Roxanne stopped for a moment and gave Gemma an appraising look. "I don't think you've ever been a broken bird," the stylist said with a laugh. "By the time I'm finished with you, though, you'll be spectacular."

Which turned out to be the case. Roxanne made no effort to adjust Gemma's already perfect haircut, but she did put just the right amount of curl and body into it, and Roxanne's deft makeup application left Gemma smiling and nodding at her reflection in the mirror.

"You like?" Roxanne asked.

"Very much," Gemma answered.

When Gemma's makeover was complete, Roxanne led her into the greenroom, where it was time to hurry up and wait. Rachel had disappeared into the studio before Gemma's makeup was finished. While she waited, Gemma pulled out a hard copy of the script she intended to use. It was supposed to be three to five minutes long and would be transferred to a teleprompter before the actual filming began. She had struggled with what to say. She had wanted to hit all the right notes— breezy, fun, lighthearted. She didn't want people to think she took herself too seriously. Guys who were interested in fun and games weren't looking for serious.

"I'm Gemma," the script read. "With a name like that it's only natural that I have a soft spot for gems, two in particular: Emeralds because they match my eyes and diamonds because diamonds really are a girl's best friend."

It seemed to her that the words in her simple introduction made it clear she was looking for someone with dollars in his wallet that he'd be willing to spend on her. Cubic zirconia? Thanks, but no thanks! Not her style.

"I'm not going to tell you my age," the script continued. "I'm looking for companionship, but I have no interest in getting married again." (Lose out on her hard-earned alimony? Not on your life!) "And I'm definitely not interested in kids. If I had wanted kids, I would have had ones of my own. If you've got kids, I'm sure they have mothers who don't need any competition in the motherhood department from me. I'll be glad to meet your kids, but I don't want to raise them or take them away from their real moms.

"Without either kids or marriage on the table, my age is none of your business. I believe in being open-minded as far as age is concerned, in both directions, up and down. If you're looking at this video and thinking I'm probably too old for you or too young, then you're probably right. So let's not even go there.

"By now you're probably wondering, 'So what does she really want?'

"In a word . . . fun! I've spent too much of my life knowing that tomorrow would be a repeat of today. I want to be able to expect the unexpected. I want adventure. A white-water rafting trip down the Colorado? I'm there. An African safari? Yes—have passport, will travel. A sunset walk along a sandy beach? Absolutely. A quiet evening of reading books in a snowbound cabin? Yes to that, too. Maybe you're into long-distance bicycling and would like to help me train, so I could do that, too. I'd also like to try my hand at ballroom dancing and bowling.

"In other words, the boring day-to-day stuff is fine for me to do by myself, but when I'm with you— whoever you are—nothing that sounds like fun is off the table, and the sooner we get started, the better."

Noelle emerged from the studio looking perplexed. "Sorry for the delay," she said. "Rachel looks great, but she keeps freezing up the moment the camera starts recording. It shouldn't be long now, but the director was wondering if you'd brought along a copy of your script. He wants me to bring it back and start loading it into the teleprompter."

"No problem," Gemma said, smiling and handing it over. "I'll be ready when you are."

With that she settled in to wait. She knew she looked good. She knew that before long she'd have men groveling at her feet, but she also knew who to thank for it—her grandmother, Natalie Hooper.

Gemma didn't actually remember the roach-infested hovel from which her grandparents had rescued her as a two-year-old, although Nana had told her about it so many times that she could see it in her mind's eye. Two days after Gemma's second birthday, Nana and Papa had gone to war with their drug-addicted daughter, Caroline.

Born with what should have been a silver spoon in her mouth, Caroline Hooper was the daughter of a small-town physician and a stay-at-home mom. Money was never an issue in their Lake Havasu home. In grade school and junior high, things were fine. Caroline got good grades and was considered an exemplary student. But once she got into high school, that all went south. By the time Caroline turned fifteen, she was a pot-smoking dropout. By the time she was eighteen, she had an out-of-wedlock baby, and a serious drug problem. For a time, Natalie and Daniel Hooper did what they could to care for both their struggling daughter and her baby girl—paying rent and utility bills, sending money and gift certificates for groceries.

Caroline had told them that she was having a party for Gemma's birthday but it would be too complicated to try to include her parents. Two days later, Natalie and Daniel turned up unannounced, expecting to deliver a stack of tardy birthday presents. They knocked, but no one answered, even though they could hear Gemma crying somewhere inside. Finding the door unlocked, they let themselves into a nightmare. The apartment was filthy. The place was littered with empty pizza boxes. Cockroaches scurried out of sight as the door opened. There were flies and bugs circling a garbage can overflowing with unwashed diapers. Natalie went straight to the wailing Gemma—dirty and hungry and inconsolable in a foul crib—while Daniel went looking for their daughter. He found Caroline on a bare mattress on the floor in the second bedroom. She had passed out cold with a syringe lying next to her.

Natalie stayed with the baby while Daniel went looking for a police officer. She had wanted to change Gemma's diaper, but Daniel told her to wait. He wanted to be sure the authorities knew how bad it was, and he was right. The cops came, and so did social services. DES was only too happy to turn the child over to a pair of responsible grandparents. A grant of temporary custody was soon made permanent.

Gemma stepped out of that filthy crib and into what had previously been her mother's life. Caroline's room became Gemma's room. The playhouse that had once been Caroline's was now Gemma's. Caroline's piano teacher became Gemma's piano teacher. Most important, Caroline's parents became Gemma's parents—Natalie her caring but disciplining mother and Daniel her doting father.

Soon after Gemma's arrival, the household's economic situation took a hit when Parkinson's forced Daniel into early retirement and he had to give up his medical practice. Still, it was essentially the same stable home with the same two loving parents who had raised Caroline, but the results with Gemma were very different. She was bright and beautiful but also cooperative, where her mother had been the opposite. Caroline had fought her parents and teachers every step of the way. As far as Natalie and Daniel were concerned, raising Caroline had been a nightmare; raising Gemma was a piece of cake.

Unlike her mother, Gemma breezed through high school and graduated near the top of her class. When it came time for her to leave for her freshman year at Arizona State University, Natalie Hooper offered Gemma her own roadmap to success.

"When your mother was your age, Caroline was out smoking dope, protesting the war, and burning her bra. You can see how well that worked out for her," Natalie counseled Gemma. "So do what I did. Find yourself some dependable young man, preferably a premed student, and marry him. You can see how well that worked out for your grandfather and me. Daniel was only a GP, of course. You'd be better off finding yourself a surgeon. Those are the ones who make the big bucks."

Unlike her mother before her, Gemma listened to every one of her grandmother's words and took every one of them to heart. Unfortunately, because she really was Caroline Hooper's daughter at heart, she ended up putting her own particular spin on Natalie Hooper's heartfelt advice. Daniel Hooper's pet name for Gemma may have been "Sugar," but she knew that when it came to "sugar and spice and everything nice," she didn't even come close. She also understood that it was entirely possible to *act* nice without actually *being* nice, but it was the best way to get what she wanted.

Growing up, Gemma had seen her mother's mistakes, and she had no intention of repeating them. As she packed her boxes to head to Tempe, Gemma instinctively accepted the idea that her grandmother had laid out an excellent game plan.

It had been left up to Gemma to work that plan to the best of her ability, and she had done a masterful job of it. Now, after years of making the best of what she considered to be a useful starter marriage, she was ready to reap some of the rewards.

Yes, she thought, sitting back and waiting her turn. *It's about time.*

Several miles across town, Ali Reynolds sighed and looked at her watch. She had known when she had agreed to do the shoot at the Phoenix Fox affiliate that it would be the same day and time that her mother, Edie Larson, would be speaking before a luncheon meeting of local Sedona Rotarians as part of her run for the office of mayor. Edie had done a number of informal coffee hour kinds of appearances, but this would be her first major speaking engagement, and one in which she would be going head-to-head with her thirtysomething opponent. As Edie's campaign manager, Ali felt she needed to be there to handle the background issues and put out any fires that cropped up. Unfortunately, the scheduled shoot for Fox's new *Scene of the Crime* news magazine had been chiseled in granite and supposedly could not be changed.

"You go do the shoot and don't worry about me," Edie had assured her daughter earlier that morning. "Brenda Riley is counting on you."

"But so are you," Ali had objected.

"You can't afford to miss the taping," Edie said firmly. "With Brenda's book due to come out the same week the show is scheduled to be broadcast nationally, she has a lot more riding on this than I do. Besides, I'll be speaking to that bunch of Rotarians, most of whom I already know on a first-name basis. How bad can that be? Don't worry. I'll be fine."

Ali shook her head in resignation. What her mother wasn't saying was that both candidates had been invited to speak at the luncheon, and this was the first time Edie would be trading campaign rhetoric with an opponent who was there with rehearsed responses.

"Why do I always end up with people counting on me?" Ali asked.

Edie smiled. "Because that's the way your father and I raised you," she said, "and we love you for it, too."

As a consequence, Ali had left her house on Sedona's Manzanita Hills Road a little before noon on that Tuesday morning to drive down into the sun-baked oven known as the Valley of the Sun. Since it was already pushing the nineties in Sedona, she knew it would be a scorcher in Phoenix. She didn't even attempt to put on camera-ready makeup for the drive down. Instead she took along the travel makeup kit she had used back in the old days when she'd been first an on-air reporter and later a news anchor.

For the better part of two years, she had known that her friend, Brenda Riley, also a former newscaster, had been working on a book about a cyberstalker named Richard Lowensdale, who, operating under any number of aliases, had victimized dozens of lonely women from all over the country, romancing them with digital sweet nothings that promised the world and delivered nothing but humiliation and heartache.

Richard's preferred victims were always vulnerable women who were considered to be high-profile in their various communities. Ali had first met Brenda Riley when they were both working as news anchors—Ali at a news desk in L.A., while Brenda did similar news desk duties at a sister station in Sacramento. Brenda had been drawn into Richard's clutches in the aftermath of a difficult divorce as well as being sidelined from her newscasting job when she'd outlived her on-camera shelf life. For Brenda, those two major losses had resulted in a booze- and drug-fueled midlife crisis. Ali had been dragged into the fray when Brenda asked for help in doing a simple background check on the new man in Brenda's life—Richard Lowensdale. Unfortunately, that supposedly simple background check had uncovered the existence of Lowensdale's full contingent of fiancées in addition to Brenda herself.

That revelation, coupled with all the other losses, had been enough to send Brenda off on another almost fatal series of benders. When Brenda had finally sobered up and wised up, she set out to expose the man for what he was. Before she could do so, however, someone else beat her to the punch. Unfortunately for

Richard, one of his erstwhile victims, Ermina Vlasic Cunningham Blaylock, happened to be a serial murderer in her own right. She had lured him into doing an illicit engineering job with the promise of a very large payday when in fact she'd had every intention of taking him out once he was no longer useful.

Ermina had carried out the cold-blooded killing with utter ruthlessness, leaving evidence behind that should have put the blame for Lowensdale's murder at Brenda Riley's door. All of that might well have gone according to plan had it not been for the timely arrival of Ali and a Grass Valley homicide detective named Gilbert Morris. Brenda's mother had alerted Ali to the fact that her daughter had gone missing. Between Ali and Detective Morris, they had not only managed to capture Ermina, they had also rescued Brenda, who, close to death, had been found locked in the trunk of Ermina's rented Cadillac.

Their timely rescue had been good for Brenda but not so good for an FBI surveillance team that had also been on the scene, intent on bringing down both Ermina and drug cartel movers and shakers who had been the end customers attempting to purchase her stock of supposedly dismantled drones. When offered a possible plea deal, however, Ermina had arrogantly refused. Rather than walking away with what would have been a hand-slap on three separate charges of homicide, she had chosen to go to trial instead. As a result, juries in two different California jurisdictions and one in Missouri had all returned guilty verdicts.

Two years later, some legal maneuverings continued, but with Ermina sentenced to life without parole in two different states, Brenda Riley, now married to retired detective Morris, was free to publish the whole story.

Scene of the Crime, a new televised true-crime weekly magazine, was prepared to give the story full-court-press treatment for its premier show, and Ali had agreed to go on camera to tell her part of the story.

It wasn't until she arrived at the television studio in Phoenix for the taping that Ali discovered that one of Richard Lowensdale's cyberstalking victims, Lynn Martinson, formerly of Iowa City, Iowa, was now living in the Phoenix area and would also be filming her segment with the same crew in the course of the afternoon.

Lynn—in her mid-forties at least, a bit on the frumpy side, and incredibly nervous—was already in the greenroom when Ali arrived. A receptionist had just given her the unwelcome news that the film crew and host had been delayed, having missed a flight connection somewhere along the way. If Ali had known about the delay earlier, she could have stayed for at least part of the luncheon meeting and driven to Phoenix immediately afterward. Now, there was nothing she could do. She went into the greenroom powder room to reapply her makeup, then settled in to wait.

Lynn, on the other hand, paced the floor and agonized over her hair, makeup, and clothing.

"Your makeup is perfect," she said, examining Ali. "Do I look all right?"

Ali had spent years in front of a camera, and she was an expert at what to do and what not to do. She didn't have the heart to tell the poor woman the truth.

"You're fine," Ali assured her. "Even if you weren't, the crew will probably have someone along who can doctor your makeup should they decide it needs fixing. Sit down. Relax. It'll be okay."

With a resigned sigh, Lynn sank down on one of the

room's several uncomfortable chairs. "I take it you're one of Richard's victims, too?" she asked.

"No," Ali said. "I'm from Sedona. I'm a friend of Brenda's and the one who ran the initial background check that started the whole unmasking of the guy we now know as Richard Lowensdale."

"Oh," Lynn said. "You're the detective, the one who figured it all out, you and that guy from Grass Valley."

"Gil Morris was the detective," Ali said. "I was a concerned bystander."

"Luckily for Brenda," Lynn said. "But I'm glad you're not one of us. Because of Richard, I ended up losing everything—my job, my self-respect. And then my son committed suicide . . ."

"I'm so sorry," Ali murmured.

Those three words of sympathy were enough to launch Lynn on a long, sad monologue, leaving Ali no choice but to listen.

"Thank you," Lynn said. "Lucas died just after I learned the truth about Richard. That's where I met him, by the way—in a tough-love chatroom shortly after Lucas was picked up on drug charges. Here I was the superintendent of schools, and my kid was in jail for dealing drugs. You can imagine how that went over in a place like Iowa City.

"When Lucas was arrested, my ex refused to take any responsibility for what was happening with our son. He blamed the whole thing on me, and that's why I fell so hard for Richard. He told me his name was Richard Lewis. It's no wonder I fell in love with the guy. Here was a caring man who was willing to listen to my troubles and who really seemed to understand what I was going through because he had a similar story. Richard claimed he had a daughter who had gone down the same druggie path Lucas was on—including spending time in juvie. Fortunately his daughter had come out all right on the other side.

"Hearing that gave me a glimmer of hope that maybe someday Lucas would be all right, too. Then I found out Richard was a complete fraud, that everything he had told me was a lie. He didn't even have a daughter. That's when everything caught up with me and I went to pieces. I couldn't go to work. Couldn't even get out of bed some days. It was then, while I was lying around feeling sorry for myself, that Lucas committed suicide. He left a note saying he was sorry but that he couldn't live in prison and that he'd rather be dead. It turns out that's my fault, too. If I had been there for him, maybe I could have saved him."

Listening and nodding, Ali didn't bother saying what she knew to be true—that kids from even the most loving of families can fall victim to suicide. Survivors are always all too ready to accept blame and to assume that something they might have done or said or might not have done or said could have made a difference.

"I'm sorry," Ali said again.

Lynn nodded and continued. "With Lucas gone, I just gave up. I ended up quitting my job. I also lost my house. My parents had retired and moved to Surprise. By then my father's Alzheimer's was getting worse and worse, so I came here to help my mom look after him. That's one good thing that came out of all that. Once I was without a job, I was able to lend a hand. Without my help, I think the stress of looking after a man who was essentially an eighty-year-old toddler would have killed my mother. Alzheimer's is hell," she added.

Ali nodded again. Lynn's tale of woe was appalling. "How's your dad doing?" Ali asked.

"He passed away about three months ago," Lynn replied. "I'm sorry he's gone, but he was really gone a long time before he died. It's not easy, but my mother and I are both starting to recover. It's hard not to feel guilty about feeling relieved. Not everyone gets that. You have to have lived it to really understand. My mother has started reconnecting with her bridge-playing friends, and she's taken up golf again. As for me? There's a wonderful new man in my life. A real one this time," she added with a shy laugh. "Without my coming out here to help my mom, I never would have met Chip."

The sudden glow on Lynn's face had nothing to do with makeup, and Ali found herself hoping that Chip was as nice a person as Lynn seemed to think he was.

Ali's phone rang. The readout showed her mother's number. A glance at the clock told her the luncheon was most likely over. "Sorry," she said to Lynn. "I need to take this." Then, into the phone she said, "Hey, Mom, how did it go?"

"Harlan Masters is full of himself," Edie muttered.

Ali laughed. "That's hardly news," she said. "Tell me something we don't know."